DEATH IN THE HAUNTED WOOD

KIM GRISWELL

Storm

Ebook ISBN: 978-1-83700-073-9
Paperback ISBN: 978-1-83700-074-6

Cover design: Dawn Adams
Cover images: Dawn Adams, Adobe Stock

Published by Storm Publishing.
For further information, visit:
www.stormpublishing.co

A Pacific Northwest Cozy Mystery Series

Murder at Last Chance Cove

Silenced at the Book Show

Special thanks to the Sitka Center for Art and Ecology for the writing residency that immersed me in the mysteries—both natural and human-made—of Oregon's Cascade Head.

Moonrise over Cascade Head cast an eerie glow over the yellow kayak as it struggled against the pull of the out-going tide. A bone-chilling breeze swept in from the sea and the marsh grass on either side of the Salmon River trembled, then hunched against the cold. Crouched on the kayak's center seat, a lone figure pulled a double-bladed paddle against the current. At the river's edge, on the branch of a long-dead Sitka spruce, a spotted owl slowly turned its head toward the movement. As its round, black eyes penetrated the gloom, it screeched a warning. Then it burst from its perch and swooped toward the paddler, its spotted chestnut-brown wings spread wide. For a moment, their gazes met as if in recognition. They were the same, these two: nocturnal predators. On the hunt, both glided toward prey in the gathering gloom.

ONE

Saffi Graywood pedaled her mint-green cruiser to the harbor café through the misty morning chill. The paved trail from Last Chance Cove RV Park to the marina district allowed her to stand on the pedals and use her hips to pick up speed. The ocean-born breeze snarled her silvered black curls and slapped her awake. Waves pounded. Gulls surfed the wind. Seals blew raspberries from the weathered docks. *Give me a break! I'm pedaling as fast as I can.*

An early-morning message from Glenn Youngkin, her favorite cookie baker and one-time prime suspect in a murder investigation, had forced her out of bed into the brisk October morning.

There's a horrible problem only you can solve! Glenn had texted.

Saffi sucked in oxygen and ignored her aching knees to pedal toward what she really needed: caffeine. Bowls of the stuff, preferably heaped with chocolate whipped cream.

When she'd first arrived in Last Chance Cove, the tiny town tucked into a coastal curve of the Pacific Northwest's Highway 101, the steamy warmth and rich smell of organic coffee had drawn her to the harborside café. Over the last four months, it had become more than just a place to get cozy with a mug of coffee. It had become the center of Saffi's cove community, the meeting spot for the oddball collection of locals who had gone from being acquaintances to friends. Some of those friends, Glenn most of all, now saw Saffi as the town's resident sleuth. She'd told him the same thing over and over: "Solving one murder does not make me a detective." But frantic messages like the one that had tugged her out of bed had become all too common.

A horrible problem? At this hour? Seriously, Glenn.

Was he prone to histrionics? *Yes.* Was he drawn to trouble like a gull to a French fry? *Double yes.* Glenn befriended every questionable character to pass through the cove. She could only hope this morning's text was about taste-testing his latest cookie creation. She could solve that problem in a few short, sweet bites. If the "horrible problem" related to checking out a potential boyfriend for murdery vibes, she would have to follow through on her threat to block his texts—at least until after crunch time.

Today's original goal, beyond indulging in her passion for coffee concoctions, had been to plow through revisions on the latest book in her bestselling *Aunt Saffi's Bedside Reader* series. The weird-but-true stories that made her books a hit were fun to find, but some articles ended up "slight"—as her New York editor, Poppy Morales, would say. What that meant varied from article to article, but, as far as Saffi could tell, the gist of it was "there's not enough *there* there." Poppy had given Saffi a two week "drop-dead" deadline. She could not let Glenn's problematic love life wreck her career.

Saffi skidded to a stop in front of Last Chance Café. The small marina café had views of the harbor on one side and the rusted hulls of fishing boats hoisted high for repair on the other. As she chained her cruiser to the bike rack, movement in the window caught her attention. Her mop-haired friend—the mirror image of Davy Jones, frontman for the sixties pop band The Monkees— stood up from his table. He gestured for her to hurry as if his morning scone had burst into flames and she was the only one who could put out the fire. Saffi straightened her shoulders and pushed through the café's jaunty turquoise front door, turned to Glenn, and held up her pointer finger.

Glenn paled. By now, he knew Saffi well enough to interpret "the finger." If she didn't get her morning mocha before talking to him, her Medusa curls would turn into snakes and sink their fangs into his throat. He sat down with an exaggerated sigh, but his impatient gaze felt like ants crawling up her neck as she headed for the coffee counter.

A Mexi-mocha with a mountain of chocolate whipped cream appeared in front of her as if by magic.

"Saw you through the window." Delilah Dunsmore, the café's barista and Saffi's new best friend, sprinkled burnt-orange specks of cayenne onto the whipped cream. They looked so much like red ink they instantly reminded Saffi of her deadline. It loomed as thick and heavy as the October clouds outside the café's window. If she didn't finish her revisions on time, Poppy would be on the phone insisting she stop "playing" RV park host and get back to her real work.

Saffi stuck her finger in the chocolate whipped cream and popped it into her mouth. "*Mmm.* You're a wizard, my friend!"

Delilah leaned her elbows on the counter and tipped her head toward the harborside window. "Glenn's had his panties in a twist all morning. If you ask me"—she wiggled her eyebrows—"it has something to do with that mysterious stranger sitting at his table."

Saffi allowed herself a glance at Glenn's companion. Something about him reminded her of a movie villain: wavy hair, triangular eyebrows, handlebar mustache. Was *he* Glenn's "horrible problem"? Saffi shook her head. She'd been watching too many horror films on the RV park's 24-hour free cable. No self-respecting villain would go out in public wearing a jacket that could have been made from her grandma's pink chenille bedspread. Still, the man at Glenn's table looked like a story dying to be told, and those were Aunt Saffi's bread and butter.

Before she could let either her deadline or her good sense stop her, Saffi grabbed her mocha and headed their way. She plastered a smile on her face, hoping to convey warmth with her honey-brown eyes rather than an introvert's queasy fear of meeting strangers.

"Saffi!" Glenn steepled his fingers. "At last. I've been telling Malcolm all about you."

Uh-oh. Saffi took a deep breath. "Nothing... unsavory, I hope." Every once in a while, the cheerful gleam in Glenn's brown eyes hardened when he looked at her. She couldn't blame him. Her solution to last summer's RV park murder had left him heartbroken. She hoped that, someday, he would forgive her.

"Glenn tells me that you single-handedly solved the murder of his cousin." The older gentleman's eyes sparked as he took her mug and slid it onto the table across from him. He tilted his head for Glenn to scooch over to the next chair.

"Glenn?" Saffi's look demanded an explanation.

Instead of offering one, Glenn moved over. He left behind a plate with the remains of October's special scone—pumpkin chocolate chip. Saffi broke off a chunk to nibble away her nervous energy.

"Saffi Graywood." Glenn waved a hand from Saffi to his table companion. "May I introduce Malcolm Morton. Actor, rogue, and stealer-of-hearts."

Click! The name triggered Saffi's memory. "*The* Malcolm Morton?" Scone crumbs flew out of her mouth. Her cheeks flamed as she brushed them off the tabletop. Glenn's friend actually *was* the villain in a movie she'd just watched, though his hair seemed to have been fast-forwarded from boot-black to feather-white. What had the film been called?

"*Horror at Haunted Hollow!*" she blurted, covering her mouth before more crumbs could escape.

Malcolm half rose and sketched a Hollywood-worthy bow. When he sat down he gave Saffi's mocha a nod.

"That looks absolutely delicious! I must have one." He snapped his fingers toward Delilah and Saffi cringed.

"Malcolm!" Glenn hissed. "You're not in LA. If you keep doing that, you'll get us kicked out."

"Really? We can't have that, now can we?" Malcolm stood and strode across the room as if he was about to accept an Academy Award. Then he slowly pulled out his wallet, held up a bill so they could see Benjamin Franklin's balding head from across the café, pursed his lips, then plunked the hundred down on the counter. "I'll have what *she's* having!" He pointed toward Saffi, who felt heat rush up her neck and into her cheeks. "And if you promise to not hold my vulgar finger-snapping against my dear friend, Glenn"—he turned to blow Glenn a kiss—"you can keep the change."

Glenn tucked his chin and hid behind his floppy brown bangs. "God. She'll never forgive me, will she?"

Nope, Saffi mouthed.

Once Delilah finished making his Mexi-mocha, Malcolm slow-walked back to the table, careful not to spill any on his pink chenille jacket.

"So, Mr. Morton." Now that she knew he was Hollywood-horror royalty, Saffi opted for the more formal address. "I'm afraid you've been misled. I am not in the business of solving murders."

"No, no. Nothing like murder. At least, not yet. What we have is..." Malcolm paused as if channeling Rod Serling introducing the next *Twilight Zone* episode. "A most unsettling mystery."

Cue ominous music. Saffi glanced at Glenn, who put a hand over his eyes.

"What kind of mystery?" As happened far too often, Saffi's curious nature overcame her common sense.

"Ah." Malcolm took a sip of his mocha, sat back in his chair, and folded his hands in his lap. "A mystery most foul."

Two drama queens at one table. Saffi bit her lip. *There goes my deadline.* She glanced toward the counter for help, but Delilah was busy pouring coffee for a scruffy-haired surfer.

"Some years back, I purchased a property up the road." Malcolm waved his hand vaguely northward.

Glenn jumped in, his brown eyes sparkling with excitement. "You won't believe it, Saffi. Malcolm owns Willow Wood!"

Saffi took a sip of Mexi-mocha and shook her head.

"It's a sixties-era theme park based on characters from *The Wind in the Willows*," Malcom explained. "A few hours north of here."

"*Wind in the Willows?*" Saffi's hands flew to her heart. "That's my all-time favorite kids' book!"

Malcolm's mustache twitched upward. "Yes. Mine as well. When I was little," he went on, "my mother pulled our camping trailer over the Coast Range from Portland for a visit every summer. We stayed in Willow Woods' RV park—the first of its kind on the coast." He closed his eyes as if looking back to his childhood. "The rides were wonderful! Mole's Caravan Cups, Ratty's River Cruise, and Toad's Wild Ride. My favorite." His smile widened until his mustache tickled his cheekbones. "Of course"—he opened his eyes—"I've seen enough of the world to know what a rinky-dink affair it really was, but at the time..." His breath came out in a hum of contentment.

"I can still taste the scones they sold in Badger's Tea House. It was built to look like a great mound of snow. The door was green. Barely tall enough for me to enter upright. My mom had to duck." Amusement twinkled in his dark eyes.

"You actually own a *theme park?*" Visions of a three-page *Bedside Reader* article danced in Saffi's head.

"The original park went belly-up in the seventies," Glenn cautioned. "The rides were sold off to a park in Utah."

"I added the land to my portfolio of properties when it went up for sale. I'm embarrassed to say I let it sit for... well, decades." Malcolm's cheeks went pink. "When I drove up a few years ago, the place was overgrown with gooseberry bushes and blackberry brambles."

The air went out of Saffi's sails.

"But," Malcolm's eyes sparkled, "the RV park was still there."

"After all those years?" Saffi found it hard to imagine an abandoned park in the soggy Pacific Northwest surviving even a single year of neglect.

"It was much the worse for wear. No power or running water. And, it had been taken over by a gang of weasels."

Saffi reread *The Wind in the Willows* every few years, so the reference to weasels made her chuckle.

Glenn rolled his eyes toward the ceiling. "He means houseless hippies."

"Yes. Yes. Hippies. Squatting in *my* park like the weasels who overran Toad Hall. Living in bunged-up vans, crumbling trailers, and broken-down motorhomes. My groundskeeper rousted the last of the interlopers a year ago. Since then the restoration has been going gangbusters. We have more than enough working RV spaces for an off-season opening and a new theme more in line with my acting career."

Glenn tapped the table in front of Saffi. "Ask him about his new theme."

As fascinating as Malcolm's story might be, all Saffi really wanted to ask was for the actor to get to the point so she could get back to her revisions.

Glenn couldn't wait. "Horror!"

A horror theme park? In the Oregon woods? Saffi saw the glint of *Bedside Reader* gold.

Over the years, Malcolm divulged, he had collected a warehouse full of horror movie props and costumes. Not just from movies he'd starred in but from classic and cult horror films. The park would have a horror movie museum. Badger's lovely tea house would become the Little Tea Shop of Horrors. He planned to hide figures around the park in places guaranteed to scare the living daylights out of visitors.

"The park will be called the Haunted Wood. Everyone loves a good scare." Malcolm waggled his fingers in front of his face like a true horror villain. "Am I right?"

Enough people loved horror movies to prove him right. Saffi, however, was not one of them. She still had nightmares about the flying monkeys in *The Wizard of Oz* and that was a kiddie film. But who was she to pop Malcolm Morton's bubble? She pressed her lips together and wiggled her eyebrows in acknowledgment.

"We're celebrating the grand reopening with a star-studded Haunted Halloween Spooktacular!"

"I can't wait." Glenn's brown eyes shone. "I've already planned my costume."

"A costume party. How exciting!" Saffi said, but inside she was wondering who in his right mind would open an RV park on the cold, drizzly West Coast in October.

"Yes, but—" Malcolm patted the pocket of his jacket and reached inside to pull out a stack of postcards. "Before the opening, I need a sleuth to uncover the villain who has been sending me these." He spread the postcards on the table.

Postcards? Were postcards his "horrible problem"? The artwork may have been vibrant when the card was printed, but it had paled over time.

"Vintage?" Saffi shuffled through the cards, her curiosity aroused.

"If they are, then so am I." Malcolm huffed. "Originals, I believe. From when Willow Wood was still open. I received the first one in August, just after I announced the park's grand reopening." Malcolm picked up the top card and handed it to Saffi.

The front of the postcard featured a cartoon badger tipping a cup toward his lips. "Visit Badger's Tea House Today!" Saffi read aloud. "Cute." She glanced at Glenn. "I'm afraid I don't see the problem."

Glenn stuck up a finger and made a turning motion.

When Saffi flipped the card over, she felt as if she'd been zapped with 220 volts of electricity. On the back of the postcard, someone had scrawled *Open this park and I will badger you... to death* in blood-red ink.

TWO

Delilah must have moved to look over Saffi's shoulder with the stealth of a ninja. When she gasped, Saffi's startle reflex sent the postcard flying. The scruffy surfer with the cup of coffee scooped it off the black-and-white tiled floor as he walked past and handed it back to her.

"Who would send such a godawful thing to a sweetheart like you?" Delilah tsked.

Malcolm shook his head and smoothed his mustache. "It boggles the mind, does it not?"

Saffi reached for another postcard. This one featured a cartoon rendering of Ratty waving from the wheelhouse of a river boat. It read, "Greetings from Willow Wood" on the front and *Rats like you should be exterminated!* on the back, in the same thick red ink. The next card featured a jaunty trailer beside a roaring campfire. "Visit Willow Wood!" Saffi steeled herself for what she'd find on the back. More red ink. Another vile warning. *Inhale the smoke and you will choke.*

Saffi counted twelve cards, each one as horrifying as the first.

Delilah put a hand to her heart as if to protect herself from the noxious vibes emanating from the vicious red scrawls.

Saffi shuffled the cards into a loose stack. "These need to be turned over to the police."

Malcolm put a hand over hers. "Which police, my dear? Some were sent to my home in Los Angeles. Others went to my post office box outside Lincoln City. And look—" He turned over card after card pointing to postmarks from up and down the coast.

"Someone who travels," Saffi murmured. "Maybe one of the squatters evicted from the RV park?"

"Yes!" Glenn's percussive clap made Saffi jump halfway out of her chair. Were her friends *trying* to give her a heart attack? "Malcolm, do you see what I mean? Her mind just spins and spins and spins."

Saffi shoved the postcards toward the center of the table. "Glenn." She shook her head. "I can't. The revisions on my book are due in just a few weeks. Even if I was qualified to investigate this mystery, and I am definitely not, there's no way I can take time away from my work."

"Glenn, dear one." Malcolm gathered up the cards. "Just let it go. Actors get hate mail all the time."

Glenn grimaced. "What about the dead badger? That's way beyond hate mail."

"It wasn't a badger, Glenn. It was an otter. Poor thing." Malcolm shook his head. "My groundskeeper found it on the tea shop steps. The park is surrounded by wilderness. Animal carcasses are not at all unusual."

"They are if they've been shot," Glenn mumbled.

The more Malcolm downplayed the incident, the more Glenn fidgeted. Saffi couldn't blame him. The path from animal cruelty to crimes against humans had been well documented. The actor could be in real danger. So could she, if she got between the postcard sender and his prey.

Stay out of it, Saffi. Focus on your work.

Glenn took a deep breath. "What about the rat poison delivered to the park office?"

A dead otter *and* rat poison! "Whoever sent those postcards is making good on the threats. You really should contact the authorities."

Malcolm spread his hands. "Misdelivered. Lennie says it happens all the time."

Saffi narrowed her eyes. "Who is Lennie?"

"My groundskeeper. Lovely man. Extremely hard-working. A tad OCD perhaps."

Two incidents, both connected to the postcards, neither reported to law enforcement on the advice of the groundskeeper. Could it be that simple? If Lennie had a grudge against his boss, Saffi could solve the case on day one and spend the next week nestled among the trees working on Poppy's edits.

Saffi's face must have gone into "sleuth mode" because Glenn put his hands in prayer position.

"Pleasey, please? You solved Linda's murder and ruined my love life in, what, a week?"

There it was. The guilt card. Saffi had wondered if Glenn would play it. Now that he had, he'd trumped every excuse card in her hand, except one—the park host excuse. She clung to it like a life preserver in a tidal wave.

"There's no way Bill would give me time off. You know what he's like."

Truthfully, Bill Kidd, the grisly-bearded park manager, would probably be delighted if Saffi joined the winter exodus from the RV park. During the season's first deluge, he'd shooed her out of the office with a twitch of his nicotine-stained fingers. "Gales like we have around here aren't for fancy-pants writers like you." At the time, Saffi's silver-streaked black curls had been sending rivulets down the front of her rainproof yellow jacket straight into her black rubber boots.

Bill was right about one thing: the park host job was an ocean away from what she should be doing, even on a sunny day. But if it kept her from feeling obligated to chase after a crazoid who killed otters and left them on doorsteps—she'd keep it, thank you very much.

Delilah, who hadn't left the table since Malcolm spread the cards on it, cleared her throat. "Uhm, actually, Saffi, I've been talking to Bill about hosting. Tips aren't so good in the rainy season and free rent would save my biscuits."

"Don't you mean scones?" Malcolm reached for the last piece of Glenn's pumpkin chocolate-chip scone and popped it into his mouth.

"Wait." Saffi scooted back her chair to get a better look at the barista. "Delilah Dunsmore! Are you trying to steal my job?"

Delilah twisted her Last Chance Café apron then let it fall. "Oh, come on. I've been listening to you moan over your morning mocha about those revisions of yours for two weeks. And when you're not in here, you're wandering around the RV park, plodding through puddles and mucking out toilets. The solution's been staring you in the face but you can't see the ocean for the marine layer. Give up the hosting job. Get your book done. Let someone who can't afford her space rent in the off-season—namely yours truly—put up with Bill's bullpucky over the winter."

Saffi's neurons were firing so fast her right eyelid started twitching.

Delilah patted her shoulder. "Breathe, hon."

Saffi took long slow breaths until her eyelid relaxed. "If I had known, I would have—"

"I know," Delilah interrupted. "You're my friend and friends help each other out, right?"

Clearly, Delilah wasn't just talking about her own situation. She was talking about Glenn and the fact that *his* friend needed help and—for some reason—he thought Saffi could, and would, give it. She turned in her chair so she was knee to knee with Glenn. "I really do have to finish this revision. I can't miss my deadline. But I'll do what I can, in whatever spare time I have."

Glenn put his hands on her knees and squeezed. "Free cookies for life!" He grinned. "As long as you *catch* Mr. Postcard Pants."

Mr. Postcard Pants. Such a Glenn thing to say, but not nearly sinister enough for the sicko who'd been threatening Malcolm for months and had possibly killed an animal to prove the threats were real. Still, for better or for worse, the name made going after a would-be killer seem slightly less terrifying.

"Fine." Saffi motioned for Malcolm to return the cards to her. She stuffed them into her backpack on top of her laptop, then rose. "If Bill agrees to hire Delilah, I'll dig around. No promises. But I'll try."

"Wonderful!" Malcolm stood and reached out to shake Saffi's hand. "Of course, this isn't a mystery you can solve from Last Chance Cove. You'll have to come to the Haunted Wood. I'll have the managers hold a site for you. Free of charge." He handed her a gold-embossed business card. "Call me when you're on the way."

Leave Last Chance Cove? He had to be kidding. Saffi's feet pumped the cruiser's pedals faster and faster as she headed back to the RV park on the paved harbor trail. Give up space 32 with the view of the Elk Creek Estuary ebbing and flowing behind her rig? If she left her space now, Bill might not let her back in. What had she agreed to? The weight of the pernicious postcards in her backpack dragged her shoulders down, and the distant bark of harbor seals sounded like laughter. Saffi glanced toward the docks where the seals lounged. *Not funny.*

As the trail intersected the road, she glanced to her right. In the off-season, she could actually cross the 101 without fear of death by semi and head up the steep hill to Troy's cottage overlooking the town. She'd first set eyes on the charter fishing-tour guide mansprawled in an armchair at Last Chance Café. Determined jawline. Eyes as steely blue as a Montana sapphire. Silver-gray hair tousled by sea breezes. Troy had awakened hungers Saffi hadn't felt in three years. If her sometimes sleuthing partner had been home, he would be the perfect sounding board. He wasn't. Troy had headed to Texas last week to visit his decades-younger half-sister Nicole and celebrate his niece's birthday.

For some reason, Saffi felt almost relieved that Troy was away for a while. Her heart had warmed to Troy quickly. Maybe too quickly. She'd met him on her first day in Last Chance Cove. The first time he had opened his muscular arms to her, she'd fallen into them like she'd been adrift and Troy was the harbor. She was ready for a harbor, but not an anchor. Her old life—the one before she took to the road in her Rambler Trek—had been anchored in her husband, Levi, in his career, his Vermont College friends and community. His death had thrown her overboard without a life jacket. Her writing had kept her head above water, and her RV had sheltered her through the storm. Over time, she'd realized that her urge to roam—to discover new places, people, and brain-expanding things—was the sea in which she wanted to swim.

Last Chance Cove had sunk its hooks into her, but her wanderlust had not dissipated. She needed to be free to go where the stories took her, including, she decided, to Malcolm Morton's haunted theme park. As she coasted into the RV park, she realized that she didn't need Troy's advice to make a decision. She would take Malcolm up on his offer, and if Bill balked about letting her keep her RV site? She would rent one with a better view when she returned. Half of the park's spaces had been empty since October said goodbye to September. It wasn't likely to fill once those winter gales Bill warned her about set in.

She leaned her bike against the rail in front of the small weather-scoured blue building that served as the park's office and marched inside. Bill didn't balk. Like the pirate for whom he'd been named, he went straight for her throat.

"You want out of your contract? I'll make *you* a deal." He held up a nicotine-stained finger for her to wait while he fumbled in the file cabinet beneath the cash register.

Saffi watched in horror as he pulled out a worn box that had once held a ream of copy paper, bound together by a thick rubber band. "Please tell me that's not—"

"My book." Bill grinned. "I've spent ten years getting this thing ship-shape. And just as I finish, lo and behold. A bestselling writer drives into my RV park. Just the person I need, I think. Unfortunately, she's so full of herself she can't see there might be a better writer sitting in the room with her."

Saffi snorted.

Bill's bushy eyebrows rose. "See what I mean?"

"Look, Bill. I'm sure you've worked hard on your novel, but I'm not a fiction writer."

"Me neither. It's a true-life tale. Begins in I-raq and ends right here in little old Last Chance Cove."

If Saffi had a dollar for every would-be writer that had begged her to read their work, she wouldn't have to write another word. Unfortunately, she didn't. Also unfortunately, she really wanted to come back to Last Chance Cove RV Park after she solved—or failed miserably to solve—the postcard problem.

"Give it here." She stuck out a hand. "But don't expect me to read it while I'm away. In fact, I won't even open the box until you let me back in the park."

After returning to her RV, Saffi stuffed Bill's manuscript box into the bottom of her closet behind her boots. "And stay there!" She pointed an accusing finger at the defenseless box. Bill's "book" explained one thing: the reason he seemed to have hated her since day one. No one resented a successful writer more than a writer who longed to be published but couldn't get a break. She felt a twinge of pity for the old pirate, but if she was going to hit the road in time to help Malcolm, she had work to do.

First, she gave the actor a call. He was delighted with her decision to head north the next day and promised to have "the very best of the best sites" ready for her arrival. Next, she silenced her phone to preempt distractions. Then she went to the row of wooden cabinets above the cockpit, opened the one above the driver's seat, and pulled out a laminated map. She moved her laptop to the sofa that filled her RV's slide-out and spread the map across the dining table. Then she dug the postcards out of her backpack and stacked them in front of her.

She spent the next fifteen minutes checking for postmarks on the backs of the cards. She marked a red "X" on every town between Last Chance Cove and Lincoln City that matched. Although she did plenty of online research for each *Bedside Reader*, experience told her that the best way to find juicy details was to go to the source. The best source for someone traveling along the coast mailing postcards? Postal workers. In her experience, small-town postal workers spent a good bit of their time chatting up anyone who came in to drop off mail, ship packages, or buy stamps.

Stamps! Now those might offer clues. So far, she knew that the person who sent the cards was not a Malcolm Morton fan. The vintage postcards indicated that the sender knew something about the original Willow Woods *and* about the actor's plan to reopen the park. A lot of people, including Saffi, chose stamps related to their interests and activities.

Saffi flipped the cards over one by one. Over the three months Malcolm had been receiving the threatening cards, the sender had chosen a mix of stamps, mostly outdoor adventures, wild and scenic rivers, and animals. Lots and lots of animals: a breaching whale, a snarling cougar, a leaping Chinook salmon. The outdoorsy type? Saffi sighed. That description fit three-fourths of the people who lived in the Pacific Northwest.

What else? Malcolm had mentioned that his groundskeeper, Lennie, might be a bit OCD. None of the stamps seemed to have come from a single sheet. They'd been chosen individually, perhaps by someone obsessive enough to cause a backup of customers at a postal counter. If that was the case, Mr. Postcard Pants might have made enough of a nuisance of himself to stick in some postal worker's memory. She made a mental note to ask Malcolm for a description of his groundskeeper. If she got lucky, one of the postal workers she planned to question might remember him.

The stamp on the most recent postcard stood out enough to jolt her to attention. It looked as if it had been issued for Halloween: a black silhouette of a cawing raven perched on a branch. Backlit by the garish yellow-green glow of an arched window, the eerie image tingled the hairs at the back of her neck. Raven. Her totem animal. She'd been attuned to Raven's messages for years. But a raven on a stamp sent to an actor she'd just met? That could only mean one thing: she'd gone too long without caffeine, and her brain was about to short-circuit.

As she spooned coffee into her French press, her tummy rumbled. Saffi glanced out the window behind the sofa. She'd been so caught up with Malcolm's mystery, the day had brightened past noon, and the only thing she'd eaten all day was a nibble of Glenn's scone. No wonder her brain was on the fritz.

While the coffee brewed, she stacked veggies on crusty bread and gobbled down the open-faced sandwich. Two of Glenn's butterlicious wedding cookies left her brain sugared up enough to go back to marking the map. By the time she finished, red Xs raced up Highway 101. Tomorrow's first stop would be in Gold Beach, Oregon. If the drive went smoothly, she could hit the post office there and in several other towns before stopping for the night. Checking distances on the map against the safe speed of a lumbering 28-foot RV, she estimated she would arrive at Malcolm's RV park by evening of the following day. None of that would happen, however, if she didn't spend the afternoon readying her rig for travel.

When it came to moving, RVs were like boats on the ocean. When she hit the road, everything that could move, would move. She cleared books, nicknacks, and loose household necessities off the dashboard, the bedside table, and the kitchen and bathroom counters. By the time she finished packing everything into cabinets, drawers, and closets, an ache had lodged in her chest. Though she'd only spent a few months in Last Chance Cove, it felt more like home than anywhere she'd been since she'd driven away from the Vermont college town where she and Levi had lived.

Stop being sappy, Saffi. She heard Levi's voice as if he'd been teasing her about her marshmallow-soft heart in person. Saffi straightened. She couldn't take her Last Chance Cove community with her, but she could bring her blog readers along for the ride.

Saffi opened her laptop and brought up her webpage. She typed "October Spooktacular" into the title block, then hesitated. She had started her weekly blog, *Travels with Aunt Saffi*, to highlight interesting places and amazing facts she found on her journeys. The comments section allowed readers to connect, to feel as if they were a part of her travels. Unfortunately, one follower—who called himself Vendergood—had gone from pleasantries to criticism to harassment. Then, he had started using her posts to track her whereabouts.

Last summer, she had kept a close eye on a silver-and-black Mini-Winnie that showed up one time too many for comfort. The hoodie-clad man driving it had never confronted her, but his presence had hovered like a dark cloud over her days. She had spotted his rig parked here and there around town for weeks. But when she'd settled into Last Chance Cove and begun to build a community around herself, he had disappeared. Would hitting the road trigger him to follow? She didn't know. But if she let a stalker take away her online community, she would be traveling into the unknown completely alone.

THREE

If a movie villain invited you to a Halloween Spooktacular at a brand-new RV park, Saffi typed, *would you dare to attend? Early this morning yours truly, Aunt Saffi, met the master of horror movie mayhem himself, Malcolm Morton, at the local café. He tossed a mystery into my lap and invited me to solve it. At this time of year, there's no place more chilling than the Pacific Northwest. Ghostly foghorns hoot warnings. Fingers of fog feel their way over the jetty. Spooking is in the air. Today's the day I unplug my Rambler and start trekking again. Stay tuned, fellow travelers!*

Saffi pushed "publish," shut her laptop, and stood. Her work-stiffened body needed stretching, and her lungs needed fresh air.

She zipped a windbreaker over her warmest wool sweater and stepped outside. The wind had whipped up, as it often did in the early evening, blowing salt-spray from the cove up and over the berm that separated the RV park from the beach. Damp air filled her lungs, softened her curls, and soothed her chore-weary body. As twilight settled over the park, the automatic lights on the lighthouse-shaped power outlets sent out their guiding glow. Thinking like a park host, she noted the ones that needed bulb replacements. Then she remembered: as of tomorrow, reporting problems to Bill would no longer be her job.

Gravel crunched beneath her sloggers as she continued along the loop to the premium RV sites along the beachfront. Unlike most of the other rows, this one was still filled. As she passed an Airstream trailer, firelight reflected off its shiny aluminum exterior. Saffi waved to the group of campers huddled for warmth around the glowing firepit between the Airstream and the glossy brown-and-gold motor coach in the next site. The happy campers lifted their wine glasses in salute.

On the other side of the motor coach, Saffi noticed a man with scruffy blond hair ducking out of a VW camper van. It was a classic—yellow and white with a pop-top that allowed a person to stand up inside. When the man turned toward her, she noticed his hand gripped a guitar.

Something about the camper looked familiar, but Saffi couldn't place him. Maybe she'd checked him into the park. "Joining the campfire?" She smiled.

"Gonna give it a try." He loped toward her with an easy surfer-dude stride. "You know how those posh retirees can be." He put a finger beneath his nose and pushed it up. "This is my ticket in." He held up the guitar.

Saffi cocked her head. "If they're so snooty, why would you want to join them?"

"Ah. I like the way your mind works. Analytical. Suspicious." He winked. "Sexy."

A blush ran up Saffi's neck, and she took an instinctive step backward.

"Don't worry. I'm harmless. Observant, but harmless. I saw you in the café this morning, didn't I?"

The hairs on the back of Saffi's neck tingled. Was this the man who'd picked up the postcard she dropped?

He raised the guitar and strummed his nails across it. "That was Malcolm Morton at your table, wasn't it? The actor." He paused mid-strum to imitate someone twirling a handlebar mustache. "Do you know him well?"

The guitar guy seemed to have moved from flirting to fishing for information. Why?

A chill wind blew curls into Saffi's face. She brushed them aside, then shrugged. "Not well." She glanced toward the campers in the next site, chatting as they warmed their hands at the firepit.

The scruffy-haired man followed her gaze. "Can you smell that?" He leaned closer. Even with the guitar between them her heart skipped a beat. "They're grilling tuna."

She'd seen enough twenty-something campers in vans to know their fridges held little more than a half-carton of eggs, a pint of milk, and enough deli meat and cheese to make a sandwich or two. Most of them were like gulls, flocking to anything that looked like a party they might crash. But this guy wasn't a kid. He had the sun-toughened skin and crow's feet of someone her own age. His short, thick hair wasn't scruffy, as she'd first thought, just beach-blown. He had the lean, healthy look of a classic outdoorsy type. His khaki painter's pants and brown leather boots were spattered with something that looked like white clay. His moss-green sweatshirt bore a black-line rendering of a bull elk with a single word scripted beneath it: *Sitka*.

"Alaska?" Saffi nodded at the sweatshirt. She could fish too. "That's quite a drive."

"Mmm." The guitar player looked down at his shirt and then back up. In the gathering dark it was hard to tell, but his eyes seemed to match his shirt. Saffi stopped herself just before she licked her lips. *Bad, Saffi.* Was it the three-year hiatus she'd taken after Levi died? Or were the men in Last Chance Cove just that much yummier than elsewhere? Both, she decided.

As if sensing her interest, he waved toward the neighboring campsite. "Care to help me crash?"

"Thanks, but no." Saffi answered before she could change her mind. If she didn't stick to her beach-walk plan—and if she downed a glass of the wine the campers were sharing—she might be more tempted than she wanted to be, given her budding relationship with Troy.

"Maybe next time." He strummed a tune as he walked away that Saffi recognized: Marvin Gaye's lament for the planet, "Mercy, Mercy Me." By the time she reached the sandy path to the beach, the song was stuck in her head. A soulful earworm.

The song always made her feel sad, as if humankind had ruined all that was good and beautiful, and there was no going back. But as her sloggers hit the beach, she looked up. A bright beam swept outward from the lighthouse. It panned across the cove and the jetty, then pointed seaward toward unseen rock formations just offshore. The fog horn's bass warning rumbled in her chest. The ocean added its elemental rhythm to the music. Peace washed through her body, and her usual "glass overflowing with peach kombucha" attitude returned.

"Saffi!"

Saffi turned toward the shout to see Delilah standing in the orange glow of decorative lights strung beneath the awning of her vintage Terry trailer waving her hands above her head. The barista looked not only anxious, but ghoulish.

Saffi waved an acknowledgment, then reluctantly left the beach to join her friend. Only a few steps beyond the protective berm that kept the highest tides out of the park, the barista's campsite enjoyed the calming susurration of waves but a bit more buffeting from the wind than Saffi's site along the estuary on the park's opposite flank.

"I've been trying to call you!" Delilah said. "Everyone's already there. Glenn. Mellie. Detective Richards. They're halfway through the appetizers and ordering a second pitcher of beer. We'll never catch up."

"Wait? Detective Richards?" Why would the town's handsome young Tolowa Dee-ni' police detective be waiting for them? "What happened? Is it Malcolm?" *Oh God.* While she'd been cleaning her RV, the postcard perp had made good on his threats.

"Malcolm?" Delilah scrunched up her face. "He's fine. As far as I know. But the party's in full swing, and the guest of honor hasn't arrived."

For a second, Saffi felt her head spin around like the possessed girl in *The Exorcist*. She must have gone pale and wobbled a bit because Delilah gave her a soft, but bracing, smack on both cheeks. "Saffi. Sweetiekins. I must have left you a half-dozen texts. Where have you been?"

"RV. Laundry room." Saffi rubbed her cheeks. "But I didn't get any texts." She reached into the pocket of her windbreaker and pulled out her phone. The home screen showed text after text, each one with more exclamation marks than the last. The final message was an emoji that looked like Edvard Munch's primal scream. That's when she remembered—she'd turned off the sound so she wouldn't be interrupted while she was cleaning, securing, and plotting tomorrow's course.

"Oops!"

Once Delilah knew what had happened, she explained the hair-on-fire messages. She had cooked up a sendoff at Beachfront Brews and invited the people who were currently guzzling and chowing down without them. Saffi still had no idea how Detective Richards had ended up in the mix, but Delilah must have had her reasons.

"Let's get going!" The barista locked her trailer and started toward the red VW Jetta parked at the edge of her site.

Saffi looked down at her sand-scuffed sloggers and the damp edges of her black jeans. She could only imagine how her hair looked—like Medusa's snarling snakes after being dipped headfirst in harbor water then hung out to dry.

"Sure. Bring it on." Saffi followed Delilah to the small red car.

As Delilah swung the car onto the smooth surface of Highway 101, she tapped her hot pink nails on the steering wheel. The air felt charged, like the moment before a lightning strike.

"OK. What's wrong?" Saffi turned toward her friend.

As Delilah glanced at Saffi, the Jetta swerved to the right. Saffi jumped so hard her seat belt tightened across her chest.

"Sorry." Delilah straightened the wheel. "OK. Remember last

summer when I said Linda Oates might not have deserved to be murdered but she did need a good talking to?"

"Sure."

"So, go ahead. Give it to me with both barrels." Delilah grasped the wheel with both hands. "I can take it."

Saffi felt flummoxed. "Give what to you?"

"The butt-kicking I deserve for going behind your back and yanking your job out from under you."

"Delilah, it's—"

Before Saffi could finish, Delilah barged ahead.

"The truth is, when I told Bill I wanted to host, he said I'd have to wait till your six months were up. Said there weren't enough RVers in the park to hire another host. But I kept pushing, like I always do. And now look what's happened. You're *leaving!*" Her voice rose into a wail. "And I pushed you out of here."

The barista pulled the Jetta into the first empty space at the restaurant, turned off the engine, and sat there with her lips wobbling. Saffi reached out a hand and patted her friend's thigh. "You didn't push me out. You pushed me to do what I should have been doing in the first place. The revisions I need to finish before Poppy kills me. And I'm not *leaving* leaving. As soon as I solve the postcard puzzle, I'll be back. And when I get back, I don't need to be checking in campers and cleaning toilets. I need to do my *real* work, researching and writing *Bedside Readers*, which earns me enough money that I don't need free space rent." She gave Delilah's leg a final pat. "You do, so the job's yours. No harm. No foul. Except... toilet duty. That's pretty foul."

That got a sniffly laugh out of Delilah and cleared the air enough for the two women to open their car doors and swing their legs out. Delilah's in snug and sexy taupe leggings under a ribbed, off-the-shoulder sea-blue sweater dress. Saffi's in sand-crusted black jeans under a windbreaker. Delilah walked around the car to link her arm through Saffi's as they made their way toward the brewpub. Just as they reached the pub's front door, it opened.

Mellie Blue—the town's most eccentric artist—reached out a hand to drag Saffi inside.

As always, Mellie looked like she'd stepped out of a Frida Kahlo self-portrait. Her long black hair had been woven into a crown, her pert lips painted poppy red to match the flowers bursting across her lemon-yellow shirtwaist dress. The black velvet shawl draped around her shoulders upped the outfit from eye-catching to elegant. Saffi sighed. *Why, oh why didn't I take time to change?*

They walked into the cacophony of a pub in full swing. Voices calling out orders. Pints thunked on counters. Silverware clanked against plates. The underlying hum of conversation gave the industrial chic dining room a beehive's buzz. Mellie danced them through the crowd near the bar toward a table by the fireplace. Thankfully, the roaring blaze took some of the chill out of the space.

"Saffi!" Glenn waved her to the chair on his left. "I saved you a seat."

On his right sat Detective Richards, his brown eyes more serious than she'd ever seen them. Since they'd met during a murder investigation, that did not bode well. The minute Saffi had settled in with a Dockyard Amber and pinched the last few calamari strips from the nearly empty appetizer plate, the detective leaned across Glenn.

"I thought you learned your lesson last summer," he said.

The detective didn't have to explain. Saffi knew exactly what he meant. Last summer's sleuthing had nearly gotten her killed, not once, but twice.

Glenn put a hand on the detective's broad shoulder. "It's not a murder, Detective. It's a mystery. And mysteries are Saffi's jam. She'll have things figured out and be back in an eyeblink." He blinked his long dark lashes in such a flirty way that Detective Richards' cheeks reddened. Then he narrowed his dark brown eyes at Glenn and set his mouth in a grim line.

"You haven't told her, have you?"

Saffi paused with a calamari strip halfway to her mouth. "Told me what?"

Glenn tugged at the collar of his black turtleneck sweater, then blew his bangs off his forehead. "Can't we let the girl enjoy her beer and nibbles first?"

"Told me what?" Saffi repeated, grasping her beer mug so hard the cold stung her fingers.

Detective Richards made a "keep talking" motion with his hands.

"OK. Fine." Glenn held up his hands in surrender. "Malcolm called a little while ago. His groundskeeper has gone missing."

Saffi's hand slid down the mug. "Missing?"

Lennie. Her one and only suspect, the person who had been involved with both the dead otter and the rat poison—who might be OCD enough to painstakingly pick out postcard stamps—was missing. His guilt had seemed ridiculously obvious. So obvious she'd pictured her visit to the Haunted Wood as a revision retreat.

Oh, Saffi. What have you gotten yourself into?

FOUR

Needless to say, the detective's reveal had burst the farewell party's bubble. Her Last Chance Cove buds took sides as they debated the merits of helping Glenn's friend versus waiting to learn more about Lennie's disappearance. According to Glenn, Malcolm had left a message for his groundskeeper just after she confirmed her decision to puzzle out the postcard mystery. He had asked Lennie to make sure the hookups were working in the site he'd promised Saffi. But when the actor pulled into the park a few hours ago, Lennie was nowhere to be found. The park managers hadn't seen him since lunchtime.

Had Malcolm told his groundskeeper that an amateur sleuth was driving north to investigate the postcards? If he had—and Lennie was behind the threats—he might have done a runner. The whole thing could be over by the time she reached the Haunted Wood. If Lennie *wasn't* behind the threats, his disappearance could be an escalation. From threatening postcards to a dead otter to rat poison to... what? Kidnapping? She hadn't seen that among the threats.

"I can hear your brain grinding all the way over here." Detective Richards rubbed a hand across his mouth. "My advice?"

Saffi pushed her beer mug away, then drew a finger through

the condensation trail, turning it into a giant question mark the detective couldn't help noticing.

"Stay home. Let law enforcement look for Lennie."

The news about Lennie had destroyed her appetite, and she didn't have the bandwidth for another round of "What should Saffi do?"

She slid her chair back and stood. "Sorry to cut out, but if I'm driving north tomorrow, I have to get up at the crack of dawn."

"And if you're not?" Glenn worried his lower lip with his teeth.

"I'll let you know."

Delilah half rose, fumbling for her car keys, but Saffi waved her back into her chair. "I think I'll walk. Gather my thoughts." She hurried from the table before her friends could stop her.

Head down, hands stuffed into the pockets of her windbreaker, Saffi rushed through the front door and plowed into a man standing in the shadows beyond the pub's entry light.

"Sorry." She reached out a hand to steady herself against his arm before looking up. She had grabbed the muscular bicep of the outdoorsy guy with the beach-blown hair. "Guitar Guy! I thought you were hitting up those retirees for supper."

"I did, but it's one and done with the over-seventy crowd. One of them actually nodded off over his tuna steak, if you can believe that."

She believed it. "I keep running into you."

"Literally." He chuckled. "Come back inside and I'll buy you a cold one."

For a brief second, Saffi considered the offer. Then she shook her head. "Sorry. I'm a few years short of falling asleep in my tuna, but I've got an early morning."

Her answer made his green eyes spark with interest. "Where you heading?"

Saffi crossed her arms over her chest. That was one question too many from someone she didn't know. The scruffy-haired guy was fishing again. *How well do you know Malcolm? Where are you heading?* He'd been there in the café, observing their table. He had "just happened" to pass by and pick up the postcard she'd accidentally flung to the floor. Had he looked at it? Did he know what it meant? Was he, God forbid, Mr. Postcard Pants in the flesh, relishing the effects his threats were having on his victim?

Chills ran up Saffi's arms and settled at the back of her neck.

"Saffi! You OK?"

She had never been so glad to hear Detective Richards' voice. "Just heading home." She sketched a wave to both men and hurried across the parking lot. After she crossed the road, she glanced back, fearing Guitar Guy would still be standing there, watching.

He wasn't. But the detective was. She offered him a grateful salute, then set a brisk pace back to the park and the safety of her tiny home on wheels.

As sunrise turned the puffy early-morning clouds fuchsia pink, Saffi wiggled to the edge of her bed, eyes still half-closed like a week-old puppy's. It had been a rough night, filled with dark dreams. One had struggled to the surface. She'd been running at top speed, crashing through thick woods. Branches slashed her face, and roots reached out to trip her. Behind her, the gasping breath of some unseen horror came closer and closer. A raven croaked, three times, and she felt herself falling... falling backward into murky water.

She'd written a "Dreams for Dummies" listicle for *Bedside Reader*, #7. If she remembered correctly, dreams of falling into water could point to suppressed emotions. *Ha!* She had plenty of those to choose from: grief, despair, homesickness, longing, the fact that she was missing Troy yet fooling herself into believing she was relieved to have a break from their growing relationship.

And fear... especially the fear of being stalked.

Last night, when Guitar Guy showed up one time too many she had leapt to a conclusion: he could be the person sending Malcolm those threatening postcards. This morning, another possibility surfaced: the stalker who'd been tracking her whereabouts. In her mind he was the hoodie-wearing man in the silver-and-black Mini-Winnie, but she'd never seen his face. Her stalker could be anyone, including the man in the van. Why did he keep showing up? Asking her to join him for a drink? Calling her sexy when she'd been grimy from cleaning and bundled in a windbreaker on her way to the beach?

She *was* analytical and suspicious, just as he'd noted. Those qualities were useful for sleuthing, but a turn-on? Seriously? *No,* the scruffy camper had noticed her at the café for one reason: she was sitting at the table with Malcolm Morton. If she had to guess, she would say Malcolm was his target, not her. She added him to her ridiculously short list of suspects: 1) Lennie, 2) Malcolm's "weasels," and 3) the outdoorsy man in the VW van. Now that he was missing, did Lennie even belong on the list? So many stabs in the dark, so few actual clues.

Saffi swung her sleep-stiffened legs out of bed. It was time to stop procrastinating and push herself toward what she knew she had to do. Something wicked was coming Malcolm's way. Glenn had pleaded, and when Raven called—even in a dream—she could not turn away.

After a cup of French brew and a microwave-warmed chocolate muffin, Saffi hung her shower-damp robe on its hook. She pulled enough layers from her built-in wardrobe to keep the chill out of her bones when she went outside to flush her RV's tanks and unhook her rig. Thick winter leggings, a thigh-length butter-soft tunic, a roomy burgundy hoodie that settled comfortably over her hips. She dug a pair of blue latex gloves out of the box beneath the driver's chair and tucked them into the front pouch of her hoodie.

"OK." She steeled herself to step out into the cold. "You've done it before. You can do it again."

Outside, fog huddled close to the creek behind her rig as if, like Saffi, it was too chilled to rise. She hurried through her routine: empty the gray and black water tanks, strap her mint-green cruiser into the carrier rack attached to the back of her RV, and unplug her rig from the 30-amp power outlet. As she worked, she thought about the advice Detective Richards had offered at the pub: *Stay home. Let law enforcement look for Lennie.*

Yesterday morning, tracking down Mr. Postcard Pants had seemed like a lark. The sender had threatened Malcolm, but not harmed him... physically, at least. Now? With the groundskeeper missing? The task of finding the postcard perp seemed much weightier, not to mention riskier.

If Lennie was a victim, who was the perp? Malcolm's "weasels"? The actor had used his groundskeeper to force the squatters out of his deteriorating RV park. Any one of them could be nursing a grudge. Boondockers—RVers who camped off-grid— came in all flavors. Those like Saffi occasionally boondocked along a coastal highway or tucked into an old logging road on Bureau of Land Management lands for the night. But those who lived off-grid full-time were a different breed. The ones occupying Malcolm's park could be anything from actual hippies to serious drug addicts to vets with PTSD. Someone like that could have fixated their grievances on Lennie as well as Malcolm. If she followed through on her promise to Glenn, she might be making herself a third target.

On a conscious level, she knew she bore no responsibility for Glenn's heartbreak. On an unconscious level? Raven's three croaks in this morning's dream might not be a call to adventure. They might be a warning. *Stay out of the woods, Saffi.*

While she stood there lost in thought, the gray tank finished draining. She detached, collapsed, and stowed the accordion-like sewer hose and the white freshwater hose, then blew out her breath. The whole operation only took half an hour, but it felt like she'd been standing in the cold morning air for days. She pulled off the blue gloves then walked across to the dumpster and tossed them inside. Her rig was ready. Was she? Perhaps regrettably, she was.

The last thing she did before she cranked the Rambler's engine was tap out a text to Troy: *Heading north for a Spooktacular Halloween. Wish you were here.* As she pressed "send," she realized just how true that was. Maybe, if he texted her back, she could entice him away from Texas for the Haunted Wood's grand reopening party.

She had timed her early-morning leave-taking to avoid the maudlin goodbyes that would make departing harder, but when she swung her Rambler Trek into the lane that led past the office, a gauntlet of bundled up well-wishers lined the way. Morning dog walkers waved. Campers blowing on steaming cups of hot coffee stopped long enough to offer a cheerful bon voyage. Glenn ran up to the driver's window, motioning for her to slide it open. When she did, he shoved three white paper cookie bags into her hands.

"Hungry Mamas, Wedding Cookies, and Baker's Tears. For the road!" He stepped back, put his hands in the pockets of his navy peacoat and locked eyes with Saffi. "Be safe!" he ordered.

Was that a hint of remorse she saw in his compassionate brown eyes?

Saffi clutched the bags against her chest. *Baker's Tears.* After she exposed his romantic partner as a killer, Glenn had poured his pain into creating the cookie—bittersweet and sprinkled with sea salt, as if showered with his tears. Had he chosen those as a reminder that she owed him? If not, he might as well have.

Beyond Glenn, Saffi spotted Delilah standing at the foot of the ramp that led to the salt-scoured blue office building. She clutched a red leash attached to Archie, the lively white terrier she'd inherited from the park's former manager. Bill stood in front of her, legs spread, arms crossed, as if barring her way inside. His gruff voice cut through the RV's engine hum.

"That is *not* a service animal. It's a mutt!"

Then he looked up at Saffi and yelled, "Your resignation is denied. Get back in here!"

"Bye Bill. Bye Archie!" Saffi waved, then blew a kiss to Delilah, who caught it and pressed it to her heart.

The first miles back on the road after months at an RV park were always challenging. Handling a 28-foot rig was more like driving a city bus than a car. Every movement felt exaggerated.

Every turn required muscle strength and intense concentration. She had no idea why the DMV didn't require a special license to drive one. At the north end of town, she stopped to get gas, air up her tires, and grab a bitter drink masquerading as a mocha. Once her 40-gallon tank finished filling, she swung her bulky rig wide to pull away from the pumps, cringing when she almost took one out anyway. *Come on, Saffi.* She gave her heart time to find its normal rhythm, then merged into the stream of traffic heading north out of Last Chance Cove on Highway 101.

She drove through redwood groves for a few miles, doing her best to keep her gaze from straying into the mysterious shadows beneath the towering trees. She didn't realize she was hunched over the steering wheel, straining to see the treetops, until she hit the rumble strips along the shoulder.

"Holy crappage!" She jerked the wheel hard enough to make her rig sway, wobbling back and forth until the Rambler settled into the lane. *Eyes on the road, Saffi. Eyes on the road.*

As she emerged from the colossal trees' deep shadows, her heart thudded so hard she could barely appreciate the expanded view. Forest gave way to fields that swept all the way to the gunmetal-gray sea. She grasped the wheel hard enough to make her fingers throb, passing dairy farms, lily fields, and multimillion-dollar mansions clinging to the edges of cliffs with barely a glance. Traffic in this section of the highway moved at a brisk 60 m.p.h. Whenever she eased off the pedal to open up a safe space between her RV and whatever vehicle she was following, a car or truck would blast past her rig, horn blaring in annoyance.

When the highway sliced through a coastal section of the Yurok reservation, the speed limit slowed to a sedate 35 m.p.h. The tiny tribal community along either side of the highway boasted a casino, a mini-mart, a gas station, and not much else. Saffi relaxed her white-knuckled grip on the steering wheel and reached for her mocha. *Still hot.* She took a long, slow pull on the to-go cup's sippy lid, then pulled a face. *Still bitter.*

As her rig lumbered past the gas station, she spotted a yellow-

and-white VW bus sidled up to a pump. If it was the camper van she'd seen last night, Guitar Guy had left the park even earlier than she had. Or maybe—her suspicious mind kicked into gear—he had followed her until she stopped for gas then driven past to keep from arousing her suspicion. *Ha! Good luck with that ruse, buddy.* If that was the case, his pitstop could be an excuse to let her get ahead of him again.

As the cars in front of her sped up, Saffi forced her attention back to the road. If she wanted to keep 16,000 pounds of moving metal between the center line and the shoulder, she had to focus on something besides the mysterious man in the VW van.

FIVE

By the time Saffi reached Gold Beach, the first red "X" she'd marked on her map, her shoulders burned like they were on fire. All she could think about was getting out from behind the wheel and massaging her muscles. The single-story Gold Beach post office hunched at the edge of the town's harbor with the slate-blue Pacific pounding into the shore on its right and the crystal-clear Rogue River surging into the sea at its rear. The US flag on the pole out front whipped back and forth in the brisk ocean breeze. She tapped the cellphone clipped to a dash mount: 8:35. Just after opening time. That boded well for finding no lines and a postal worker with time to chat.

She hurried toward the post office with her palms pressed to her curls, hoping to keep her hair from puffing up like a dandelion gone to seed. One look in the door's reflective glass told her she'd failed. Once inside, she noticed a bulletin board filled with "Wanted" posters. *Wanted: Drug Trafficking. Wanted: Robbery of Postal Employee. Wanted: Shooting of a Postal Truck Driver.* Each poster promised a reward of up to $50,000, offered by the US Postal Inspection Service.

The US Postal Inspection Service! If her amateur sleuthing didn't turn up any clues, that was who Malcolm should contact.

The middle-aged postal worker behind the institutional-white counter stopped spraying it with disinfectant, wiped it down with a paper towel, and tossed the towel into a trash can against the wall behind her.

"Blowing up a storm out there, isn't it?" The postal worker nodded at Saffi's hair.

The woman's uniform—light blue shirt, dark blue slacks—did not flatter her figure, but it wouldn't flatter any woman. It was a man's uniform, military cut. The dark blue eagle's-head logo on the woman's shirt looked like it was about to fly off her chest and gouge someone's eyes out. Saffi's maybe.

"I should have worn a cap."

"No use." Notably, the dark brown bun at the back of the woman's head was pulled so tight it stretched her cheeks toward her ears. "It would have blown halfway to Agness by now."

Saffi had no idea where Agness might be, but she had a feeling if she kept quiet and listened, she would find out. She glanced at the woman's name badge. *Brenda.* Brenda was just the kind of worker she'd hoped to find behind the counter. Talkative.

Brenda pushed her rectangular glasses up her short straight nose then pressed her hands on the counter. "So, I don't see a package or an envelope, you must need stamps."

Saffi nodded. "Do you have any nature- or Halloween-themed stamps?"

"Got both. Single or sheet?" Brenda unlocked a drawer beneath the counter, pulled it open and started rooting around in it.

"Single. I just need a few."

The woman dug a bit deeper. "These are fun." She held up a half-filled sheet of Halloween stamps.

Excitement buzzed through Saffi's body. The stamps looked just like the one affixed to the most recent postcard the actor had received. Spooky silhouettes in ghastly-colored windows.

"This may sound strange, but I was hoping for a raven."

"Somebody already snagged that one, unless you want to buy a whole sheet?" She pulled an intact sheet out of the drawer and waved it enticingly.

Saffi pursed her lips as if considering. "Hmmm. I just need one to send a postcard."

Brenda's cheerful demeanor shifted. "The guy who bought the raven stamp said the same thing. Then he took fifteen minutes choosing one stamp." Her eyes narrowed.

Clearly, Brenda's patience was wearing thin. "I'm traveling, so I'll probably buy more postcards along the way. I'll take that." Saffi reached for the full sheet of Halloween stamps, hoping to get back on Brenda's good side. "You must have an amazing memory."

The postal worker shook her head. "Who needs a memory when Yelp is forever?"

Saffi scrunched her nose. "What do you mean?"

"The guy took so long someone posted a scathing review. You wanna know what she said?"

Saffi gave what she hoped was a sympathetic nod.

"'Beware of this post office. Especially Brenda. She showed a customer every stamp in the drawer. By the time I reached the window, it was 5 p.m., and she said she couldn't serve me because it was *after hours!*'"

Saffi did her best to keep a straight face. "So you remember him." She hadn't yet asked Malcolm for a description of Lennie, but if Brenda could describe the guy, she would.

"You bet I do. I got written up because of that guy. His face is right here." She tapped the center of her forehead then proceeded to give Saffi a description worthy of the "Wanted" posters she'd seen in the lobby. *Male. Caucasian. Tall. Fifties. Wearing a green sweatshirt.*

Saffi's belly clenched, and her hands went cold. "Was there a picture on the sweatshirt?"

Brenda scratched her nose. "There was. Some kind of wild animal."

Saffi pictured the bull elk on Guitar Guy's sweatshirt. "Any words?"

"Just one. Sitka."

Brenda's description exactly matched the guitar-playing camper from Last Chance Cove. That, combined with his suspicious behavior, moved him to the top of Saffi's suspect list. If he was the postcard perp, this investigation could be over before it started.

There was one problem: she didn't know his name. As Saffi climbed back inside her rig, she mulled over how she might track him down. If she saw him again, she could start a conversation. Get him to divulge his name. Copy his license plate info. That would give her his state of residence, Alaska, most likely. She needed the same info she would gather from campers back at the RV park.

Saffi smacked herself on the forehead. He'd camped in her park. If he hadn't been a stealth camper, all she had to do was call the office. If she was lucky, Delilah would answer the phone.

She wasn't.

"Miss me already, huh?" Bill's chortle came through the phone. "Well, it's too late. Delilah's taking to the job like a shark to chum."

The image of fish guts in the water turned Saffi's stomach. "Is Delilah there? I'd like to talk to her."

"Nope on a rope." Bill sniffed. "So, whatta ya want, other than to hear my manly voice?"

Since she'd already left the job, what Saffi wanted wasn't legal for her to have. But knowing Guitar Guy's name was too important. She sucked in a breath, giving herself time to think. What would make Bill give up the goods? He loved nothing more than putting women in their "place." Maybe she could play on his misogynistic urges.

"I met this camper at the cove last night. Up in the front row? He was in a VW van. Space, uhm, thirteen. Right by the beach path."

"You met a dude, did you?" Bill snorted. "Troy's away so it's time to play?"

Don't react, Saffi. Let his dirty-old-pirate mind wander where it will.

"It's not like that, Bill. He's interested in, uhm... movies," Saffi said the first thing that came to mind. Thanks to Malcolm, that was films. "I told him I'd send him the brochure the Chamber of Commerce hands out about movies filmed along the Pacific coast."

"But you were so busy not fooling around on Troy, you forgot to get his deets."

Saffi punched her own thigh to keep herself from pouncing on the gleeful pirate. "I forgot, yes. But it's nothing to do with—"

"Uh-huh. It's just that brain fog women your age—"

Now he'd done it. "Bill! Get a grip. Yesterday was long and busy. My mind was elsewhere. I didn't get his info, OK. Now give it to me before I burn that manuscript I have stowed in my closet!"

"Whoa. Hold on, now. I'm getting it." Was that a hint of desperation in the old conniver's voice?

Saffi heard something that sounded like Bill flipping through last night's registration cards.

"Space thirteen. Space thirteen. I got twelve, fourteen, fifteen, sixteen. Thirteen, huh? You sure?"

"I'm sure."

"Looks like your heartthrob didn't register."

Saffi's breath caught. So he *had* been a stealth camper.

"Oh, wait!" Bill broke into her thoughts. "Here it is. Somebody misfiled the darned thing. You, probably."

Saffi caught her lip between her teeth to keep from reminding him of all the times she'd had to reorder the registration cards after his turn in the office.

"OK. His name is Charles Horseman. He's got a P.O. box in Los Angeles. His email address is charleyhorse@snailmail.com."

Saffi groaned. "Bill. Did you check his driver's license?"

"Course I did."

Right. Saffi could almost see the spittle splattering the office phone. Poor Delilah.

"Charley Horse at snailmail.com?" She waited, giving him

time to pull his head out of his posterior. It didn't happen. "Bill, come on. Who's foggy now? It's a fake name. Bogus email address. What about his license plate? That must be real."

"License plate? Why would you need that to mail a brochure?" Bill barked. "Wait a minute." A few seconds passed as Bill's brain caught up with his mouth. "You're snooping for clues!"

"Fine. You caught me. Just give me the guy's license plate."

"Heck no! You shouldn't be asking for any of this stuff! I could lose my job."

"Bill, this is important. If you don't want to give it to me, pass it to Detective Richards. He already knows why I would ask."

"I'll think about it, but if you do anything to my manuscript, I'm gonna come for you. *Capiche?*"

Why did "tough guys" lapse into pseudo Italian when they wanted to intimidate someone?

"Catch me if you can." Saffi held the phone away from her ear for a few seconds to enjoy Bill's increasingly frantic pleading. "*Hasta la pasta*, Bill!" She used her own favorite phony phrase before pushing the red button to hang up.

Charles Horseman. Really, Bill? The whole thing made her leg muscles clench. But they loosened as she thought about what she'd learned. The guy in the VW camper van was traveling incognito. That meant he had something to hide. Did the P.O. box location tell her anything? If he was the culprit, being in Last Chance Cove the same day as Malcolm visited was no accident. He could have followed Malcolm up the coast from Los Angeles. He could be following him still, all the way to the Haunted Wood, fully prepared to make good on more of his threats. It was time to stop ruminating and hit the road.

Saffi checked the next red "X" on her map, then folded it away. She cranked the Rambler's engine and secured her phone in the mount on the dash. Catching sight of the three bags of Kevin's Kookies, she opened the Hungry Mamas, bit into the yummy goodness of oatmeal, chocolate chips, raisins, and pecans—her all-time favorite nut. She washed the chewy cookie down with a water-bottle chaser. *Thank you, Glenn!*

"Port Orford! Here we come!"

Moments later, Saffi's exuberance met the reality of the road. As she turned left onto the long, narrow bridge that spanned the Rogue River, wind whapped the side of her rig with the force of a giant's fist. *Whoa!* The steering wheel jerked right, and Saffi cranked it back to the left and held tight. To her relief, the Rambler's weight kept it from tilting sideways and flopping over the stumpy concrete rail between her and the choppy water below.

Saffi's heart pounded. What had made her think she could handle this drive? Four months of staying put had turned her into a road wuss.

After about half an hour of white-knuckling the road, she wound through a forest dense with sword ferns, rhododendrons, Douglas fir, and western hemlock. She emerged into Port Orford, the second "X" she'd marked on her map for today. Despite the cheerful blue trim on the town's white postal building, her inquiry about a tall white man possibly wearing a green Sitka sweatshirt elicited a grim, "No! Next!" The pasty postal worker behind the counter glared her out the door.

Another forty minutes took her to her third stop: Bandon. The red-brick post office was another strike-out. The two postal workers bustling behind the counter actually laughed when she asked if they remembered a guy buying single stamps.

The older of the two, a stocky man with the dark skin, square jaw, and coarse black hair of someone with Filipino ancestry, hefted a package off the counter and dropped it into a rolling bin behind him. "Which guy?" he asked when he turned back to Saffi. "The one that just went out the door, or one of the hundreds of other guys who buy stamps here each and every week?"

Saffi clenched her teeth in a contrite grin. "Is that the dumbest question you've heard today?"

"Oh, no. Willis Bunker came in here earlier. Asked me if he could pop the bubble wrap."

His female co-worker, a freckled redhead sporting round, black Harry Potter glasses, pulled a face. "The first time he came for the bubble wrap, he didn't even ask. He just went postal on the stuff."

The Filipino guy grinned. "You ducked under the counter. Remember?"

The redhead blushed. "I thought he had a gun... OK?"

The black-haired worker's eyes held enough fondness in them that Saffi figured he harbored a secret crush on his co-worker. "Willis is a Vietnam vet with PTSD." He turned to Saffi. "His therapist told him to pop bubble wrap so he'd be less jumpy about sudden sounds. Now, I think he just does it for the fun of it."

"It *is* fun." The redhead nodded. "But if you want to play..."

"... you gotta pay."

The two dissolved into a laughing fit.

Saffi sighed. These two had been working together long enough to finish each other's sentences.

"So, what are you, some kind of detective?" the male worker asked.

While Saffi debated how much to divulge, she read his nametag. "Well, Vincent, I'm doing a bit of research for a book I'm working on." She crossed her fingers behind her back to witch away the lie.

"A writer! I'm a writer, too." The redhead's hazel eyes shone with excitement and curiosity. "Tell me about your book."

"Oh," Saffi waved a hand to downplay her accomplishments. "I write nonfiction. Weird-but-true stories about this, that, and everything."

"Like *Aunt Saffi's Bedside Readers*?"

Saffi squinted at the young woman's nametag. *Laurie?* Was the lettering getting smaller, or was it time for glasses?

"Those books are great. WindRiver Books down in Old Town carries them. Hey!" Laurie scrounged a piece of paper from the recycling bin and pulled a chained pen toward her. "What's your name? If you get those stories of yours published, I'd love to read them."

"Saffronia Graywood." She reached out and shook Laurie's hand. "But my friends call me Saffi."

Laurie's squeals followed her out the door and lifted Saffi out of the doldrums she'd been sinking into. Her last two post office stops had been big, fat sleuthing fails. Her brilliant idea to haunt post offices had gained her two clues: someone had bought a raven stamp in Gold Beach, and that person matched the description of the man in the yellow-and-white camper van. The only reason Brenda remembered anything about the guy who'd bought the raven stamp was the online review that had led to being written up by her supervisor.

Back in her rig, Saffi set her phone's GPS to direct her to WindRiver Books. The minute she pulled onto the highway, the sexy Aussie male voice she'd chosen for her cell's navigation system said, "In fifty feet, turn left." She obliged, guiding her rig under an arch with a *Welcome to Old Town Bandon* sign.

She wrangled her Rambler into an RV spot in the town's free parking lot, then scurried toward the blue locator dot on her cell-phone's map. Brisk ocean air swirled around her, lifted her curls, and freshened her energy after the post office's stuffy interior. She spotted the WindRiver Books & Gallery sign swinging in the breeze the minute she turned onto Second Street. Once inside the warm and welcoming store, she bought a cozy mystery she hadn't read, signed the store's stock of *Bedside Readers*, and got a lunch recommendation.

Tony's Crab Shack was a few blocks west near the town's tiny port. "Look for the red awning," the bookstore cashier told her. The shake-roofed building's awning definitely stood out from a distance. As Saffi got closer, she saw colorful windsocks bucking the breeze and crab traps piled in stacks. The building housed a bait-and-tackle shop as well as the crab shack. A good sign, she decided. The seafood would be fresh.

She blew through the door on a salty breeze and stopped in front of a deli counter loaded with fresh fish on ice. After glancing at the chalkboard menu above the counter, she ordered a cup of chowder and a crab cake, slipped a tip into the "Crew Appreciation Jar," and took her food out back to the town's glass-enclosed picnic pavilion. Gulls begged for bites, but she was way too hungry to share.

Being inside the pavilion allowed her to enjoy both her food and the view across the mouth of the Coquille River all the way to the sea. The wind couldn't reach her, but she could still see its effects. Seabirds fought against its force, some blown backward, others straining to stay in place. The bob and sway was a dance Saffi could have watched all day, if she hadn't needed to make more miles before she camped for the night. She scraped the last spoonful of chowder from her cup and picked crab-cake crumbs from her burgundy hoodie. Gulls careened and caterwauled just outside the pavilion, but Saffi held firm. "Sorry, mates."

When she stepped outside, the wind hit full force. Saffi reeled. A nearby warbler's cheerful twitter sounded like laughter. She blushed and glanced over her shoulder to see if anyone else had seen her drunken stumble. Then she tossed the empty containers into the trash bin and headed in the direction of the parking lot. As she crossed the street, she noticed a van parked so close to her Rambler's nose she would have to back up before pulling out.

What a nincowpoop! Saffi co-opted one of Bugs Bunny's favorite insults as she clenched her fists and marched toward the vehicle. Within a few strides, her boots skidded to a halt. She was storming straight toward a yellow-and-white VW camper van.

What should she do? Casually walk up and say, "Why are you following me?" Or "What's up with those threatening postcards you've been sending to Malcolm Morton?" Or, better yet, pull out her cellphone and call—

A sinking feeling sucked away her cockiness. She was on the road with no backup. No Detective Richards, no Delilah, no Glenn. No resources beyond her own brain and abilities. What had she been thinking? Collecting clues to solve a crime made for a great board game, but in real life, every clue led closer to an actual criminal. As she stood there, stiff with uncertainty, the VW's wheels spun sand into the air as the driver hit the gas. By the time she reached her rig, she had her key in hand. If she could catch up with the van, she might be able to write down its license plate.

She didn't need the key. Her automatic steps were extended. That could only happen if her door was ajar. Saffi felt as if she'd been gut-punched. She yanked the door open and stumbled up the steps before she could even think about whether she should go in or stay outside and call the cops. She paused in the kitchen space and forced herself to take long, slow breaths, the kind that would lower her heart rate and stop the vein in her throat from pulsing. That gave her time to take in details: her raven pillow still rested on the couch with her Pendleton-wool throw draped behind it. Her kitchen and living room cabinets seemed undisturbed. When she walked to the back of her rig, she found nothing amiss. Had she forgotten to lock her door? Maybe the wind had blown it open.

Saffi shook her head. *No!* The wind was blowing shoreward, the wrong direction to force the door open. It was more likely to slam it shut. She clambered down the stairs and back outside to check the door for damage. The metal plate around the keyhole hadn't been scraped or bent. She saw no evidence of a forced entry. She must have left it unlocked. Her belly felt sick. How could she have been so stupid?

The keys, Saffi? Remember? Levi's voice echoed in her head and she *did* remember. The RV dealer where they'd purchased the Rambler Trek had warned them that standard RV keys could open just about any RV lock. He'd recommended upgrading to a coded keyless lock. At the time, the cost had been off-putting. Now, it seemed a small price to pay for security. The first chance she got, she would have the lock replaced. At least nothing seemed to be missing.

Back inside, Saffi closed the door to let the steps retract. Then she locked it and checked the handle to make sure no one could enter. If she hadn't been traveling, she would have had a glass of wine to settle her nerves. But driving an RV even slightly impaired was not on her to-do list. She scooted into the captain's chair and resettled her cellphone in the dash mount. Now, all she needed was to check her next destination on the map. She reached toward the passenger seat where she thought she'd left it. The map wasn't there.

It wasn't under the passenger seat or beneath the captain's chair. It wasn't in the cabinet above her head. A pulse started to pound in Saffi's temple as she checked place after place. It wasn't on the couch, on the dining table, or in the bathroom. It was gone, and so—she soon discovered—were the threatening postcards she'd carefully tucked into her backpack.

Her entire investigation had driven away in that VW van.

SIX

Saffi made two calls: the first to ask Detective Richards if it would be worthwhile to inform local police about the break-in, the second to warn Malcolm about the man in the yellow-and-white van. The detective insisted that she file a report, even though he acknowledged that the follow-through might be little to none.

"Get it on record, so that if anything else hap—" He took a long pause. "Look, Saffi, no matter how good you are at digging into details, this isn't someone you're investigating for a book. File a report. Let the police do their jobs. Stop the sleuthing and stay off this guy's radar."

He didn't say the words "before it's too late," but Saffi heard them nevertheless. Her response did nothing to reassure him—or herself, for that matter.

"I'll get it on record. Then I'll get back on the road."

She expected the call to Malcolm to include a little less drama. Unlike Detective Richards, who saw her as an amateur without a clue, the actor saw her as his sleuthing salvation. She should have remembered: drama was Malcolm Morton's middle name.

"Oh, Saffi!" Malcolm's voice was filled with relief. "Are you almost here? Losing Lennie has shaken me to my core."

Saffi frowned at her cellphone. "Lennie's still missing?"

"Missing? Darling, he's not missing. He's dead!"

"Dead?" Saffi couldn't seem to squeak out more than one word.

"His body was found in the river. Trapped beneath our dock." Malcolm breathed into the phone, deep, heavy breaths as if the weight of what had happened rested on his chest. "I can't believe any of this is happening to me. It's like something out of one of my own movies!"

Saffi's grip on the phone tightened. How could Malcolm be *so* insensitive? He wasn't the one dead under the dock. Saffi gulped down her gorge as the horrific image flashed into her mind. A dock, a river, a fall... all three had shown up in her dream. Maybe Raven's message wasn't some subconscious mumbo jumbo about guilt at all. Maybe Raven was guiding her to Lennie's body the same way he'd led her to the body on the beach last summer.

"Did Lennie drown?" *Please say it was an accident.*

Malcolm sighed. "The local sheriff seems to think it's foul play. He's questioning everyone in the park as if we are suspects in some dreadful made-for-TV movie. Poking around all over the place. The museum. The tea shop. Lennie's tool shed. He even inspected my roadster, if you can believe it!" The actor harrumphed. "What the fool thinks he'll find in there, I'll never know."

"Malcolm, I don't know. This changes things."

"Saffi, darling, things can't change! They really can't." For a second, the bite in the actor's voice reminded Saffi of the way he'd snapped his fingers to get Delilah's attention at the café. Then his voice warmed. "You must come! You're the only one I know who has actually solved a murder. Glenn assures me that you will give the case the attention poor Lennie deserves."

Saffi grimaced. *Thanks a lot, Glenn.* The fact that Malcolm had already labeled Lennie's death a murder rang alarm bells. It could have been an accident, even if the sheriff had decided to question everyone. Why was he so sure Lennie had been killed?

"Maybe you should postpone the park opening. Just until the case is solved. You don't want to expose your guests to this level of danger, do you?"

The cellphone went silent as if Malcolm was considering her suggestion, but when he spoke again, he was adamant.

"Invitations went out a month ago. RSVPs are coming in by the... by the dozens. My guests are troopers. The show must go on and all that. Besides, the local paper splashed our grand reopening across the front page of this week's paper. No, my dear. We must keep the pedal to the metal, just like our dear friend Mr. Toad."

Saffi chewed a nail to keep from saying what she was thinking out loud. *All of Toad's adventures ended in crashes or jail time.*

"You'll catch the perpetrator and put an end to his shenanigans. I just know it. What was that silly name Glenn called him?"

"Mr. Postcard Pants," Saffi mumbled.

For her, the name no longer held any charm. Murder was miles away from mischief. Detective Richards was right. She had to file a police report. The perp in the yellow-and-white van deserved a place on law enforcement's radar, and Malcolm's. Before she rang off, she described the camper van and its driver and told Malcolm about the stolen postcards.

"There's the sleuth Glenn told me about!" he said. "You'll have this thing solved before you arrive and you can relax and... what writing task are you supposed to be doing?"

"Revising." Saffi ended the call with a sigh. Right now, all she wanted to revise was her decision to leave Last Chance Cove.

The young police officer who took Saffi's report had ruddy cheeks and spiked blonde hair. He looked like he'd be happier on a surfboard than stuck in a musty wood-paneled room taking down the details of a break-in with nothing missing but a road map and some postcards.

"Are you sure you didn't leave your RV unlocked?"

Saffi scrunched her lips then forced a smile. "Yes. I'm sure."

When he asked the question again a few minutes later, Saffi held up her hands. "You have all the information you need, Officer.

I don't want to waste any more of your time." She was out the door and into her rig before he could close his gaping mouth.

The break-in left her on edge. Though she hadn't seen the VW van since it spun out of the parking lot, the hair on the back of her neck prickled as she drove, and she couldn't get over the feeling of being followed. Her gaze kept drifting to the dashboard rearview camera screen. After she hit the highway's rumble strips multiple times, she swore. "Eyes forward, Saffi!"

She rolled down the hill into Coos Bay after 5 p.m. Part of her was relieved that the post office was closed. A man had died. Maybe it had nothing to do with the postcards. Maybe it had every-thing to do with them. Either way, she was too exhausted to grill any more postal workers, especially at the cranky end of a long day.

A few miles up the road, she stopped to gas up, fill her water bottle at her kitchen sink, and take a long-overdue potty break. A private bathroom was the benefit she most appreciated about RV travel. No thigh-clenching waits for a public restroom. No disgusting facilities to endure. Just a rest stop in her own home sweet rolling home.

With sunset fast approaching, Saffi kept her rig as close to the speed limit as she dared, hoping to reach the campground she had targeted for tonight's stop before the sun sank below the horizon. There were far fewer travelers on the road at this time of year than there had been when she drove to Last Chance Cove at the begin-ning of last summer. Not having tailgaters biting her bumper helped her relax into the drive.

She swung her rig into Honeyman State Park, just south of Florence, so close to sundown that the Latina ranger cautioned her to wait for morning before walking the trail to the dunes.

"Get an early start in the morning and you'll avoid most of the dune buggies," she said as she handed her a parking permit to post in her windshield.

"Dune buggies?" Saffi must have looked as bewildered as she felt. How could there be dune buggies in a state park?

"Yep. You can drive the things right out onto the dunes from H Loop."

Once Saffi drove deeper into the park, she understood the ranger's warning. The campground was heavily forested, the deep shadows foreboding. Night was about to fall and at this time of year it would fall hard and fast. She backed her rig in, leveled the jacks, and hooked into water and power. The park had an RV dump station—which she would take advantage of on the way out—but no onsite sewer hookups.

Despite the ranger's warning, Saffi's body whined for a good stretch. *Please, please, pleasey-please* don't sit down. Sitting was the last thing she wanted to do. She wanted to walk through the gathering dark toward whatever story the dunes at the edge of the campground had to tell. She stuffed her cellphone, a battery-operated flashlight, a bottle of water, and a protein bar into her backpack, locked her rig, and pocketed her keys. Then she followed the asphalt back to the main entrance, gave the ranger an apologetic shrug and looped around to the trail that would take her to the dunes.

It didn't take long to see the error of her writerly ways. The path was narrow, fully immersed in shadow, and slippery with mud. In some places, dark pools of water lurked just a misstep away. She thought about turning back, but the scent of earth and sea and tree kept her boots marching forward as her lungs filled with nectar-sweet evening air. Within ten minutes, the smell shifted from moist forest to sunbaked sand.

Saffi hurried toward the gap in the trees where the trail gave way to dunes. Within a few steps her stride turned to a sandy slog. Moments later, she stood, mouth gaping, at the view that had inspired Frank Herbert's sci-fi masterpiece, *Dune*, and its water-starved planet, Arrakis. Massive dunes, ground from the backs of the Coast Range by the mighty Pacific then sculpted by the wind, towered above her. She stood with her boots in shadow, but sunlight bathed the dune's crest. If she reached the top before sunset, the view would be nothing short of spectacular. How could she resist?

At first, the climb seemed doable, but the higher she went, the more vertical the dune became. Sand rolled beneath her boots, dragging her halfway back with every forward step. Her backpack tugged at her shoulders, and she shrugged it off. The extra weight was not helping. She chugged down enough water to sustain her, took a few bites of peanut-butter chocolate protein bar, then washed them down with more water for good measure. She rustled in the bag for her cellphone. She would need it for photos once she reached the crest. Then she left the pack behind. No one else was crazy enough to be hiking up the dune at twilight. It would be safe.

Saffi climbed... and climbed... and climbed, but, with every step, the summit seemed farther away. The shadows at the base of the dune deepened and crawled upward. Darkness consumed her tracks. The light at the dune's crest turned golden. The smartest thing she could do would be to turn around, head back to the forest trail before it became too dark for safety.

She took a break, licking salt from her lips as she debated. *Up or down? Make a decision.* Watching the sun set from the top of an Oregon dune was nearly irresistible, but the ranger's warning rang in her ears. Her legs had grown tired, her breath as labored as a woman a decade older. Her shoulder muscles ached more than they had when she'd climbed out of her coach. *Down*, she decided.

Just as she turned to descend, her ears caught the buzzing whine of a dune buggy at full speed. She couldn't see it, but as the sound increased, two beams shot outward above her head. The buggy was coming over the dune, straight at her. Her only hope was that it would go airborne. Saffi flattened herself against the sand, and not a moment too soon. The machine soared over her quaking body to land a few feet from where she'd been standing moments before. Her heart pounded, but the buggy's engine drowned out all other sounds. Turning onto her back, Saffi let the dune cradle her as her breathing slowed. As her body stilled, something else caught her attention—the sound of the buggy scrabbling in the loose sand as it reversed. The vehicle's blue-white halogen headlights pointed in her direction, and Saffi's vision blurred. Every muscle in her body clenched as if expecting the buggy to screech forward and grind across her.

To her infinite relief, it didn't. Instead, the driver turned off the engine. The crash of waves against the distant shore filled the air. Saffi struggled to sit up, raising her forearm to shield her eyes from the blinding headlights. A figure emerged from the buggy's protective metal cage, a black silhouette coming toward her out of the light. She held her breath; her hearing sharpened until she could hear the scrunch-shush of boots in the sand.

For the second time since she left Last Chance Cove, she felt absolutely alone. She had put herself at the mercy of fate—made herself a target of Malcolm's enemy. And if that was who slogged toward her right now, she was up a sand dune without even a backpack to smack into his knees.

SEVEN

When a woman's voice called out, Saffi's lungs expanded with air and her heart unclenched.

"You OK?" A leather-gloved hand reached toward Saffi.

"I probably peed my pants, but I'm fine." She put a knee in the sand, gripped the hand, and let the woman hoist her to her feet. "You scared the crap out of me."

"Yeah, well I told you not to come out here this late, didn't I?"

Once Saffi was on her feet, she recognized the ranger from the check-in booth. She busied herself brushing off the seat of her pants, then the back of her hoodie to let her embarrassment cool before she faced her. "You did."

"And you didn't even make it to the top." She clicked her tongue and shook her head.

"I would have, if you hadn't almost decapitated me." Saffi hated the whine in her voice.

"Operative word, *almost*." The ranger tucked her arm through Saffi's and tugged her toward the dune buggy. "How about I make up for it with the ride of your life?"

If she'd been so inclined, the twinkle in her hickory brown eyes might have lured Saffi into more than just a buggy ride. Since she wasn't, she settled for a heart-thumping, wind-whipping rumble up, over, and around dune after towering dune as sunset washed the sand with a glow as orange as a Halloween pumpkin's shell. The ride ended with a short roll down a sandy slope into H loop, where the ranger tucked it into the first parking space and cut the engine.

"We'll have to walk from here." She leaned close and whispered, "It's quiet time."

Saffi's legs actually wobbled when her boots hit the pavement. Who knew riding in a dune buggy required so much muscle? All that clenching and clinging and whooping and hollering and holding on for dear life. She had sand in her hair, her clothes, her ears, even up her nostrils, but Saffi could not have cared less. The ride was... thrilling, that's what it was.

"That was unforgettable, uh, uhm...." She raised her brows at the ranger in question.

"Val."

"Saffi." She held out her hand, and Val slipped off her leather driving glove and grasped it firmly.

"Saw that on your registration form." She stuck both gloves in an inner pocket of her forest-green uniform jacket and zipped it closed.

"It's short for Saffronia," Saffi said.

"Ah. Unusual. Like mine, which is *not* short for Valerie, so don't even go there."

"OK. I'll bite. What's it short for?"

The ranger kicked a stone with the toe of her boot. "Valencia," she said softly.

Saffi chuckled. "Like the orange?"

"My mother was a picker in the groves down south."

"South as in southern California?" Saffi asked.

Val nodded. "Mom said Valencias were the sweetest oranges she'd ever tasted, and I was the sweetest *bebé* she'd ever seen."

"Aw. That's adorable."

As they sauntered past site after empty site, the ranger rubbed her hands together.

"Should have kept those gloves on." She saluted a trio of campers roasting marshmallows over a roaring blaze inside a fire ring.

The walk worked the kinks out of Saffi's legs. She hadn't felt so good in... well, forever. Maybe it was all the oxygen she'd inhaled yelling her head off as Val whipped the buggy left, then right, spewing sand in their wake. Lost in the after-glow of the ride, she didn't realize they'd passed her RV site until Val stopped in front of the ranger's cabin near the park entrance.

"I'm not much of a drinker, but I've got some kombucha. Or hot chocolate? If you want to come in."

The moment of absolute loneliness Saffi had felt on the dune came back, and she could not resist. She paused at the door to take off her sand-filled boots and brush sand off her thick socks. Then she bent over and gave her curls a good shake before following Val inside. The one-room cabin was roughhewn, but the coarse wood made it feel sturdy, safe. Val waved Saffi toward a small gray couch positioned in front of a woodstove. Just beyond the couch was a full-sized bed tucked tight with blankets and piled with pillows, some flannel-covered, some faux fur. What looked like a down-stuffed duvet lay folded across the foot of the bed. The woodsy style made Saffi want to nestle into the couch and not move. Unfortunately, the moment she sat down, her metabolism cooled and she went from thrill-ride hot to lounging-around cold. She bounced her sock-clad feet and rubbed her arms to rev herself up.

"Don't worry." Val knelt in front of the stove, opened the glass-windowed door, struck a long-handled match and held it to the crumpled paper beneath the kindling. In seconds, fire blossomed along its edge. "Warms up fast in here."

Saffi smiled, thinking of her own tiny living room. "Small spaces do that."

"So." Val skirted a wooden café table with a single chair and stuck her head into the fridge in her petite kitchen. "I've got pumpkin spice and apple ginger. Both homemade." She glanced over her shoulder at Saffi.

"Wow. You make your own kombucha? I'm impressed."

Val's cheeks pinkened and she shrugged. "Some of my job postings have been pretty remote. It was make my own or do without."

"Both those flavors sound great but, to be honest, I'm feeling a bit too chilly for a cold drink," Saffi admitted.

"Hot chocolate it is! As long as you like it Mexi-style."

Val chopped a fat round tablet of Ibarra chocolate into small pieces while a saucepan of milk warmed on the woodstove. When the milk started to simmer, she added the chocolate and stirred with a wooden spoon as it melted. She sprinkled cinnamon and cayenne pepper into the pan, then whisked the ingredients into a froth before pouring the steaming mixture into mugs. As spicy smells permeated the room, Saffi tucked her feet beneath her, and relaxed into the "I Love Oregon" cushion propped against the couch arm.

"Your place is super cozy."

Val handed her one of the two steaming mugs, and Saffi held it between her palms, letting its warmth toast the chill from her fingers.

Val sat at the other end of the couch and chuckled. "You wouldn't have said that if you'd seen it when I first arrived. Or smelled it." She tweaked her nose. "I swear, the ranger before me must have been tanning animal hides in here."

Saffi couldn't stop a shiver of revulsion. "Glad I missed that."

"Listen, Saffi." Instead of lifting her mug to her lips, Val set it on the floor. "I didn't run into you on the dunes by accident. I was looking for you. And I brought you here because I wanted..." Val hesitated.

Uh-oh. Had coming inside given Val the wrong idea?

"To warn you," Val finished.

Saffi stiffened, nearly losing her grip on the mug. "Warn me about what?"

Val waved toward Saffi's mug. "Drink your chocolate before you spill it."

Saffi took a sip and tried to lick away the froth before it dribbled down her chin and onto her hoodie. As usual, she did not succeed. "Oops!" She grinned. "I'm pretty sure my husband, Levi, fell for me because I'm such a mess."

"I can see the appeal." Firelight danced in Val's hickory brown eyes. "If I were a few years older, I might fall for you myself." The ranger deftly stuck a pin in Saffi's ballooning ego.

Saffi sputtered into her hot chocolate, sending so much foam onto her hands Val jumped up to fetch a kitchen towel. After Saffi dried most of the stickiness from her hands, she handed it back with a wry grin. "The husband comment?"

Val laughed. "The straight woman's fallback when she thinks I'm flirting."

"OK. Since my perimenopausal charms hold no appeal"—Saffi quirked her brows—"why *did* you bring me here?"

"Like I said, to warn you." Val set her mug at her feet. "About an hour before you arrived, a camper pulled up to the window. He told me he was supposed to meet a friend at a campground outside Florence, but he couldn't remember which one. He described you and your rig."

Saffi stopped with her mug raised halfway to her lips. Guitar Guy had already grabbed the postcards and her map. What else could he want?

Val patted her arm. "Don't worry. I told him there was no one in the park matching his description and sent him on his way."

When Saffi breathed a sigh of relief, Val shook her head.

"He came back. After you'd checked in."

A chill ran through Saffi's veins. "He's here? In the park?" She set her mug on the floor and started to rise, but Val leaned over and put a hand on her arm.

"It's OK. Sit."

Saffi sat, but her body vibrated like a rocket about to blast off.

Val finally picked up her mug. She balanced it on one knee while she talked. "I told him he had the wrong park. We didn't have a single Rambler on the premises. Gave him a few other places to check, and he drove off."

Saffi put her face in her hands. "Thank God you were the one at the booth," she mumbled through her fingers.

Val shook her head as she blew on her hot chocolate, then took a sip. "It wouldn't have mattered. With all the wackos in the world, no park ranger would give out information about a woman traveling alone. Besides, since you *are* a woman, if you'd been meeting someone, you'd have asked me if he'd checked in. If he hadn't, you'd have called him and texted him until he showed up to get you to stop. Am I right?"

Saffi grinned. "Naturally."

Val reached a hand across the couch toward Saffi. "Is this guy stalking you? I could put out an alert on his butt. He wouldn't be able to get a campsite anywhere on the coast."

Saffi pictured the outdoorsy guy with the guitar on a "Wanted" poster, and then, because her libido apparently couldn't control itself today, she pictured him on one of those "hottest men" calendars. *Hottest postcard perps?* Maybe not.

"Thanks," she told Val, "but that's probably not necessary. The thing is, I've been investigating some... threats."

Val's brows shot up. "Are you some kind of private detective?"

"No." Saffi blew her unruly curls off her forehead. "I'm a writer."

"A, uh, what?"

"Yeah. Ridiculous, isn't it? I helped solve a murder last summer and then deluded myself into thinking I knew how to track down bad guys."

"How bad?" Val uncurled from the couch, stepped to the front window, and lifted the edge of the curtain to peer into the darkness.

"I'm not sure, but worse than I thought when I started this misadventure. Someone sent threatening postcards to a friend of a friend. The horror film actor, Malcolm Morton?"

"Ooh!" Val dropped the curtain edge. "His movies give my goosebumps goosebumps. I love them!"

"Yes, well, it's gone way past postcards. Malcolm's

groundskeeper may have been murdered. And this guy in the VW camper van just keeps"—Saffi threw up her hands as if warding off a blow—"showing up... wherever I go."

Val's green eyes went wide. "Good grief. What are you going to do?"

Saffi hesitated. She could imagine what Val would do. She would pull on her black leather gloves, throw a shovel in the back of her dune buggy, and buzz after the guy. When she caught up with him, she would whop him so hard little cartoon birdies would fly in circles around his head. But Val was Val, and Saffi was an aging writer who spent too much time pounding a keyboard to pound anyone in real life. Not that she'd want to. If she ever figured out who sent those threatening postcards, she would gleefully hand him over to the nearest law enforcement officer and then pulverize his reputation in a *Bedside Reader* article.

Saffi drained the cooling chocolate in her mug. "Honestly, Val. I don't know. Maybe I'm done with sleuthing. But right now, I'm going to get some sleep before I get any loopier than I already am."

"Before you go." Val held up a finger. "The guy who asked about you wasn't driving a VW van. He was in a Mini-Winnie."

A cold fist clenched Saffi's belly. It had been months since she'd last seen the silver-and-black rig, but as soon as she'd gone on the move, it had shown up again. Her stalker was back, and her Spooktacular blog post had probably started his engine.

EIGHT

Despite the bomb Val dropped the night before, sleep came quickly. She slept like a log—one that had been blown over in a gale, crashed to the ground, then tried to pull itself upright by its branches and roots. In the process, her bedding had been destroyed. She gave the jumbled sheets and blankets a one-eyed glare and shuffled into the RV's tiny kitchen to boil water for her morning coffee. Once her French press had been filled, steeped, and plunged, she poured the aromatic brew into her favorite mug, the one with the raven.

She pulled the thick terry robe she'd thrown over her flannel jammies closed and cinched the belt tighter to keep out the early-morning chill. Then she carried the steaming mug outside to breathe in the morning air. When she reached the picnic table, she froze. Her backpack was perched atop the table's weathered wooden planks. She'd left it on the dune, then forgotten all about it. Saffi took a sip of the smooth Honduras roast in her cup, hoping a shot of caffeine would jingle a few brain cells.

Val! The ranger must have found the pack and dropped it off while she was still sleeping. What a thoughtful thing to do! Saffi smiled. Were her things still inside?

She dumped the contents out on the picnic table. Water bottle, flashlight. Had Val snitched her half-eaten protein bar? Saffi gave the bag an extra shake hoping the protein bar would tumble out. It didn't. Instead, stiff paper rectangles rained down on the table. It took Saffi's brain a few seconds to register what she was seeing. Malcolm's postcards! They'd been stolen in Bandon. How could they be in her pack now?

Only one person could have returned them, and it wasn't Val. It was the man in the VW van. The man who had broken into her RV: Guitar Guy, AKA Charles Horseman. Saffi knew better than to put one and one together and come up with "guilty," but the description Brenda, the Gold Beach postal worker, had given her of the man who bought the raven stamp had been a dead-on match to Charles Horseman—or whoever the man with the silly pseudonym really was.

She might be done with sleuthing, but, clearly, sleuthing was not done with her. This guy had followed her all the way from Last Chance Cove, stolen Malcolm's postcards—and her map, which was still missing—and then returned the cards. If he was the post-card perp, why would he do that? No amount of caffeine could combobulate her brain enough to figure that one out. His finger-prints must be all over the cards. If she could get them into the hands of law enforcement, she'd have physical evidence to pin at least one crime on the perp: the RV break-in. And that might put her one step closer to closing this case.

If she'd been in the cove, she could have asked Detective Richards to get them examined. Of course, he probably would have refused and told her to stick to writing. She drained her coffee mug, wishing caffeine settled her nerves instead of making them sizzle.

After a day on the road, the mystery she'd set out to solve—who sent those threatening postcards to Malcolm—had shifted like grains of sand on a dune. It now included not one but *two* stalkers dogging her steps, a break-in, a theft, and—possibly—a murder. Were all those things connected? If so, how?

Think, Saffi!

She was missing something, something important. The post-card threats had been leveled at Malcolm, not at his groundskeeper. But the cards had not stopped the actor. They hadn't even slowed him down. He was going ahead with the grand opening of the Haunted Wood, despite three months' worth of threats. Frustrated, and angrier than ever, the person behind the threats could have decided to take his terror campaign to another level. But why go after the groundskeeper?

The answer whapped her between the eyes. Lennie had been at the Haunted Wood, in harm's way. Malcolm had not. Which meant—how could she have missed it? If the postcard perp had been haunting her drive northward and breaking into her RV to steal a map and a handful of postcards, he could not have been at the Haunted Wood killing Lennie.

Saffi took a deep breath. It was time for pj tai chi. Standing between the picnic table and a massive rhododendron separating her site from the next, she slid her feet out of her sloggers to connect with the earth. Body grounded in mountain pose, she sank into her hips and did her best to ignore the pokes and jabs of pebbles and pine straw as she began her practice. Slow stretches to earth and sky. Hands calming the waters, fanning the wind, moving clouds, focusing the arrow of intention. She inhaled oxygen fresh from the evergreens that surrounded her, and—with hands pressed together in a final namaste—she gave back gratitude to the Earth for the energy it shared every morning.

Saffi brushed the prickles from her bare feet, slipped on her sloggers, and picked up her empty raven mug. It was time to get ready for the road. Unhooking from water and electric went quickly but when she maneuvered her RV into the park's dump station, the black tank took its own stinky time draining. As she waited, she checked her phone to see how long today's drive would take. If she moved at a good clip and didn't stop along the way, she would arrive in two hours.

She missed her stolen map with the starred post offices, but her gut told her stopping at them would be a waste of time. She'd glommed onto grilling postal workers because the cards were the only clues she had to follow. The tactic had given her a suspect, but dawdling along the way would not get her closer to solving the case. There would be pitstops, of course. There were too many cliffs and curves between Honeyman State Park and her destination to drive without a break. When a message from Delilah pinged on her phone describing the caramel-meltdown-mocha she'd once had in Yachats, Saffi knew just where that stop would be.

She eased her rig away from the dump station and crawled past the check-in booth on her way toward Highway 101. As she passed, Val came running out, waving a sheet of paper. Saffi braked and slid open the driver-side window.

"I spotted that VW van you told me about!"

Saffi nodded. "I'm not surprised." She shared what she'd found on the picnic table, and Val grimaced.

"He must have walked to your site. His camper van was parked right there." She pointed to a few lined spaces near the park entrance. "And I got this!" She waved the paper then handed it through the open window.

Saffi gasped. "His license plate! Oh, wow." She waggled a finger at Val. "Naughty, naughty."

Val fluttered her eyelashes. "I do what I can for my friends. And, being a *writer*," Val gave her a conspiratorial wink, "I'm sure you'll know just what to do with that."

"Absolutely." Saffi folded the sheet of paper, then half rose from the driver's seat and tucked it into the back pocket of her jeans. "Sit on it. At least, until I can find someone with access to a DMV database and the credentials to use it."

As Saffi released the emergency brake, Val stepped back. "Be safe, Saffronia Graywood!"

"*Nos vemos*, Valencia Orange!"

"Not if I see you first!" Val teased, and Saffi decided that she would definitely stop at Honeyman on her return trip. She'd never had Ranger Woman for a friend before, but every friend she found along the Pacific coast made her feel like she was finding her way home.

Saffi set a spine-jarring pace along the stretch of highway between Honeyman and Florence. She slowed to city speed limits as she chugged through town, then sped up again, remembering from her map that she would soon be clutching the steering wheel in terror.

The map was right.

The road climbed cliffs so high she felt dizzy when her gaze shifted toward the sea. Her Rambler Trek strained like an aging bull going uphill and pulled at the reins like a racehorse on the way down. When the highway dipped down to sea level straightaways, signs reminded her that the Oregon coast paralleled a deadly earthquake subduction zone. As if she could stave off "The Big One," she sped up and held her breath between each *Entering Tsunami Hazard Zone* and *Leaving Tsunami Hazard Zone* sign.

A few heart-thumping highway loops later, Saffi pulled into the tiny cliffside village of Yachats and found a sandy spot alongside the road near the Green Salmon Coffee Shoppe to ease her rig off the pavement. Before going inside, she took time to call Detective Richards. With an argument already on the tip of her tongue for why he should run the VW van's license plate, she started talking the minute she heard his voice. It took a few seconds to realize she'd reached his answering machine. Why she'd thought he would be in the office at 7 a.m., she wasn't sure. When the machine beeped, she left a message explaining about her backpack showing up and read off the plate number along with a plea. "I don't have any other law enforcement contacts. You know I wouldn't ask unless—" The machine cut her off mid-sentence, which was just as well. The detective knew her well enough by now to know she would not only ask, she would pester him until he answered.

The caramel-meltdown-mocha she ordered was everything

Delilah had promised and more. In fact, it was so good she wanted to savor it instead of sipping as she drove. She cranked her engine and followed the signs to Yachats State Park. She parked her rig to give herself an ocean view while she sipped scrumptious coffee, munched a sunrise bagel sandwich, and wrote a blog post based on the sustainability practices of the Green Salmon crew. From mopping floors with rainwater to heating the space with forest service slash—woody debris left behind from logging operations— the cozy coffee shop conserved energy in some of the most creative ways Saffi had ever seen. "What's the wildest, weirdest, or coolest way you conserve?" she asked her followers. She reread her post, fixed a few errors, and then hit "publish."

Feeling good about writing *something*, she stowed her laptop and slid into the captain's chair. The road bumped and curved and sang as the Rambler's wheels gobbled up the last miles before her destination. Tuning into a radio station on the edge of the continent was next to impossible, so she belted out pop songs from the sixties, seventies, and eighties—making up lyrics when she couldn't remember them. Once she reached the outskirts of Lincoln City, the last town before Malcolm's Haunted Wood, she pulled into the first gas station advertising propane for sale. Some RV resorts had propane onsite for refills, but Saffi had no idea if Malcolm had included that perk in his park plan. If she wanted her teeny home cozy-warm during October's chill afternoons and nights, she needed to top off her tank.

Stopping gave her an unexpected update on the park and even added a few new clues to her decidedly short list. When the station attendant finished filling her propane tank, she went inside to pay the bill he had scribbled out and spotted the local paper. Malcolm had told her about the front-page article celebrating the park's reopening. The photo showed a white banner strung between two Douglas firs. In ghoulish red letters complete with simulated blood drips, the banner read: *Malcolm Morton's Haunted Wood*.

Saffi bought the paper and took it back to her coach. Since no other rig was waiting for a propane refill, she spread the inky newsprint out on her dining table and sat down to read. The header was what Malcolm had intimated: *Horror Film Star Celebrates Grand Opening!* The article contained much of the same information the actor had shared with Saffi when they'd met. His fond memories of Willow Wood had prompted him to buy the dilapidated park when it went bankrupt. He held onto the land for decades. Now in "the twilight of his career" he had time to devote to his pet project: restyling Willow Wood as a "haunted" park, complete with a horror movie museum and spine-chilling surprises lying in wait in the woods.

"For all those horror fans who want a jolt of fear with their evening stroll," the reporter, whose byline was Brian Bennion, quoted Malcolm, "I have the original Creature from the Black Lagoon among many other movie ghosts and ghouls guaranteed to scare your socks off." The article went on to mention Malcolm's "Little Tea Shop of Horrors" and the attached RV park, stating that it would open before Halloween and could accommodate a limited number of guests, by reservation only.

The next part of the article was more than just news; it put her sleuthing self on high alert. Local real estate developer Cecily Raymond, who the reporter called "the force behind Riverside Ranch near Cascade Head," had offered a scathing opinion of Morton's grand vision.

"More like grandiose," Raymond was quoted as saying. "Malcolm Morton is not a developer. He's a B-list Hollywood fop hoping to fan the flames of his long-dead fame. But locals shouldn't worry," Raymond continued. "When Morton's park flops—as I'm sure it will—I'll make him an offer he can't refuse. The long-delayed Riverside Ranch extension will be back on the drawing boards with the new and better features our upmarket buyers crave."

The article went on to outline the possible benefits of both projects for local taxes and businesses and seemed biased toward Cecily Raymond's real estate venture. If the man in the van hadn't stolen those postcards, the real estate developer would have gone to the top of Saffi's list of suspects. While researching a *Bedside Reader* article, she had stumbled on a university study that put murder motives into four main boxes: love, lust, loathing, or loot. When it came to the Haunted Wood, Cecily Raymond had something at stake. Something the size of a mountain of money.

NINE

Saffi had expected the Haunted Wood to be easy to find, with a highway sign pointing to the turnoff and a lighted resort-style sign at the park entrance. Instead, she spotted helium balloons printed with Malcolm's image in his most famous horror movie roles. They bobbed above a tumbledown fence that seemed to be melting into the ooze along a roadside ditch. *Malcolm as Dracula, Malcolm as The Wolfman, Malcolm as a killer clown.* One balloon every fifty feet or so.

The images startled Saffi so much she nearly drove her rig into the ditch beneath them. What she didn't do was spot the turn into the park: a narrow gravel road gouged out of the thickest brambles Saffi had ever seen. She blew past the "entrance" and slowed to take the next right turn. Big mistake. The surface road she wandered onto was narrow and winding with no possible turn-arounds for a 28-foot rig. If Malcolm's plan had been to locate a tourist attraction in the middle of nowhere, he had succeeded.

Saffi poked her cellphone on its dash mount, hoping her GPS could help her loop back to the main road. Fifteen minutes later, she took a right turn onto the Salmon River Highway at a burned-out shell of a building. Her cellphone identified the blackened hulk as the Otis Café and labeled it "permanently closed." The two-lane road ducked under Highway 101 then curved around to merge into it. Seconds later, Saffi spotted more of Malcolm's creepy balloons along the right-hand side of the road. She gritted her teeth. A left-hand turn into a narrow drive was always easier than a right-hand turn, but the entrance to Malcolm's Haunted Wood consisted of several feet of earth and gravel humped over a metal culvert with a drainage ditch on either side. She sat in her lane, engine humming, unwilling to risk what wasn't just her RV, but her home, to a "bridge" that seemed certain to collapse under the weight of a 16,000-pound machine.

Nobody in their right mind would drive an RV over that. Saffi took her hands off the wheel and pressed them into her jiggling knees to give herself time to think, but the distant blast of an airhorn brought Saffi's chin up. Her eyes went to the rearview camera screen. The grainy black-and-white view showed a semi-truck coming off the mountain about a half-mile behind her. A second blast of the airhorn told her all she needed to know. The truck driver didn't have enough room to brake for a stopped vehicle. She could turn into the park or put her foot on the gas and hope to accelerate fast enough to avoid being plowed into the pavement.

She turned.

As the semi roared past, the back of her coach swayed. If he'd hit her, Saffi realized, it would have been her own darned fault. She should not have stopped in the middle of a heavily traveled highway to size up a turn. Truthfully, she'd never attempted one with so little wiggle room. She'd seen Levi do it plenty of times. When he did, she closed her eyes, clenched her hands, and breathed deeply until it was all over. Now it was up to her. One mistake, and her left "duallies"—dual back wheels—would slide over the side and her RV driving days would be over. The vein in the middle of her forehead throbbed so hard she could feel a headache brewing.

With the danger from the semi past and no other vehicles in sight, she took a few seconds to judge her angle of approach. She inched forward until she could swing her front tires to the left and bring her backside over enough to center her rig in the lane above the culvert. Then she pressed the gas and eased the RV across. Just past the ditch, brambles scraped along her coach like a witch's claws on metal. Saffi grimaced. *Thanks for wrecking my paint job, Malcolm!*

Once her RV cleared the brambles, Saffi found herself on a narrow, freshly graveled road. She locked the fear and anger she'd been feeling in a box, fully prepared to pop it open in Malcolm Morton's face if the marvelous RV park he'd described didn't emerge from the wilderness sooner rather than later. At this point, she felt misled, put upon, and downright disappointed in Glenn's friend.

Up ahead, the gravel road turned to asphalt, broken and humped by tree roots, the remains, perhaps, of the road to the original theme park. Saffi's RV bumped along at a butt-bruising pace. To take her mind off the discomfort, she scanned the open field to her left. About fifty yards from the road, the field became wetlands. Snowy white egrets lifted their spindly legs as they stalked through cattails and tufted hair grass. A blue-crested kingfisher plunged headfirst into what could only be water. Closer to the road, a gray hawk with an orange-and-white barred chest perched on a moss-speckled limb, its red eyes scanning the soggy field for mice or other prey.

Even inside the closed and moving vehicle, Saffi could smell plant life, green, growing, and thriving in the mud and muck of it all. The river Malcolm had mentioned must wind through the wetland's grassy hummocks. Saffi half rose from the driver's seat but could see neither the river nor the dock under which Lennie's bloated body had been found.

Farther along, she noticed patches of something that looked like bamboo at the road's edge. An invasive species, probably planted by the park's original builder. To the right of her coach: nothing but forest. In the park's prime, Malcolm had told her, plywood cutouts of the gentle creatures from Kenneth Grahame's

Wind in the Willows enlivened the shadows beneath the trees. Now, according to the article she'd read, movie monsters lurked in the wood's evergreen canopy. Saffi shuddered.

As time ticked by with no resort in sight, she began to think she'd made a colossal mistake bringing her RV down what looked more and more like an abandoned road. Her energy waned. The long and harrowing drive, the near-death experience at the park entrance, and the stress of the past two days had sucked away the excitement of the chase for Malcolm's tormentor. She was left with a growing suspicion that the Haunted Wood was nothing but smoke and mirrors. If she didn't reach something that looked like an RV park soon, she would turn around—she had no idea how or where—and go back to Lincoln City. Surely a town seven miles long would have an RV park with an open space she could tuck into for the night.

Just when she'd given up, she spotted another balloon. Tied to a low-hanging tree limb, it bobbed like a Halloween goblin wearing the face of Malcolm Morton in his prime: teeth bared, eyebrows arched, eyes scary-wild. A few yards past the balloon, the road curved away from the wetlands and into the forest. The white banner with the blood-red letters she'd seen on page one of the local paper loomed ahead. It stretched from tree to tree just a few feet above the roof of her rig. Beyond it, she finally saw evidence of something straining with all its might toward the designation "resort."

Saffi's spirits lifted as she drove toward the cluster of buildings ahead. On her right sat Malcolm's Little Tea Shop of Horrors—a small, quaint, stone-fronted café with ivy dripping from its roof and icing-pink café curtains in its front windows. If not for the gigantic Venus flytrap movie prop drooling on the front stoop, Saffi would have called it "charming." Just beyond the tea shop stood an enormous red-roofed barn with a sign that proclaimed it to be "Malcolm Morton's Haunted Horror Museum." Parked along the side, she spotted what could only be Toad's infamous red roadster, or Malcolm Morton's car.

"Wow!" she breathed.

The only other structure was just beyond the barn, directly in front of her rig where the crumbling asphalt road ended. It looked like a slice of ancient redwood had been laid on its side and hollowed out to make space for a park office. Dangling above the door set in the center of the log building was a lighted sign that should have been posted at the highway turnoff: "Welcome to Malcolm Morton's Haunted Wood. Enter at Your Own Risk."

She had arrived.

The minute Saffi parked her RV in front of the office and turned off the engine, a couple emerged from the office. The man—short and round with a pointed nose and button-brown eyes behind round wire-rimmed glasses—had a tiny sprig of a mustache which twitched like whiskers when he beamed a smile at Saffi. He looked for all the world like Mole from *Wind in the Willows*. The woman—long and lean—towered over him.

"You must be that writer woman Malcolm told us about." She rubbed her hands together briskly then stuck her thumbs under the red suspenders clipped to the waistband of her faded green cargo pants.

Ratty? Saffi stared in wonder at another character straight out of Kenneth Grahame's children's book. Malcolm could not have chosen a more perfect pair to host a *Wind in the Willows*-themed park, but they seemed incongruous in a park designed to induce shivers.

"Saffi Graywood." Saffi returned the man's smile and gave the woman a nod. "Malcolm said he'd hold an RV space for me."

Ratty snorted, gave a brisk nod toward the mostly empty sites, then introduced the pair of them. "I'm Bev. This is Bob. We're the Joneses. Malcolm hired us to manage the RV park, such as it is." She glanced at Bob, whose button-brown eyes rolled skyward behind his round glasses. "We were coming to the end of a summer gig at a park just outside of Yellowstone. Beautiful place, right on the river. All the amenities." Bev's striking eyes, the rare blue color of glacial ice, glowed with the memory.

"Outside of Gardiner? I stayed there one time." Saffi remembered the place fondly as well.

Bev gave Saffi the nod of kinship RVers who had stayed at the same park shared.

"I spotted Malcolm's ad for a couple to manage his new 'resort.'" Bob made air quotes.

"Sounded like just the ticket," Bev broke in.

Saffi's gaze ping-ponged between the two as the couple finished each other's sentences.

"Winters are wet here." Bob blinked and pushed his glasses up his nose.

"But temperate," Bev continued.

"Thanks to the ocean." Bob pointed his nose in the direction from which Saffi had come. "You can't see it from here."

"But at night, you can hear it." Now Bev's eyes held the dreamy look of someone as besotted with the sea as Saffi herself.

"Almost makes the move worthwhile."

"Almost." Bev's lips tightened over slightly protruding teeth.

Saffi was about to ask what they meant when Malcolm himself called out.

"Saffi! At last!"

She turned toward his voice and spotted him striding out of the red-roofed barn. He'd replaced the pink chenille jacket with a white-silk kimono that appeared to be streaked with blood.

"Malcolm!" Saffi rushed toward the actor, terrified that the postcard perp had made good on one of his threats. "Should I call nine-one-one?"

The aging actor laughed so hard he had to bend forward to catch his breath. Once he did, he stood tall and twirled, letting the kimono billow around him. Then he took a bow. "This kimono was once worn by the absolutely luscious Shirley Yamaguchi."

Saffi stared at the blood-stained kimono. She had written about the actor who had worn that silken robe for her fifteenth *Bedside Reader*. If she remembered correctly, the article had been called "Real-Life Propos"—a nod toward *The Hunger Games* books she'd been devouring at the time. During the Second World War, Yamaguchi had starred in heart-palpitating romances featuring Chinese women who fell for hunky Japanese invaders. The equivalent, Saffi mused, of Katniss Everdeen falling for one of the Capitol soldiers patrolling District 12.

"Her birth name was Yoshiko," Saffi said, "not Shirley."

"Ah. Yes." Malcolm acknowledged her comment, then went on as if he hadn't heard it. "Shirley's kimono is part of the 'Villains and Victims' exhibit I'm putting together. Isn't it lovely?" Malcolm arched his triangular brows, twirled his mustache, and struck a damsel-in-distress pose. Even gone white with age, the actor's famous facial features reminded Saffi of his most villainous roles. The movie star Malcolm Morton, she recalled, had never been the victim. He'd always been the one to deliver threats.

Was that why he hadn't known how to react to the threatening postcards? At first, he had waved them off as the usual tripe actors received from the murmuring masses. Then he had gnawed his nails as he awaited the arrival of his savior: Saffi Graywood. Writer. Researcher. Sleuth. So far, savior of no one, except perhaps Glenn, who was not behind bars for a murder he had not committed, thanks to Saffi's sleuthing.

Saffi stopped ruminating long enough to notice the grimace of discomfort on Malcolm's face. The backward-leaning pose had apparently been too much for his aging body.

"Sorry," she apologized. "I'm sure it was quite lovely before *that* happened." She gestured toward the bloodstain blossoming down the front of the white-silk kimono.

Malcolm straightened slowly, clutching his back. "Bev, darling. Get my chiro over here. My sacroiliac needs an adjustment."

Saffi's eyes widened. Did the actor really have a chiropractor on call out here in the literal sticks?

"Bob, show Saffi her site." He turned a smile on her that would have been filled with nothing but enthusiasm if not for the pain behind his eyes.

As they walked toward her RV, Malcolm gasped. When she

turned to check on him, he pointed toward her Rambler as if it was one of the movie monsters he claimed haunted the forest.

"Darling, tell me that monstrosity isn't yours. I've been picturing you tootling up the coast with a lovely little trailer just like the one my mother towed behind her Oldsmobile wagon." His lips pursed. "Did you hire a driver?" He glanced around as if expecting a hulking teamster to saunter over with Saffi's keys dangling from his thick masculine fingers.

Saffi planted her feet shoulder width apart and put her hands on her hips. "I certainly did not. That big girl is *my* baby. I've driven her back and forth across the country and up and down both coasts."

"On the interstates, yes? Not on—" He flapped a hand in the direction of Highway 101. "A woman couldn't possibly..." He trailed off as if finally noticing the tightness of Saffi's lips, the fury building in her eyes.

"Let me get this straight." Without actually meaning to, she took a step toward Malcolm that forced him to limp backward. "You thought I could track down the person who sent you those threatening postcards, but not drive a Class-A RV?"

"Yes, well, no... it's just." Malcolm pressed a hand against his back as if to remind her of his pain. "I just adore vintage trailers. You know, like the ones in those postcards. They remind me of my mother."

Saffi's eyes widened. "The postcards that threatened your life if you didn't shut down the park?"

Malcolm ran a hand through his thick white hair then gave Saffi a sheepish grin. "Yes. Those very ones."

She leaned into the actor and lowered her voice. "I'd like to talk to you about those, when you have a minute."

Malcolm's eyes widened. "Have you discovered—?"

Saffi glanced at Bob and back at Malcolm, hoping he'd get the message that the discussion would be better in private.

"Bob,"—she turned toward the Mole-like half of the management team—"let's go see that RV site."

Bob glanced at Malcolm, and then nodded. "Hope everything works," he muttered.

That comment elicited a glare and a huff from Malcolm. "Bob isn't sure if Lennie finished hooking up your site before he, uhm, drowned or whatnot." Then he turned and waved Bev toward the office. "My chiro?"

Bev went, but her eyes held the most murderous look Saffi had seen in months. How long had the Joneses been here? If the Yellowstone gig ended in August, they could have been stuck here for months waiting for the park to open—long enough to sour the pair on the Haunted Wood as well as account for the ice-blue daggers Bev had just shot into its owner. Especially if he showed the same cavalier attitude toward all of the staff he'd just shown to poor Lennie.

Saffi hopped into her rig, buckled herself into the captain's chair, cranked the engine, and nodded to let Bob know she was ready to roll. As she inched forward, he pointed toward a Jayco Eagle travel trailer and mouthed the word "ours" as they passed. Saffi gave him a thumbs up and mouthed "sweet." Next, he pointed toward a 40-foot toy hauler with slide outs on both sides at the end of the first row and opened his arms wide to warn her to swing out before she made the turn. Saffi made it with plenty of room to spare. Still leading the way, Bob walked the length of the toy hauler and stuck out his arm to signal a left turn at the park's second row of finished sites. As she turned into the row, Saffi's mouth fell open and she lost her grip on the steering wheel. She barely grabbed it in time to keep from taking out a sign or two.

When she pulled into her own site, number 14, she turned off the engine and sat for a moment, staring out the windshield as her heart galumphed in her chest. The yellow-and-white VW camper van with the license plate she'd now committed to memory was one row away from the spot reserved for her Rambler. The man who called himself Charles Horseman lounged in a camp chair by a stone-circled fire pit outside the van, casually strumming his guitar.

TEN

Saffi might not be able to see the ocean, but she felt its influence enough to pull an oversized Vermont College sweatshirt over the ribbed turtleneck she'd worn for the drive. The sweatshirt had been Levi's. He'd worn the fabric soft over many years of supporting the school's Lake Monsters baseball team. She kept it as a comfort item for days when she needed to feel him nearby. Seeing Guitar Guy camped directly across from her site made this one of those days.

The mirror over her bathroom sink showed the mess putting on the sweatshirt had made of her hair. The figure staring back at her was a perfect fit for a haunted RV park. Determined to at least *try* to look presentable before she marched over to confront Charles Horseman, she scrunched her fingers through her silver-streaked black curls. The trick usually tamed the curly mass, but she could almost hear the mirror chuckle. "The *scariest* of them all!"

Saffi knocked her knuckles against the glass, thinking that— under these circumstances—that might be better. "I'll take it." She squinted her honey-brown eyes and curled her lips in an evil sorceress sneer.

The man who had become her nemesis hadn't moved from his spot beside the flickering fire. She felt—and willfully ignored—his stare as she plugged into the electrical outlet and attached her rig to water and sewer connections. Bev and Bob's eye-rolls had led her to suspect she would be living off-grid during her stay at the Haunted Wood. She was pleasantly surprised to find the hookups professionally installed, providing more than just the essentials to, by her count, five full rows of RV sites.

Tasks complete, she rolled her blue gloves off her hands and tucked them, inside out, into the back pocket of her jeans. She squared her shoulders and shook off her fear. Last summer, she had faced a killer and survived. Surely she could face a guy who sent threats through the mail.

Saffi Graywood: boldly going where no woman in her right mind would go. Great plan.

As she strode across the gravel lane, the hunk with the beach-blown hair opened a guitar case that lay on the ground beside him. He carefully tucked the instrument into its red-felted folds, shut the case, and clicked the metal latches. Then he stood and walked into her personal space like a long-lost friend. The small gap he left between them buzzed as if electrified. Saffi felt a magnetic pull in her chest and forced herself to lean away so she wouldn't topple right into him. *What in Raven's name was wrong with her?* And why hadn't her erstwhile totem bird shown up to warn her away from this guy?

"I don't know about you, but I was expecting this place to be full." He glanced over his shoulder to scan the empty rows, then turned back to Saffi with a perplexed frown. "Isn't the grand opening on Halloween?"

If he hadn't been stalking her all the way up the coast, she might have enjoyed the way he smelled of woodsmoke and man musk, or appreciated the intelligent gleam in his moss-green eyes.

"Charles Horseman." He held out a hand and before she could stop herself, Saffi took it.

His grip was as warm as the sparks spiraling off his campfire, his palm leathered by hard work. He didn't hold back as some men did but gave her hand a firm shake. He also avoided squeezing the bones of her hand together—one of those "I'm the man and you're not" moves of insecure men. Saffi returned the favor. Not too soft. Not too hard. Just right.

"Saffi Graywood." She had to tilt her chin up to look him straight in the eyes, but she did, giving him her best "I've been watching you, too, and I know you're up to no good" glare.

He tipped his head in acknowledgment, then kept talking as if they were RV buddies catching up on the road. What was this guy up to?

"There's a trail to the river just over there." He jerked a thumb toward the grove of trees behind the log-shaped park office. "Bev says the elk herd comes around for a drink about this time of day."

Elk! Saffi caught her breath. "There's an elk herd here?"

"Sure is. They range all over this area. All the way up to Cascade Head." He nodded vaguely west.

"Cascade Head?" Saffi pursed her lips. "I've never visited, but I think I saw it on the map you *stole* from my RV."

Charles Horseman—or whoever he really was—ran a thumb along his upper lip. "Not here." He glanced toward the office. "Walk with me, and we'll talk."

"Walk with you?" Saffi put her hands on her hips, and her voice rose with each word. "Into the deep dark forest toward the river, where, I'm guessing you know, a man was recently found dead?"

Horseman reached out and tried to grab hold of her arm. All he caught was a flap of her oversized sweatshirt, but it was enough to allow him to pull her closer. He bent toward her, his breath warm and scented with something that smelled like cardamon.

"Have you been drinking chai?" She looked accusingly into those green eyes.

"I have. Despite its creep-show vibe, the tea house serves the best chai I've tasted since I left LA. I think it might be homemade."

Saffi tried to step away, but he tightened his grip just as footsteps crunched in the gravel behind her.

"So!" Someone clapped, and Saffi turned her head to look over her shoulder, spotting Bev a few steps away. Like Saffi, she'd donned another layer against the chill. A beige cable-knit fisherman's sweater now covered her Henley and suspenders. "You weren't kidding when you said you knew our famous guest. Even better than you admitted, it seems." She raised her brows at Saffi and gave her a not-at-all surreptitious thumbs up.

A flush of embarrassment surged from Saffi's chest all the way up to her cheeks.

"We've been getting to know each other for a while." Charles pulled Saffi into the crook of his arm. His bicep bulged against her shoulder.

Saffi had no idea what he was playing at, but when she opened her mouth to correct him, his squeeze tightened into what felt like either a warning, or a threat.

"Bob and I like to keep watch over women on the road by themselves." Bev's eyes cooled to the glacial blue Saffi had seen earlier. "All kinds of predators out there." Despite what Saffi had taken as a warning, Bev gave Charles an oversized wink before heading to his fire to warm her hands. "Malcolm asked me to invite both of you to the tea house for supper. Please say you'll come. I'm not sure Bob and I can handle another evening of 'oohing' and 'aahing' as Malcolm reminisces about his Hollywood glory days all by ourselves."

Saffi wriggled out of Charles' grip and brushed off her shoulder as if brushing away "Mothstra," Malcolm's radiation-mutated foe in an atomic-age big bug movie. The memory of the skull-faced moth threw a dose of water on the heat she'd felt with Charles Horseman's arm around her shoulders. The warmth had reminded her of Levi, then of Troy, and now of how much her heart—and her body—ached for companionship. Manly hugs aside, she needed to focus on what mattered: the case she'd driven all this way to solve. To do that, she needed to know what Charles Horseman was up to, and if a hike in the forest with the man in the VW van would get her closer to a solution, she supposed she'd have to hike. Still, she wasn't about to go down that trail without telling someone where to find her body if she didn't return.

"We'll be there." She accepted the dinner invitation for both of them. "But first, Charles has been nice enough to invite me on a hike to the river."

"Great idea!" Bev straightened. "Let me know if you see the elk herd. I've gotten some dramatic shots of them during the blue hour."

The "blue hour," Saffi knew from writing about photographer's tricks, was the magic hour before sunset when indirect sunlight turned the world blue and eliminated the pesky shadows that could screw up a spectacular shot. Bev must have dabbled in photography quite a bit to know how to use fading sunlight to her advantage. And if she had spent much time near the dock at trail's end, she would be the perfect person for Saffi to pump for information about what might have happened to Lennie, Malcolm's groundskeeper.

After Bev retreated to the office, Saffi whirled on the guy she'd been calling "the postcard perp" since Bandon. "The next time you manhandle me like that, I'm going to stomp my bootheel into your toes and scream bloody murder." She glared.

Charles held his hands up. "I'm sorry, OK? I just—" He glanced toward the office where Bev's head had appeared in the window above a computer monitor. "I can imagine what you must be thinking, but I'm not who you think I am."

"It's not who I think you *are*. It's who I think you're *not*, Mr. Charley Horse. Although, the excruciating pain part certainly fits."

"You're gonna have to do better than that." He set his jaw. "I've been fending off charley-horse jokes since kindergarten. My name really *is* Charles Horseman, and I have a card to prove it."

Anyone with online access and half an hour to spare could create a business card and get a box of 500 shipped for $25. Saffi had done it herself when her publisher declined to have a card printed for her. She was just about to tell him that when he wrangled a well-worn wallet from the back pocket of his jeans and flipped it open. On one side was a driver's license issued to Charles J. Horseman of Los Angeles, California. On the other side was something that would cost way more than twenty-five bucks to fake: a gold badge that read *Inspector, United States Postal Service.*

"Shall we?" He tipped his head toward the trail and gestured with one arm.

She nodded. "Let me lock my RV first." Then she squinted at him. "For all the good it will do with you around."

ELEVEN

The moment they stepped beneath the trees, the light dimmed and the temperature dropped. The scrabble of unseen creatures in the underbrush might have sent her scurrying back to the RV if not for the man striding confidently beside her. Saffi's heart sank. In her mind, she'd amassed enough evidence to put the guy in jail, and he was, what? Some kind of trumped-up mail carrier?

"What does that badge mean, anyway? You're a... mailman... who investigates crimes?"

The man beside her chortled. "Mailman. Good one." He glanced toward her, then shook his head. "Professional investigators don't just grab whatever garbage they find lying around, grind it all together, and turn it into mush."

Saffi stopped. The vein in her temple started throbbing like it had on the road. She wanted to stomp past him and keep stomping till she reached the river, but if she did that, she'd probably give herself a stroke. "Did you just call me a garbage disposal?"

He arched his brows but said nothing.

Saffi crossed her arms. "Look, if you feed me garbage you're going to get ground garbage. Give me useful information and I'm a... blender. Truth in, smoothie out." She quirked an eyebrow in challenge.

He turned to face her, crossing his own arms to mirror her stance. *Classic law enforcement tactic to make a perp feel comfortable.* Saffi remembered the move from an article in *Bedside Reader*, #6, called "Grill 'Em Like a Steak."

"I'm not some mailman who stuck with the job long enough to get a promotion, OK? I'm a federal law enforcement officer." His weathered face took on the seasoned look of a professional... something. But a postal inspector? When she'd seen the info about the US Postal Inspection Service on the "Wanted" poster in Gold Beach, she had pictured mail carriers relegated to the backroom with stethoscopes. She'd imagined them listening to brown-paper-wrapped packages held together with too much duct tape to find out if they were ticking.

"Federal law enforcement. Like the FBI?" Saffi tilted her head.

Charles grimaced. "I'm surprised you haven't slapped us into one of those *Bedside Readers* of yours. We're the oldest law enforcement agency in the country. Been around since 1775. That means the FBI is a bit like *us.*"

"Wow. You look really young for your age." Saffi couldn't resist the jibe, but she also couldn't resist little-known history. She tucked the article idea into her brain's "to-do" file.

"Go ahead, laugh. Some of the crimes we go after might seem small. Like romance scams. Ever heard of those?"

A memory jolted Saffi's heart, and she hugged her arms tighter over her chest. Years ago, not long after her mom had died, her dad had been sucked in by a guy in Kazakhstan pretending to be a beautiful young woman who needed him to save her from a sex trafficker. "She" had written love letters. Sent photos by mail. Pleaded with him to send money so she could come to America and be with him. By the time Saffi realized what was happening, her dad had lost half his bank account.

Charles reached out to touch her shoulder as if he had read her mind. "It's not just about wiping out people's bank accounts, Saffi. Hearts get broken."

Had he just said that? Whoever this guy was, he was not only right, he was sensitive. What were the odds?

Saffi would never get over the guilt she felt for not spending more time with her father after her mom passed. Just as Charles said, the mail-fraud phony had broken her father's heart, right along the crack left by her mother's death. He'd wasted away. If Saffi could have gotten her hands around the neck of the man who had done that—

"You get it. I can tell from that murderous look in your eyes." Charles gave her shoulder a squeeze. "We go after minor scumbags just as hard as we do major ones, drugs and arms dealers who use the mail like it's their own personal delivery system. It might take years, but we don't stop digging until we put them in cuffs."

Saffi rubbed her arms. The sad memory, along with standing still for so long, had allowed the chill settling over the forest to sink into her bones. Something else had started to sink in as well. A federal agent—someone who investigated the kinds of crimes he'd described—was not looking into a few postcards received by an aging actor. If he was after Malcolm, something far more serious was at stake. The best way to find out was to ask.

"You're investigating Malcolm Morton, aren't you?"

His face closed down faster than she could pull down the blinds in her RV windows. "I'm not at liberty to discuss an active case."

"You followed me and stole my bag because you thought I was involved in whatever you think he's done. Must have been pretty disappointing to find nothing but a few postcards and half a protein bar. If you'd followed Malcolm instead of me, Lennie might still be alive."

Her new "friend" the postal inspector pressed his lips together. The leathery skin of his face reddened as he shoved his hands into his back pockets. Saffi couldn't seem to stop herself from making it worse. "Inspector or not, those postcards you took don't belong to you, and, if I'm correct, stealing mail is a federal offense. I could have you arrested, you know." She shook a finger in his face.

He spluttered in disbelief. "By who? Me?" He took his hands out of his pockets and rubbed them through his short hair until it was a scruffy, sexy blond mess. "You're exactly as analytical and suspicious as I remember."

"It's my job to be."

"No. It's *my* job." He put his hands on his hips and sighed. "And you're right. I blew it. Someone died, and, if Malcolm was involved, some of the responsibility for that falls on my shoulders. I followed *you* because Malcolm transferred materials to you, and that made you look like a suspect. And following *suspects* is what I do."

"I'm not a suspect. *You're* a suspect!" Saffi could have kicked herself. She'd just delivered a line straight out of an elementary school smackdown. "Besides, if I'm a suspect, why did you give back the cards, and why are you telling me any of this?"

Charles—Charley—blinked rapidly. What should she call this guy? Mr. Inspector Man?

"Because you were cleared. You're not using the mail to commit crimes. You're a writer turned wannabe detective and"—now it was his turn to shake a finger—"you are treading ground that could make you the killer's next victim."

Saffi was about to offer a rebuttal when it hit her: he sounded just like Detective Richards. "Who cleared me?"

The postal inspector's lips twisted, and he squinted as if trying to decide how much to share. "I got a call from a detective in Last Chance Cove. He'd run my license plate—thank you very much for that—found out who I am, and called to warn me about you."

So! Detective Richards had not only listened to her message, he'd followed through. She would have called to thank him if he hadn't thrown her in front of the mail delivery van.

"You robbed me. What do you expect, an apology?"

"Nope." Charles clapped his hands and rubbed them together like he was about to start a fire. "I expect you to enjoy your stay at the Haunted Wood and leave the investigating to me. Also, please, call me C.J. I've heard enough charley-horse jokes to last a lifetime." He gestured toward the trail. "We'd better get going before the light fades."

Saffi started walking. He'd talked about the postcards as if the threats had nothing to do with his investigation. Was that why he'd given them back? She stretched her legs to keep pace with his longer stride, being extra careful to not trip on a root and fall at his feet. Wouldn't he just love that? At least... until he had to heft her back up again, Saffi chuckled under her breath.

"So, C.J., this trail walk was a ruse to get me out of Bev's earshot, right? Now that we've cleared the air, why don't we turn around?"

"Are you kidding?" His face glowed like a kid's. "Elk!"

As she pictured the second-largest member of the deer family—called "wapiti" by native tribes—Saffi felt the same glow wash over her. She adored the cows with their doe eyes, regal reddish-brown necks, and taut bodies the color of chamois. And the bulls! The racks she'd seen on those guys! Majestic, with deadly potential.

"Are there elk herds in Alaska?" She took her eyes off the trail long enough to glance up at C.J.

"What do you mean?" He frowned.

"The first time we met, there was an elk on your sweatshirt." She reached out to touch the spot on the brown wool sweater he wore now. "And the word *Sitka*. I thought you were this rugged camper dude from Alaska." Saffi laughed. "So much for my sleuthing skills."

"Guess you'd better leave the detecting to the pros." He hurried forward, either avoiding the Alaska question or afraid she'd start another infantile argument. Saffi being Saffi, she couldn't stop herself from wondering. Was he still hiding something? And, if so, what?

As the trail ended, the view opened up, and there they were in all their splendor: a herd of elk blowing steam from their snouts and jostling each other as they made their way toward a spot about five hundred yards downriver. Her mouth rounded into a silent "wow" of wonder. Seaward of where they stood, the huge animals were black-paper silhouettes cut from twilight's blue glow.

C.J. gave a low, soft whistle. "Ten points at least on two of those big boys."

He pointed out a pair of massive bull elks at the back of the herd, one watching over the cows, the other edging toward the females from the periphery. Just as Saffi caught sight of them, the guardian turned his shaggy brown neck and eyed the other bull. Seconds later, he threw back his head and bugled, a high-pitched whistle that ended in a grunt.

C.J. bent toward her. "He's warning the other male away from his harem. It's mating season. If the other bull doesn't back off, they'll fight."

Saffi held her breath. She'd watched videos of bull elks in rut fighting for females, but it was rare to see such a sight in person. With C.J. standing close enough for her to feel the tug of his magnetism, she had to almost physically pull herself away. Troy might be in Texas, but she didn't want to be the kind of woman that flitted from one man to another in the aftermath of losing a husband. Suddenly, she felt a bit squeamish about watching the bulls battle it out.

"Shh..." C.J. put a finger to his lips and waved her toward the dock for a better view.

The moment Saffi stepped onto its weathered wood, a chill rose from the river below to engulf her. She folded her arms and grasped the loose sleeves of her comfort-sweatshirt, tugging its warmth against her chest. Maybe the shiver that racked her body came from the chill wind blowing upriver from the sea. Maybe it came from the twinge of guilt she felt about Troy. But at least some of it came from the fact that Lennie's body had lain beneath this very dock, swollen and still, just a day ago. A human being had died. Would his loss leave gaping black holes in someone's life as Levi's death had left in her own?

Another shrill bugle tore Saffi's gaze from the dark ripples visible between the dock's worn planks. The intruding elk had not backed away. She looked up just in time to see the guardian male lower his head and charge. The harsh clack of antlers as the bulls locked horns and wrestled for dominion ripped the last vestige of serenity from what should have been a peaceful place. Despite her doubts, Saffi could not tear her gaze away. The battle was too savage, too elemental for her to do anything but watch.

In the distance, the herd's "bachelors"—years too young to duke it out—paced the field's perimeter. With no chance of winning a mate for themselves, all they could do was watch, and place their bets on which bull in his prime would prove strong enough to pass on his DNA.

TWELVE

The flicker of electric candles inside mounted coach-style lamps gave the Little Tea Shop of Horrors an eerie glow. When Saffi got close enough in the gathering dark to see the exterior clearly, she could tell that the "stone" blocks were actually faux-stone panels. From a distance, they looked real enough to trick the eye. The ivy dangling off the roof caught her attention next. If she hadn't been able to tell by touch, the smell would have given the trailing vines away. Green plastic, not growing plant life. Saffi crinkled her nose. *Smoke and mirrors.*

Stepping inside the café was like walking onto the set of Malcolm's one and only horror-themed musical. Minus the singing, for which Saffi was eternally grateful. Set in a quaint café with mismatched tables and chairs, the movie pitted the actor's character against that most terrible of terrors: people-eating plants. Glancing around the café, she spotted sticky sundews, bulging pitcher plants, and spiky flytraps. They looked so real, she reached out to touch one. *Fake.* Probably for the best. It would take a café full of bugs—or patrons—to satiate that many meat eaters.

Given the décor, she could only imagine the culinary horrors the tea shop's cook might concoct, but the smells coming from the kitchen made her mouth water: cardamon, curry, ginger, and the savory scent of samosas frying. When a young woman with silky black hair and peach-brown skin bustled out of the kitchen carrying a basket filled with fresh naan, Saffi decided she'd stepped through a portal into an Indian restaurant. The jewel-toned snakeskin sari the young woman wore looked exactly like one she'd seen in a Hollywood remake of a Bollywood movie. Hopefully not. If Saffi remembered correctly, the movie ended with the shapeshifting snake woman exacting bloody revenge on the character played by tonight's host.

"You see, Saffi? You see?" Malcolm waved her over. "The grand opening nears and we are ready to amaze the masses!"

Malcolm's math didn't match Saffi's. If every RV site filled for the opening, five rows times eight spaces equaled forty drivers, plus their guests. Masses? Hardly.

She'd hoped to have a moment alone with Malcolm, but it looked like that would have to wait. As the last to arrive, she joined Malcolm and "friends" at a spindle-legged oval table, the tea shop's largest. Bob hopped up to pull out the empty seat between himself and C.J., as gentlemanly as Mole himself. Bev sat beside her husband, and their famous host sat across from Saffi on the other side of a carnivorous centerpiece. This one featured red-veined pitcher plants, their hungry mouths open to reveal insects embedded in what looked exactly like liquid. Saffi shivered. Stomach-churning, if they'd been real.

"At the Haunted Wood," Malcolm continued, "you won't just see movie memorabilia in a museum. The costumes in my collection will be worn." He waved his right hand toward the server like an Academy Award presenter. "Exquisite, yes?"

The server was young—still in her teens, Saffi guessed. The peaches in her cheeks ripened as Malcolm drew everyone's attention to the snakeskin sari she wore.

"Careful, dear," the actor warned as the girl slipped tongs beneath a flatbread triangle glistening with ghee. "It's impossible to remove butter from silk."

Saffi arched a brow at the actor. "You're lucky I'm not serving. I would have had ghee stains from stem to stern before I even reached the table."

The young woman turned her head to hide a smile from her employer.

"Yes, well. It's a good thing you're a writer, not a worker." He pressed his napkin against his mustache, staining the white linen fabric with the clarified butter he'd warned the server about.

Saffi huffed. "I'm sorry. The only people who think writers don't work are those who've never written a word in their lives."

Malcolm flapped his napkin, folded it into a triangle, then laid it across his lap. "You sound just like every scriptwriter I've ever worked with. If I ad-lib dialogue, they whine as if every word on the script had been written in blood."

Saffi was beginning to think that wouldn't be such a bad thing —if the blood in question belonged to Malcolm Morton. By the end of the meal, she might need to add her own name to the list of suspects. How had he seemed so charming when she'd met him at Last Chance Café? The Glenn effect, she decided. She adored the cookie baker, so she had assumed his friend would be just as sweet and quirky. That's when she remembered Glenn's ex, Last Chance Cove's recently jailed city manager, whose most outrageous quirk turned out to be murder. Maybe Glenn chose his male friends for their clothes, not their kindness.

Compared to the server's sari, Malcolm's frumpy Prince Albert style jacket left more than a little to be desired. The black broadcloth jacket had a velvet collar that must have looked smart at one time, but the nap had been worn to nubs. When Malcolm caught her looking and struck a pose—eyebrows raised, eyes wide, thumbs stuck under the lapels like a proud peacock—she gasped.

"That's not—" Saffi's hand shook as she pointed at the jacket.

"It is! It is." Malcolm ran a thumb along the velvet lapel. "The very one Professor Marvel wore in *The Wizard of Oz*."

C.J.'s leg was so close to Saffi's she could feel his muscles tense. She glanced to her right but his eyes were focused on his plate as if spooning coriander chutney onto naan mattered more than life itself.

"I read somewhere that the costume designer found thirty jackets in a secondhand store," Bob mumbled around a mouthful of the flatbread.

Somewhere? Aunt Saffi's Bedside Reader, # 4 perhaps? Saffi suppressed a smile by sucking melted ghee off her lips.

"Yes, yes!" Malcolm sat up straight. "The director and wardrobe man chose this ratty old thing to give Professor Marvel the look of an aristocrat who'd seen better times. 'Grandeur gone to seed,' I think they called it."

"Did it really belong to that writer fella, Frank Baumgartner?" Bev gestured with her fork, coming so close to her husband's left eye Saffi feared for his sight.

"L. Frank Baum," Saffi corrected. "And it did. At the time, people thought the story was a marketing scam, but according to the movie's publicist, it was true. There's even a letter from Baum's tailor, verifying he'd made the jacket for him."

Bev's fork clanked against her plate. "Those flying monkeys still give me nightmares."

"Me too!" Saffi, C.J., and the teenage server chorused, and everyone at the table laughed.

It was the last bit of merriment the evening had in store. As course followed course, sweat broke out on the teenaged server's brow. Saffi could hardly imagine the amount of discomfort and stress she must be feeling. She was now doing her utmost to keep food off the sari she wore as well as the priceless jacket Malcolm had thought was a good choice for enjoying a messy meal. Samosas, curried chicken, palak paneer—the spinach and farmer's cheese dish was Saffi's favorite—all arrived and were placed in front of each diner without incident. The tastes made Saffi's eyes roll with pleasure. If the tea shop continued to serve food this delicious, diners would come in droves, despite the "horrors" promised in the café's moniker.

By the time dessert was announced, the waistband of the black slacks Saffi wore had stretched as far as it could. She had just vowed to not eat another bite when the server came out of the kitchen balancing a silver tray on one hand. Five white ceramic ramekins filled with Saffi's favorite Indian dessert: gajar ka halwa. *Delish!*

Just as the girl bent to place a cardamon-scented dish of sugary carrot goodness in front of Malcolm, he flailed out his arm to accentuate the retelling of a dramatic moment in one of his films. The milky carrot dessert smashed against the front of the sari. It oozed down the silk to land with a plop on the beaded slippers she wore on her dainty feet.

Malcolm's face went from jovial host to horror villain quicker than anyone could say "Oops!" The table went so quiet Saffi thought she could hear the actor's blood seething. Before it did, the girl turned, set the tray on the closest table, and fled from the room, sobbing what sounded like "Nanaji!" as she ran to the kitchen.

A few minutes later, a full-bellied Indian grandpa with frizzled white hair marched out of the kitchen. His white chef's jacket bore all of the cooking stains Malcolm had pestered the server to avoid.

"Malcolm, what is it you are doing to my granddaughter?" he demanded. "If you keep haranguing the girl, we will have to be leaving. Is that your desire?"

Malcolm half rose from his chair, but the chef's intimidating girth seemed to make him think better of it. "No! Sunny, please. Locals can't run this place. The whole town is nothing but burger joints and fried fish."

"And my granddaughter is... my *granddaughter*, you understand?"

"Of course. Of course I do, it's just... the costume. It's..."

Sunny's black eyes flared. "If you wanted it clean, you should not have forced my grandchild to wear it." His words seethed with resentment, and his clenched teeth gave him the sinister look of a Bollywood villain.

Malcolm folded his napkin and placed it on the table in front of him. He looked at each of his guests in turn, then at the glowering chef. "Perhaps we should call it a night."

As they gathered their things, Saffi looked longingly at the halwa.

"Nanaji!" The girl leaned toward her grandfather and whispered in his ear, then he looked at Saffi and offered a sincere smile. "I'll make the to-go cup for you, yes?"

Saffi's mouth watered. "And the others?"

He put his hands on his meaty hips and sighed. "Yes. Yes. But not for you!" He shook his finger in Malcolm's face. "Your dessert is, what did you tell my granddaughter? 'Impossible to remove from silk.'"

Oh, she liked this guy. Saffi folded her hands in namaste position and gave the chef a slight bow. He barely contained his grin, but his granddaughter did not. They both bowed in return, saluting the god within her as she had done for them, before returning to what was clearly their domain and not Malcolm's—the kitchen.

THIRTEEN

As Saffi walked down the steps into the damp chill of a coastal Oregon night, she added Sunny's name to her mental list of suspects. Once she let go of the certainty that C.J. had sent the postcards, suspects paraded in front of her like perps in a police lineup. Cecily Raymond, with money as her motive. Bev and Bob Jones, lured by Malcolm's promise of a resort-style post to a place that was anything but, and now, Sunny. She liked the Indian grandfather's gumption, and she was going to *love* the halwa she clutched in her hand, but that flare in his eyes burned hot. There was far more to the look than the irritation of a single evening. Sunny and Malcolm had some kind of shared history. Maybe that history had given him a reason to send those threatening postcards. Malcolm's condescending behavior, perhaps? Here, in the land of ocean waves, windswept forests, and hummocky wetlands, his Hollywood sense of entitlement stacked the deck against him.

"Saffi! Wait!" C.J. caught up with her a few yards away from the café, but a glance over his shoulder seemed to stop him from saying more.

Hearing voices, Saffi turned to see that Bev and Bob had come out of the café on C.J.'s heels and were hurrying to catch up.

"Hey, you two. We'll be showing Malcolm's films in the

museum every evening once the park officially opens," Bev said. "Bob and me are screening one of them tonight, if you'd like to join us."

Behind his wire-rimmed glasses, Bob's eyes were as round as a kid's at a concession stand. "Popcorn!" He grinned.

Saffi glanced at C.J. She almost missed the slight shake of his head but not the caution in his green eyes.

"I think I'll just eat my dessert and turn in," Saffi begged off. "After two days of driving, I'm about to drop."

"Mind if we do that together?" C.J. asked. "Van's kind of cold this time of night."

Saffi stiffened. Was he propositioning her? His moss-green eyes were all tease until he held up his to-go container and wiggled it in her face.

"Dessert?"

From Bev's brow twitch and sideways smile, Saffi gathered that the postal inspector had just reinforced the idea that they were more than casual friends. One part of her wanted to give him a piece of her mind for using that tactic without consulting her. Another part wanted to solve this case as quickly as possible. If that meant keeping C.J. close, so be it. Now that she thought about it, the postal inspector might be a better actor than their host. First, he'd convinced her he was a surfer dude with a guitar, vanning his way up the coast. Now, he'd shifted his role to the resident sleuth's man friend. He was good, she had to admit.

"Catch you tomorrow." Bev waved, but Bob had already made a beeline for the barn and the theater-style popcorn popper Saffi imagined waited inside.

C.J. put his hand behind her elbow and guided her toward her rig without a hint of what he was really up to. She fumbled her keys out of the pocket of the windbreaker she'd thrown over her black slacks and turtleneck on the way to dinner. Once she'd unlocked the door, C.J. followed her up the steps like an agent requisitioning her RV for a vital mission.

"I need a beer." He set his dessert down on the counter, then opened her fridge and poked around without even asking.

Some mission.

"Please," she gestured toward the bottles of dark ale tucked securely in a pocket of the refrigerator door, "be my guest."

"Want one?" He held up the bottle he'd snagged, but Saffi waved it away.

"If I drink that, I'll be asleep before you tell me what set off your postal inspector Spidey senses."

C.J. twisted the top off the brown bottle of ale. While he commandeered the couch, Saffi took two spoons out of a kitchen drawer and held them up. C.J. shook his head. "Too sweet for me. It's all yours if you want it." He nodded at the to-go cup he'd set on the counter.

Saffi snatched the cup and put it into the fridge before he could change his mind. Then she squeezed into a padded dining chair at one end of her small table so she could dig into her gajar ka halwa without, she hoped, spilling most of it in her lap. "It was the jacket, wasn't it?" She took a bite of warm carroty goodness, licked her spoon, and then her lips.

He nodded. "Good guess."

Saffi wasn't going to let him get away with that. "Not a guess. I knew it because your-your—" She pointed her spoon toward his muscular thighs while trying to keep her eyes from lingering. "Your legs went all tense when Malcolm said the jacket was the real deal."

C.J. leaned back against the couch cushions and crossed one leg over the other, resting the bottle against his chest. He'd brought the mixed smells of woodsmoke, evergreen, and Indian spices into her space. Somehow, that made the RV feel homier, almost as if she were back in Vermont, eating Indian takeout with Levi while they relaxed in front of a roaring fire.

Saffi sighed. When would everything stop reminding her of her old life? She had been on the road, traveling and writing, seeing new sights and meeting new people for three years. When she'd opened up to Troy, she had been sure she was ready for something real. Yet here she was, confusing C.J.'s investigating tactics with actual flirting and, she had to admit, enjoying the attention.

"Detective Richards warned me about your powers of observation." C.J. pulled her back to the topic at hand: L. Frank Baum's jacket. "He's sure they'll be the death of you one day."

I just bet he is. Saffi shoved another spoonful of the bright orange dessert into her mouth to keep from blurting out a retort. Detective Richards wasn't exactly wrong. Twice last summer she had almost died because she'd puzzled out answers ahead of anyone in law enforcement.

"Writers have to hone their powers of observation, just like 'real' detectives."

"I'm sure they do, but they don't carry sidearms to protect themselves when they poke the wrong bear."

"Humph!" Saffi protested around the halwa she'd just spooned into her mouth. "You've never attended a writer's conference in Texas." She'd seen plenty of Lone State authors packing more than pens in their purses. "So, come on. Are you going to share what you know, or was this just a ruse to raid my fridge?"

C.J.'s weathered jaw tightened. His moss-green eyes clouded as he studied her for a moment. "Given our little chat on the trail, what do you think?"

It was Saffi's turn to eyeball him. As she did, she let what she knew about him unspool in her mind. He'd approached her at Last Chance Cove, chatted her up, invited her to join him at the fireside. He'd followed her, but, unless he was crap at his job, he hadn't bothered hiding his presence. Once she'd arrived at the park, he hadn't wasted time equivocating. Instead, he'd showed her his badge and walked her down the trail to talk. Unlike the tight-lipped Detective Richards, Postal Inspector C.J. Horseman showed signs of being a collaborator.

She looked him in the eye. "You've decided to share."

C.J. uncrossed his legs and leaned toward her. "That jacket Morton was wearing is connected to the case I've been working. It was part of a shipment from a movie studio to the Smithsonian a few years back. The shipment 'disappeared'"—he made air quotes—"between LAX and Reagan International."

Saffi grasped the edge of the table. "Malcolm's a thief?" What had Glenn gotten her into? He was going to owe her more than a few bags of cookies, scrumptious though they might be, when she returned to the cove.

C.J. took a long pull on his beer, then wiped his mouth with the back of his hand. "Hard to say. Morton's been on our radar before as a possible receiver of stolen goods. He may have purchased the jacket from the person behind the heist. The actual thief was probably a baggage handler."

Saffi paused with her spoon halfway to her mouth, which was a mistake. The bright orange plop landed on her black sweater. She plucked the spoonful of dessert off her sweater and popped it into her mouth without thinking. When C.J. chuckled, her cheeks went hot.

"What? It's too good to waste." She put the spoon down beside her mostly empty cup and tucked her hands between her thighs before she could embarrass herself again. "A baggage handler? Aren't those guys screened before they're hired?"

C.J. shrugged. "A lot of airlines outsource the grunt work to independent companies. The jobs are tough. Long days hunched inside the belly of an airplane. Working outdoors no matter the weather. Heat. Wind. Rain. Ice." He paused to take a swig of his beer. "Mostly young guys. Strong backs. But not paid well enough to resist a side hustle."

"How would someone like that know the value of a Smithsonian shipment?"

"They wouldn't. They're just someone's inside man. Their job is to put the right package in the right place so that someone else can pick it up and pass it to the person who *does* know what it's worth. My LA team has been haunting the dark web ever since the heist."

"Any luck?"

"We've spotted a few items listed on the shipping manifest up for sale. But tracking the buyers?" He shook his head. "They're protected by so many layers it's like peeling an onion the size of Jupiter. If you do get to a username at the onion's core, linking *four_tea_thieves* with a live human being is almost impossible."

Saffi stifled a laugh. "Forty thieves. Good one." Her knowledge of the dark web was about as thin as onion skin, but she knew an *Arabian Nights* folktale allusion when she heard one. "What were the other items listed for sale? Besides the Oz jacket? If Malcolm shows up wearing another one, I can let you know."

"Sorry. That's confidential. But if you notice anything suspicious, I hope you'll share." C.J. drained his ale, stood to rinse the bottle in the sink, then turned as if looking for the recycling.

"I use a brown paper bag," she said. "But I haven't set one out yet. Just leave it on the counter."

He did, then he stepped down into the short stairwell. "Promise me you won't ask Malcolm or anyone else about that jacket. Now that I've actually seen him with one of the stolen items, I can get a search warrant. I don't want him spooked before that happens. Malcolm needs to think you're poking around after those postcards, and nothing else."

Fine. She was here to investigate the postcards anyway, and, if she heard him right, he'd given her the green light to go ahead. *Sweet!*

She saluted. "Yes, sir, Mr. Postal Inspector, sir." Then she stood as well, preparing to lock the door after him. With C.J. one step down the stairs, the two of them were now face to face.

Instead of looking away, he stared straight into her eyes. "Don't make me regret telling you this, Saffi. If you put anything I tell you in confidence into your next *Bedside Reader*, I have handcuffs, and I'm not afraid to use them." His eyes twinkled so much there was no way to miss the innuendo.

As she locked the door behind him, she couldn't help taking that image back to her bedroom and tucking it beneath her pillow to spark a few dreamland delights.

FOURTEEN

Saffi's morning tai chi stretches did little to unkink her back and shoulders. She'd spent too much time driving and sitting around dinner tables and too little time stretching her legs and sticking her nose into places Detective Richards and C.J. thought it shouldn't go. But if she didn't nose out the person threatening Malcolm with those postcards, she'd never wipe the slate clean with Glenn. Deep down, she knew she didn't owe him anything. He'd gotten mixed up with the wrong man and covered for him. That was on him. But for the last few months, she'd seen too much sadness haunting his sweet brown eyes. She wanted to see them sparkle again.

On the way to talk to Bev and Bob in the office, she stopped by the tea shop for breakfast. The Little Tea Shop of Horrors was a sit-down place. It lacked the walk-up counter she enjoyed using at Last Chance Café. When Saffi was on deadline, she could duck in and out almost faster than Delilah could talk. The reminder of deadlines made Saffi feel ill. She needed something in her belly, and quick.

She took a table with a view facing into the forest. Morning sunshine bathed and brightened the grove. Although redwoods dominated the forest surrounding Last Chance Cove, here she spotted Douglas firs and western red cedars, draped in lichen thanks to year-round moderate temperatures and coastal fog. The trees towered over an understory lush with tree ferns and thick with rhododendrons. Tall as they were, these sentinels were second- or even third-growth trees. The area's old-growth forests had been logged out long ago. If she walked among the trees, she would see massive tree stumps, evidence of elders that would put their descendants to shame. The forest teemed with creatures far more interesting than Malcolm's movie prop monsters.

A cough at her shoulder made her jump.

"Sorry." Last night's teen server stood at her elbow holding out a menu. When Saffi took it, the girl touched the tip of a ballpoint pen to her order pad and waited.

No fancy saris today, Saffi noted. The teen had pulled her silky black hair into a ponytail and wore jeans with a T-shirt. An apron with a Venus flytrap drooling down its front protected her casual clothes. She'd pinned her name badge through the plant's tongue, proof, to Saffi, that the girl had her grandfather's spark.

Saffi squinted at the badge. "Juh-yoh-tee?"

"Like Jee-oh-tea, but fast," the girl corrected with a smile.

"Jyoti." Saffi ran the sounds together. When the girl grinned, Saffi pointed at the menu. "Do you really serve Poison Mushroom Chai?"

"Uh, no. They're not poisonous." Jyoti rolled her eyes. "Malcolm insisted. I doubt we'll sell a single cup of that stuff."

Saffi pulled her pointer finger down the list as she read. "Ghoulish Green Tea. Gotcha Matcha. Black Dragon Latte." She looked at the server with a plea in her eyes. "These sound, uhm, horrifically, ah... good. But if I don't get a coffee my brain will implode."

When Jyoti reached out and flipped the menu, Saffi let out a sigh of relief.

"That's more like it. Killer Clown Caramel Latte. Mad Scientist Mocha. Frankencoffee." Saffi laughed, then tapped a finger on Mad Scientist Mocha. "Easy on the cayenne." Despite the terrifying names, Malcolm's coffee menu drew heavily on the coffee drinks Delilah steamed up in Last Chance Café. She was pretty sure Mad Scientist Mocha would taste exactly like the Meximocha Malcolm had consumed the first time they met. Maybe he'd tucked a menu under that pink chenille coat of his.

After flipping the menu to the front, then to the back, Saffi screwed up her lips. "Food?"

"The breakfast menu's at the printer," Jyoti said. "Today we have Decomposed Omelets, which are basically egg-and-veggie scrambles, or Creepy Crumpets." The server's eye-roll was back.

Malcolm's horror theme would either drive customers away or have them vying for space at the tables. If he'd set up the park closer to LA, she had no doubt it would be the latter, but out here, where nature stole the show on a daily basis? Saffi feared Malcolm's dream would sink as fast as the helium balloons along the highway.

"As long as they're not topped with worms, I'll have the crumpets."

Saffi couldn't watch Jyoti grind the beans and tamp down the grounds or see steam rise from the oat milk she'd ordered, but she could hear the operation happening. She could also smell the rich aroma of coffee as the young server carried a mug to her table. She set it in front of Saffi along with her breakfast order. The crumpets came toasted, with generous dollops of bilious green curd. Two foil-wrapped eyeballs on the side of the plate watched as Saffi poked a finger into the green goo and gave it a tentative lick.

"Mmm."

"Lime curd!" Jyoti giggled.

The crumpets smelled yeasty, as if freshly baked. The first bite made Saffi's taste buds delirious: crispy, chewy, and delicately spongy, they were nothing like the crumpets she occasionally found in grocery stores.

"Your grandfather?" Saffi lifted one brow.

Jyoti nodded. "He's a genius. I don't know why he let Malcolm talk him into wasting his talent in this place." She bit her lip and looked over her shoulder as if making sure her grandfather was out of earshot. Then she leaned toward Saffi and whispered, "Malcolm has some kind of weird... I don't know, hold over him? One day he was head chef at my family's Indian restaurant on Ventura Boulevard, the next day he was packing his bags for this place." She waved a hand in disdain. "Mom begged me to come with him. To try to find out what was going on. We've been cramped together in Nanaji's toy hauler for two months. If he hadn't let me bring my Fiat, I'd have gone stir crazy by now."

Before Saffi could tease more information out of the girl, the café door opened. Chill, ocean-scented air swept in. Jyoti stiffened, then bolted for the kitchen. Saffi's window-facing seat forced her to look over her shoulder.

It wasn't the cold that had sent the girl running. It was Malcolm. He stood in the doorway dressed exactly like his character in *Dating Dracula*. When he saw he had Saffi's attention, he spread his arms wide to reveal the red silk lining of his black cloak. With his thick white hair and mustache, he looked more like a vampiric grandpa than the dashing sex-and-blood-starved Drac of his youth, but, Saffi had to admit, he still looked fangtastic.

He strode across the room to Saffi's table, swirled the cloak off his shoulders, nearly smacking her in the face in the process, then slapped a newspaper down on the table in front of her.

"Good morning to you, too."

He slid the paper closer and tapped a finger on the title. His face turned as red as the town-crushing fruit in his killer tomato movie.

"Malcolm Morton's Haunted Murder Trap," Saffi read aloud. "Oh, my."

"Please tell me you've solved this thing." Malcolm draped his cloak over the chairback across from her before taking a seat.

When she'd arrived yesterday, she was sure she knew exactly who had sent those postcards. Now, she had nothing but suspects. It was too soon to throw any of them under the steamroller of Malcolm Morton's dreams. Without telling the actor anything about the lawman in the van, she laid out her thoughts so far. The postcard perp clearly knew plenty about Malcolm, Willow Wood, and the actor's vision for the new park. The perp's stated goal was to keep the park from opening. She wasn't ready to share her suspect list, especially Sunny and the Joneses, all of whom seemed to have beefs against the boss. The actor would probably fire them on the spot, tossing out innocents along with potential suspects and killing her investigation before she could make progress. Instead of suspects, she focused on possible motives. Whoever had sent the cards had something to gain if Malcolm capitulated, perhaps someone who wanted his land. "Although the stamps made me think the perp might be someone who cared about nature. An environmentalist, perhaps."

"Brilliant!" Malcolm sat forward. "We *have* had a few sign wavers over the months. *Save the Wetlands. Planet over Profit. Keep the water clean and the forest green.* I rather liked the rhyming ones." He twirled his mustache. "One of those Sitka people got right in my face. Wanted to know why there were no environmental impact reports on file."

Saffi choked on the bite of crumpet she'd just taken. *Sitka?* Had she taken C.J. off her suspect list too soon?

Malcolm pushed a glass of water toward her and kept talking while she washed the clog down her throat. "I told her there had been no change of usage since the last permits were issued, so no report was needed. She was livid, but what could she do?" Malcolm shot a hopeful glance toward the kitchen. Saffi had a feeling Jyoti would stay in there for as long as she could.

If the Sitka person was female, it wasn't C.J. That was a relief, but also a worry. Two people somehow connected to a town in Alaska was one too many for her. The protesters Malcolm described seemed pretty tame, but the Pacific Northwest had a long history of eco-terrorists spiking trees, derailing trains, setting fires, knocking out power stations. If the postcard perp was an environmental activist gone loco, Malcolm and everyone in the park could be in danger.

Saffi unwrapped a chocolate eyeball and popped it in her

mouth, hoping the soothing sweet would help her think. "Malcolm, what's the Sitka connection? I don't get it."

"Sitka." He waved a hand. "It's just up the road."

The last time Saffi had looked Alaska was not "just up the road," but before she could ask, Malcolm tapped a finger on the newspaper. "The reporter who wrote this showed up less than an hour after Bev found Lennie's body."

Saffi startled. "Bev? Bev found him? How awful for her."

"Of course it was awful, but did you hear what I said?" He put both elbows on the table and leaned forward. "That newshound arrived before the sheriff. I shouldn't be surprised, I suppose. The Haunted Wood is the biggest thing to happen to this town since Willow Wood closed."

For a second, Saffi thought she saw a satisfied gleam in Malcolm's eyes, but when he squeezed his forehead between his right thumb and forefinger, genuine sadness seemed to sag his shoulders.

It didn't last. Seconds later, he sat up straight and snapped his fingers in the general direction of the kitchen. "Jyoti! My tea, if you please."

As Malcolm's Bog Fog Latte steeped at his elbow, Saffi read the article beneath the attention-grabbing header. The intro probed the "suspicious death" at Malcolm Morton's horror-themed park.

"According to Sheriff Raymond, it could take weeks to determine whether the groundskeeper's death was an accident or the result of foul play." As Saffi read aloud, something tugged at her memory. Something about the sheriff? Nothing rose to the surface, so she kept reading.

Unlike the intro, the rest of the article read like a press release. The Haunted Wood opening would be the event of the Halloween season. There would be more stars in attendance than in the night sky. A costumed "Spooktacular" would take place on the grounds. There would be treats aplenty and "the King of Horror" would have so many ghoulish tricks up his sleeves attendees would be sharing the story for months, if not years.

"With murder afoot, all you Halloween boys and ghouls should watch your backs. Be there... and be scared!" Saffi looked up from her reading in time to see Malcolm mouth the final words along with her. He wasn't angry about the article at all. He was delighted.

She folded the newspaper and passed it back to him. "All news is good news, eh, Malcolm?"

The actor took a sip of his Bog Fog, then sighed. "Successful openings don't happen without the press, my dear. If I can put the Haunted Wood on the front page, why shouldn't I?"

Put it on the front page? Saffi scooted her chair back. "You called that reporter!" she seethed. "Your groundskeeper is dead and you're drumming up publicity!"

Malcolm twirled his mustache like the villain who'd taken bites out of a bevy of beautiful necks in *Dating Dracula*. "Admit nothing. Pay no price."

Saffi threw a ten down on the table, but Malcolm handed it back. "As I promised, everything here is on the house."

Saffi snatched the bill from Malcolm's hand and slapped it back down on the table. "That tip is for Jyoti." Then she walked around the table and leaned toward his ear. "But here's a tip for you, Mr. Morton. While those boys and ghouls are watching their backs, someone is watching you. And you just announced to the world that the show will go on, despite a death on the premises. Didn't you star in *Attack of the Murder Hornets*? You know exactly what happens when you kick a hornets' nest."

Malcolm pressed his lips together so tightly they trembled. Then he pushed back from the table, stood, and grasped the back of his chair. "You can't possibly think I've forgotten those awful postcards. Or poor Lennie's death. Are you even trying to discover who is behind this terror campaign? For all Glenn's talk of how brilliant you are as a sleuth, have you found a single suspect?"

"Yes, Malcolm." Saffi winked. "I have."

And so has C.J. Horseman, PSI.

FIFTEEN

Her encounter with Malcolm had left her more determined than ever to talk to Bev. She needed to know how the park host had come to find Lennie's body and whether she'd seen anything else that could be added to Saffi's small stack of clues. As she hurried toward the office, sunbeams slanted through the trees, striping the log-shaped building with light. When she opened the door and poked her head inside, she found Bob working solo, his round body wedged into the rolling chair in front of the computer.

He looked away from the monitor and blinked as his eyes adjusted. Saffi had done the same thing herself more times than she could count. Looking into a computer screen dried her eyes more than anything, except walking directly into the wind.

"Saffi!" Bob turned the chair toward her. The Halloween-orange safety vest he wore was even worse than the yellow one she'd handed over to Delilah when she passed along her park host job. Bob's vest bulged over a black sweatshirt with matching sweatpants.

"Can I help you with something?"

Every time Bob's button-brown eyes blinked behind his round wire-rimmed glasses, Saffi thought of Mole from *The Wind in the Willows* and smiled.

"Actually, I was hoping to talk to Bev. Malcolm told me, she, uhm, found Lennie's body?"

Bob pushed both hands against the chair arms and wrestled himself out of its grip. "She doesn't want to talk about that. Even I can't get a peep out of her. She's traumatized."

"I don't want to upset her, but..." She casually picked at a dried patch of chocolate eyeball that had somehow adhered to the green turtleneck she'd put on this morning. "The reason I'm here is to figure out who's been sending those threatening postcards to Malcolm. If I can talk to Bev, I might be able to find out if Lennie's murder is connected."

"*Choo!*" Bob sneezed, tugged a handkerchief from his vest pocket, and blew his nose. Then he pushed his glasses up his nose and crossed his arms over his orange vest. "Why would Bev know anything about those postcards or Lennie's murder? She didn't see a thing."

Except, you just said you couldn't get a peep out of her, Saffi mused. "I understand. If I wasn't on deadline for my next *Bedside Reader,* I wouldn't push. As soon as the opening is over, I have to book it back to Last Chance Cove, whether I figure this out or not."

Bob snorted, then brushed a finger across his whiskery mustache. "If you don't, Malcolm will probably send you a bill for your stay."

Saffi raised both brows. "Will he now?"

"You wouldn't believe the things he's asked us to do since we got here. Things *way* beyond a park manager's duties."

Saffi wasn't about to pass up that kind of opening. "Such as?" She used C.J.'s mirroring tactic and crossed her arms, hoping to put Bob at ease.

"Such as setting up those movie props in the forest so they'd scare folks half to death." Bob trembled. "In Malcom Morton's world, nothing is real." Bob snorted. "Not even his name."

Saffi startled. "His name? What do you mean?"

"Malcolm Morton's a stage name. His real name is Kenneth

Grahame. That's why he loved Willow Wood when he was a kid, and why he bought this run-down has-been of a park."

If Malcolm had been anything but an entertainer, the name change would have set off alarms. But plenty of actors adopted stage names. Saffi had written a piece for *Bedside Reader*, #8 about actors whose careers went from stalled to stellar after they opted for more "star-worthy" names. Krishna Pandit Bhanji wasn't getting call backs until he became Ben Kingsley. Movie theaters couldn't fit Helen Mirren's birth name—Ilyena Lydia Vasilievna Mironov—on marquees. Michael Keaton had been born Michael Douglas, but someone famous already had that name. The name of a famous children's book writer would have been equally problematic for a movie villain in the making.

"Bob!" Bev stalked into the office, giving him a look that could only be interpreted one way: *close your blabbing mouth*. To cover up the uncomfortable moment, she bustled over to a metal tray at the end of a long wooden shelf bracketed to the curved back wall.

"This came while Malcolm was away." She held out a postcard. "He didn't even want to look at it. Asked me to give it to you when you arrived."

Saffi's first instinct was to shrink away from the vintage card Bev held out to her.

Come on, Saffi. That's a clue and you have a book to finish. Despite the fact that Saffi hadn't breathed a word of what she was doing to Poppy Morales, her editor's voice had been in her head for long enough to recognize the Brooklyn accent urging her to get on with it.

The vintage card featured a pumpkin-headed girl staring wide-eyed at a raven perched on her outstretched arm. An owl stood at her feet. The front of the card read "Don't you dare try to frighten me." The word "frighten" had been scratched through and replaced with the word "find." How many people had Malcolm told about Saffi's mission to find the postcard perp? *Not helpful, Morton. Not helpful.*

The raven on the card made Saffi's senses tingle. It seemed to be watching, waiting for her to read the rest of the message. She steeled herself, then turned the card over. On the back, the sender had scribbled a bone-chilling ending to the sentence on the front: *Or you will be... nevermore.*

"It's another one of those cards like Malcolm's been getting, isn't it?" Bev's brow furrowed. "Don't you dare try to find me, or you will be nevermore."

Saffi wasn't surprised that Bev had already read the card and probably every other card that had come to Malcolm at the park. But the fact that she could quote the card, almost as if she'd written it herself, turned Saffi's blood cold.

"I'm amazed you get mail deliveries here."

"*Choo!*" Bob sneezed, then sniffed.

Bev tugged the hankie from his pocket and tweaked his nose. "Seasonal allergies." She pulled a face. "Bad this time of year."

In October? Saffi had a feeling there was something more to Bob's sneezes. Maybe Mr. Mole had a "tell"—like a poker player whose eyelid twitched whenever he picked up a dud card. She mentally added sneezes to her list of things to track as she prodded the pair for information.

"We get deliveries from local businesses," Bev responded to Saffi's remark. "But no mail delivery. There's some kind of form Malcolm needs to fill out to get the park's address into the postal system database, but has he bothered? No." Bev rolled her eyes. "Instead, he rented a post office box in Neotsu, between here and Lincoln City." Bev stuck out a thumb in a somewhat southerly direction.

"And somehow it's *our* job to pick up the mail." Bob stuffed himself back into the office chair.

Something else struck Saffi as she flipped the card back to the front. The raven wasn't looking at the pumpkin-headed girl. It was looking straight at Saffi. Raven wanted her to pay attention to something, but it wasn't what was written on the card.

Saffi's brain clicked. She flipped the card over to check out the postmark, as she'd done for all of the other cards. A soaring eagle stamp had been pasted to the card. But no postmark. This postcard had not been mailed. *Cue creepy music.* Saffi shivered.

"You picked this up at the post office?" Saffi waved the postcard toward Bob.

Bev jumped in. "I found it this morning when I sorted yesterday's mail. Stuffed in with more of those RSVPs for the shindig."

Bob's chair squeaked as he sat forward. "Any takers?"

Bev shrugged. "Haven't looked, but if Malcolm gets one more 'thanks but no thanks' he's going to blow a gasket."

Were Malcolm's Hollywood friends declining his invitation? Saffi tucked that away to think about later and focused on the postcard. If the threat had not been mailed, someone had stuck the card into the stack of mail Bob brought back from the post office. That could only mean one thing: the sender had access to the RV park office. Perhaps, Saffi speculated, that someone was inside the hollowed-out log office with her right now.

"Choo!" Bob sneezed hard enough to roll his chair backward.

Saffi held out a hand. "Are you OK? That's some allergy. What did you say you're allergic to?"

Bob patted one vest pocket after another. "I must have forgotten to take my allergy tab this morning." He located his handkerchief and gave his nose a noisy blow.

"Let me make you a coffee." Bev took Saffi by the elbow and guided her out of the office in much the same way C.J. had steered her last night. Every instinct told Saffi to pull away, but that wouldn't get her any closer to the truth. Going with Bev might.

Or it might get you stuffed under a dock. Great! Now Detective Richards' voice was in her head. She brushed it away.

"Sorry about that," Bev said once she got Saffi outside. "Bob has some interesting tics, and I could see that one was triggering your sleuthing side."

If she didn't want suspects to know what she was thinking, Saffi realized, she'd have to work on her "resting sleuth" face.

Bev walked her across to the first row of RVs and unlocked the

Jayco's door. "Welcome to our pride and joy!" The park manager waved her inside.

Saffi stood at the bottom of the trailer's retractable entry step, weighing the risk. As she did, she heard the thrum of guitar strings. Seconds later, an overly enthusiastic voice broke into the lyrics of a Bon Jovi song about swearing to be there for someone.

She tilted her head as if listening and smiled toward the yellow-and-white camper van. *I hear you, C.J. And if I go in here, you'd better be.*

"It's a little early in the day for a serenade." Bev pushed past Saffi. "Ya comin' in?"

Saffi followed Bev into a trailer that looked years newer than her Rambler. Slide outs on either side opened up an enviable amount of space for a kitchen, dining area, and living room. The TV on the far wall was bigger than the window above the dining table in Saffi's rig. "Wow!"

"She's a sweetie, alright." Bev walked to the center of the main room and leaned her hip against a kitchen island.

Saffi felt a drool coming on. "I would kill for that much counter space."

"It's a good thing we have it." Bev pointed to two top-of-the-line milk frothers plugged into an electrical outlet. Beside them sat two French press coffee pots.

Saffi widened her eyes. "That's uhm... why?"

After a moment's hesitation, Bev shrugged. "In a word? Bob. That one there"—Bev pointed toward one of the two frothers—"started slowing down a bit. It just needed a bit of scrubbing to get the magnet that spins the aerator working again, but before I had time to do that, Bob had ordered a new one. I tried to get him to return it, but he went on and on about how fast it would be to froth milk for two drinks at once."

"And the second press pot?"

"He drinks decaf. I drink *actual* coffee, if you get my drift."

"I get it." Saffi took a step toward the counter. "With two

frothers and two press pots you can make a full-caf and a decaf latte at the same time."

"Yes, ma'am. I learned a long time ago that if one of Bob's tics ain't actually gonna kill me, I might as well ignore it. He does the same for me."

Saffi strolled over to one of two gray pleather recliners across from the entertainment center, then looked to Bev for permission to sit.

Bev nodded her OK then busied herself with coffee making. "I'm guessing you don't write all those books without being fully caffeinated."

Like any writer would at the mention of her work, Saffi immediately warmed to her host. "You know my *Bedside Readers*?"

"Bob's got a whole shelf of them."

Saffi pursed her lips in question. "He didn't say a word."

Bev shook her head. "He's not that kind of fan. Keeps himself to himself, does Bob."

With a million-selling series under her belt, Saffi had met all kinds of *Bedside Reader* fans. Gushing. Timid. Challenging. Eager. She was grateful for every one of them. At least, every one that hadn't morphed from fan to stalker. She was already regretting yesterday's blog post about sustainable café practices. Her stalker had used it to do two things: chastise her for driving a gas guzzler and let her know he was tracking her movements. "At nine miles per gallon, how far from Yachats would a single tank take you?" he had written. Her Green Salmon post had revealed exactly where she'd been. *Way to go, Saffi!*

"Hello?" Bev stood at the kitchen island, tapping her foot and holding up one of the two French press pots. "Coffee?"

Saffi pulled her wandering brain back inside the trailer. "Sorry. I'd better go with decaf. I had a mocha at the tea shop. If I have more than one caffeinated drink in an hour, my brain gets completely discombobulated."

Bev bypassed the faucet over the sink for what looked like a miniature version of the same thing to its left. When she stuck the

French press under it and pulled the lever at its back, steam rose from the water.

Instant hot water? Saffi was beginning to think it was time for an RV upgrade. "That came with your rig?"

"No. When Bob ordered a second electric tea kettle, I blew a gasket. Sent the dupe back and installed this little beauty."

When the lattes were frothed and poured, Bev brought one to Saffi. "Cup fits in the holder." She gestured toward the cupholder in the recliner's arm.

Saffi took a sip. Even though the coffee was decaf, it was full-bodied and smooth. Her tongue detected no bitterness. She smiled her approval to Bev, who had seated herself on the small sofa in front of the trailer's back picture window. Behind Bev's head, Saffi had a distant view of C.J. adding a log to his campfire. As if sensing her gaze, the postal inspector looked up. Their eyes didn't meet, of course. He was too far away.

It hit Saffi that the distance didn't matter. The RV's windows had been tinted for daytime privacy. Looking out, Saffi had a clear view. Looking in, C.J. wouldn't be able to see a thing. So much for being there for her. Saffi could only hope that a woman who could make a barista-worthy latte had something besides murder on her mind. She picked up her coffee, took another sip, then plowed ahead.

"Bob doesn't have allergies, does he?"

Bev leaned against the sofa back and crossed her long legs. "Told me he did, when we first met. We'd both been through a marriage or two. I figured his exes couldn't deal with all that sneezing and nose-blowing. After a few months, when he got comfortable with me, his 'allergy'"—Bev, who held her coffee mug between her hands, made air quotes with her pinkie fingers—"disappeared."

Saffi had been right. Bob's sneezes were his "tell," but maybe what they told had more to do with nerves than guilt.

"Don't get me wrong. Bob's a great guy. The sweetest man

you'll ever meet. And, unlike those other jerks I hooked up with, he would do anything for me."

Anything? Saffi had to wonder if that included covering for his wife. If she had killed Lennie and then pretended to find his body, would Bob back her story? Right now, the clues that put Bev on Saffi's suspect list didn't amount to much: her obvious antipathy toward Malcolm and the fact that she'd discovered the body beneath the dock. It was time to find out whether Bev was truly traumatized, or covering up her own guilt.

"Earlier, at the tea shop"—Saffi turned to look through the window behind her—"Malcolm told me that you were the one to find Lennie's body. What a terrible experience."

Bev shrugged. "It just happened, that's all. I walk out to the dock every evening with my camera, taking pictures of the elk herd, if they're there. Sunsets. Great blue heron. Got some eagle shots you would *not* believe."

So much for being traumatized. Bev was either deflecting Saffi's question or finding the groundskeeper's body under the dock was all in a day's work at the Haunted Wood. If it was deflection, Bev was a pro. Instead of giving Saffi an opening for more questions, she jumped up to grab her iPad and started showing her photos she'd taken from the dock. Shot after shot of the elk herd, including one of two bulls with horns locked in battle. A river otter mama clutching her baby to her belly. An eagle, wings out, claws extended, caught in the exact moment his muscular legs dipped into the river to extract a wriggling fish.

Bev had a keen eye, Saffi had to admit. These were as good as those Troy—also an amateur photographer—took, and his were on the walls at Last Chance Café. A wave of warmth washed over her at the memory of Troy sharing an album of his favorite shots while they cuddled on the love seat in his cottage above the sea. Not for the first time, Saffi wondered why she'd left the cove—where she'd just begun to feel at home—for this wild postcard chase. If Troy hadn't gone to Texas... if she'd known Malcolm then the way she was beginning to know him now... she might have resisted the plea in Glenn's brown eyes.

Bev seemed to have sensed she'd lost her audience. She was a fingertip away from shutting down her iPad when Saffi noticed a different kind of photo: a figure in a kayak, silhouetted against a Halloween-orange sunset, lifted one end of a double-bladed paddle as if in greeting.

"Friend of yours?" Saffi pointed at the image.

For the first time, Bev stiffened. "I wouldn't say that, no."

Saffi waited, hoping the silence would pull more out of Bev. It didn't. Instead, it brought the park manager to her feet.

"Time to get back to work." She walked to the sink and rinsed out her cup. "And now that you know Bob's nervous sneezes had nothing to do with those postcards, you can put that noggin of yours to figuring out who sent them."

SIXTEEN

As Saffi stepped down from the Jayco, C.J. flagged her down, as if he'd "just happened" to be strolling by. He put a casual arm around her shoulder, reinforcing the fiction of their close friendship.

Bev locked her RV door then gave them a wave as she walked past on her way back to the office.

"I get what you're doing and why," Saffi said, "but if that hand goes any lower, you might lose a few fingers."

C.J. leaned toward her black-and-silver curls. "Message received. Did Bev spill any beans?"

"A few. And I got—" She started to reach for the postcard she'd slipped into the pocket of her hoodie.

C.J. tightened his grip on her shoulder. "Not here."

As they walked away from the office, Saffi realized just how insular the RV park community was. A few buildings, a few RVs, a trail, a dock. Close quarters. The people who had been here awhile would have gotten to know one another well enough to either become friends or get on each other's nerves. From what she'd seen so far, it was the latter, not the former. She also realized that—other than the trail or the forest—there was nowhere on the grounds she and C.J. could go where they would not be observed, maybe even overheard.

"I was thinking about driving into town," C.J. said. "I see you don't have a toad."

A toad, in RV jargon, was a vehicle towed behind one's rig. For long stays in places like the Haunted Wood, RVers with rigs as big as Saffi's needed a vehicle for trips in and out of town. In Last Chance Cove, she could walk or bike for necessities such as groceries, toiletries, and, of course, books. The Haunted Wood was within biking distance of town, but she had no interest in becoming a grease slick beneath an eighteen-wheeler's tires. Though she hadn't been in the park long enough to run out of anything, it didn't take guessing to figure out that C.J. wanted to talk privately about what she'd learned.

C.J. led her toward his VW camper van. When he opened the door to usher her inside, he held up a hand.

"Sorry. I haven't had a passenger in a while." He slid open the doors in the body of the van and poked around till he came up with a squashed brown paper bag. He punched it open, then started stuffing the items on the passenger seat and floorboard inside: empty to-go cups, used napkins, a crushed raisin box, the wrapper for a peanut-butter chocolate protein bar.

"You *ate* the other half of my protein bar?" Saffi snatched the offending item before he could bag it.

C.J. gave her a sideways grin. "Investigating is hungry work."

Saffi shook the empty wrapper at him. "This is my favorite flavor, and it was the last one in the box."

C.J. grunted. "Mine too. If it had been one of those frou-frou lemon blueberry ones, I'd have left it." He tossed a windbreaker, a pair of sandy flip-flops, and the Sitka sweatshirt he'd been wearing the day they met over the seat into the camping compartment.

Was he complimenting her taste while admitting he'd scarfed down her protein bar? Mr. Postal Inspector was nervy. She had to give him that. The sweatshirt though... that flashed her back to the beginning of her journey and Brenda's description of the man who held up her line picking out a stamp.

"You bought a raven stamp from the Gold Beach post office!" she accused.

"I, uh, what?" The look of confusion that creased his face seemed genuine. "No."

"Are you sure? The post office worker gave a perfect description of you."

"It wasn't me."

"Male. Caucasian. Tall. Green sweatshirt."

C.J. laughed. "Half the men in the area fit that description."

"Wearing a *Sitka* sweatshirt?"

"OK. Maybe not half the men. But way more than one. It wasn't me."

His eyes held the kind of sincerity that came from telling the truth... or being a pathological liar. She remembered the way she'd felt when she spotted C.J.'s van on her trip northward. Curious at first. Then somewhat suspicious. And finally, in all honesty, incensed. After he'd broken into her RV in Bandon, she'd been sure the weathered man with the guitar was the postcard perp, not a protein-bar-snatching law enforcement officer.

Saffi crossed her arms over her chest. How did anyone get good at this sleuthing thing? Clues that pointed in one direction could shift like a weather vane when the winds changed and point in the opposite direction. Maybe it was like writing a solid article. She needed at least three credible sources to confirm a story. Was one disgruntled postal worker enough to put a badge-carrying postal inspector back on her suspect list? Brenda's description needed more noodling, but the Sitka sweatshirt still set off alarm bells. If it wasn't C.J., who was the tall white dude with the green sweatshirt?

"I think it's safe to get in now." C.J. stepped back. "I'll just—" He waved the full trash bag toward the dumpster between the tea shop and the office.

Saffi stepped into the van and buckled into the passenger seat. The vehicle smelled like woodsmoke and evergreens with a whiff of dirty socks, the first clear clue she'd had all day: it was time for C.J. to visit a laundromat.

As they bumped along the driveway back to Highway 101, Saffi debated telling him what she'd learned from Bev. He had told her to stick to the postcard mystery, and she'd tried. OK, she hadn't tried, but why should she? The postcard threats had to be tied to Lennie's death. How could they not be?

She hadn't learned all that much, but she decided to share what she knew: Bev had discovered Lennie's body, but when Saffi asked her about it, she had changed the subject. "Believe it or not, she pulled out a photo album and showed me her nature photos. She's really good."

Now that she thought about it, the fact that Bev loved nature was a clue. The majority of stamps on the postcards had featured nature in one way or another. When she mentioned that to C.J., he nodded. "Good observation. I'll see if I can find out more about Bev."

Saffi nodded. "Thanks. There was one photo, though. A silhouette of a kayaker paddling toward the dock. The person seemed to be waving one end of the paddle at Bev."

C.J. stiffened. "And that's a big deal because...?"

"Because when I asked her if this person was a friend, Bev said 'not really.' And then, she jumped up and said it was time to go back to work. That has to mean something, doesn't it?"

C.J. seemed to be mulling over her question, then he shook his head. "Whatever connection you're trying to make, I don't see it. I also don't see what a kayaker has to do with those postcards you're supposed to be investigating."

"Right. Stick to the postcards," she mumbled. So much for sharing with the pro.

After that, C.J. drove in silence, concentrating on keeping semis off his bumper while maintaining a safe distance between the van and the traffic ahead. As they approached a busy intersection, Saffi noticed a post office on the left-hand side of the road. "Is that Neostu?" She leaned forward and pointed.

C.J. glanced to his left then nodded.

"Bob told me Malcolm has a PO box there."

"Makes sense. It can take a while to get a new address into the postal database." C.J. went on to explain that the Haunted Wood might never have mail delivered directly to the office. "There's only so much time in a day, and with only one address on a road"—C.J. shrugged—"the mail carrier isn't going to drive down there."

Since they were on the topic of postal delivery, Saffi decided it was time to show him the latest postcard. She slid her hand into the pocket of her hoodie, pulled it out, and held it where he could see the vintage card with its haunting Halloween theme.

He flicked his eyes sideways then his weathered jaw hardened. "Malcolm received another threat?"

Saffi nodded. "Bev gave it to me when I was in the office this morning. Said it came in yesterday's mail, but look at this." She tapped a finger on the stamp to emphasize the absent postmark.

C.J. took his eyes off the road long enough to glance at the card. In that moment, the light went from green to red and the car in front of him stopped. He slammed his foot on the brake pedal hard enough to jolt the camper van to a stop. Saffi jerked forward into the shoulder belt.

"Sorry," he apologized. "Put that away until we're parked, would you?"

A few seconds later, he nodded toward a sign for Roads End State Recreation Site and signaled a right turn beside a lighthouse replica. The road took them between two shopping centers and past a turnoff for the Chinook Winds Casino. It rambled past houses and a jumble of time- and wind-weathered cottages then turned into a parking lot loop at the brown wooden sign for the recreation area.

Saffi cast a look at C.J.

"Taking this privacy thing a bit far, aren't you?"

He parked, shut down the VW, opened the driver's-side door, and the mighty Pacific Ocean shushed her voice. Saffi inhaled salt-laden moisture, and her body relaxed into the moment. Bob had told her the ocean was close. Bev had said she could hear it at night. But Saffi had been so immersed in Malcolm's Haunted

Wood, she'd hardly felt its presence. Now that she did, she realized how much she'd missed it. She stepped out of the van and stood for a moment, watching waves roll toward the shore. It was like recognizing the face of a lost loved one. *Be still my heart.* Saffi smiled.

"After squatting by that campfire all morning, I need a stretch. You up for it?"

More than anything.

Saffi sighed out the worries she'd been holding in her gut since she set off on this wild perp chase. She scrambled after C.J. down a short path between hills covered with ice plants. The path emerged onto the shore where a narrow lazy creek meandered toward the sea. Her blue sloggers—the ones with busy bees and perky daisies—wobbled over fat round pebbles at the creek's edge, then sank into beach sand. Thank goodness she'd stuffed her sock-clad feet into those this morning instead of her sneakers.

"We can stretch our legs while we talk," C.J. said, then outpaced her within a few steps.

Sloggers are not made for playing catch-up. Instead of following him down the beach, Saffi plodded toward firmer sand at the edge of the waves. If he wanted to talk, the postal inspector could go her way, or drive that bus of his back to the highway.

It took him a few yards to notice she wasn't beside him, but when he did, he altered his course and joined her on the firm sand.

"I was headed toward the rocks." C.J. pulled a dark blue knit cap out of the pocket of his windbreaker and covered his scruffy blond hair. "Thought you might like to see where the cormorants roost."

Saffi turned toward where he pointed. A scrabble of huge black rocks—hardened lava, Saffi supposed—stepped into the sea.

"Why not?" She stuffed her curls into her hoodie and tied it shut to keep the cold wind blowing off the ocean from making her left ear ache as they walked northward. As they got closer to the rocks, Saffi saw white patches of what could only be guano and heard the chuttering coos of cormorants as they stretched their oily black wings to dry them in the wind.

"There must be hundreds of them!" Saffi shaded her eyes. Their feathered attire was gloss black from their head crests to their tails, but white from the tip of their pointed orange bills, down their long necks to their bulging bellies.

"*Corvus marinus*," C.J. murmured. "The sea raven."

A shock went through Saffi's body. "Sea raven," she whispered an echo.

"So." C.J. turned to face her. "Let's see that postcard."

For all his expertise, the postal inspector came up with the same conclusions Saffi had reached earlier. "No postmark, so it wasn't mailed. You say Bob picked up the mail?"

Saffi nodded.

"Either he stuck it in the stack himself, or someone else added it to the mail after he brought it back to the office."

"Exactly." Saffi huddled into her hoodie. "Which could mean that someone who works at the park wants me to stop looking for them."

C.J. sucked his lips and made a funny little squeaking sound. "Maybe."

"Maybe?" Saffi stuffed her hands into her pockets.

"It's been quiet since you arrived," C.J. said, "but when I pulled in yesterday all kinds of people were coming in and out. Delivery guys. An electrician. The sheriff. That real estate lady. An ecologist from Sitka who's mapping the wetland."

Sitka again?

"Malcolm told me someone from Sitka got in his face a while back. Something about the park not having an environmental impact statement? What I don't understand is why someone from Alaska would come all the way to Oregon to map wetlands or get involved in a protest against the Haunted Wood."

C.J. narrowed his moss-green eyes in confusion, then smacked the postcard he held in one hand on the palm of the other and laughed. "That's why you asked me if there were elk herds in Alaska. You thought my sweatshirt came from Sitka, Alaska!"

"Uh, yeah. What else would I think?" Saffi was beginning to

feel as if she was the butt of some joke only C.J. understood, and she didn't like it one bit. The tone of her voice must have tipped him off because he apologized.

"You're right. It's the most logical conclusion."

"It is. So?"

"So, I could tell you, but it would be a lot more fun to show you." He turned back the way they'd come.

"Show me what?"

"Sitka!" C.J. waved for her to follow.

As he shouted the word, the cormorants startled and rose skyward. Wings flapping in unison, they flowed into a line pointing southward. Then, as if answering some unseen call, they swerved toward where Saffi stood, swooped over her head, and coalesced into a "V." Then the sea ravens arrowed north, straight toward a massive green headland in the distance. Saffi had no idea where they were headed. She only knew that Raven—her totem animal whose messages she dared not ignore—expected her to follow.

SEVENTEEN

C.J. drove back the way they'd come but passed the turnoff for the Haunted Wood. The van crossed over the Salmon River, according to a sign Saffi struggled to read before they sped past. To her left, the river cut a winding path through a wide marsh. Though she couldn't see it, she was certain it emptied into the Pacific just beyond her view. For a second, she thought she glimpsed the same emerald green headland she'd spotted from the beach. C.J. took the next left-hand turn, almost directly opposite the road she'd used yesterday to loop back to the 101 after she'd missed the road into the RV park.

"Three Rocks Road," she read aloud. She pictured three rocks, one balancing atop another, the kind hikers or park rangers left to mark trails. Then she imagined three pebbles scattered in the road. Finally, she pictured three boulders sliding off a slope to land on top of a vehicle. "Any particular three?" she asked.

"Yep. Three big ones. Just offshore where the Salmon River dumps into the sea. There's all kinds of legends about the place. A glowing cave. Bigfoot bones. A ghost ship. Treasure chests."

A little bell went off in Saffi's brain. "That's just the kind of mysterious lore my readers love." If she could find out more, this trip might be worthwhile, even if she didn't catch any criminals.

Once again, C.J. read her mind and volunteered the information she needed before she even asked.

"If you have time, you should head down to the history museum in Lincoln City. They have tons of information about the area."

Saffi furrowed her brow. "How do you know so much? I thought you were from LA."

"Ah, well, I work there. But I've spent a lot of time here. Family connections."

Family connections? Here? Her sleuthing senses went on high alert. Coincidences happened, sure. All the time. But the fact that C.J. Horseman might have every reason to travel Highway 101 from southern California to here, with insider access to every post office along the way, made her want to zap his name back to the top of her suspect list. From the moment he'd shown her his badge, she'd trusted him without question. Had that been a mistake?

Maybe it wasn't the badge. Maybe it was the captivating green eyes.

Enough! Saffi shushed her inner snark.

C.J. stopped the VW at an intersection. To the left, a sign pointed to Knight Park. "There's a boat launch down there. The only public launch near the mouth of the Salmon River."

Saffi craned forward to look around him but couldn't see a thing.

"Could the kayak in Bev's photo have launched from that park?"

C.J. sucked in a sharp breath, tilted his head as if thinking, then shrugged. "Probably, unless it was someone with access from Cascade Ranch. They have a clubhouse a mile or so up the road."

Cascade Ranch. Wasn't that connected to the real estate developer who'd trashed the Haunted Wood in the newspaper? "I think I read something about Cascade Ranch. They're adding an extension?"

"No." C.J.'s head shake was forceful and his mouth set in a grim line. "That's Riverside Ranch. Different project, a bit upriver.

Cascade Ranch has been here since the sixties. The guy who developed it cared about this place. He even set aside land for Sitka."

Whatever that is. If Saffi had been a nail biter, she'd have been chewing them by now.

"Riverside Ranch is all about making money. As much as possible and to heck with the consequences to the ecosystem."

Instead of turning left toward Knight Park, C.J. went right. Saffi caught sight of a small wooden sign and sat up straighter: Sitka Center for Art and Ecology. "Sitka!"

The narrow road curled through forested land before opening out into an area with rolling hillsides to the right, and—if you squinted past the tiered, wood-shingled condos—the Pacific to the left. A small herd of elk grazed the grass. One female cropped tufts so close to the road that Saffi could have rolled down the VW's window and touched her copper-brown snout, if she'd dared.

She felt her eyes go wide with wonder. "What is this place?"

"A little bit of heaven." C.J. smiled.

That, she could see, but what else? C.J. stayed mum until he'd parked the van in the shadow of a massive Sitka spruce. Saffi looked through the side window, up, up, and up through its moss-covered branches until C.J. came around to open the van door. He ushered her onto a path that led to a small grouping of rough-hewn wooden buildings, weathered gray-white over time by the elements. The tallest was shaped something like a hexagon with a large round window in its upper story. She caught sight of a blue sign with white lettering beside what appeared to be the main office.

"Sitka Center for Art and Ecology." Saffi glanced at C.J., still waiting for an explanation that hadn't come.

C.J. strode through the door without knocking. A gorgeous young woman with strawberry-blond hair draped over her shoulders looked up. Her eyes lit with something that could not be mistaken: love. Before Saffi even had time to speculate about whether she and C.J. were an item, he lightly rapped his knuckles on the top of her head.

"Saffi Graywood, meet my daughter, Meredith."

Whoa! Did C.J. have a wife back home in LA? If so, he'd been fooling her on more levels than she wanted to admit.

The young woman behind the desk stood, stuck out her tongue at C.J. and reached her hand toward Saffi. "Mere, please." She pronounced her shortened name "mare"; combined with her last name, Saffi couldn't stop a smile from breaking out. Mere gave Saffi's hand the same Goldilocks shake her dad had when they first met: not too hard, not too soft. Her eyes—the same moss-green as her father's, Saffi now noticed—held consideration and warning: "Any friend of my dad's is a friend of mine. Unless you break his heart, then watch out." She smiled, but set her teeth to show Saffi she meant business.

So, not married. Unless C.J.'s daughter was a lot more liberal than Saffi would ever be. Given how unlikely anything more than a "fake" relationship with C.J. might be, Saffi felt safe from daughterly retribution.

"To what do I owe this unexpected pleasure?" Mere moved from behind the desk toward her dad, giving and receiving the kind of hug Saffi hadn't had since Troy left for Texas. People with close relationships took hugs for granted. They were a battery you could plug into whenever you needed a charge, a jolt, a reminder that you mattered to someone. When they were gone... the longing for human connection never went away. Since Levi's death, she had welcomed hugs whenever she could get them. Right now, she felt just a little bit jealous. She and Levi had not been blessed with children. A series of miscarriages, the last of which had nearly cost her life, had been enough to shift Saffi's focus from babies to books. Life dealt blows, but the Chumbawamba song that had gotten her through that time still guided her: she got knocked down, but—after wallowing in misery for a bit—she always got back up again.

C.J. pulled out of the hug and stepped back to include Saffi in the circle. "Saffi would like to know a bit about Sitka," he told his daughter.

"Ah, well—" Mere started, but her dad stopped her.

"Careful what you say. This is *the* Saffi, of the *Aunt Saffi's Bedside Reader* series. Apparently, anything you say can and will be used in a future book. Unless you have the ability to arrest her if she reveals confidences."

His eyes went from warm to just a hint of cool as if he wasn't kidding around. He was reminding Saffi—and maybe his daughter —that some things were not fodder for the masses. Mere raised both brows.

"I'd better keep Sitka's deep dark secrets a secret, then." She gave Saffi a wink.

If one of those secrets involved yelling at Malcolm Morton about the possible environmental impacts of his project, fine. If it involved threatening postcards or worse? Not so fine. Saffi held up two fingers on her right hand and put her left hand over her heart. "I swear to keep secret that which must remain secret but reserve the right to divulge anything and everything else."

Mere smacked her hands and rubbed them together. "Good enough. Shall we?"

She waved Saffi and C.J. toward the office door they'd entered moments ago. On the way out, they passed a shelving unit filled with Sitka gear: T-shirts, caps, water bottles, sweatshirts, including one exactly like C.J. had been wearing the first time they met. Brenda's ID of the man in the green sweatshirt had not narrowed the suspect field as much as Saffi had thought.

Once outside, Mere led them along paths that wound around the wooden buildings. Saffi saw statues, a totem pole, a giant stone wheel balanced atop a stone pedestal. She used her cellphone to snap photos of the grounds through the wheel's wide eye before moving on. As they walked, Mere talked, describing the history and purpose of the Sitka center. It was, Saffi learned, a place that fostered a synergy between the arts and nature. Printmakers, sculptors, photographers, ceramicists, musicians, writers, ecologists, biologists, foresters... the list of those who had come here to work, teach, or learn went on and on.

They passed a wooden bench so perfect for a quiet moment beneath the beam of sunlight streaming through the trees that Saffi took a time-out from the tour. Father and daughter stepped away to catch up and give her a bit of solitude.

The peace that washed over Saffi was deeper than she had experienced anywhere except at the edge of the Pacific. It was as if she'd stepped off the treadmill into a world so still, so silent, she felt —for perhaps the first time in her life—that she was not outside of nature observing it. She was a part of it. As moments passed, she realized that nature wasn't silent at all. A constant conversation swirled around her. Birds called, squirrels chattered, wind set the trees to talking. Beneath it all, she could hear the drumbeat of waves crashing into the shore.

As she rejoined her guides, fresh energy surged through her body, enough to revise a book or write a new one, and more than enough to solve the postcard mystery. After all, Raven's seafaring siblings—the cormorants—had pointed her in this direction. There were clues here, and Saffi was determined to find them.

Mere continued the tour past artists' studios where creatives worked on projects inspired by and connected to the unique, and protected, environment of Cascade Head Conservancy. She stopped at a small building with a red door, guarded by three small hooded figures that could have been Jawa from the planet Tatooine in the Star Wars movies.

"This is the writer's studio." Mere smiled. "I wish I could show you inside, since you're a writer, but we have a resident working in there right now."

After the tour ended, Mere suggested a walk. Saffi could not have been happier.

"I feel like all I've done for the last few days is sit on my behind in the driver's seat of my RV." She gave Mere a sideways grin.

"So, you're vacationing at the Haunted Wood like my dad?"

Mere lifted a reddish-blond brow, then glanced at her father as if checking to see what Saffi might already know.

"When she's not writing, Saffi sticks that cute nose of hers into business better left to law enforcement."

Saffi halted. A compliment to get on her good side followed by a dig to put her back in her place. Two could play that game. "Unfortunately, the gorgeous green eyes of law enforcement miss things I happen to see."

Mere burst out laughing. "She has your number, Dad." She leaned toward Saffi. "He's always done that. Turned on the charm right before he reminds you of his superiority in all things."

The walk Mere suggested led them down Sitka's long drive then turned right onto an asphalt road crumbling along the edges. The road sloped downward then swooped left toward the river where it ended. Startled from its fishing by their approach, a great blue heron spread its immense wings and lifted skyward. It flew across the river to a beach on the opposite shore then stalked back into the water, beak down, hoping to spot the silver wriggle that meant a snack was at hand.

When Saffi looked away from the heron toward the sea, she gasped. "Three Rocks!"

The mouth of the Salmon River was a short meander from where they stood. Just beyond it, as C.J. had said, three massive rocks emerged from the water. The flicker of wings caught her eye as a flock of cormorants circled the three rocks before landing. The sound of Mere's voice broke through the birds' chuttering, and Saffi turned toward her.

"Sorry. What was that?"

Mere pointed to a wooden building behind her with the same time- and weather-worn look of those up the hill at Sitka. The deck behind the building had a picnic table. If Saffi could have a place like that to write, she'd be in heaven—as long as it wasn't pouring rain, of course.

"That's the Cascade Ranch clubhouse," Mere said. "They let Sitka staff and residents use it when nothing else is going on." She led them around the building to large racks stacked with canoes and kayaks. The image of a kayaker waving one end of a paddle at Bev popped into Saffi's mind.

"Do you kayak?"

Mere grinned. "Since I was a kid." She turned to her dad. "My grandfather was a marine biologist. He used to guide kayak tours along here." The look she gave her father was filled with shared memories.

C.J. picked up a river-worn stone and skipped it across the water. "My dad thought firsthand experience of pristine coastal lands would boost support for land conservancies."

"Back in the seventies, Poppa Horse testified before Congress in support of the CHSRA." Mere beamed. Her eyes shone, and she patted her chest as if barely containing her pride.

Saffi shook her head. The initials did not ring a bell. "The CHSRA?"

"All of this." C.J. held out an arm and turned in a slow circle. "Those marshes out there," he pointed across the river, "the estuary, Cascade Head and much of the forest on this side of Highway 101 are part of the Cascade Head Scenic Research Area. Set aside by Congress."

Mere wrapped her arms around herself. "Poppa Horse would have done anything to protect this place."

Mere's nickname for her grandfather was too adorable for words. What wasn't adorable was that word: *anything*. Bob would do anything for Bev. Poppa Horse would do anything for this pristine place. Would Mere do the same? Someone had taken a kayak upriver to the Haunted Wood's dock, and it could have come from exactly where she now stood. Just as the thought crossed her mind, a lone cormorant flapped its way upriver to land on a moss-covered rock in front of the clubhouse deck. It spread its oil-black wings wide and gurgled.

I hear you, sea raven.

Mere glanced at her dad with a mischievous grin. "Remember

those guys Poppa Horse took care of when you were in high school?"

Saffi turned to C.J. "You grew up here?" He'd been vague when he told her he had "connections" here. Clearly, those connections ran deep.

C.J. lifted his brows. "Yeah. A couple of clowns from my school used to cruise around in kayaks. Took potshots at cormorants, otters, gulls. Anything that moved."

Standing in this place where water met sea, Saffi saw living creatures in every direction, and her heart sank. Heron silently stalked through the marsh. Fish glided through the clear water. Birds swooped and screeched over and around the Three Rocks. Seals snoozed on the sand bank across the river. People hunted for food in rural areas, she knew that. Adults and kids alike. But taking potshots at wildlife just for the fun of it? The bile in her belly started a slow burn.

Mere pursed her lips and glared. "Poppa Horse caught them at it on a school day. Paddled out and dumped 'em in the drink, then called their parents. Now that he's gone, I keep an eye on this place. Anyone who messes with this," she spread her arms wide, "messes with me."

What might have been a flash of fear crossed C.J.'s face. It disappeared so quickly Saffi thought she must have imagined it. But she knew exactly what might have triggered it.

EIGHTEEN

Mere, as it turned out, was a sculptor. After a short riverside stroll, she led them back to Sitka, and her proud father forced her to show Saffi what he called her "real" work.

"She's brilliant," he bragged.

They followed Mere past the office, up some steps, and across a deck to one of the studios they'd passed earlier. When Mere opened the door and ushered her inside, Saffi gasped.

"Why are you sitting behind a desk when you can do—" Saffi waved toward shelves filled with sculptures, some simple white clay forms that seemed to be in process. The color of the clay triggered an itch in Saffi's brain, but she was too fascinated by Mere's work to scratch.

C.J.'s daughter's completed works were so colorful and whimsical Saffi would have wrapped them all up and shipped them home, if she'd had a home big enough to hold them. The finished figures looked something like marionettes with wires raising a hand in greeting here or to stifle a yawn there. One figure had a lop-eared rabbit slumped over its bald head. Another straddled a Cinderella-worthy carriage that seemed to be made from the skirt of her ball gown. A blue bird nested in the curls piled atop her head. The colors were rich—reds, yellows, blues, oranges. Every finished piece featured pictures painted and fired into permanence in the industrial-size kiln that stood in the center of the room. And within those pictures were other pictures, as if each sculpture was a world that contained other worlds. C.J. was right. His daughter was brilliant.

There was no way she belonged on Saffi's list of suspects, kayak or no kayak.

"I did a residency here a few years back. Now I mind the office a few times a week to earn my time on the kiln," Mere answered Saffi's question. "I have a cabin upriver. It's a quick paddle each way. When the weather allows, of course."

Saffi stifled a groan. She did *not* want this brilliant artist, who just happened to be C.J.'s daughter, to be a killer. And what reason could Mere possibly have? One clue wasn't enough to put her on the list.

But it's not one clue, Saffi, it's three. Mere had been kayaking since her youth. Her grandfather had been part of protecting this area from development, and she'd made it clear that she would do the same. Plus, she regularly paddled the river, right past the Haunted Wood. Reluctantly, Saffi let her gaze roam the room again. Her heart sank when she spotted something she'd missed. A handful of upside-down signs leaning against a wall. She wandered as inconspicuously as she could toward the signs, asking questions about Mere's work.

"I'd love to have one of your pieces. Do you sell in galleries?"

Saffi pulled out a sign and glanced at its message as Mere talked about the string of galleries who represented her work.

"One in LA, thanks to my dad!" She gave him a wink.

C.J. nodded, but his expression had turned dour.

"I have a few pieces in Gold Beach, a place that's half-coffee shop, half art gallery. Not the best outlet," she confided, "but I also have one in Newport. And Portland, of course, but if there's anything here that strikes your fancy, I'm happy to cut out the middle man."

As Mere talked, Saffi's brain made connections. For decades, nature had been reclaiming the land Malcolm had purchased. When bulldozers and woodcutters and electricians and plumbers started streaming down the lane to Malcolm Morton's Haunted Wood, Mere had probably seen them as invaders. For someone who loved Sitka, reopening the park would be a massive leap in the wrong direction, perhaps a danger to the conservancy itself. Malcolm could not have done a better job of making himself a target of environmental activists if he'd tried. Mere, Saffi now suspected, was the "Sitka person" the actor had described. The artist seemed like the kind of young woman who wouldn't hesitate to get in the face of the "great" Malcolm Morton.

Saffi half hated herself for what she said next. "I'd love to spend more time with the pieces before I choose. Maybe I should come back without..." She pointed to C.J., whose glower told her he knew exactly what she was doing, and if he could stop her, he would.

If what she'd said about buying a sculpture had not been true, Mere's delight as she dug a card out of a drawer and handed it over would have pierced Saffi through the heart. As it was, she could barely look the artist in the eye as she offered her thanks for the tour and said goodbye.

As Saffi and C.J. walked back to his van in silence, she could feel his green gaze boring into her. He didn't open the VW's door for her this time, and, from the way he slammed the driver's side door, she gathered that his unerring ability to read her thoughts told him that his plan had not only failed, it had backfired.

He didn't say a word all the way back to the park. When he pulled the van into his site, he clicked the key to turn off the engine. Then glanced at Saffi. "It's not her," he said, his voice dark with worry. "Mere's a spitfire, but there's no way she had anything to do with Lennie's death. She's a protector. Not a destroyer."

"And the postcards?" Saffi's stomach clenched as C.J.'s weathered face reddened, his jaw hardened. Had he known all along that his daughter could be a suspect? If so, why had he taken her to Sitka? The answer came easily. He must have known that Saffi's cute nose would sniff out the Sitka connection sooner or later. Maybe he thought the best way to keep Mere off her suspect list was introduce her. Too bad he hadn't warned his daughter to get rid of those protest signs.

Back at the park, Saffi barely had time to fill the electric tea kettle and click it on before someone pounded on her door. "Hang on!" she called. She moved her bland white mugs and the Japanese dragon teacup aside, peering into the cabinet in search of the raven mug she'd bought from her artist friend Mellie Blue. When she didn't spot it, she grabbed the closest one and dropped a tea bag inside.

"Saffi! I know you're in there!" Malcolm's voice rose to stage level before she could get the door open. "I've been looking for you all morning."

"What is *wrong?*" she demanded.

Malcolm stood at the bottom of the steps dressed like a sun gone supernova: yellow pants, an orange knitted jacket, a bright red pullover, and a scarf striped in all three colors plus white.

"Is that?" She pointed to a blood smear on his right sleeve. Instead of answering, he grasped her arm and almost pulled her off the steps.

"Malcolm! Stop." She grabbed the stairway's wooden handrail and dug in her heels.

"You have to come. Now!" He turned and hurried away, a yellow-and-orange blur that fully expected her to follow.

Saffi took time to turn off the kettle before stuffing her feet back into her sloggers and clomping down the steps. She spotted Malcolm disappearing through the rustic rolling doors of the museum. She locked her RV and took a deep breath. She hadn't had time to check out the barn yet, so she readied herself to note every detail inside Malcolm's museum. The first detail to catch her eye stopped her in her tracks. Saffi blinked, and blinked again.

Everywhere she looked, blood dripped: from the walls, the horror movie posters, the creatures. Blood-red handprints marred the surfaces of display cases, even the popcorn popper had a red-fingered smear down its side. It looked like a scene from Malcolm's one and only slasher film: *Blood for Blood.*

How could the actor stand there so calmly, arms crossed over his body, face slightly miffed rather than terrified? Where was his flight response? Her legs ached with the tension of trying to stand still rather than turning to flee. Malcolm, on the other hand, tapped his foot as if waiting impatiently for her to... what, scream?

The clues clicked into place.

"It's not real, is it?"

Saffi walked close to one of the defaced posters and stuck a fingertip into a red handprint. She held it to her nose and took a sniff. In her fifth *Bedside Reader*, she'd written an article about the evolution of fake blood in cinematography. Before technicolor, chocolate syrup was the go-to goo for simulating blood on screen. This wasn't chocolate, but it wasn't blood either. It lacked the metallic scent that differentiated real blood from fake. She dared a tiny lick of the gore on her finger and tasted the sickly sweet flavor of Karo corn syrup. Along with non-dairy creamer, lots of red food coloring and a drop of blue, the fake blood covering Malcolm's museum could very well have been made from the recipe actor Bruce Campbell had whipped up for his *Evil Dead* character.

"When did this happen?" Saffi asked.

"I have no idea." Malcolm ran a hand through his wavy white hair, then tweaked the curls of his mustache. Saffi thought she noticed a faint pink tinge in the white whiskers. "Everything was fine when I went to bed last night." He pointed upward toward an enclosed loft that ran across the back of the barn.

"Is that where you stay while you're here?" Saffi asked.

Malcolm nodded briskly, then walked to the middle of the museum and pulled out his cellphone. She expected him to call the police. Instead, the actor turned in a slow circle, clicking picture after picture.

"Did you report this?" Saffi walked toward him, taking in a row of plexiglass cases. Each one contained an iconic costume from one of Malcolm's films. The dark brown mink stroller Malcolm had worn as Victor Frankenstein in *Sea of Ice and Blood*. The flowing black Rasputin robe decorated with intricate cord work and trimmed with black fur from *The Demon Monk*. The L. Frank Baum jacket he had worn to dinner last night. All of the cases had "bloody" handprints, but only one showed a stain on the costume itself: the blood-stained kimono Malcolm had been wearing yesterday when she arrived.

As Saffi strolled through the museum, she couldn't find a single item that had been damaged, not even the movie posters, since they, too, were encased in frames behind clear plastic. It would take plenty of elbow grease to clean up the mess, but no real damage had been done. When she pointed that out to Malcolm, he slapped his cellphone against his palm.

"No damage?" He shook the phone at her. "Just look at this place. We open in four days, Saffi. Four!"

She was about to explain the concept of hiring a cleanup crew when a throat cleared behind her. Saffi whirled just as Malcolm shouted a greeting.

"Ben! Come in, come in." Malcolm hurried toward the newcomer, hand extended.

"It's, uh, Brian, sir. Brian Bennion." The young man who shook Malcolm's hand looked like he'd just walked off a college campus. He had russet curls, worn long and loose. His blue eyes blinked behind scholarly glasses as they adjusted to the bright white glare of LED ceiling lights. He pushed his glasses up his sharp nose before sticking out his hand to shake the actor's.

"You said there was another, uh, incident."

Saffi's gut clenched. Instead of calling the police, Malcolm had called a reporter! Wasn't Brian Bennion the reporter who had written the front-page article about the park's grand opening? Given the shrinking staffs of newspapers in the Internet news age, the college-age kid had probably also been the reporter Malcolm had notified after Lennie's body was found. He had, after all, said "another incident."

If the bloody mess in the museum turned out to be nothing but a publicity stunt, she was going to roast Malcolm like a marshmallow on a stick.

"An incident. Indeed, indeed." Malcolm guided Brian into the museum and showed him the damage, meanwhile raving about the priceless artifacts inside their plexi-protected cases. Saffi heard him sharing which film each item had been featured in and who had worn each costume. To Saffi, he sounded more like a carnival barker than a vandalism victim. "Come one, come all, to Malcolm Morton's Museum of Blood-Soaked Horrors!"

The longer she watched, the more her blood pressure rose until it pulsed against her temples. She had to get out of here before she gave the reporter a *really* juicy headline: "Bedside Reader Author Goes Berserk." She'd never hear the end of it. Poppy, her New York editor, had set a Google alert to notify her of every mention of Saffi Graywood, Aunt Saffi, or *Bedside Readers*. One of those would pop up on her screen, and Poppy would know what Saffi had been up to for the last few days: sleuthing instead of revising.

While Malcolm regaled the young reporter with stories of stardom past, Saffi's brain set to work figuring out who had spent the night painting the museum blood red. The actor himself? Someone else on the premises? Or someone from outside the park? If Malcolm had done it, the motive would probably be garnering more publicity. If someone else in or outside the park had done it, it had to be the postcard perp whose motive was clear—harass the actor into shutting down the Haunted Wood.

She couldn't search Mere's cabin or Cecily Raymond's house—wherever that might be—for evidence. But if all that blood had been concocted at the Haunted Wood, it had probably happened in a kitchen. Bev and Bob had a large enough kitchen in their Jayco, but she hadn't spotted a single drop of red on the pristine counters. If they'd mixed up fake blood at some point, they'd done a professional job of cleaning up after themselves. The tea shop kitchen was a strong possibility, since it was a restaurant kitchen with commercial mixers. Either Jyoti or her grandfather could have mixed a batch of red gore. Was there a kitchen in the actor's loft?

With Malcolm distracted by the reporter, now would be the perfect time to sneak inside and nose around.

Saffi waited until Malcolm led Brian to a row of creatures. The actor posed with one after another—Malcolm and Mothstra, Malcolm and Frankenstein's monster, Malcolm and Crocodilia—encouraging the young reporter to snap pictures. Both men were much too busy, she hoped, to notice an author-turned-sleuth tiptoeing toward the ornate metal staircase that curved upward into the loft. When she reached the top stair, there was no door to stop an intrusion. She stepped directly into a reproduction of an Art Deco-style theater lobby. Her mouth fell open, and wonder flooded her body as her memory took her back in time.

Over the years, grand theaters like the one Malcolm's loft evoked had been replaced by cookie-cutter multiplexes. Those were now giving way to home theaters. Why go out to a movie when you could stream the latest blockbusters without getting off the couch? Saffi knew why. The elegant décor, the massive screens, the seat-shaking boom of surround sound, the smell of buttered popcorn, and the taste of salt as you licked it off your fingers, one by one.

She pulled herself out of her memories to focus on the loft. The main room was rectangular, and huge, stretching the entire width of the barn. Its floor had been covered—wall to wall—in red carpet with a repeated pattern of a rearing white Pegasus in front of a purple cloud. The walls had been painted pale blue with a cream, red, and gold-foil cornice just below the ceiling. A leather sectional dominated the center of the room. The black-and-white animal skin draped over its back looked both sleek and fluffy.

The wall across from the sectional featured rich red trompe l'oeil curtains. They bracketed a massive home theater screen and looked real enough to have just opened for the night's feature. Speakers had been placed strategically around the room. On the back wall, another ultra-realistic painting, this time of a projection booth window, complete with what looked like a vintage carbon arc projector. A feeling of anticipation washed over Saffi as if at any second the projector would click to life, and a bright beam would dance figures across the screen.

She was so entranced by the room, she forgot for a moment that she had stolen her way up here with a mission—to find out if the loft had a kitchen. Once she remembered, she took a step toward one of the two doors leading off the main room.

A familiar voice chuckled. "I knew you wouldn't be able to resist."

NINETEEN

When Saffi turned, she noticed that Malcolm's mustache had grown pinker since she last saw him. He must have gotten blood on his hands—metaphorically, at least—while pointing out the mayhem below to the reporter. Malcolm's habit of twirling his whiskers probably accounted for the pink tint she'd seen earlier as well, but had it come from discovering the mess? Or had he been responsible for the fake bloodbath?

Saffi took a deep breath and turned in a slow circle to take in the room again. "This place is... glorious."

Malcolm stood straight, shoulders back as if readying himself for a close-up. A wide smile pushed the tips of his mustache up his cheeks and made his eyes sparkle. But after a few seconds, his shoulders drooped. He wandered across the room and sank into the leather sectional.

"Glorious. And yet, all an illusion." Malcolm's eyes saddened. "My days in the spotlight are over, my dear. This is my last-ditch attempt to keep them alive."

"This?" Saffi waved a hand to take in the room. "Or this?" She spread both arms wide to embrace the entire Haunted Wood.

"All of it. I need this grand opening to be big! Bigger than big! These postcards, the threats, Lennie's death? You *must* discover who is behind these despicable deeds before something else happens!" He leaned forward and covered his face with his hand.

She had seen him use that move in movie after movie, probably to fake feelings he couldn't quite conjure. Saffi walked to the sectional, sat down beside the actor, and angled her body to face him. Out of the corner of her eye, she saw a red smear on the black-and-white animal skin she'd noticed earlier. Was it still wet? When she reached out to touch it, the skin quivered, expanded, then slipped off the back of the couch onto her lap, warm, wiggling, and scratching for purchase.

Saffi screeched, dumped the creature off her lap, and scrambled to her feet. Its head turned toward her. Its glowing green eyes both judge and jury.

"What *is* that?"

Malcolm chuckled. "*That* is Tomago. She's a Maine Coon."

Saffi's hand shook as she pointed at the... could it possibly be a cat? Stretched on the back of the sectional it had been, what? Four feet long? And when it hit her lap, it landed like twenty-five pounds of fluff-covered flesh. "*That* is a *cat?*"

"Now you've insulted her. She'll never forgive you, you know. Not unless you pick her up and whisper sweet nothings in her ear."

Saffi loved cats. She did. But if she tried to pick up a cat half her size, she'd throw her back out. Instead, she sat down and bent toward the cat, giving her a gentle scratch under the chin. "Sorry, uhm, sweetie." Then she sat up and patted her lap, inviting the monster cat to jump up.

Tomago was not that easy. She narrowed her eyes, lifted her tail, and flounced away.

Malcolm chuckled. "I'd say she'll warm up to you in time, but she's persnickety about such things."

Saffi brushed at the cat hairs clinging to her hoodie and examined a fresh rip in her jeans. Then she lifted her gaze to the actor. "She had a bit of... red... on her coat. Want to tell me about that?"

Malcolm's gaze hardened. "As you can see, she's free to come and go." He waved toward the stairwell. "Likes to prowl, that one.

With that mess downstairs, I'm surprised she doesn't look like someone tried to slaughter her."

Saffi pictured Tomago stretched along the back of the couch oozing blood and was grateful she hadn't found her that way. The thought reminded her of why she was here: to find out if Malcolm was behind the vandalism. "Look, do you really want me to solve this? Even if it takes the park off the front page?"

The wide-eyed, affronted look Malcolm gave her slowly narrowed into scrutiny as she held his eyes with hers. His lips thinned.

"Glenn was right."

"About what?" Saffi narrowed her own eyes in return.

"You keep digging and digging until someone's life is ruined."

Saffi jumped to her feet, fists clenched. "He did *not* say that."

Malcolm squinted. "And you would know this because?"

"Because... because..." Saffi sucked in a breath. *Because he's my friend. Because he's kind, not cruel. Because I can't bear for that to be true.* In the end, the most evident reason surfaced. "Because Glenn idolizes you. If he thought I'd ruin your life, he would not have asked me to get involved."

Malcolm settled into the leather sectional, resting his head against the back cushion as if beyond exhausted. "You have an uncanny ability to ferret out the truth when you put your mind to it."

Saffi put her hands on her hips and stared down at him, trying to use the height advantage to look intimidating. "I have been putting my mind to it since Glenn convinced me to help you. Would you like to know what I've concluded so far?"

"Of course, of course. I want nothing more." He sat up again and rubbed his hands together in anticipation.

"I can't solve this case if I don't know what's real and what's Malcolm Morton's movie magic."

Malcolm raised his angular brows. His lips tipped into a grin. Then he stretched them wide to expose the tips of his canines. The minute facial moves made him look as evil and deadly as the

Wolfman character he'd played in *Love Bites*. "No, darling. You can't."

Saffi turned and stomped toward the curving staircase. Fury pounded through her veins.

"Saffi!" Malcolm called out. "Come back!" When she didn't, his pleas turned to wolfish howls. By the time she reached the museum's concrete floor, the howls had been cut short by an old man's hacking cough. If she hadn't seen how easily he could manipulate her by shifting from one character to another, Saffi might have felt sorry for him.

Despite Malcolm's machinations, she'd learned two vital things from the encounter. One, what was at stake for Malcolm Morton was not love, lust, loathing, or loot. It was *legacy*. And from what she could tell, his legacy didn't just matter a little. It mattered a lot. Two, Malcolm Morton's acting skills were downright scary. If she wanted to solve this case—and she did—she'd have to pry off the actor's masks to get to the truth. Fortunately, she'd already met a few people who might be more than happy to expose the "real" Malcolm Morton.

When she made her way downstairs, the barn door was wide open. A cluster of people hung about outside like looky-loos at a car wreck. Brian Bennion dictated notes into a cellphone app. Bev and Bob whispered together on the fringes. Jyoti, minus her grandfather, Sunny, folded her arms as if protecting herself from the latest Malcolm madness. C.J. stood to one side, his eyes locked on the man who had planted himself between the onlookers and the museum's interior. Big and beefy, with the belly bulge of a high school linebacker gone to seed, the man wore a brown and tan uniform. A gold star pinned to the left side of his tan shirt identified him as Phil Raymond, sheriff of Lincoln County.

"Listen up, everybody!" Sheriff Raymond tucked a thumb into his utility belt and held up his other hand. "I need you all to go back to whatever you were doing so I can do my job." He looked at each person in turn until he got a nod or some other acknowledgment, but when he spotted C.J., his distinctive gray eyes widened in surprise before flicking to the next person.

Malcolm must have called the sheriff after all. Saffi chewed her lip, trying to decide if she should approach him. Before she could, he whipped toward her like a predator spotting prey.

"Who are you, and what were you doing in my crime scene?" he demanded.

"Saffi Graywood." Saffi held out her hand, but the sheriff ignored it. "Malcolm took me inside to show me what had happened."

"Oh, he did, did he?" The sheriff looked over his shoulder, craning his neck as if expecting the actor to appear onstage. "And why would he do that with law enforcement on the way?"

Saffi screwed up her lips. *To tell, or not to tell?* That was a question with no good answer. *Tell,* she decided. "I've been looking into some threats Mr. Morton received through the mail."

Sheriff Raymond squinted at her. "Are you some kind of private dick?"

Are you kidding me? Across the way, C.J. rolled his eyes and mouthed the word "sorry" as if apologizing for all lawman-kind.

"No. Just a friend of a friend."

"I swear. You ladies need to stop reading those—whattaya call 'em? Snuggly mysteries? The more you read, the more you think amateurs solve crimes. That, Miz Grayforest, does *not* happen in real life." He took off his brown felt hat to run a hand over a few sweaty strands of hair doing their darndest to keep the bald at bay.

Saffi thought Detective Richards might beg to differ, given she'd handed him the solution to last summer's murder in Last Chance Cove. But maybe not. He'd been the first to tell her to stay out of the postcard case. Clearly, he would not be the last.

"I do love a good mystery." Saffi forced a smile. Better to let the sheriff see her as someone dreaming of solving mysteries like the heroes in the books she read rather than a capable woman who might solve the case before he could tie his boot laces. Which were, she had noticed, untied, as if he'd stuck his feet in them and clomped out the door in a big hurry. Whoever had called him must have reported real blood slathered all over Malcolm's museum. *The man himself?* Most likely.

Out of the corner of her eye, Saffi saw Jyoti slip away and head toward the tea shop.

"Just so you know"—she turned her attention back to Sheriff Raymond—"Brian arrived not long after I did. He spent quite a bit of time inside." Saffi nodded toward the young reporter. He tipped his head so that his russet curls partially hid the cellphone he was whispering into.

"Bennion!"

The young man snapped to attention.

"Didn't I tell you what would happen if you showed up at a crime scene before I arrived again?"

The reporter shrugged. "It's the job, Sheriff. You know that. If someone calls in a tip, I have to follow it."

"Hmph!" The sheriff straightened his shoulders and tucked his other thumb into his belt.

Did they get this guy from central casting? If he was the walking stereotype he seemed, getting information out of him would be like squeezing milk from an oat. Of course, oat milk was her favorite non-dairy option, so someone must know how to do it. She glanced at C.J. The postal inspector's sun-weathered face had darkened as he scrutinized the sheriff. At first, she thought he was sizing the man up and not liking what he saw. Then she remembered: C.J. had grown up here. From the look on his face, he knew a few things about Sheriff Raymond she might find useful.

"So, Ray. What do you think?" C.J. tilted his head toward the museum. "Could this be connected to your murder investigation?"

"Well, Charley Horse, it's hard to tell, isn't it? With amateurs on the scene." The sheriff's use of the nickname C.J. despised confirmed her guess that the two of them had a history.

"Don't sell yourself short," C.J. shot back. "You don't get elected sheriff without a year or two under your belt."

C.J.'s dig seemed to hit home. The sheriff squared his shoulders, puffed out his chest, and sucked in his belly in one swift move, almost as if he'd practiced the "lawman look" in front of a full-length mirror. She expected him to light into C.J. Instead, he whirled toward her—the classic move of a bully when challenged. Go after someone weak enough to intimidate, like a woman. Saffi mentally rubbed her hands together. This was going to be fun.

"If Malcolm brought you over here, where is he?" he demanded.

Saffi locked her hands together behind her back and tilted her head. "In one of my favorite mysteries, the detective said, 'To find the answer you must connect the dots that others don't see.'"

The sheriff's mouth set in a line so tight his lips trembled. "I asked you a real question, Miz Grayson. I expect a real answer."

He wanted real, so she gave it to him, pointing to the floor where one blood-red splat led to another, and another, and another… all the way to the bottom of the curved staircase leading to Malcolm's loft.

Sheriff Raymond resettled his hat on his head. Then he scanned the group. His gaze slashed past C.J. and landed on the reporter. "Bennion! You're the only local in this crowd, so I'm gonna trust you to shut these doors and make sure no one goes in here. Ya hear?"

The only local? She dared a glance at C.J. His nostrils flared, and his hands clenched at his sides.

Brian reached out a hand as if to stop the sheriff. "I've got a story to report. I can't just loll around here all day." He nervously tapped his pointer finger on his phone.

"If I say you can, you can," Sheriff Raymond threw back over his shoulder as he lumbered toward the curved staircase.

Brian cursed under his breath. He put his back and thigh muscles into wrestling the rustic rolling door closed, but the thing seemed to be stuck. C.J. huffed in exasperation. Then he stepped forward and gave the huge door a single shove that rolled it into place.

"Dude!" Brian held his hand against his chest. "I almost lost a finger!"

Saffi stepped close to Brian and whispered, "Good thing you already filed that article, huh?"

Brian Bennion's eyes widened behind his glasses. "I, no... what?"

Saffi took a step back to look him in the eye. "Come on. You weren't whispering into your phone to warm up your vocal cords. You were dictating a story, which you just sent"—she tapped his phone screen—"to your editor."

His face reddened, and he pushed his glasses up his nose as if to cover his embarrassment.

"Be careful." She focused her honey-brown eyes on his. "Writing puff pieces to promote the Haunted Wood could bring tourists into town, but there's something darker going on here. How do you know the source of those tips isn't behind it?"

Brian's eyes widened, and he shoved his phone into the back pocket of his jeans. Then his gaze roamed from the museum to the trailhead. "I guess I don't." He rubbed the sharp point of his nose with the back of his hand.

"This first tip I got was about a dead badger. I thought it was a hoax. Those things don't even live on this side of the Cascades. But, hey, if Malcolm Morton wants a bit of hoopla around the opening of his park, and I think our readers will be entertained, why not?"

"Entertained?"

"These days it's all about eyeballs and clicks, and the oddball stuff that's been happening around here draws both of them."

Saffi couldn't argue. She used the same strategy to choose *Bedside Reader* topics.

"But then Lennie..." Brian's face paled, and he licked his lips as if they'd gone dry. "I was there when they pulled him out from under that dock. Do you have any idea what that's like?"

Brian's question shot her back to last summer. She could still smell the wet dog on the blanket that had been wrapped around her shoulders after she'd found a woman's body, shrouded in seaweed, rocking in the tide at the edge of the Elk Creek Estuary. Seeing death like that, when you weren't used to it, shocked a person into numbness, but, in time, details reemerged. Brian might remember something useful if she could coax him to talk. Would he? She'd just called him out for touting Malcolm's park in a news article. She had to try, and the best way to get him to open up would be to share her own experience.

"I do know," she said. Then she shared with him what she had found and how she had felt. She even shared her amateur investigating and that she'd figured out who the killer was, just in time to almost get run over by a truck.

"You're snooping around this case, too, aren't you?"

Brian's accusation hit home. "Malcolm brought me here to try to find out who has been sending him threatening postcards," Saffi divulged. "Lennie's death might be related to that. If it is, anything you could remember might help me figure out who is behind all this." She waved her hand in the general direction of the museum and trailhead. "Do you remember anything that might help? Anything at all?"

"Besides the fact that his head was bashed in? No." He tucked his russet curls behind his ears. "I was too busy puking my guts out and then getting yelled at by the sheriff for contaminating his crime scene."

Lennie's head was bashed in? No wonder the sheriff had said his death could be "foul play." Not a peep of information about the investigation had been released to the community since she'd arrived yesterday. No speculation. No warnings. Sheriff Raymond seemed to be holding his clues close to his chest.

Brian Bennion, on the other hand, had a few more cards to deal. "I'll tell you this for no extra charge: the first person Sheriff Raymond called after he got a look at the body was his wife."

His wife? "Why would he do that?"

He shook his hair loose and pushed up his glasses. "Lennie

used to work for her. He was groundskeeper at Riverside Ranch before Malcolm hired him away."

Saffi's confusion must have shown on her face.

Brian squinted at her. "The sheriff's wife? Cecily Raymond?"

Boom! No wonder she'd felt an itch when she first heard the sheriff's name. She'd read about Cecily Raymond in the article Brian had written about the park opening. "Sheriff Raymond is married to the real estate developer?"

Brian nodded.

"The one who's planning to scoop this place up the minute it fails?"

A smirk, followed by another nod.

A breeze blew through the trees, bringing with it the somewhat fetid smell of wetlands. Saffi pulled the sleeves of her hoodie over her hands, then tucked them under her arms. Malcolm's groundskeeper had worked for the person with the most to gain if the park closed. Her husband, the sheriff, had wasted no time calling her. Coincidence? Not likely.

It seemed even less likely that Lennie would have left a groundskeeping position with an exclusive subdivision for a chancy gig at Malcolm Morton's Haunted Wood. Maybe he'd taken the park job for another reason: to be Cecily's Raymond's eyes and ears at the Haunted Wood and help her figure out how to shut it down. Maybe someone had caught him snooping and shut *him* down first.

<h1 style="text-align:center">TWENTY</h1>

Saffi had hoped to catch up with C.J., but by the time she finished talking with Brian, the postal inspector had disappeared. She still needed that cup of tea Malcolm had stopped her from making, but dealing with the vandalism and delving into what Brian knew had gobbled up the rest of the morning. What she needed now, was food. She aimed her steps toward the Little Tea Shop of Horror, hoping to bring a bit of order to the chaos surging in her brain, or at least consume enough carbs to fuel it.

Jyoti arrived with a menu just as Saffi settled into her favorite table, the one with a view into the woods. She ran a finger down the lunch specials. Creature Kabobs with Black Lagoon Sauce. Mac and Sneeze. Gravestone TLT. *What was Malcolm thinking with this menu?*

"The 'gravestones,'" Jyoti pointed her pinky at the last item, "are made out of the yummiest tempeh you ever tasted, stuffed into a toasted pita with butter lettuce and sliced tomato."

"Sold!" Saffi slid the menu toward Jyoti, who wrote down her order. "I trust my taste buds to your expertise."

"Chips or crudités with that?" Jyoti asked.

A fistful of crunchy potato chips might soothe the feathers

Sheriff Raymond had worked so hard to ruffle, but she opted for the opposite of what she thought he would choose.

"Crudités." *Take that, Sheriff Stuffed Shirt!*

As Jyoti reached for the menu, Saffi put a hand on top.

"Something else?" The young woman raised a thick black eyebrow.

Saffi shook her head. "No. Well, yes, but not to eat." While she was here, she hoped to find her way into the kitchen. When she made the mistake of glancing that way, Jyoti's dark eyes narrowed.

"If you think my grandfather had something to do with that mess in the museum, you can think again."

"I'd love to rule him out." Saffi tapped a finger on the menu. "Do you think he'd give me a look at the kitchen?"

"The kitchen?" Jyoti's black ponytail was already swinging toward "no" when Saffi held up a hand.

"Look. Malcolm has the most to gain from the notoriety of this vandalism, so he's already at the top of my list of suspects. The sheriff, on the other hand, doesn't know Malcolm the way we do. He'll be looking elsewhere for a culprit. Given the preference he just displayed for locals, he will probably look at park guests and new arrivals."

"What do you mean?"

"He told that young reporter to shut the barn door—a little late since it's after the fact. But—" Saffi shrugged. "He tasked him with keeping people out, because he was the only *local*."

Jyoti's lips quivered with anger. When she glanced toward the kitchen, Saffi pushed a bit harder.

"If your grandfather has nothing to hide, he won't mind a little look-see, will he?"

Jyoti pulled a face. "You don't know my grandfather. Behind that door"—she pointed her pen toward the kitchen—"he is the raja of all he surveys." She tugged her lip between her teeth, but when Saffi wiggled her eyebrows and smiled her encouragement, belief in her grandfather shone in the young woman's eyes.

"Nanaji!" she called as she headed to the kitchen.

Beyond that, Saffi had little idea what was said. She heard what sounded like a harsh refusal, then a soft voice, pleading, encouraging, then rising in pitch enough that Saffi could make out what was said.

"Your daughter, my mother, wants you home. Where you belong! Where *we* belong. How is it that you put this-this *actor*—" Her voice lowered again as she hissed out the word like an expletive, followed by a mumble far below Saffi's ability to eavesdrop, fine-tuned as it might be.

At last Sunny's voice sweetened. "Yes, *Beta*. If you want me to do this, I will."

When Jyoti strode back to Saffi's table, her eyes shone with tears, but her gait exuded confidence. "You can poke around all you want, but not until after you have eaten. Yes?"

Saffi gave a small nod, resigned to the fact that—if Sunny had been mixing up a big batch of fake blood—he would scrub down the kitchen and remove any evidence while she ate. She bore the wait with somewhat impatient grace, but when she took her first bite of her TLT, the savoriness of the sauce that oozed out made her forget all about sleuthing.

She caught the drip running down her chin and licked it off her finger. "Is that... almond butter?"

Jyoti grinned. "Yes. Also coconut milk. Curry sauce. Fresh chili. Maple syrup. Don't you just love it?"

Saffi loved it so much she made a "go away" motion with her hand so she could savor every bite. Tempeh didn't taste this good where she came from. Sunny must have marinated it in the sauce for hours, and if he spent that much time preparing a single menu item, surely he didn't have time to make fake blood. It was official. Her taste buds had fallen in love with Sunny. If he turned out to be involved in the postcard threats and vandalism, she would be devastated.

Why *was* this man here, wasting his talents at a tea house in the Oregon woods? If she could answer that question, she would be one step closer to understanding the mysterious Malcolm Morton. Of that, Saffi was certain.

She finished the pita sandwich, demolishing six paper napkins and doing permanent damage to the front of her hoodie in the process. She filled her glass from the pitcher of cucumber water Jyoti had placed on the table, cleansing her palate for the crudités she'd been ignoring. In keeping with Malcolm's horror theme, the veggies had been arranged to look like a face caught mid-scream: matchstick carrot hair, a poxy face made of cauliflower florets, radish round eyes with green olive pupils, and bright red-pepper-strip lips. The red lips encircled a ramekin of cucumber raita, the gaping mouth—Saffi supposed—in which she was meant to dip the veggies... if she dared. *Bwa-ha-ha!*

Of course she dared. She plucked a cauliflower cheek out of the poxy face and plunged it into yogurt dip made crunchy with chopped cucumbers. Cool fresh mint balanced the warm hint of roasted cumin. She was too full to eat an entire screamfest of veggies, so when Jyoti came out to invite her into the kitchen, she asked for a to-go container.

"I can't eat another bite, but it would be a crime to waste an ounce of your grandfather's food."

A grin spread across Jyoti's face. "You see it, don't you? This place is so far beneath him. You'll help me persuade him to leave. I know you will."

Saffi squeezed the young woman's hand in reassurance. She hoped her next steps would lead the investigation away from Sunny, but, until they did, she had a kitchen to examine.

As she expected, Sunny's kitchen was spotless, without a trace of telltale red fingerprints. Either he had cleaned up while she ate as she'd feared, or he had nothing to do with the fake blood incident. She was already sighing in relief when she noticed the chef move in front of a cabinet and bump the door shut with his bottom. He looked at the ceiling and then at the floor. Then he swept his gaze around the kitchen as if checking for anything amiss. He pursed his lips and folded his hands on his belly as if satisfied.

Oh, Sunny. I hope you don't play poker.

"May I?" She gestured toward the cabinet.

"Please." He squeezed his face between his hands as if mimicking shock. "I am embarrassed for you to be looking in there. It's my hodgepodgery."

Saffi had no idea what a "hodgepodgery" was, but she wanted one. She lifted her hands and shrugged.

"You know." Sunny wiggled his thick white brows at her. "The place where I store bits and bobs. Empty jars, expired goods, dirty cloths and such. I can't be running back and forth to the dumpster all day, so I stuff them in there until closing time."

Saffi stepped toward him, folded her hands over her stomach to mirror his pose, and waited. A few seconds later, Sunny heaved a great sigh and stepped aside.

She opened the cabinet and knelt on one knee to peer inside. Sunny hadn't been kidding. If the rest of the kitchen looked like this, the local health inspector would slap a "C" rating on this place and shut it down. At the front of the cabinet was a line of empty, unwashed jars. Behind those, she found bags of chickpea flour and super-size containers of garam masala, cumin, and turmeric. Not empty, she noted, but full enough that she had to move them to the floor to look behind them. There, she found cleaning supplies and pinkish rags still damp with what smelled like bleach. Saffi glanced over her shoulder to see Sunny pressing his eyelids with his fingertips as if he couldn't bear to look.

Mixing food and cleaners was a big no-no for food handlers. Sunny was too good at what he did to make such an amateur mistake. In his haste to hide the evidence, he had stuffed the front of the cabinet with enough items to hide what he'd used to clean the fake blood mess. Behind the cleanup supplies, in the very back corner, she found the most damning evidence of all: two containers of concentrated food coloring—one red, one blue.

When she pulled them out, Sunny sighed, then settled his shoulders. "They are all natural. The red comes from beets. The blue from butterfly pea flowers. Such lovely colors. I couldn't bear to throw them away."

Jyoti, who had stood in the kitchen doorway chewing her nails as Saffi searched, gasped. "Nana, no! You didn't!"

Sunny walked toward his granddaughter and put his hands on her shoulders. "Sometimes, Beta, one must do things that look bad to make something good happen."

Jyoti stepped away. "Is that what you would tell me if you found evidence of a-a *crime* in my room?"

Sunny's shoulders slumped, then he turned to Saffi with a contrite smile. "My clever granddaughter is always hitting the nail exactly on its head." He thumped his own head for emphasis.

Saffi sat back on her heels, hoping she wouldn't have to beg Sunny to haul her to her feet. "Just tell me one thing. Was the bloodbath Malcolm's idea? Or yours?"

Sunny licked his lips, then pressed them together as if determined to keep silent.

"Tell her!" Jyoti demanded. "Tell her now, or I will call Mom. Do you want her to learn that her own father is capable of such things?"

"No, Jyoti! Please! Malcolm, he—" He shifted his eyes to Saffi, then back to his granddaughter.

A voice broke the silence. "Holds the note on the restaurant in LA?" C.J. strolled past Jyoti, commandeering the room as he leaned against the spotless counter beside where Saffi knelt and crossed his arms.

Sunny groaned. "How is it that you know this? You are, what, a van camper? And you!" He glared at Saffi. "You are a writer of *Bedside Readers*, are you not? Your books are highly entertaining, I must admit, but has writing them prepared you for a career in law enforcement?" He waggled his head back and forth. "I think not. And yet, here the two of you stand. In my kitchen. Preparing to ruin my reputation, destroy my family's business, for... what?"

The jibe Malcolm made earlier stung Saffi afresh. Was he right? Did she dig and dig and dig until she ruined someone's life?

Her thighs were on fire from kneeling, but when she tried to stand, her back kinked. She cast a pleading look at C.J., and he took the hint, offering a hand to hoist her to her feet.

"Thanks." She shut the cabinet door, pressed her hands on the counter, and did a mini-cat stretch, hoping to loosen her back before the muscles froze up. Before she turned to face Sunny and Jyoti, she glanced at C.J., her brows raised in question. He gave a slight shake of his head that she took to mean he did not want to break cover just yet.

"Look." She turned around. "From what I saw this morning, no real damage was done. If Malcolm put you up to this, you were doing what your employer asked."

Sunny pursed his lips. "Will you be telling the sheriff what you have found?"

C.J. chuckled. "If we let Ray form his own conclusions, he'll chase his own tail until he bites it."

Sunny nodded briskly, then he took off his white chef's jacket and waved them out of the kitchen. "Sit. I will bring chai and nankhatai. Then we will talk."

Over tea and buttery shortbread cookies, Sunny explained why he had come to the Haunted Wood and how Malcolm had convinced him to splash fake blood all over the museum. Malcolm Morton had been visiting Sunny's restaurant on Ventura Boulevard for decades. One year, Sunny had faced a series of setbacks. His tandoor oven needed to be replaced. A roof leak had to be repaired. When Malcolm heard the family couldn't find enough financing to cover these major expenses, he stepped up.

"He loaned me the money. Just like that!" Sunny snapped his fingers. "One friend to another. Now, I have chance to repay his friendship. He wants very much for this park to succeed."

Jyoti stood. "I understand friendship, Nanaji. I also understand how you might feel that you owe Malcolm. But committing some kind of *crime*?"

So many emotions crossed Sunny's face, Saffi couldn't keep track. Embarrassment, reflection, calculation, anger—perhaps at

Malcolm for putting him in this position—all dissolved into a single emotion: regret.

"Can you forgive me, Beta?"

Jyoti unclasped her hands and rushed into her grandfather's arms. "Always."

At that moment, the café door opened, and Malcolm backed inside, talking nonstop as if trying to keep someone at bay. Sheriff Raymond pushed his way past the actor, eyes scanning the room until they stopped on Sunny.

"Mr. Dhaliwal?"

Sunny tensed. "Yes, I am Mr Dhaliwal."

The sheriff strode toward their table and stopped so close behind Saffi's chair she crinkled her nose at the vinegary smell of his sweat, a sign of diabetes if she remembered correctly from her "Ooh-ooh That Smell!" article for *Bedside Reader*, #16. She was about to push back her chair to force him to move, but his next words froze her in her seat.

"Mr. Dhaliwal, you are under arrest for vandalism and theft."

"Theft! Of what?" Jyoti demanded.

"A priceless jacket once worn by the Wizard of Oz."

TWENTY-ONE

Malcolm moved like a chess piece to stand behind Sunny's chair, as if countering the sheriff's words. "I told you, the fake blood was a publicity stunt." The actor put a hand on Sunny's shoulder. "As for the jacket, Sunny wouldn't dream of taking it. He's one of my oldest and dearest friends." The knuckles on Malcolm's hand whitened as if his grip on the chef's shoulder tightened.

Sunny's jaw clenched in response, but, beyond that, he didn't move a muscle. He seemed frozen somewhere between defiance and resignation.

Saffi glanced at C.J. The postal inspector was as focused on the two men as she'd been, despite the fact that his face was an unreadable blank. He'd come here to investigate the Smithsonian shipment heist, and the Baum jacket was central to his case. What must he be thinking, now that it had gone missing?

The sheriff's eyes kept shifting from Malcolm to Sunny and back again. The skepticism on his face said he highly doubted a famous actor could be friends with the Indian cook in his café. He fumbled with his utility belt until he located and unhooked a pair of handcuffs.

"If you didn't want me to arrest him, you shouldn't have told me he was the vandal."

Sunny shook off Malcolm's hand and rose to his feet.

"You *told* him?" The chef slammed the table with both hands. "I only did this thing because you asked me to."

Malcolm tugged at the collar of his red turtleneck, then grabbed the loose end of his yellow-orange-and-white-striped scarf and flung it over his shoulder with enough drama to draw all eyes to him.

"Sunny, darling. Sit. Sit."

When Sunny did not sit, Malcolm moved away from his chair.

"Look, don't worry. There's no way I will allow this-this *person* to arrest one of *my* employees."

Don't you mean one of your oldest and dearest friends? Saffi arched her brows at C.J., and he tilted his head her way as if his curiosity had been piqued as well.

The sheriff dangled the handcuffs on one finger and grinned. "I'd like to know how you're going to stop me, given Mr. Dhawali here just confessed."

"Dhaliwal!" Sunny and Jyoti barked at the same time.

Something about the jacket theft tugged at Saffi's memory. Something she'd seen earlier, as she walked through the museum. She let the scene play out like a movie in her head. The fake blood. The posters. The costumes. The film froze in front of a display case with a bloody handprint smeared over its door lock, and Saffi remembered.

"Wait!" She shoved her chair back and stood. "The vandalism and theft aren't related!"

Sheriff Raymond shook the cuffs at Saffi. "Oh, let me guess. You found a clue the professional law officer missed. Am I right?" He gave an exaggerated wink that made Saffi want to smack his smug face. She didn't because... well, he was right.

"They're not," Saffi insisted. "Shall I tell you how I know?" In lieu of smacking him, she returned his exaggerated wink.

C.J. suppressed a chuckle with a hand over his mouth and a fake cough, but the amusement in his moss-green eyes gave him away. The sheriff scowled.

"There's nothing you know that Malcolm hasn't already told me!" He yanked a spiral-bound notebook out of his shirt pocket. Once he got it loose, he flipped a few pages and started reading aloud. "Victim, M. Morton, wore jacket to dinner. On his way to bed, victim *returned* said jacket to display case. Upon waking, victim discovered museum vandalized. Fake blood everywhere. During crime scene examination, victim discovered jacket *missing* from said display case."

As Saffi listened to the litany of how Malcolm had been "victimized," she wove through the café's mismatched tables toward the front window. She stared past the giant carnivorous plant daring visitors to enter the tea shop toward the mostly empty rows of RV sites. She ran her tongue over her teeth, tasting the lingering flavors of almond butter and spicy chai as she placed the morning's events on a timeline. She started with the moment the actor pulled her out of her Rambler and ended when she sat down in the café to order lunch. When she was sure she had the pertinent details in the right order, she turned to the sheriff and pointed at the notebook in his hand.

"So, everything you know about what happened is in there?" She tapped her chin. "I should get one of those."

"You need more than a field notebook to solve crimes, Miz Grayforest."

"Graywood," she corrected. "And you're right. You also need to ask questions of witnesses."

The sheriff slapped his notebook against his leg. "What do you think I've been doing the whole ding-danged morning?"

"Here's the thing, Sheriff. *Three* people went into that museum before you arrived. You told one of them off for entering your crime scene. *Me.* You ordered another one to guard the barn door. *Brian.* And you interviewed one—and only one... him." She pointed at Malcolm. "I'm curious. Why not interview Brian, or me? He's a reporter. I'm a... what did you call me? One of those snuggly mystery readers. Both things train one to notice details. Perhaps we made useful observations."

The sheriff squeezed his notebook so tightly the spiral binding bent in the middle. "Such as?"

"Now that you ask"—she gave him her widest smile—"I *did* notice something in the museum. Something that might change your mind about the vandalism and theft being related."

"Oh, they're related." Sheriff Raymond stuffed his notepad into his shirt pocket, stopped playing chess—if he ever had been—and marched straight toward Sunny. Just before he reached the chef, C.J. pushed his chair back and stood, effectively blocking the sheriff's path.

"Let's hear her out, shall we?"

They stood chest to chest, a lawman standoff if Saffi had ever seen one. She tried to keep her lips from twitching upward but failed miserably. Oh well, if Sheriff Stuffed Shirt didn't already know what she thought of him, he was about to find out.

"Thank you." She sucked the smile into a straight line and nodded at C.J. "Sheriff, I can confirm that Malcolm wore the Oz jacket to dinner last night because I was present. I can also confirm that the jacket was returned to its case."

The sheriff put his hands on his hips. "Is that a fact?"

"It is. I saw the jacket in the display case when I walked through the museum this morning."

"Well, there you go. The jacket was there, and now it isn't. Case closed."

C.J. rubbed his chin. "You might have missed something, Ray. If Saffi saw the jacket in the case *after* the vandalism happened, there's nothing to tie Mr. Dhaliwal to the theft."

"That's right." Saffi walked over to Sunny and stood beside him. "The jacket had to have been stolen between the time I went through the museum and the time Malcolm noticed it was missing."

The sheriff's lips twitched sideways into a frown. "Morton?" He whirled to face Malcolm, who had edged away from Sunny as Saffi explained what she'd seen and now stood near the café entrance. "What are you playing at?"

Malcolm struck an offended pose, feet together, hands gripping the lapels of his orange jacket, scarf quivering as he sucked in short, little breaths. Just as he opened his mouth to reply, C.J. interrupted.

"Ray? Could we?" He waved a hand toward the kitchen.

"Oh for the love of..." The sheriff's face turned the color of plum pudding, but he stalked into the kitchen leaving C.J. to follow.

The rest of them turned toward the kitchen like satellite dishes trying to pick up a signal. C.J. kept his voice to a low rumble, but Saffi had a good idea why he wanted a kitchen confab. He had decided to fill Sheriff Raymond in on the case he was investigating and make it clear that the county lawman had no jurisdiction over it. Her guess was confirmed when the sheriff raised his voice in defiance.

"I have a confession, Charley Horse. I'm taking Diwali in."

Saffi covered her face with her hands and shook her head. Every time the sheriff mangled Sunny's last name it got worse. Had the man even heard of Diwali, the Hindu festival of lights?

"You're not taking my grandfather anywhere!" Jyoti jumped to her feet, nearly knocking her chair over in the process, and stormed toward the kitchen. C.J. kept her from ending up on the other end of the sheriff's handcuffs by putting an arm around her shoulders and guiding her back to her seat.

"Malcolm?" He speared the man at the door with a pointed green stare. "Do you intend to press charges?"

"For what? Fake vandalism?" Jyoti jumped to her feet again and ran to Malcolm, tugging on the lapels of the actor's orange knitted jacket. "If my grandfather goes to jail, who's going to cook for the Spooktacular?"

Saffi had to give it to the young woman. She knew the actor well enough to pull the right strings.

Malcolm backed out of Jyoti's grip, smoothed his lapels, and straightened his striped scarf. "Sheriff, I have no intention of pressing charges."

I should hope not, since it was your ridiculous idea! It was all Saffi could do to not shout the words out loud.

"Now, if you don't mind, we have a grand opening soon and much work still to be done."

Sheriff Raymond's eyes bulged, and his face went two shades brighter. Saffi feared he might actually go into cardiac arrest. She scanned the café for a defibrillator, but either Malcolm hadn't bothered to have one installed or it was in the kitchen.

"Ever since you and your fancy-pants... *entourage*... arrived, you have been wasting law enforcement time and resources!" the sheriff sputtered. "What makes you think you can call the station and scare the bejeezus out of my deputy so you can get this place on the front page again? She thought someone had recreated the *Texas Chainsaw Massacre* over here."

Malcolm's mouth fell open. "But I didn't call. You just"—he flapped his hand at the sheriff—"showed up."

Saffi gasped. *If Malcolm hadn't called the sheriff, who had?*

"You can't possibly think I'm that foolish." Malcolm ran a hand through his wavy white hair. "I called Ben. I wanted publicity, not some arrest-happy county sheriff."

The arrest-happy sheriff clenched his jaw so hard Saffi thought he might break a tooth.

"My wife was right. This place needs shutting down, and if I can find a way to do it before that *guh-rand* opening you're planning, I'll do it."

TWENTY-TWO

For Saffi, what came to mind next was a line often used by mystery writers: *The plot thickens.* She'd stumbled on the source of the original line—*"Ay, now the Plot thickens very much upon us"*—while researching the origins of familiar phrases. This one had been lifted from a seventeenth-century satirical play. Saffi loved discovering where phrases originated. In fact, she loved the exercise enough to include word and phrase origins in every *Bedside Reader*. They were a fan favorite, too. If the search for the postcard perp had been the plot of a book, it would now have thickened to the consistency of overdone oatmeal, and she could toss it in the bin and be done with it. *If only!*

After Sheriff Raymond's dramatic exit from the café, Malcolm disappeared into the kitchen with Sunny. They seemed to be arguing, but the only words Saffi heard made no sense: had Malcolm really said he needed to "keep the weasel at bay"? Probably not.

Jyoti put a closed sign in the front window, C.J. excused himself, and Saffi hurried after him. She caught up just before he reached his site. "You know that guy, don't you? The sheriff."

"Good old Ray. Still taking potshots." C.J. rubbed his eyes, then shrugged. "Let's say, I know him well enough to wonder how he ever got into law enforcement. He was voted 'most likely to end up *behind* bars' in his senior year." C.J. chuckled for a second then sobered up.

Potshots? The word nudged a memory, something C.J. had told her. "Is he—"

C.J.'s eyes clouded. "Look, I need to report in. That jacket was the first bit of physical evidence I've found. Now that it's gone..." He lifted a hand, then turned away, striding quickly toward his van.

He looked as discouraged and exhausted as she felt. Since she'd arrived at the Haunted Wood, she'd been spinning in a vortex of Malcolm Morton's creation. She needed a nap, but first, she needed Delilah Dunsmore, barista, legendary Mouth of Last Chance Cove, and her best friend.

"Saffi Graywood!" Delilah whooped so loudly Saffi had to hold her phone at arm's length to keep from losing her hearing. "*The* Saffi Graywood? The one who promised to call but disappeared into the morning fog never to be heard from again? Do you have any idea what I've been imagining since you left?" Delilah sucked in a deep breath but kept going before Saffi could answer. "First I thought you'd been kidnapped by a family of Bigfoots. *Bigfeet?* Whatever you call 'em. Then I thought you'd driven your RV into a tunnel and never came out the other side. I read about interdimensional portals in one of those *Readers* of yours. Let's see..." She paused long enough for Saffi to hear background noises: a dog panting, tires on damp pavement.

"Is that Archie I hear? Are you driving?"

"Yes, and, no. Of course not."

Before she could ask about the sounds, Delilah went on with her litany of things she'd imagined had happened to Saffi when she didn't *bother* calling. "You stopped to potty and fell into the Devil's Churn."

Saffi had actually considered a stop at the popular visitor's center outside of Yachats. If she *had* fallen into the water churning through the narrow chasm, she would not have been the first careless person to do so. Fortunately, the parking fee and small lot kept her moving.

Delilah rattled on without waiting for Saffi to comment. "Then you drove too fast around a curve, and your RV flew off a cliff into the Pacific. But here you are," she huffed, "safe as Vienna sausages, calling me on the phone. I have no words."

Saffi burst out laughing. Delilah had more than enough words for both of them, and Saffi's heart felt happier than it had in days, just to hear them.

"You might not believe it, but those things aren't half as looney as what's really been happening."

"Well... that sounds like a story worth waiting for. Make it good, and I just might forgive you for making me wait—"

"Two days?" Saffi cut in drily.

"Two and a half, but who's counting? More than two days of not knowing if you were squarshed like a skunk in the middle of the road and stinking to high heaven. Archie, scooch your fluffy behind over and give me some room."

Saffi imagined the scruffy white terrier sprawled across the tiny sofa in her friend's vintage Terry trailer. Delilah had adopted the little guy after the murder of his owner last summer. She heard a bit of scrabbling, which probably meant Archie had chosen an even more comfy place for his snooze: Delilah's lap.

"OK. I'm ready. Dish."

Saffi dished, giving Delilah a day-by-day breakdown of what had happened since she drove out of Last Chance Cove RV Park. She shared her fears on the road—the man in the yellow-and-white van showing up everywhere she went, having her RV invaded, the missing postcards, the half-eaten protein bar... that part sent Delilah into a giggle fit. When Delilah stopped laughing, Saffi told her that the man in the camper van had turned out to be a postal inspector, and that he was responsible for the break-in, the post-card theft, *and* eating the other half of her protein bar.

"Yes, but what does he *look* like?"

Saffi could almost see Delilah's red eyebrows twitching.

"Rugged. Outdoorsy. Good-looking, if you like the scruffy-surfer-dude-turned-lawman look."

"Oh, mama." Delilah whistled. "I told Troy not to go chasing off to Texas right after the two of y'all got together."

Saffi waved away her concern, forgetting for a second that Delilah wasn't actually sitting on the other end of the couch with her feet up.

"C.J.'s here for work. So am I."

"C.J.? Already on a nickname basis, are you?" Delilah chuckled. "You can't fool an old fooler like me, girl. You're up there *avoiding* work. But that's OK. You needed a break from those revisions. I saw a new white streak pop up in your hair last week."

What? No! Saffi clutched her black curls. "They're silver, Delilah. Silver streaks."

"Uh-huh. Sure they are. Well, go on, spill the rest of the black-eyed peas."

She did, describing the various denizens of the park and surrounds in the kind of detail that would keep her friend's laugh pealing through the phone. When she told Delilah that Malcolm had stolen her coffee specials and given them gag-inducing names, the barista hooted again.

"Course he did, the old charmer. Is he still parading around in that pink bedspread?"

"No need. He's got a whole museum filled with costumes. You won't believe what he wore to dinner last night." She went on to describe the Wizard of Oz jacket, the vandalism, and the subsequent theft. Delilah punctuated the story with gasps and squeals.

Before she ran out of steam, Saffi shared the one thing she didn't want to admit: Glenn's friend was a riddle she had yet to solve.

Delilah snorted. "More like a Rubik's cube, if you ask me."

She was right. Multiple times a day the cube twisted, the colors changed, and a whole new puzzle appeared. The solution, which had seemed a click or two away at the beginning, now seemed more out of reach than ever.

"You know what I do with coffee fails?" Delilah asked.

"What?" Saffi stretched out on the couch and pulled the Pendleton blanket off the back to ward off the chill seeping through the RV's uninsulated walls. "I pour it down the sink and start from scratch."

Go back to the start? That would mean re-examining the postcards. Why not? She snuggled deeper into the soft blanket and felt her eyes closing as Delilah's voice rumbled in her ear.

"Saffi!" A voice echoed in her head over and over, then something pounded, as loud as hailstones against the metallic sides of her RV. "Saffi!"

She couldn't move. Something was holding her down, binding her legs. She kicked and kicked, dislodging herself from the clutches of... a cozy throw. Something hit the floor with a loud thump. Saffi blinked, struggling back to consciousness. She'd been talking to Delilah and then—*Oh, no! Had she fallen asleep while her friend was still talking?* She tucked her chin into the shoulder of her hoodie to wipe away the drool oozing out of her mouth, then turned sideways, peering at the floor to see what had fallen. Her phone.

"Saffi!"

Saffi sat straight up. Someone was really out there.

"Mrr... an... ang... on!" She stumbled off the couch and fumbled her way toward the RV door in the darkness. On the way, she tripped over her shoes and planted a hand against the stairwell wall to catch herself, shoving her palm into the light switch.

"Owie, ow, ow...!"

Why *was* it dark? It had been late afternoon when she'd phoned Delilah. She flipped the switch, flooding the interior with light, then tried to suck the pain out of her palm.

Just as she was about to unlock the door, she stopped herself. *Who was out there?* Her sleep-addled brain hadn't recognized the voice. She flipped on the outdoor light and squinted at the face on the other side of the small window in her door.

That's when it hit her: the drool, the bedhead, the total dishevelment that was Saffi Graywood when she first woke up was in full view of C.J. Horseman, postal inspector, looking—how was this fair?—like he'd just hosted a segment of *Oregon Outdoor Adventures*. He had a teasing grin on his non-drool-smeared face, and smile crinkles framed his moss-green eyes.

She unlocked the door, held up a finger, and sprinted for the bathroom. Before he could open the outer door, she slid the wooden door between the bathroom and living room closed with a satisfying thud. She clenched her fists and steeled herself before turning toward the mirror. Then she almost face-planted into it.

It doesn't matter, she told herself. *Sure, he flirted with you, but that was a disguise. He's here for work, nothing more.*

"I've already seen you," C.J.'s deep voice rumbled. "You might as well come out."

Saffi clenched the sink with both hands. *Oh, no you don't. I'm not coming out until my curls are tamed, there isn't a trace of drool on my face or*—she pulled her hoodie out from her chest—*a massive smear of yummy-smelling TLT sauce on my top.* She wrenched off the hoodie and tossed it into the shower.

By the time she slid the door open, C.J. was pacing the floor. She'd washed her face, brushed her teeth, pulled a wide-toothed comb through her curls, then yanked on a long-sleeved burgundy T-shirt with "Hold on while I overthink this" written in white script across the front.

C.J.'s eyes went right to the words and, of course, her chest. After a few seconds, he realized what he was doing and looked up, a blush rising up his neck.

"I was just"— he flapped a hand—"reading. Your shirt. Not..." His voice trailed off.

"Don't worry." She quirked her lips into a teasing smile. "I won't overthink it. So!" She clapped her hands then rubbed them together. "What's up?"

C.J. glanced around her tiny space as if trying to remember why he'd pounded on the door. "Uhm... well. I just, hadn't seen you for a while, and... your lights were out."

Was he looking out for her? *Aw. Sweet.* She patted him on the shoulder. "All is well, but thank you. I was thinking about looking at the postcards again. The ones you stole? See if they might jog something loose up here." She thumped a knuckle on her head.

"In there?" He nodded toward the backpack sitting between the two captain's chairs then grabbed it and rumbled inside before she could stop him.

She lifted an eyebrow. "Looking for another protein bar?"

"Maybe..." He smiled wide enough for dimples to dent his cheeks.

"Sorry." She shook her head. "All I have left are those lemon-blueberry ones you loathe."

"In that case," he pulled out the stack of postcards, "how about you share what you learned from Brian Bennion. You had that boy babbling like a brook."

"I did learn a thing or two."

She cleared the junk off her dining table to make space to lay out the cards. Some were familiar: the "badger you to death" card, the "rats like you" card, and the "you will choke" card. Others she'd barely glanced at.

C.J. pulled out the second dining chair tucked at the end of the table. He placed it beside hers and sat down elbow-to-elbow, so close she could smell the evergreen-and-woodsmoke scent of *eau de outdoorsman*. Somehow, she kept her hands steady as she placed card after card in rows across the tiny table. If Troy had responded to the text she'd sent before she'd left the cove, she might have been more inclined to block out C.J.'s yumminess. Being ignored did not make the heart grow fonder. Levi, Saffi told herself, would *never* have ignored her text.

Her inner voice fact-checked her. *Unless... he was teaching, or biking, or having a beer with colleagues after work, or...*

Saffi shook herself back to the mystery at hand. She filled C.J.

in on everything Brian had told her. Malcolm had been tipping him off to stories that might garner publicity for the park. The reporter had been present when Lennie's body was dragged from the water and seen that the groundskeeper had been bludgeoned.

C.J. rubbed his hand across his mouth. "I asked Ray if they'd found water in Lennie's lungs."

Saffi knew from last summer's case that a drowning victim would have water in the lungs. Someone who died before going into the water would not. "What did he say?"

"That he had no intention of sharing information about a murder investigation with a trumped-up postman."

Saffi stifled a laugh. She'd thought the same thing at first. "Still, he let something slip, didn't he? Lennie was murdered."

C.J. grinned. "He did. And thanks to you, I now know the probable cause of death. Shall we?" He waved toward the cards spread across the table.

The two of them scrutinized the front side of the postcards so long that their breathing synchronized. C.J. reached across her to flip the top left card over, his left arm pressing into her right as he stretched forward. Saffi's breath caught.

Stop it, stop it, stop it. This is work!

She frowned, trying to concentrate on the cards. Warm vintage scenes of characters from *The Wind in the Willows* on one side. Vile words of warning on the other. A lovely scene of Badger sipping tea in front of a roaring fire had "Cozy Up with Badger" on the front. C.J. flipped the card over and read the words "and you will burn." A picture of Toad in his red motor car waving his jaunty driving cap read, "Willow Wood... Just a Short Drive Away."

Saffi flipped this one over. They both leaned forward to read the back, their heads so close she could feel his breath on her cheek. *From certain death*, the sender had scribbled in blood-red ink. The chill that crept along her skin made her realize why she hadn't studied all of the cards the same way she had the first few. She couldn't bear to have her memories of Kenneth Grahame's classic friendship tale forever shadowed by the postcard perp's awful additions.

"Who would do this?" She shook her head and pushed back her chair. "I'm sorry. I just can't."

C.J. put a hand on her arm and gave it a reassuring squeeze. "Why don't we have some tea?"

Saffi raised an eyebrow. "Can I splash whiskey in mine?"

"Only if you've got enough for two."

She had emptied the electric tea kettle and started filling it with fresh tap water when she stopped and turned toward C.J. "Spiked tea's not going to cut it. How about we go straight for the good stuff?"

"Thank God." C.J. turned his chair and stretched out his long legs.

As the warm golden glow of single malt Scotch drove the chill from Saffi's bones, they discussed the postcards, the missing L. Frank Baum jacket, and the fact that Malcolm Morton's determination to open the Haunted Wood might have been the death of Lennie and could actually be the death of him. As the evening progressed, C.J. somehow ended up on the couch beside her. When Saffi stated her fear for Malcolm's safety out loud, C.J. left the couch and walked back to the table.

"If the person who sent these is the same person who killed Lennie Lonigan, you could be right."

C.J.'s words and the loss of his body heat made Saffi feel as if the sun had gone down twice in one day. He set the small glass tumbler with what remained of his Scotch on the table and picked up a postcard from one of the rows, holding it up so she could see. It featured a smiling Mole with his whiskery nose stuck into a teacup. "Who takes something this cute and turns it into a scene from a horror movie?"

Saffi stiffened. Badger's quaint tea shop turned into the Little Tea Shop of Horrors flashed into her mind. *Malcolm Morton, that's who.* She didn't say it out loud. Not yet. But Malcolm knew the original park and Kenneth Grahame's characters better than most.

He had opportunity: he had traveled the route between LA and the Haunted Wood multiple times over the past few months. He could have stopped to send cards to himself along the way. But what was his motive? Publicity?

No. If the postcards were a publicity stunt, why had he encouraged her to track down the sender instead of splashing them all over the news? It made no sense. If he'd shown the postcards to Brian Bennion, he could have been building interest in the park for months. As far as she knew, he hadn't. Saffi walked backward through the whirls of her brain. At no time during her search for the postcard perp had Malcolm breathed a word of the cards to the newspaper. They stood apart somehow. That could mean Malcolm wasn't behind them. But if he wasn't, whoever sent them knew about the original park and had access to vintage Willow Wood cards.

Mere was too young to have visited the park, but she was a local. She probably knew at least something about the history of the land she was trying to protect. Cecily Raymond? Depending on her age, she could have visited the park in its heyday. As a real estate developer, she would have known about the prior usage of the land she wanted to develop. Would either of them know where to find vintage Willow Wood postcards? Saffi swigged down the last of her single malt as she tried to figure out where she would find such a thing if she needed it in her research. A light went off.

She looked up at C.J. "Does the Historical Museum in Lincoln City have a gift shop?"

He took his tumbler to the sink and washed it, making himself at home in her tiny space. "I haven't been there in years, but they used to have one."

"Any chance they sell vintage Willow Wood postcards?"

He double-snapped then clapped. "I do like the way your mind works."

Analytical. Sexy. She hadn't forgotten their first interaction at Last Chance Cove RV Park. The teasing glint in his eyes said he remembered, too.

The Scotch warming her veins made her want to stand, walk slowly toward the man leaning against her counter and fall into his arms like a saloon girl from an old-time western. Regrettably, as far as Saffi was concerned, her brain did not know when to zip its lips and let nature take its course. Instead, it spewed out an irrefutable fact. *Eighty-proof whiskey rarely leads to good relationship decisions.*

Fine! Tonight, she would take her thoughts to bed and send the luscious lawman on his way. *More's the pity.* Tomorrow, she would visit the museum and, hopefully, find out what she needed to know: was Malcolm Morton as generous as Badger, helpful as Ratty, and kind as Mole? Or had he sent those postcards to himself and lured her to the Haunted Wood for reasons she might not have the skills to detect?

TWENTY-THREE

The sun peering through her pink curtains gave her bedroom a rosy glow. *Morning? Already?* The chill seeping through the thin walls of Saffi's RV made her want to hit "snooze" on her alarm and snuggle deeper into the covers. As she reached a hand toward her phone, she remembered—the Historical Museum. The sooner she visited, the sooner she would know if the vintage postcards could have come from there.

She steeped French press coffee as she readied herself for the trip into town. Halfway through the cup, she realized she didn't have a way to get there. She wasn't about to drive her RV over that graveled culvert again, at least, not until it was time to head home.

Saffi chewed her lip. What to do? Bev and Bob had a car, and, obviously, so did Malcolm. Who else might have one?

Jyoti! Her coffee cup rattled in the saucer as she set it on the counter. Even though she'd yet to see it, the young woman had told her she had a Fiat. It must be tucked away inside that 40-foot toy hauler, the only RV on the premises she hadn't been inside. If she could talk Jyoti into a trip to town, she might be able to learn more about her grandfather's relationship with Malcolm *and* investigate the vintage postcards.

Half an hour and a lot of cajoling later, Jyoti left the tea shop in her grandfather's care and unlocked the toy hauler. Within minutes, a tiny green Fiat with a beige convertible top hummed down the ramp and bumped onto the ground behind the RV. When Jyoti opened the car door and waved, Saffi clapped. It took a few more minutes and Saffi's help to walk the back of the toy hauler closed and latch it in place.

"Wow!" Saffi had to duck her head to wrench herself into the tiny car's front seat. "This is adorable. Can I have it?"

Jyoti grinned. "Absolutely not. Ladybug is mine all mine."

"She suits you." Saffi glanced over her shoulder to see that it was, unbelievably, a four-seater. The only passengers she could picture back there were small children, and elves—the short kind from Disney movies, not the tall kind from J.R.R. Tolkien's *Lord of the Rings*. Hobbits might fit, if they didn't have those big furry feet. *Dwarves?* No. Saffi shook her head. Where would they put their axes?

"Lincoln City here we come!" Jyoti glanced playfully at Saffi as her finger hovered over the switch to open the convertible top.

"No. No, a thousand times no!" Saffi put her hands together in prayer position. Like most Oregon coast mornings, this one had arrived with the ghost of winter on its breath. Despite the Merino wool sweater beneath her Patagonia jacket, she would freeze to death with the top down.

"Just kidding." Jyoti winked and moved the stick shift in the console to "D" for drive.

They drove the same route she'd taken with C.J., but in the tiny green ladybug of a car the barreling behemoths behind them made her heart thump double-time. "Can this thing go any faster?"

When Jyoti punched the gas, Saffi grabbed for the handle above the door and held on tight. The golf course, post office, and strip mall passed in a blur, and when Saffi noticed the highway curving left ahead of them, she pointed a finger and gritted her teeth. Jyoti pressed the brake as they went into the curve, then pumped the gas to ricochet into the long straightaway that was Lincoln City. They passed a convenience store on the right, a Pig 'N Pancake on the left, a bank, another bank, a used car lot, an antique mall, and a long string of restaurants, hotels, and gift shops. In the middle of town, Jyoti pointed to a brick building with blue-and-white trim.

"Bob's Beach Books! That's where I'm going after I drop you off. I could have sworn I bought the next book in the fantasy series I was reading, but it's gone missing."

Saffi glanced at the books in the window with envy as the Fiat passed. She'd much rather wander through the stacks in search of a book to cuddle up with than hit the local history museum.

"It's not the first time that's happened."

Saffi frowned. "Wait. Books have gone missing?"

"Not just books. My favorite mug, my grandfather's souvenir pocket knife. Malcolm's lost a few things too, like those fancy soaps he loves so much." She rolled her eyes.

Mugs? Saffi still hadn't found her raven mug. Was there a thief on the grounds? And, if so, had that person upped their game to include the Oz jacket?

The car lurched right, and Saffi looked up just as Jyoti jockeyed the Fiat into the parking lot of a massive shake-shingled building with gaudy red trim.

"Is this it?" Saffi ducked her head, trying to read the sign through the Fiat's windshield.

"According to my GPS? Yes!" Jyoti hunched over the steering wheel to scrutinize the building. "What do you expect to find in there?" Her nose crinkled.

Saffi had spent enough time in small museums to have a ready answer. "Weird and wonderful things. You should join me."

Jyoti pressed against the seatback as if appalled at the thought. "You mean 'dry and dusty,' right? Thanks, but no. Books are my jam. I'll be back in about an hour."

Instead of a docent, the museum had a floor sign. "Self-guided tour," Saffi read aloud. "OK." She stuffed a ten-dollar bill through the slot in the plastic donation box and followed an arrow that pointed to her right. She hurried through a homesteading exhibit that would have put Jyoti to sleep and cringed over a logging exhibit with saws wide enough to fell redwood trees. When the next turn took her into an exhibit featuring all things "Willow Wood," she perked up.

Brightly painted cutouts of Ratty, Mole, and Badger adorned the walls. She spotted a table and chairs rescued from Badger's Tea House and a park replica that included the rides Malcolm had talked about in Last Chance Cove. Here at last were artifacts from the theme park the actor had loved.

Saffi bellied up to a glass case filled with memorabilia, including—she bounced on her toes—postcards exactly like those sent to Malcolm.

"I see you're interested in Willow Wood." A trim woman in a mauve pantsuit, starched white shirt, and leopard-skin kitten heels joined her in front of the glass exhibit case.

At last, a living, breathing human being who might be able to answer some of Saffi's questions. She tapped on the glass above the postcards. "I collect vintage cards like these, from classic roadside attractions. You don't sell them, do you?"

"We do." The woman pointed the way Saffi had been heading. "In the gift shop at the end of the self-guided tour. I'll meet you there when you've seen all of the exhibits." Her red lips parted in a smile that revealed a line of lipstick smeared across her top teeth. Somehow, that made Saffi feel better about being sentenced to trudge through a fish-canning exhibit. Saffi emerged into the gift shop like a bear from a cave, blinking in the glare of fluorescent lights and gasping for fresh air.

"I find local history fascinating, don't you?" The woman tucked a stray hair into the champagne bun at the back of her neck. What was someone so chic doing in a historical museum gift shop? When she asked, the woman was delighted to tell her.

"I volunteer once a month. I was a history major in college

before I got my real estate license and learned how to make *real* money." The knowing wink she gave Saffi made her cringe. She squinted at the badge pinned to the woman's jacket and took an involuntary step backward.

"Are you OK?" The woman, whose nametag read "Cecily Raymond," reached a manicured hand toward Saffi.

"Sorry." Saffi shook off her surprise. "I probably need water." She walked to the chiller cabinet at the other side of the gift shop, partly because she really *did* need water, and partly to give her heart a chance to make its way back down from her throat to her chest cavity. Cecily Raymond, the developer trying to claw the Haunted Wood property away from Malcolm, volunteered at the Historical Museum. What were the odds?

She twisted the cap off the water bottle and guzzled half of it down before turning back to the counter Cecily guarded. "You said you might have vintage cards from Willow Wood. Can I see them?"

Cecily slid open the glass door behind the display case and pulled out a photo binder. When she opened it up, Saffi saw pages filled with vintage postcards and photos slipped into plastic sleeves.

"Let's see." Cecily bit her lower lip demonstrating how she'd ended up with a line of lipstick on her teeth. "I think—" She pointed toward a once-colorful postcard then shook her head. "No. That flume is from an actual logging camp, not the log ride they had at Willow Wood." She flipped through a few more pages. "I'm terribly sorry. The last time I checked we had plenty of Willow Wood postcards. Someone must have sold them." She looked up, and when her eyes met Saffi's they gleamed like marbles.

Oh, really? "Can I have a look?"

"Of course." Cecily turned the book around and handed it to Saffi. "If you see anything you want to purchase, let me take it out. We can't be too careful with these precious bits of local history."

Saffi flipped through the binder, looking for anything that screamed "Willow Wood." She was about to turn a page when she saw a photo of a woman clutching a black-and-white speckled hen. The woman wore a straw hat. The hen, bizarrely, also wore a hat... crocheted from gray yarn and tied beneath her beak in a bow. Saffi tapped on the woman and lifted her eyes to Cecily who still hovered nearby.

"Who's this?"

"That is Sylvia Smith with her famous Barr Rock hen, Speckles. She knew her letters, our Speckles."

"I'm sorry." Saffi pecked her fingernail against the case. "She what?"

"Speckles laid eggs with letters on them."

How had she not heard of this fabulous feat?

Saffi held up a finger. "Could you hold on for a sec?" She pulled her cellphone from her pack, opened her notes app, and typed an entry under the title *Animal ABCs*. "Do you have anything else about Speckles? I'd love to include her in my next book."

Cecily sniffed. "All the local papers, as well as Ripley's *Believe It or Not*, told Speckles' story years ago."

Saffi nodded like a sage of all things news-related. "Perfect. The more sources I can check, the better."

Cecily pulled another book from the glass case. She opened it to a section filled with yellowed articles with crumbling edges, all about Speckles. Saffi scribbled down the names and dates of the papers so she could search their online archives later.

"This is fabulous. Thank you!" Saffi gave Cecily a genuine grin.

"What's your name, dear? Maybe the local bookstore has something you've written." Cecily sounded both curious and condescending.

Saffi tried to picture the posh real estate developer with a stack of readers on her bedside table, and failed. *Get ready for the blank stare.* "It's Saffi. Saffi Graywood. I write the *Bedside Reader* series."

The real estate developer's eyes went wide enough to contain dollar signs. "You're Aunt Saffi!"

"Guilty as charged."

Cecily pulled a business card from the pocket of her mauve blazer and forced it into Saffi's hand. "If you're looking for a second home in the area, Riverside Ranch is the *only* development worth considering."

Saffi imagined telling Cecily about living in a 28-foot RV. The woman would keel over in a dead faint.

"I'm so sorry we don't have any Willow Wood postcards." Cecily broke into Saffi's gleeful imaginings. "Are you planning to write about the park?"

Saffi brought her thoughts back to the search at hand. Cozying up to Cecily could lead to clues, and she needed every one she could collect.

"Your museum's Willow Wood room definitely sparked my interest." What was a little white lie among erstwhile friends? "The park must have been wonderful. Did you go there when you were little?"

"Oh, no." Cecily patted the bun at the back of her head. "I was just a baby when it closed."

Saffi shut the book of clippings and pushed it back toward Cecily. "I read in the local paper that someone is reopening the park, but with a different theme. Horror, I think?"

Cecily's nostrils twitched like she'd stepped in poo. "Horror. Can you imagine? Taking a place beloved by a generation of children and turning it into a creep show. Malcolm Morton thinks he's all that and a tin of caviar, but he's not."

"You know the actor?" Saffi widened her eyes as if impressed by what she'd heard.

"Oh, I know him," Cecily fumed. "And I'll tell you something free of charge. There are things going on over there—*terrible* things. If my husband, the *sheriff*, gets called over there one more time, he will shut that place down." A breath later, her eyes widened, and her lips smacked shut as if she realized she had spilled her true feelings. "That's just between you and me, Saffi dear. If you put it in one of those books of yours, I'm afraid I'll have to sue."

"My pen is capped." Saffi mimed putting the top on a ballpoint pen. Then she dug her wallet out of her sling pack, paid for her bottled water and a vintage photo of Speckles the hen, and hurried to the door, grateful to find Jyoti's Fiat idling at the curb.

TWENTY-FOUR

Saffi intended to keep her promise: she wouldn't put Cecily Raymond into a *Bedside Reader* article. She would, however, put her at the top of her list of suspects. She needed to get back to the Haunted Wood before Malcolm pulled another stupid publicity stunt. If she didn't, Sheriff Raymond would not hesitate to shut down the park. Of that, she was sure. But as Jyoti battled the northbound traffic out of town, Saffi's energy level plummeted, and her stomach grumbled.

Jyoti glanced sideways at her. "Did you eat before you dragged me out of the tea shop?"

Saffi had to think about it but, no. All she'd had this morning was a cup of French press coffee. "Malcolm said there wasn't any decent food in town. Was he right?"

Jyoti's sleek black ponytail swung back and forth. "Uhm. No. Whenever he's up here, he gets Nana to cook for him. Malcolm's knowledge of the local food scene probably dates back to his childhood."

She sped the Fiat up and jockeyed between cars to get around the pokey drivers and rubberneckers. Saffi watched restaurant after restaurant blip past the side window.

"You must have someplace special in mind."

"I do, but we have to hurry. They close at two."

"So, a breakfast place."

"And lunch. The best on the coast, not counting the tea shop, of course." Perfect peach circles suffused Jyoti's cheeks. Saffi found the young woman's pride in her grandfather both touching and warranted. Jyoti signaled for a right turn, eased the Fiat into the small packed lot of the Otis Café, and parked in an empty space near the back.

The Otis Café. The name triggered the memory of a burned-out hulk.

"This place used to be outside of town, didn't it? Just beyond the Haunted Wood?"

Jyoti raised her thick eyebrows. "Did you miss the turn?" When Saffi nodded, she chuckled. "Everyone misses it. That entrance is ridiculous."

Saffi couldn't disagree. It was.

She followed Jyoti out of the Fiat and into what looked like a repurposed fast food joint. The minute she stepped inside, the smell of fresh-baked bread told her this wasn't fast food—it was home cooking. Onions, bacon, cinnamon, maple syrup: the mélange of smells made her mouth water.

They followed the host to one of the two open tables. He handed them menus and rushed off to greet the customers that came in on their heels. Unlike the tea shop at the park, this café was packed with diners. An elderly couple at the table on their right dug into a shared plate of pancakes turned purple by the Marionberry syrup they kept squirting onto the stack. On their left, two men whose uniforms identified them as cable installers carved up chicken-fried steaks and biscuits smothered in gravy. Saffi tapped the menu on the table and frowned at her companion.

"Jyoti, the Little Tea Shop of Horror will never draw this much business. Not even with the park full and Sunny in the kitchen. Malcolm has to know that."

The teen gave her customary eye-roll. "Does he? I doubt it.

Malcolm has these memories of Willow Wood as a thriving park, filled with tourists."

Saffi laid the menu on the table, pressed her hands on it, and leaned forward. "The original park only lasted a few years, even though it was family-friendly and had *rides*."

Jyoti shrugged. "Nana's restaurant back home draws a lot of actors like Malcolm. They're stars or wannabe stars or used-to-be stars. They all think the sun shines out of their..." She trailed off in a grimace. "You know. And everything they shine that light on will turn to gold."

Saffi thought back to what Bev and Bob had told her: many of the invitations Malcolm sent out were coming back with regrets. With or without the postcard perp, Malcolm's dream might not last past opening night.

Jyoti tugged at the menu under Saffi's hands. "Ready to order?"

Saffi came out of her reverie, but the menu stayed shut. There were too many other things to look at. One sign on the wall advertised whole pies to go: Marionberry or Walnut. Another sign informed her she could buy black molasses bread, pumpkin bread, or walnut cinnamon rolls to take home to her RV. *And gorge until your clothes don't fit,* the snarky voice in her head chided. Why, Saffi wondered, couldn't the voices in her head understand the critical role carbs play in brain function?

"Check out the specials." Jyoti pointed to a white board.

Saffi read the first item scribbled in green marker under the title "Worth the Weight."

"Cinnamon-roll bread-pudding French-toast with two eggs." She turned to Jyoti, eyes wide with disbelief. "They're kidding, right?"

"Nope. Let's split! Half the calories"—Jyoti patted her flat belly—"and all the yum."

"Sure, why not?" Saffi handed the menus back to the waitress who sidled up to their table.

"You must have been here before." The young redhead's round cheeks dimpled with her smile.

"Nope. But she has." Saffi nodded at Jyoti, who ordered the special.

"Anything besides water to drink?"

"Coffee!" they chimed.

Saffi sighed. "This place is evil." She could feel her arteries harden just thinking about the food she was about to eat. "I'm surprised Malcolm hasn't jacked it up, put it on a trailer, and carted it off to the RV park."

"*Shhh...* don't tell him." Jyoti put a finger to her lips. "He just might do it."

By the time they'd finished stuffing their bellies, Saffi knew the only way to burn off *that* many calories was to walk back to the park. When she suggested it to Jyoti on their way back to the car, the young woman's eyes bugged out.

"No way! Once you get out of town there's not a sidewalk in sight. You'd be roadkill before you walked a mile." Jyoti clicked her key fob to unlock the Fiat's doors. "Hop in. I need to get back to work before my grandfather—"

"Fires you?" Saffi laughed, and Jyoti joined in. With her grandfather in the kitchen, her job was safe, whether she wanted it to be, or not.

Early-afternoon sun filtered through the trees as they bumped down the gravel road toward the RV park. Saffi cracked her window to breathe in the soothing mix of pine, cedar, mint, and earth. Then she spotted a Malcolm Morton balloon, sagging toward the ground but still tethered to the trunk of a Douglas fir. The juxtaposition of nature and horror made her spirits sink as well. Was that how the postcard sender felt?

Saffi considered her suspects. The person who pasted nature and ecology stamps on all those postcards didn't seem like a Cecily Raymond. Cecily wanted to profit off the land, but Mere? Mere wanted to conserve it. For someone who loved this land the way she did, it must feel like Malcolm Morton had slit open her beating heart and squeezed lemon juice into the wound. The thought of investigating C.J.'s daughter made her feel sick. That, or the fact that she'd eaten her weight in sugar, gluten, and cholesterol at the Otis Café.

Back at the park, a "closed" sign in the tea shop window told her Sunny had shut down the café, whether for lack of customers or lack of a granddaughter to take orders, Saffi didn't know.

"I'd better check on him," Jyoti said. She let Saffi out of the Fiat by the museum and drove toward the toy hauler.

Saffi's visit to the museum hadn't shortened her list of possible postcard perps. It had made the list even longer. Mere Horseman, Bev and Bob, Cecily Raymond, or the man himself—Malcolm Morton. This seemed as good a time as any to probe the possibility that the postcards were a publicity stunt, just like the fake blood in the museum. Finding the museum's doors padlocked, Saffi made her way to the office. Bev and Bob were both inside, but they had no idea where Malcolm might be.

"How are the RSVPs coming along?" Saffi asked. With the costumed Spooktacular three days away, the actor might feel pressure to pump up the publicity. Who knew what he might do next?

Bob sneezed, and Bev handed him a tissue.

"Malcolm came in earlier hoping for a stack of 'yesses.'" Bev stuck her thumbs under her suspenders and pulled them away from her red-and-white striped Henley, then let them snap back into place.

Ouch! Saffi gritted her teeth. How did her breasts take that kind of abuse?

"When he opened 'em up and found a bunch of regrets—"

"He stormed back to the museum—"

"And pulled the barn door closed behind him."

Saffi's head had ping-ponged between Bev and Bob so many times she wasn't sure who had said what. She thanked them and got out of there before she gave herself whiplash. She wandered back to the barn, tugged on the padlock—which was secure—then skirted around the side. Malcolm's red roadster was gone.

Now what? Should she take a fat-burning walk or go back to her RV and work on the revisions she'd been avoiding? She was about to choose the latter when Jyoti returned from the toy hauler waving a sticky note.

"Malcolm and Nana went to the post office to pick up a shipment for the Spooktacular. I think I'll get the café ready for tonight." She left with a backward wave.

The post office! Saffi glanced toward C.J.'s campsite. The yellow-and-white camper van was gone. Had the postal inspector followed Malcolm and Sunny? Maybe he thought their excursion had something to do with the stolen Oz jacket.

She remembered a tidbit from an author podcast about mysteries. "If you want to solve the crime before the sleuth, pay attention to who benefits."

Who might benefit from the theft of L. Frank Baum's jacket? Surely not Malcolm. He needed it for his museum... although... Saffi leaned against the barn door. Why was that jacket on display anyway? It had nothing to do with horror movies and Malcolm had never worn it in a film. Maybe he had put it on display just so it could be "stolen."

Saffi thumped a fist against her forehead. *Think!*

She kicked loose the memory of Malcolm and Sunny arguing about keeping a weasel at bay. That seemed absurd... unless the weasel was related to C.J.'s case. A partner in crime Malcolm had stiffed? Someone so scary the master of horror had fled up the coast to disappear into the Haunted Wood?

For the first time since she'd arrived, Malcolm, Sunny, and C.J. were away from the grounds. Jyoti was busy in the café. Saffi glanced toward the hollowed log office building. Bob and Bev were both still inside. There couldn't be a better time to finish her aborted search of Malcolm's loft.

TWENTY-FIVE

With Malcolm off the grounds, she could snoop through his loft like she'd failed to do when he caught her there. C.J. had refused to share his list of items from the Smithsonian shipment. If she could get into Malcolm's closet, she could make her own list. To share... *or not!* Saffi chuckled. All she had to do was pick the padlock on the barn door without being seen.

She'd briefly considered writing a lock-picking how-to for homeowners who'd lost their keys. Despite the fact that most of her articles were meant to entertain or enlighten, she included at least one piece per annual that taught the reader something useful. The lock-picking article was one of countless ideas that didn't pan out. No matter how clever she thought her ideas were, some stories ended up in her computer's trash can. Exciting leads failed to meet her three-times verified standard. Research trails went cold. Real-life tales turned out to be so horrifying she put them back under the rocks where they'd been hidden.

As for the lock-picking article? After viewing a few online videos, she realized that anyone who wanted to pick a lock could watch a tutorial and... *open sesame!* She had, however, bought some lock-picker's tools which were back at her—

"Need to get in there?"

Saffi jumped higher than she had in years, then bent forward to catch her breath and, hopefully, give herself time to stop looking guilty. Finally, she turned toward the voice.

"Bev!" Saffi rolled her shoulders.

"Didn't mean to scare the pants off you. Malcolm told us to help you in any way we could." The amusement in Bev's ice-blue eyes told Saffi she was fully aware that the boss would not have padlocked the barn unless he wanted everyone—including Saffi— to stay out. "He can't wait for you to nail the guy who sent those threats."

If Bev knew how to get past Malcolm's padlock without risking charges for breaking-and-entering, Saffi was all ears. "I thought I'd check the display case," she said. "See if I can figure out how someone got in there to steal the Oz jacket."

Bev's brows furrowed. "Are the theft and the postcards connected?"

Saffi lifted her hands. "In all honesty, at this point I don't have a clue. Which is why I'd like to nose around in there." She jerked a thumb toward the barn.

"Well, these might help." Bev held up a ring of keys big enough to unlock every case in the place.

Saffi couldn't stop her eyes from narrowing. "Malcolm keeps a whole set of keys in the office?"

Bev snorted. "Course not. These were Lennie's. Found them in the mud after they pulled him out of the river."

Saffi sucked in a breath. Bev had Lennie's keys? If she'd found them after his death, why hadn't she given them to the sheriff? Or Malcolm, for that matter.

"Aren't those, uhm, evidence?"

Bev shrugged. Clearly, she didn't care one way or the other. "You need 'em, or not?"

Saffi needed them, and the park manager's eyes said she knew it, but if Saffi took them, she might be making a deal with the devil. Bev wouldn't tell Malcolm that Saffi snooped in the barn and Saffi wouldn't tell Malcolm that Bev had the run of the place. In *The*

Wind in the Willows, Ratty—the character Bev had reminded her of from the moment they met—was a loyal friend. Saffi wanted to trust her. Could she?

No. Not really. Bev had discovered Lennie's body. Taken his keys. Closed the photo album she'd been enthusiastically sharing when Saffi asked about the kayaker waving a paddle in greeting. What, exactly, was Bev Jones up to?

The park manager shook the key ring, its jangle an invitation Saffi couldn't resist. She took the keys.

"Drop them by at the office when you're done." Bev wandered toward the massive log that served as the park office with her hands stuck into the back pockets of her green cargo pants. A cloud of mystery surrounded the park manager, and, so far, Saffi could not see beyond the mist.

Crucial minutes passed as Saffi tried key after key in the padlock. Sweat beaded her brow, and dark curls drooped into her eyes. *Seriously, Saffi? The guys on the lock-picking videos took less time and they didn't have keys!* Finally, one of the keys clicked. Relief flooded her veins as the padlock released. She pulled the lock out of the staple, opened the hinged hasp, and heaved the sliding door open. Then she hung the lock from the staple again hoping that, from a distance, the door would appear locked when she pulled it closed behind her.

Key ring dangling from one hand, she took several slow breaths to settle her nerves. The museum now smelled of corn syrup *and* bleach. In the few hours she'd been away from the park, someone had sponged away most of the fake blood. They had, she noted, left bloody handprints strategically placed on display cases, posters, and the theater-sized popcorn machine. A Malcolm Morton touch, if she'd ever seen one, though she doubted the actor had done the cleanup. Sunny had probably been conscripted to undo the damage Malcolm had forced him to do the first place.

OK. She squared her shoulders. *Enough time wasted. Let the sleuthing begin!*

When she passed the case that had held the Oz jacket, she

paused. A new item already hung from the half-body mannequin inside—a yellowed duck-cloth straight jacket she recognized from one of Malcolm's early films. He'd played a dallying husband whose wife had gone berserk after catching him in an affair. An axe with bloody prints on the handle rested against the straight jacket. Saffi shuddered as her thoughts went to Lennie. Someone had walloped the groundskeeper hard enough to kill him, but she had no idea what had been used. An axe? A kayak paddle? A handy branch found on the trail? If the sheriff had stumbled on the murder weapon, his "this is my jurisdiction" mindset meant he wasn't likely to share the information with her.

Saffi wound through the exhibits, making her way toward the spiral staircase beneath the loft apartment. The steps gonged as she jogged up them, and the cellphone in her sling pack thwacked against her ribs. She slowed as she neared the top to peek above the top stair. She heard a hiss and glimpsed a blur of movement an instant before something massive swatted her head.

Saffi fell backward, grabbing for the metal railing. If she plummeted to her death on the concrete floor, she would never forgive herself. Neither would Poppy, since she hadn't finished her revisions. Her hands found purchase, and she clutched the cold metal, holding tight to give her legs time to steady. Her heart pounded, and her breath came in raspy gasps until she forced herself to take a long slow breath in, then another out. Within seconds, the deep breathing did its job, slowing her heart rate and filling her lungs.

Once her feet felt secure, she released her grip and touched her head, wincing. Her hand came away sticky with blood. Someone had attacked her, and that someone was in Malcolm's loft, determined to keep her out. Glenn's friendship meant the world to her but risking actual death to assuage her guilty feelings? That was not the act of a sane woman.

Today, Saffi decided, was not a good day to die. Today was a day to retreat while she still could. She'd already started backing down the stairs, slowly, one by one, when she heard a noise, soft and rumbling like a finely tuned motor or—Saffi stopped—the purr of a very large cat. *Tomago!*

The Maine Coon had swatted her off the stairs, probably in retaliation for the lap-dumping Saffi had given her.

"Tomago?" She inched upward. "Nice, kitty, kitty, kitty." She felt like the too-dumb-to-live victim in one of Malcolm's movies, walking knowingly into the monster's lair. "Be a good girl and don't kill me. OK?" She kept her voice low and soothing as she eased her head above floor level again, sure that at any moment, Tomago's claws would slice her face open.

They didn't. She spotted the black-and-white Maine Coon sashaying toward the leather sectional. When she reached it, Tomago made a mighty leap onto the back of the couch, then pawed at the leather before flattening herself into her favorite position, lying in wait for her next unsuspecting victim. Saffi collapsed forward onto the red-and-purple art deco rug, nose to nose with a rearing Pegasus. She rested her head for a minute, then pushed her upper body off the floor, hoping any bloody smudge she'd left behind would blend in with the rest of the red.

Was there a bathroom in this place? And did it have a first aid kit?

She tiptoed across the home theater-style living room, trying not to attract the attention of the guard-cat. When she reached the closest door, she opened it and gasped loudly enough to elicit a purr of what sounded like agreement from Tomago. It would be a crime against interior design to call the room she stepped into a "bathroom." Both bath and boudoir, the opulent room looked like it had been designed for Joan Crawford, not Malcolm Morton. A gold-sided clawfoot tub dominated the room's center. Black-and-white ceramic tiles covered the floor. Saffi pulled the door shut behind her, a precaution against Tomago using the tiles as camouflage to launch another attack.

A brass tray stretched across the tub, filled with bath bombs, vintage bubble-bath bottles, and natural-bristle body scrubbers. Saffi picked up a gold-wrapped bomb and sniffed. Coconut, vanilla, and the bitter orange scent of bergamot. A black bomb molded into the shape of a rose smelled like crushed rose petals with a hint of lemongrass. These must be the fancy soaps Jyoti had mentioned, some of which had gone missing. She was tempted to heist one herself, but this was the actor's home away from home, not a hotel expecting guests to filch the fine toiletries.

Blood dripped down her forehead, reminding her that she needed to find a bandage—hopefully before she bled all over the lambskin rug in front of the bathtub. After poking around a bit, she found the medicine cabinet recessed behind a fan-shaped mirror with black glass and gold trim above a white ceramic pedestal sink. Inside the cabinet, Malcolm had thoughtfully provided a box of adhesive bandages in various sizes, one of which fit over the owie Tomago's paw had left on her head. The scratch was tiny, hidden beneath her black curls, and bleeding like a wound ten times its size. Head wounds did that, she remembered from one of the medical texts she kept in her RV for research. Cat scratches needed cleaning, but she'd do that at home. In the meantime, she stuck a bandage over the wound and tucked the wrapper into the front pocket of her jeans. Best to leave no trace of her presence.

Now... she scanned the room... *if this was both bath and boudoir, where was Malcolm's closet?* She still hadn't spotted the toilet—or, based on what she'd seen so far—the bidet. Her guess? It was hidden behind the lacquered screen to the left of the sink.

On the opposite side of the room, Malcolm had draped a black-and-gold paisley dressing gown over a tufted gold-velvet chaise longue. The wall behind the chaise was covered in black-and-gold art deco wallpaper. The pattern reminded Saffi of the flowing champagne fountain her editor had rented for the launch of her tenth *Bedside Reader*. She had a hazy memory of that particular party, thanks to the ever-flowing bubbly.

A slight misalignment of the wallpaper pattern brought Saffi back from the ghost of parties past. Closer examination revealed a nearly invisible door. When she spotted the knob and opened it, a motion-sensor light illuminated a massive walk-in closet. And in that closet: gleaming built-in wooden cabinets, shoe racks, drawers, and shelves, all filled with decades of movie glamour. Silks and furs. Cashmere and linen. Gold lamé and burgundy velvet. Every item looked as if it had been crafted in a costumer's workshop. The walk-in smelled of the hopes, dreams, and successes of generations of actors, after they'd been doused in dry-cleaning fluid and spritzed with lavender. If Glenn saw this room he would literally swoon. Fortunately, a cushioned bench had been placed in the center of the closet, perhaps for just such an occurrence.

Saffi sat down on the bench to survey her surroundings. She had no idea how to even begin compiling a list of items that might have come from the Smithsonian shipment. She spotted the pink bedspread jacket Malcolm had worn the first time they met hanging between a red puffer vest and a quilted silver satin jacket. When she pulled the latter out, she found a gold scorpion embroidered on the back. Neither the puffy vest nor the scorpion jacket seemed to fit the actor's Old Hollywood style. She slid her cellphone out of her sling pack and snapped pictures of both items, then opened the notes app to start a list.

Inside a shoe-shelving unit, she spotted pristine black-and-white wingtips and polished brown loafers beside a pair of filthy white sneakers with a bright red Nike swoosh. She snapped pics and added the oddity to the list of items that didn't seem to match Malcolm's style.

As Saffi knelt down to get a closer look at the bottom row of shoes, something warm thrummed against her hip. *What the heck?* Saffi tumbled onto her side then scrambled to her knees, looking over her shoulder to see what was in the closet with her.

"Tomago!" She used the cushioned bench to push herself to her feet then brushed off her jeans and watched cat hair join the dust motes drifting to the floor. "How did you get in here?"

The Maine Coon turned and walked away as if in answer to her question, then squeezed herself through a narrow opening at the end of the room opposite the bath. As the tip of the cat's twitching tail disappeared, Saffi grabbed the edge of the door and pulled it open. With far more grace than Saffi had managed getting back to her feet in the closet, the twenty-five-pound cat sprang onto a king-sized bed. It proceeded to use the green silk-upholstered headboard as a scratching post. Saffi was debating whether to intervene when Tomago glanced over her shoulder as if daring her to get between a cat and her prey.

Saffi might have tried. The green silk looked vintage, after all. But a distant screech froze her in place. *The barn door!* She'd closed it on her way in. A few seconds later, boots rang on the metal staircase, and a voice yelled "Saffi! You still in here?"

She abandoned Malcolm's upholstery to his larger-than-life cat and fled, back through the closet and into the boudoir, closing every door she could remember opening as she went. Bev topped the staircase, waving her away from them. "Safer to use the fire exit."

"Fire exit?"

"This way!" Bev led her through the living room to a door hidden in the trompe l'oeil projection booth behind the couch.

How many doors had Malcolm hidden in this place? How did Bev know where they were, and why was she leading Saffi out the back instead of down the stairway?

Saffi followed Bev through the door and clattered down the fire escape on the park manager's heels. At the bottom, Bev put a finger to her lips and listened. When car doors slammed and voices headed their way, instead of toward the front of the barn, Bev swore. "Back here." She hurried Saffi behind a large wooden shed.

"Has this been here the whole time?" If it had, Saffi should probably hang up her sleuthing hat and call it a day. The shed was half the size of the tea shop. This was her third day in the park, and she hadn't bothered to truly explore the grounds. *Bad Saffi.*

Like the barn, the shed was padlocked, but Saffi still held a key ring that would probably get her inside. She jingled the ring with a question in her eyes.

Bev shook her head. "Nobody's been in there since—" She snatched the keys. "The shed was Lennie's domain. No friends, no family... as far as I could tell, the man's entire existence was taking care of the grounds and those tools."

Other than Malcolm, no one had said a word about the groundskeeper, until now. "What was he like, Lennie?"

Bev's ice-blue eyes met Saffi's. "Can't say I really got to know him. Kept himself to himself. But he was watchful." Her gaze hardened. "Like you."

Was that a warning, or was Bev hinting that Lennie's watchfulness had gotten him killed? The shed might have been Lennie's domain a few days ago, but now? It was a locked space that could offer clues to his murder. She needed to get inside. Before she could pressure Bev to change her mind, a beeping sound caught Saffi's attention.

"Is that a backup alarm?" She edged toward the corner of the shed and peered around. What she saw made her stand up straight and step forward. A tow truck, with Malcolm's red roadster on its bed, was backing slowly along the side of the barn. Malcolm and Sunny stood to one side. Both men looked badly shaken.

Bev tugged at her arm and made a "stay put" motion with her other hand, but Saffi ignored her.

"Malcolm!" She ran forward. "What happened?"

The actor slumped against Sunny, who put his arm around him. "The brakes failed."

A jolt went through Saffi's body. The postcard with Toad driving his roadster! What had it said? "A short drive away from certain death," she whispered.

"Nanaji!" Jyoti ran down the tea shop steps and careened into her grandfather, knocking Malcolm aside. "What happened? Are you OK?"

Sunny patted her back, whispering comforting words into the top of her head. Malcolm wandered away, coming to a wobbly rest at Saffi's side.

"We were just tootling along without a care in the world," he murmured. "Heading toward the post office. The light changed, and I hit the brakes... nothing. I managed to steer off the road, straight onto the golf course."

Saffi gasped and clutched at Malcolm's arm. "Dear God. Are either of you hurt? Do you need a doctor?"

"We're fine, we're fine." Malcolm waved away her concern. "But my lovely car." He shook his head and wandered toward the front of the roadster. The front wheels were crumpled toward each other. One of the roadster's bug-eyed headlights had been punched out. The other wobbled like an eyeball fallen from its socket. Clods of grass and dirt choked the front grill.

"I believe Malcolm has just made his first hole in one!" Sunny made light of the crash, probably for his granddaughter's sake, but his dark eyes held a haunted quality Saffi had not seen before.

"Yes." Malcolm laughed along for Jyoti's benefit, then clapped his hands together and leaned toward Saffi. "The tow truck operator checked the brake lines," he whispered. "From what he could tell, the front two were cut, just enough that when I hit the brakes, they ruptured. The pedal went straight to the floor."

A sickening sense of dread flooded Saffi's body. The postcard perp had struck again.

TWENTY-SIX

After the roadster wreck, failure settled over Saffi like a shroud. She trudged back to her RV, exhausted, defeated, with barely enough energy to toast bread and spread it with hummus before taking to her bed. She read a little, munched her toast, and slumped into sleep without even brushing the crumbs off the covers. During the night, her brain gnawed away at the case, sending her images of rats scurrying through the park, a gunman sniping at otters, a blood-red car careening off a cliff. She awoke with the realization that she'd let herself be pulled off track by Malcolm Morton's theatrics and a certain green-eyed lawman intent on solving a heist worth millions.

Yesterday, instead of focusing on the job she'd come here to do, she'd dug through Malcolm's wardrobe looking for clues that would help C.J. solve *his* case. She'd let herself be pulled toward the postal inspector like iron filings to a magnet. Exciting? Yes. She'd been widowed, but she was far from dead. Something about the way he read her mind, his teasing flirtation, or the blaze of intelligence behind his moss-green eyes made her want to... what? Show off her sleuthing skills? Show him up? *Arrgh! Get a grip, woman.*

On her fourth morning at the Haunted Wood, she was no closer to identifying the postcard perp than she'd been when she arrived. But the sender? He or she crept closer every day, turning threats into reality… one by one. The dead otter for the badger card, the rat poison, and now, the roadster wreck. Malcolm and Sunny could have been killed!

Today she needed to knuckle down. She could count suspects who'd been on the grounds or close enough to follow through on the threats on one hand: Bev, Bob, Mere, Cecily Raymond, and Malcolm (although, if he'd wrecked his own roadster he was more psycho than the character he'd played in *Deranged in Denver*). After Bev's reluctance to unlock the shed behind the barn yesterday afternoon, she knew exactly where to start.

She showered, ate a light breakfast while watching an online tutorial, grabbed her lock-picking tools from the kitchen drawer, and headed to the tea shop for sixteen ounces of sweet caffeinated goodness. As Jyoti steamed her Mad Scientist Mocha, Saffi poked her head into the kitchen to check on Sunny.

"Fine as chickpea flour," he assured her. "Do not be worrying your head." As he waved her out of the kitchen, she couldn't help noticing the way his shoulders sagged, as if the world had landed on his back and he had forgotten how to stand straight.

Jyoti turned from the coffee station to catch her eye, stress lines creasing her otherwise seamless forehead. "If anything else happens to my grandfather, I will—" She clenched her hand around the to-go cup she'd just filled and capped. Mocha shot from the spout. "Oh!" She let go and backed away, shaking hot coffee from her hands. "I'm so sorry. I'll make you another one."

Saffi reached for the dripping, sticky cup. "This one will do just fine."

The look of gratitude Jyoti gave her nearly broke her heart. She had to find the culprit behind the push to close the park before someone else got hurt.

Saffi cut between the tea shop and the barn, sipping coffee and trying to act nonchalant. Once behind the barn, she tugged on the shed's padlock. It didn't fall open at the touch of her magic fingers, but she'd come prepared. She took a long slow pull of perfectly spiced mocha, then set the to-go cup down by her feet. A few pokes and clicks with the right tools and… *presto unlocko!* She'd be ready to find what Bev wanted to stay hidden.

The October chill made her eyes water and blurred her vision. She blinked and squinted, poked, prodded, and worried the lock with picks that had been "guaranteed foolproof" by the online ad that had bamboozled her into buying them. What had made her think she could pick a lock? She'd been at it for so long her upper arms ached and had yet to feel a single pin drop in the way the tutorial described.

"Looks easy in those videos, doesn't it?" Warm air whispered along her neck. If she hadn't recognized the voice, she would have stabbed C.J. with either the metal tension tool or the hook she held in her hands… or both, one to each thigh because… *why?*

"Why do people keep sneaking up on me?"

"Ah."

There was that soft, warm whisper again.

"I take it this is not the first lock you've tried to pick."

Saffi could have stepped away from the shiver he kept sending down her neck, but it was the kind of shiver she liked to lean into, not avoid.

"Give me those… before you hurt yourself, or worse still, me." He gently removed the tools from her clenched fists and went to work on the padlock. A few probing stabs later, the lock slipped open. "After you." He took a bow and stepped aside to let her enter.

As she wandered into the shed, he reached down to pick up the to-go cup she'd set on the ground. "Forgot your coffee!" He licked sweetness from his thumb.

Great! She had just become the kind of sleuth who needed a man to show up, open doors, and gallantly present her with a sticky to-go cup.

Or the kind of sleuth who takes help when it's offered, Saffi my love. Levi's voice in her head settled her ruffled feathers. Besides, she didn't just take help from men. She was an equal opportunity help taker. Yesterday she'd grabbed that key ring from Bev without hesitation, even though, clearly, the woman could be a murderer. Or at the very least, a secreter of things she didn't want Saffi to see.

Going from mellow morning light into semi-darkness blinded her for a few seconds. As her pupils widened, she saw a light switch just inside the door and flipped it up. C.J. wasted no time following her inside and shutting the door against potential watchers.

They both scanned the room, taking in the carefully stowed gardening and maintenance tools and equipment. Hammers, trowels, shovels, a digging fork, rakes, a tree-limb lopper and more hung from utility hooks spaced along one wall. Jars holding nails and screws and bolts lined the back of a workbench on the opposite wall. Screwdrivers, wrenches, and tools Saffi couldn't even name hung from the pegboard above it. An extension ladder leaned against the back wall. A wheelbarrow balanced on its front wheel was propped against the wall beside it. There were power tools, too: a leaf blower, a chain saw, a drill, and a sander among them. The place smelled of gas and oil, sawdust and dried sweat, the latter smell probably came from the overflow of wadded-up towels and T-shirts in a basket beneath the workbench.

C.J. put his hands on his hips and whistled. "Quite the shop. Looks like Lennie kept it spick-and-span." The look on his weathered face was both admiring and envious.

"Bev told me he didn't have friends or family. This place was his world." Saffi noted a few cobwebs drooping from the ceiling, a reminder that Lennie hadn't been here in days and would never darken the door again. Would anyone care? Anyone at all?

She sagged against the workbench. "I thought I'd find something besides tools in here."

"Why?" C.J. frowned.

"Bev, she..." Saffi sipped the last of her now-cold coffee. Then she waved the empty cup toward the door as if expecting the park manager to barge inside and ask what the heck she was doing in Lennie's shed.

C.J. put a hand on her shoulder and gave it a squeeze. "I know that look. You noticed another one of those clues Ray missed, didn't you?" He put his other hand down on the workbench as if to block her there until she confessed her deepest darkest secrets... or desires. His body was close enough for heat to transfer to her own. That outdoorsy mix of evergreen and smoke that permeated his clothes was an aphrodisiac she wasn't sure she wanted to resist. As she felt herself starting to lean closer, she stopped.

What was it he'd asked her? Something about missed clues?

Instead of leaning into him, she ducked under his arm and stepped away from the pull of his body to gather her thoughts. He'd trusted her with the truth of his identity. He was extremely easy on the eyes and helpful with a lock pick. The least she could do was share a measly clue or two. She tapped her chin, then nodded.

"After Lennie was killed, Bev found his key ring in the mud. Instead of handing the keys over to the sheriff, she kept them."

C.J. stiffened. "Why would Bev tell you about the keys? Kind of incriminating, aren't they?"

Why did he have to be so smart? She sucked in a mouthful of tepid air then blew it out with her confession. "I was trying to break into the barn, OK? She said Malcolm told them to help me, so she did. Then I... I kind of poked around in Malcolm's loft."

C.J. wiggled his eyebrows. "And into my case? Despite the fact that I explicitly asked you not to?"

She ducked her head. "I know. I know. But"—she pulled her phone out of her sling—"I was thinking about your list of items—"

"The one I didn't show you." He smacked his forehead with his palm. "Nothing intrigues an amateur sleuth more than an unanswered question. I told you: that list is confidential, and it's going to remain so."

Saffi tabbed open her notes app and held up her phone. "I understand. I do. That's why I made a list of my own. Look!"

C.J. leaned forward squinting at the screen. "Red puffer vest.

Silver satin jacket. Scruffy Nikes." His eyes narrowed as he stepped back. "How did you get that?"

"What?" Saffi thumbed off her phone and zipped it into her bag.

"My list, Saffi. My list!"

What was he talking about? "I did not steal *your* list. These are things I found in Malcolm's closet. Look!" She switched to the camera app and clicked through the pictures she'd taken.

C.J. ran a hand through his scruffy blond hair. "And you photographed these particular items because...?"

Saffi scratched her nose. "Malcolm has a style. Old Hollywood. Dramatic. These things don't fit."

"You're right."

"About what? That they don't fit?" His reaction to her list said more than he'd been willing to tell her. Some, or all, of those things were part of the stolen Smithsonian shipment.

Thoughts flashed through C.J.'s eyes. When they settled into certainty she hoped he was about to answer her question. He didn't. Instead, he asked about Bev.

"Bev let you use the keys to get into the barn, but not the shed?"

Saffi nodded.

"Why?"

"I don't know." She turned to scan the shed again. "There has to be a reason."

Lennie's tools hung in neat rows, some blunted by use, some freshly sharpened, but all squeaky clean. Even the concrete floor looked scoured. Malcolm wasn't kidding. His groundskeeper must have been a bit OCD—not a bad quality in someone whose job was to keep the park in top shape. Her eyes settled, finally, on the one incongruous thing: the overflowing laundry basket. It was so full she wondered if Lennie had been struck down before he had time to wash his shop gear. Did the park even have laundry facilities? They were either hidden from view like the maintenance shed or Malcolm hadn't bothered to install such conveniences. If the

Haunted Wood ever filled up, that decision would come back to bite him in the butt.

She knelt down in front of the bench and pulled the basket out, then gingerly picked through the oily rags, grimy towels, and sweat-stained T-shirts. C.J. continued to lean against the workbench, legs crossed at the ankles, hooded green eyes watching her every move. As she neared the bottom of the basket, her hand grasped more than cloth: a solid object wrapped inside a large blue shop rag. She clutched the wrapped object, which was heavier than she'd expected, and pulled it onto her lap.

"Find something?" C.J. uncrossed his legs and straightened.

"Not sure."

Unlike the other rags in the basket, this one looked new. When she unwrapped the towel and got a look at what was inside, Saffi lost her grip. She caught the object against her belly before it rolled off her thighs, rose slowly, then placed it on the workbench, a hunched black bird statuette that glowered like a grumpy grandpa awakened from a much-needed nap.

"Is that a—?"

Before Saffi could say "raven," C.J. shouted, "The Maltese Falcon!"

"Wait." Saffi stepped back. "The *actual* falcon? From the Bogart movie?"

C.J. touched a fingertip to the tip of the bird's thick curved beak. "It was in the shipment. At least, one of them was."

Outside, a bird scolded in a rasping voice. *Raven? Hang on*, she sent a mental message. *This is important.* "One of them?"

"The studio had more than one made for the film. Its twin sold at auction for four point one million a few years back."

Saffi whistled. This wasn't some tchotchke; it was a treasure worth stealing. This had to be the reason Bev didn't want her to search the shed.

"Oh, gods. I can't believe I almost dropped it." As Saffi pressed the statuette to her chest, her fingers felt an aberration on the back of its head. A raised blob, part tacky, part flaky. She turned the bird slowly, then almost dropped it again. "C.J.! Is that?" She held the statue out to him. Just as he grasped the falcon and leaned in for a closer look, the bird outside croaked again.

"Brr-oak! Brr-oak!"

Another cry joined it... and another, followed by the sound of heavy birds landing on the roof's spine, one after another after another. It took longer than it should have, but Saffi finally heard Raven's warning in the unfamiliar cries.

"We need to get out of here!"

C.J. tossed the rag back over the statuette and crooked it under his arm in a football carry. "Let's go!"

At that moment, metal clinked against metal, and the padlock snicked shut.

"Hey! There's someone in here!" C.J. slammed the shoulder opposite the stolen falcon against the wooden door. The crash reverberated through the walls, but the door held.

Saffi heard something splash against the shed's wooden sides. "Gas!" She pressed her nose into the crook of her arm. The splashing was followed by a series of clicks that made her moan out loud. She heard the same sound every time she tried to light the propane burner on her RV's stove. Utility lighters like the one flicking outside never lit on the first strike, at least not for her. They also ran out of fuel just when you needed them most. *Please, please!* She pressed her hands over her nose in prayer position.

A few seconds later, the birds that had landed on the roof shrieked, their startled cries sounding almost human. Their wings pounded in concert as they lifted skyward. By the time their voices faded into the distance, Saffi smelled smoke. Gray tendrils reached through the shed's cracks and crevices seeking someone to strangle.

"Take this!" C.J. held the rag-wrapped falcon toward her, and she took it, hands shaking. "Saffi." He touched her cheek and lifted her chin with one strong finger. "I am *not* going out like this, and neither are you. You get low. I'll get us out of here."

She sank to the cold concrete floor while C.J. prowled the shed like a wolf. He picked up tool after tool, brow furrowed, as if calculating each tool's odds of freeing them before they passed out from smoke inhalation. Smoke started to fill the shed and shove its way into her lungs.

As she cradled the falcon against her side, it smacked against something hard in her sling bag. *Her cellphone!* Despite C.J.'s much-appreciated manly efforts, her instincts were the opposite of a damsel in distress. She had a cellphone, and she knew how to use it.

Malcolm Morton was the last person she wanted to call, given the evidence she'd found in his walk-in closet, but she had no choice. His was the only local number in her phone. She put a fingertip to the actor's name in her recent calls list and pressed.

TWENTY-SEVEN

Voices shrieked. Fists pounded. Saffi heard it all as if from a distance, everything blurred by the white haze that burned her chest and stifled her breath.

"The hose! Get the hose!"

Was that Bev's voice? She could get them out of here with a twist of a key. Why didn't she?

"It's in the shed." Bob's explosive sneezes barely registered over the cacophony of shouts and screams.

Another voice—authoritative, booming as if from the center of a stage to reach the farthest rows at the back of the house—broke through the madness.

"Sunny! Jyoti! Fill those buckets!"

She heard splashing and scooted backward until she hit the ladder leaning against the back wall. Lack of oxygen jumbled her thoughts. *Was someone adding fuel to the fire?*

"More, Beta! We need more water!" Sunny shouted.

Not gas. Water. She closed her eyes against the smoke's relentless sting and let her fogged brain try to make sense of other noises: the wrench of metal, the groan of wood, the grunt of exertion. Something splintered and metal rang on the concrete floor. Saffi's eyes sprang open as light exploded into the shed.

"Saffi!" C.J. turned back for her at the same time Malcolm Morton pulled the door wide open and pushed his way inside.

"Out, out, out!" He tried to shove the immoveable object that was C.J. Horseman. "Bob! Help!"

Once C.J. was outside, Malcolm rushed toward Saffi, tucked an arm under hers and jerked her to her feet. She kept her grip on the falcon, but the shop rag flopped open, exposing the glowering black statuette. Malcolm's mouth opened in surprise, bringing enough smoke into his lungs to make him choke. He shook his head as he tried to clear his throat. "Come along, Aunt Saffi!" He coughed. "Glenn would never forgive me if I let you burn."

As Malcolm led her toward the light, Saffi tripped over the crowbar C.J. had dropped after wrenching the door open. Even though her lungs were screaming for clear air, she paused to look back into the smoke-filled space that could have been her tomb. Her eyes sought out one particular thing—something she hadn't seen before and did not see now. A cough racked her chest, and she bent forward, gasping for breath.

Malcolm gave her arm another tug. "I called Fire and Rescue. They'll be here soon. Let's get away from this infernal smoke, shall we?"

The next hour felt like a week... a month... a lifetime.

Saffi and C.J. had both been checked by paramedics. Both had pulse oximeters stuck to their fingers to check their oxygen levels, after which Saffi had an oxygen mask pressed over her mouth and nose and C.J. was deemed fit to go back to his van. Once her oxygen levels rose to a safe level, a female paramedic escorted her to her Rambler and settled her on the couch.

"You'll be hoarse for a while," she warned. "But if you have trouble breathing or feel confused, have someone drive you to Samaritan."

"I hate to sound confused, but... aren't *you* the good Samaritan?" Saffi blinked. Her lids felt heavy, her eyes like they'd been scoured with pot scrubbers.

The paramedic chuckled. "Not as good as the hospital in Lincoln City."

Saffi relaxed against the raven pillow that cushioned the arm of her couch. As she dozed, she heard the croak of birds, felt the weight of webbed feet on her sternum, heard the whoosh of wings rising, rising, rising out of the smoke, into the wet and welcoming clouds. Something plopped on Saffi's cheek and burned through skin to bone in white-hot agony.

Remember, Raven whispered.

The first thing she did when she awakened was kick off the blanket and run to the bathroom. She fumbled for the light switch in the gathering darkness, flicked it on, and turned her head to stare at the burn on her cheek.

There was no burn. Her skin was porcelain-white, flawless. She had been so sure...

Wash your face, Saffi.

She turned the faucet to cold and splashed water on her skin until she remembered. The shed. The Maltese Falcon. The padlocked door. The smoke. The croak of a single word in her ear: *remember*.

What? She rubbed her arms. What part of this horrible afternoon did Raven want her to remember?

The last thing she wanted to do was leave the warmth and safety of her Rambler. But she had to. Someone had tried to kill her, kill C.J., to protect the secret hidden inside that shed. The secret she'd found—not just the Maltese Falcon, but what she'd discovered on the back of its head: a blob that looked and felt like dried blood. She'd lost track of the falcon statuette. Had someone scooped it up, either to hide the evidence or safeguard it?

The smell of smoke suddenly overwhelmed her, and she tipped her nose toward her hoodie, then her hair. She was definitely the source of the smell. The only solution: a shower and fresh clothes.

So be it!

Three-quarters of an hour later, she was squeaky clean and smelling of coconut and argan oil shampoo. She blow-dried her hair into a halo of black-and-silver curls, then brightened her cheeks with pink cream blush. Her lashes were once thick enough to forgo mascara. She stroked on a bit for special occasions but tonight, with her eyes still reddened and smoke-sore, she refused to risk poking herself in the eyeball.

Minimalist makeup in place, she dug through the cabinets above her bed to find her softest knit tunic: chocolate-brown Merino wool. She slipped that over a satin tank top and French-cut undies. After today's ordeal, her skin craved both luxury and comfort. Every cell in her body wanted to celebrate the fact that she had lived to sleuth another day. She struggled to pull thick soft fleece-lined leggings up her slightly damp legs, and then tugged them over her hips. She stood barefoot in front of the mirrored closet in her bathroom, loving the tiny room's cozy feel and not the slightest bit envious of Malcolm's walk-in wardrobe. Especially since he seemed to have resorted to theft to fill it.

Once she'd pulled on her softest cotton socks, she sat on the couch to slide her feet into handmade butter-soft Italian leather boots, because living small didn't just mean living simply, it meant choosing quality over quantity. Finally, she shrugged into her down coat, armoring herself with warmth and an extra layer of protection before she walked down the steps into a place filled with more liars, thieves, plotters, and murderers than she could ever have imagined.

On the Oregon coast, sunset came with a sudden drop in temperature. When the cold outside air hit her smoke-bruised lungs, she started coughing and couldn't stop until she zipped her down jacket all the way up to her chin. Once the hacking eased, she tucked her hands into the jacket's deep pockets. The smell of smoke still lingered in the air, but the moist breeze snaking upriver from the Pacific would soon wash it clean. It would take much longer to wash away her fear.

All around her, the chirps, clicks, and hisses of insects rose from the forest and wetlands from which the park had been carved. She heard the sharp *peent* of a nighthawk hunting its evening meal. More than a few of those insect voices would be silenced before the hawk's hunger had been sated. An owl hooted: the first she'd noticed since arriving at the Haunted Wood. And, as Bev had promised, when night fell, she could hear the soothing voice of the ocean, singing its forever song.

Dust-to-dawn light fixtures on the park's buildings and at the end of each row of campsites cast puddles of soft light. She glanced toward C.J.'s site. No flames flickered in the fire ring tonight but a yellow light glowed inside his VW van. She was hungry. The light breakfast she'd had this morning had long since burned away, but instead of heading straight to the tea shop, she turned her steps toward the van. She rapped her knuckles against its flank, and, a few seconds later, the side panel door slid open.

"Let me get my jacket."

Either C.J. had read her mind again, or his own hunger matched her own. When he stepped down from the van, he gripped both of her hands, leaned toward her until his forehead touched hers.

"That curious mind of yours was almost the death of us today. Will you stop now?" He shrugged his shoulders and grimaced, as if feeling the pain of bruises inflicted by the shed's unyielding door.

Saffi stared into eyes shadowed with the same fear she knew must be haunting her own as she considered his question. "And let whoever tried to burn us alive get away with it? What do you think?"

C.J. chuckled. "I think I'd better buy fire insurance."

The locked shed. The stolen statue with its sticky, flaky residue. Evidence, she felt certain, that someone would not hesitate to kill and kill again. The danger she'd dragged them into felt closer than ever. "Do you have the falcon?"

C.J. nodded.

"And do postal inspectors travel with those handy-dandy blood-detecting gizmos CSIs carry around on TV shows?"

He lifted his blond brows. "This one does."

"And...?" She waited, arms wrapped against a chill that came from more than just the October evening air.

"And you were right. The falcon has traces of blood on it."

"We found the murder weapon!" Saffi bobbed up and down in excitement.

"Maybe." C.J. put a settling hand on her shoulder. "Let's keep that to ourselves for now, shall we? RVs burn faster than sheds."

Saffi knew that all too well. Last summer, an arsonist had set fire to a 40-foot coach. It had burned to a hulk in ten minutes flat. "My lips are locked."

C.J. rubbed his thumb across her mouth as if wondering what it might take to unlock them. *Not much,* Saffi realized as her toes lifted her closer to his level. A bubble of anticipation surrounded the moment, cutting them off from the world. Then... it burst.

"Dude!" Someone hooted from the next campsite.

Saffi's heels smacked into the ground and something that felt like middle-school first-kiss guilt made her glance around. Somehow, she hadn't noticed the gleaming Airstream in the next site. Colorful lights strung from its awning danced across the grinning faces of three bearded hipsters huddled beneath it. They lifted bottled brews in salute, the rolled-up sleeves of their flannel shirts showing off impressive tattoos.

C.J. gave the younger men a nod then linked his arm through hers. Now that she'd noticed the Airstream, she took a minute to scan the park. While she slept, it had started to fill. How had the noise not awakened her? The trauma seemed to have acted like a sleeping pill. The new rigs were varied and interesting. Three spaces down from C.J.'s site was a zeppelin-shaped trailer that looked like it might have landed instead of parked. On the back row at the edge of the forest, she spotted a compact Casita with a jaunty porthole in its door, and a vintage Terry trailer that reminded her so much of Delilah's tiny home she could have wept.

"The revelers have begun to arrive," C.J. said.

The RSVP-regrets Bev had shown her made her think

Malcolm's big bash would be a bust, but the Spooktacular was on! It might be a tiny bubble, like those burbling from an uncorked champagne bottle, but the party just might float.

TWENTY-EIGHT

As they stepped inside, the tea shop—which teemed with people—
went silent. Then Malcolm rose from the largest table, the one
they'd shared the night he wore the Oz jacket, and started clap-
ping. One by one, diners at various tables joined in, new—though
somehow naggingly familiar—faces beamed smiles as if she'd done
something special when all she'd done was sleuth herself and C.J.
into a wooden box surrounded by flame. Bev and Bob rose from
one of the small tables, faces unreadable until Bev lifted her wine
glass and tilted it toward Saffi. Bev met her eyes, but Bob looked
down, sneezing into the napkin that had been in his lap.

A voice echoed in her head. "Get the hose!" Then another:
"It's in the shed."

Saffi's nostrils flared, and she hardened her lips into a tight line.
But it wasn't, was it? She'd scanned the shed for a hose. Given
Lennie's neat-freak tendencies, it would have been easy to spot.
Bob's sneezes told her he was up to something, but if she wanted to
know what, she'd have to keep digging.

Saffi unzipped her coat and turned back to the table just as two
of Malcolm's companions rose to face her. One had henna-red
curls and blinged-out nails that flashed as she clapped. The other

had dark brown bangs that failed to hide the apology in his soft brown eyes.

Saffi burst into tears and ran into their arms.

"You're here! How are you here?" She sobbed into the gap between Delilah's and Glenn's shoulders, trying not to get snot on their clothes. She clutched at them, as if they were life preservers and she had been bobbing in the ocean for days with no help in sight.

Delilah stroked her hair. "It's OK. You're OK."

"I'm so sorry. So sorry," Glenn whispered. "I can be such a stupid spiteful bit—"

Saffi pulled back, then dragged the sleeve of her down jacket across her eyes and reached into her pocket for a tissue. When she couldn't find one in either pocket, someone handed her a cloth dinner napkin, and she honked carbon-black mucous into its folds. Crying her eyes out had released the mess clogging her sinuses, and her head felt clear for the first time since she'd emerged from the shed.

Delilah took the napkin and stuffed it into the pocket of her jean jacket. When Saffi tried to protest, she held up a hand. "What are best friends for?"

That set Saffi to blubbering again. It took a trip to the restroom, half a roll of toilet paper, and multiple paper towels to clean herself up enough to face the room again. Back at Malcolm's table, she found C.J. ensconced between Delilah and Glenn, both of them leaning toward him as if they were sunflowers and he was the sun at first light. Saffi chuckled. She couldn't blame them one bit.

"Saffi, darling! Sit!" Malcolm pulled out the empty chair between himself and a man Saffi didn't recognize, though his glasses, trim beard, and goatee reminded her of someone. Maybe one of Levi's colleagues at the university? The actor introduced him as Matt.

"And this lovely lady is Kelly Jo." Malcolm gave a little bow to the beautiful black woman seated between Glenn and Matt. Her shoulder-length hair, spiked bangs, and warm, slightly crooked smile made her look like a teenager, though the eye contact she made with Saffi showed the confidence of a much older woman.

"Saffi Graywood." Malcolm finished the introductions and resumed his seat.

"Matt. Kelly Jo," she repeated their names to help her remember as she smiled their way. "A pleasure to meet you both." Saffi shrugged out of her down coat and hung it off the back before starting to sit.

"We've been discussing the small issue of a misappropriated museum shipment," Malcolm continued.

Saffi's hip hit the edge of the seat instead of the middle and she flailed out a hand, grabbing hold of the table to keep herself from falling. Water and wine glasses rattled. Glenn saved his just before it spilled in his lap.

"I told Malcolm these things were better discussed in private, but..." C.J. shrugged and lifted his hands palm up. "Ever the showman."

Saffi centered her bottom firmly in the seat before giving Malcolm her full attention. "Do tell."

"Seems our Mr. Horseman isn't really a camper. He's a federal agent!" Malcolm wiggled his eyebrows and twirled the tips of his mustache like Hercule Poirot about to reveal the solution to a whodunit.

"Postal inspector." C.J. tapped the table then shook his pointer finger at the actor.

Of course, Delilah jumped right in, insisting that C.J. explain the role of a postal inspector and asking with her eyes if they were all as ruggedly handsome as he was. Glenn wanted to know if he'd come to the Haunted Wood in pursuit of Mr. Postcard Pants. Saffi shot him a look of dismay. Things had gotten way too serious to use the silly nickname they'd bandied about in the safety of the Last Chance Café.

"Not at all. Despite the fact that my *life* was threatened and I nearly *died* in a car crash," Malcolm cut in just as C.J. opened his mouth to answer, "our postal inspector has been hunting something else. A very valuable shipment went missing in transit, and—you won't believe this!" He reached toward Delilah's knee, but she blocked the move so quickly and effectively the actor couldn't fail to get the message: *This isn't Hollywood and I'm not a dewy-eyed starlet.*

"Ahumm." Malcolm cleared his throat to cover his embarrassment. "Apparently, C.J. has been helped by Saffi, our amateur sleuth who was *supposed* to be finding out who sent me those horrible postcards." His dark eyes slid Saffi's way. She returned the look, glare for glare. "They have located items from the stolen shipment right here in our very own Haunted Wood."

In your very own closet, Saffi seethed.

A throat cleared behind the actor, and he turned. "Ah! Thank you, Jyoti, dear." He spread his arms wide. "Dinner is served."

Jyoti's arrival relieved the tension that had been ratcheting up around the table since Malcolm began his exposition. She set a basket heaped with hot garlic naan glistening with ghee in the center of the table. Around the bread, she placed bowls of yellow dahl, potato chickpea masala, and spinach-green saag paneer. As they sampled the appetizers, the actor lost his audience to side conversations. Saffi asked Matt if he'd ever taught at Vermont College.

Matt laughed "The closest I've come to a professorship was playing a high school principal in a rom-com."

Saffi nearly choked on the bite of naan she'd just taken. "I'm sorry. I—"

Matt waved away her apology. "I get that a lot lately. It's either the glasses, or the goatee." He stroked his chin and posed.

"Does it drive you nuts? People thinking they know you but not making the connection."

"Completely understandable. I'm much smaller in real life than on a movie screen." His humble grin immediately put Saffi at ease, then he shifted the conversation to her search for the postcard perp. He even shared tips on amateur sleuthing he'd learned from a voice-acting gig, including, *Every sleuth needs a mystery-solving crew;* and *If you can't sniff out the culprit, have a snack.*

Kelly Jo, who had somehow managed to pull Glenn's attention away from C.J., glanced over her shoulder and whispered something that sounded like, "Ooby-ooby-oo." Saffi raised her brows, but Matt did an eye-roll and kept talking. By the time the main dishes arrived, they had formed a two-member amateur sleuthing club. It disbanded by unanimous consent when Jyoti started describing the supper delights Sunny had prepared for the table: shrimp poached in coconut milk, crispy nutty fish pakoras, and grilled salmon kabobs.

As dinner conversation died down, Malcolm took the opportunity to retake center stage with stories of his forays on the "dark web."

"In my experience, there is no easier place to find goodies." He used his napkin to dab coconut milk from his mustache. "I know, I know." He waved the napkin at Glenn to keep him from interrupting. "Some of the people on there are a bit shady."

Glenn snatched the napkin and threw it down on the table in front of the actor as if challenging him to a duel. "A bit? Malcolm. Stealing a postal shipment is a-a what, a federal crime?"

He glanced from Malcolm to C.J. and back.

"Exactly." C.J.'s jaw clenched.

Malcolm picked up his napkin and returned it to his lap. "Fortunately, Mr. Horseman understands that *I* had nothing to do with the theft. If I'm willing to return all of the items despite a not-insignificant monetary loss—and I am, I am—he's going to let me off with a hand slap. Isn't that right, C.J.?" The actor's hand trembled as he stabbed a fish pakora with his fork and lifted it to his mouth, evidence that his blasé attitude was all pose.

C.J. folded his hands and pressed his lips against them. "If the information you shared about the seller leads us to the thief, yes."

Apparently, while Saffi napped, C.J. had been busy. He had contacted his superiors who had contacted the Smithsonian.

Everyone was thrilled that the shipment would be reclaimed, and no one had any interest in pursuing the end buyer. They wanted the seller.

"There!" Malcolm smacked the table so hard it jumped. "Problem solved."

"Now, Saffi." He focused the dark, gleaming eyes she'd seen in way too many horror movies on her. "About those postcards."

She clenched her napkin tight enough to strangle Malcolm as she waited for him to berate her about her lack of progress. He didn't. Instead, he reached into his jacket pocket and pulled out an object that had become all too familiar: a postcard. When he handed it to her, she sucked in a breath. It wasn't a Willow Wood postcard. It was another Halloween postcard. The Historical Museum in Lincoln City must have been the source of the Willow Wood cards, exactly as she had deduced. Once the ones they had on hand were gone, the perp had resorted to vintage cards of a similar era. This one, like the last, had a Halloween theme: a boat on a river beneath a full moon. The ghastly crew of rowers had Jack-o-lantern heads and glowing yellow grins. The card's front read, "Have a Haunted Halloween!" The blood-red inscription on the other side sent a chill to Saffi's toes: *See you at the Spooktacular!*

If not for the string of threatening cards that had come before, this could have been a friendly note responding to Malcolm's invitation. Of course, a friend wouldn't have signed the card with a giant bloody X. Saffi put the postcard down on the table and wiped her hands on her napkin, just in case it really *was* blood.

She had just opened her mouth to tell Malcolm he needed to show this one to the sheriff when the tea shop door slammed open, and the man himself strutted inside. Two wary deputies trailed behind him, ogling the tea shop and the diners now frozen in silence. As the law officers scanned the room, Saffi secreted the postcard Malcolm had just given her in the pocket of the down coat hanging off the back of her chair.

Sheriff Raymond's eyes roamed the room before landing on the actor. "Malcolm Morton! Just the man I've been looking for." He walked across the room and slapped a folded document on the table in front of Malcolm.

"This so-called haunted RV park is a clear and present danger to nearby public and private properties, and I am shutting it down!"

TWENTY-NINE

As the sheriff tried to roust diners out of the tea shop, Saffi's fingers tightened on the edge of the table. She'd had enough of the local lawman's lackadaisical approach to law enforcement. "I would think you'd have better things to do," she seethed. "Like catching a murderer? Or an arsonist?"

The sheriff skewered her with a look meant to silence, but Saffi was fed up. She could have died today, but where was Sheriff Raymond? Colluding with a conniving wife who wanted the land? If Malcolm hadn't put a hand on her arm and leaned toward her, she'd have been on her feet.

"Never confront a snake head on," he whispered. "Plan a distraction so it's looking the other way. Then sneak up on it. Grab it behind the head, then snatch its tail before it can whip you off your feet." He winked. "That little tip came from a rattlesnake wrangler working the set of *Venom Vengeance*."

The master of movie madness had hit the viper on its triangular head. *A distraction.* Ideas bubbled up, but the one Saffi found herself most drawn to involved three suspects and their fingerprints. One of whom, if found guilty, would permanently distract Sheriff Raymond from his quest to close the Haunted Wood. Saffi patted Malcolm's hand, took her leave of her fellow diners, and crooked a finger at C.J.

"I need a favor," she said when he met her near the door.

"Will there be smoke inhalation involved?" C.J. teased.

"Probably not. But first you'll have to follow me back to my RV."

C.J.'s eyes darkened with feeling. "Count me in."

"Delilah, Glenn!" Saffi waved for her friends to follow. "This way!"

C.J.'s shoulders slumped. "Suckered again."

They gathered jackets, bags, and—in Glenn's case—a to-go box of leftovers he'd begged from Jyoti, and headed outside. On the short walk, Saffi had questions.

"Malcolm seemed surprised when he saw the falcon statuette in the shed."

"Falcon? What falcon?" Delilah asked.

Saffi explained about the Maltese Falcon as they strolled toward her RV. Her friends could barely contain their excitement. Saffi had to shush them before the entire campground discovered the whereabouts of the valuable black bird.

C.J., who was walking a few steps behind, cleared his throat. "Malcolm claims it was stolen from his loft."

Saffi stopped so fast he almost ran into her. "And he didn't report it because...?"

From the way he pinched the top of his nose and closed his eyes, Saffi could tell that C.J. was more than a little fed up with Malcolm Morton.

"Malcolm's an expert on movie memorabilia," he reminded them. "If the items he claims to have purchased weren't hot, they'd have been sold individually, at auction. Probably through Sotheby's. *Not* on the dark web."

Glenn clicked his tongue. "The old rascal. I thought he was flamboyant, not felonious."

"Who has the falcon now?" Delilah asked.

"It's safe," C.J. answered without giving out any details, but

Saffi understood. If she had a multimillion-dollar bird in her possession, she wouldn't tell a soul where it was hidden.

With those nagging questions cleared up, Saffi tucked her arms through Delilah's on one side and Glenn's on the other. "And how is it that the two of you managed to show up right when I needed you?"

"Honey, we've been on the road since the morning you called me." Delilah snorted.

Saffi remembered the sound of tires on wet pavement when she'd called her friend the day before yesterday. "You said you weren't driving!"

"I wasn't." She peered around Saffi to tilt her chin at Glenn. "He was."

They had planned to burst on the scene, yell "Surprise!" and immediately demand a guided tour of the Haunted Wood. Instead, they'd found Saffi napping and been forbidden to wake her, thanks to her recent near-death by flaming shed.

Glenn finished the apology he'd started earlier, complete with the entire "b" word he'd called himself. Saffi told him she would only forgive him if he never called himself or anyone else that again. His soft brown eyes sparkled with amusement as he locked his lips with an invisible key, then immediately unlocked them again.

"Saffi Graywood, you are the most forgiving bit—"

Delilah put a fingertip to his lips. "Stop running your mouth like a bathhouse toilet before she changes her mind."

Saffi's chest swelled with something that felt a lot like love. Having them here gave her exactly the lift she needed to regain her confidence. With their help, she would kick the postcard perp back into whatever hole he—or she—had crawled out of. She unlocked the door of her Rambler Trek and ushered everyone up the stairs, eager to share her plan.

After shedding boots and coats, Delilah and Glenn squeezed C.J. between them on the couch like a very tasty clam.

"Be right back." Saffi dug the postcard Malcolm had handed

her earlier from the pocket of her down coat as she cut through the bathroom to her bedroom. She tossed her coat on the bed, then rummaged through her sling pack for three small white cards. Back in the living room, she turned the captain's chair around to face her guests. She stretched her Merino wool tunic to her knees, sat down on the cushioned seat, and got down to business.

"The postcards Malcolm gave me in Last Chance Cove have been handled by too many people too many times. There is little to no chance of getting a decent print off them." She glanced at C.J., who nodded. "But this card," she held up the one that promised, or threatened, to meet the actor at the Spooktacular, "wasn't mailed. It was hand-delivered to the park office." She flipped it over to show that the card bore no postmark. "I'm thinking that ups the odds of finding a good print." She lifted her eyebrows toward C.J.

He tilted his head. "Possibly. But unless the person is in the national database we won't find a match."

Saffi spread the three business cards across her lap. "True. But if the prints on the postcard matches a print on one of these, we just might have our perp."

"Ooh!" Delilah and Glenn both scooched forward to get a better look, effectively squishing C.J. tighter between them. The postal inspector unzipped his jacket and mansprawled, trying to reclaim his space.

Was that sweat on his forehead? Saffi repressed a smile.

When C.J. held out a hand for the cards, she hesitated. Did she really want to do this? Risk a schism after he had helped her, shown her more respect than any other law enforcement officer so far? By giving him the business cards, she would be disclosing the three people who were at the top of her suspects list. One of them would not make him happy. She gave him an apologetic look as she handed him the cards.

He glanced at the top two cards but when he reached the third, he bolted to his feet, face grim. "Tell me you're kidding."

Delilah and Glenn flattened themselves against the couch cushions, their faces a mix of surprise and confusion.

Saffi stood to face C.J. and put a hand on his arm. "I'm hoping to rule her out."

He shook her hand off and stepped away. "You're playing with lives here, Saffi. If I put these into the system and people's lives get destroyed, you won't face the consequences, they will."

Saffi flinched. *Glenn was right. You just keep digging and digging...* Malcolm's accusation rang in her ears. A hot rush of emotion washed over her. Defensiveness. Embarrassment. Remorse. But she hadn't done anything wrong, had she? Saffi lifted her head.

"C.J. Someone *is* playing with lives, but it's not me. It's the person who sent those cards. Lennie was murdered. Malcolm and Sunny could have been badly injured in that car wreck. You and I?" She clutched the sleeve of his jacket and stared past the betrayal in his eyes to find the common ground of their shared near-death experience. "If the person who sent those cards shows up at the Spooktacular, determined to kill again, and-and I haven't done everything I could. I couldn't live with that. Could you?" She held his gaze, but his anger did not soften. Instead, he shoved the business cards into a coat pocket and headed for the door.

"If you think my daughter could kill someone, you're a piss-poor judge of character. And it looks like I am, too."

"C.J., I—" He was out the door before she could plead for understanding.

On a normal night in Last Chance Cove, Saffi, Delilah, and Glenn would have stayed up talking till the foghorn lulled one of them to sleep. This was not a normal night. The tension left in C.J.'s wake and the reason for his reaction, which they'd demanded she share, left Glenn reeling. Saffi wasn't sure if he would explode or collapse.

Ever the peacemaker, Delilah pulled herself up from the couch and clapped. "I, for one, am exhausted." She glanced down at Glenn, hoping he'd stand as well. "Archie won't forgive us if we stay out past his bedtime." She nudged his foot. "Come on."

"Archie's here?" Just the thought of the saucy white terrier—

former service dog, current pampered pet—brought a smile to Saffi's face. Since she'd saved the terrier from the sneaker wave that swept his owner's body into the sea last summer, she was almost guaranteed doggy kisses. She could use a bit of affection right now, and Archie might be the only one willing to give it.

She was wrong. When Glenn finally stood, he moved toward her, took her hand, and then pulled her into a hug. "This sleuthing business isn't for wimps, is it?" Saffi felt tears rising and tried to blink them back. "I get it now."

"What?" Saffi sniffed.

"How much courage it takes to do the right thing. Last summer, I didn't have it, but you did. For Malcolm's sake, I hope C.J.'s as courageous as you are, my friend."

THIRTY

First thing next morning, she got a faceful of Archie kisses, along with an invitation to join Delilah and Glenn on an early-morning trail walk. Her lungs ached from yesterday's ordeal, but her heart ached even more. The look on C.J.'s face when he stormed out of her RV had kept her awake for hours. He had been furious. For all she knew, he had tossed the business cards she gave him on a campfire on the way to his van. If he had, her fingerprint plan had gone up in flames.

"Saffi!" Delilah snapped her fingers. "If those worry lines on your face get any deeper you're going to trip over them. Let's walk!"

Delilah led them past the tea shop to a crooked signpost that read *Trail of Terrors*.

"Malcolm swears this trail will scare the pants off visitors." Delilah led them into the shadows beneath the trees.

Like much of the mischief Malcolm got up to, Saffi wasn't sure a terrifying trail was a good idea. Maybe the sheriff was right. A life spent enacting onscreen horrors might have blurred the line between what was acceptable in movies but forbidden—or an actual crime—in real life. Maybe out here in the coastal Oregon woods, Malcolm Morton *was* a menace.

In response to Delilah's "scare your pants off" comment, Glenn gave an exaggerated cinch to the thick black leather belt holding up his white jeans. His boyish grin helped ease the last bit of awkwardness between them.

"Careful," she warned. "Those jeans already look tight enough to do permanent damage."

Before the last word was out of her mouth, Archie started growling. Saffi whirled in the direction his nose pointed. A few seconds later, he almost pulled his leash out of Delilah's hand as he charged beneath a rhododendron. Before she could stop him, Archie sank his teeth into the furry leg of—

"Bigfoot!" Delilah swooped back a leaf-laden branch. "I knew you were hanging with these guys instead of me!" She wagged a finger at Saffi.

Archie tugged so hard the eight-foot ape-man hidden behind the screen of spindly green shrubs tumbled like a felled tree.

"If Bigfoot falls in the forest and there's no one around to hear it..." Saffi murmured.

Glenn's eyes went wide. "Was he really there at all?"

"See no Bigfoot. Hear no Bigfoot. Come on Arch!" Delilah tugged him out of the bushes. "We've got miles to go before we eat."

The rest of the walk went about the same. Archie barked. One of Malcolm's creatures lost a terrier-sized mouthful of fluff, scale, or hide. The trail wiggled and wound past Douglas firs and Sitka spruce, the Creature from the Black Lagoon and the Mummy. Ferns, moss, and mushrooms sprouted from fallen trees. So did a motion-sensitive witch's hand and a chomping Venus flytrap.

They ducked out of the woods at trail's end laughing about the bone Archie had ripped from a dangling skeleton. He refused to drop it and carried it clutched between his canines as proudly as a wolf who'd brought down its own prey.

"What a mighty hunter you are, I—" Saffi looked up from feeding Archie's ego and stopped mid-sentence. None of Malcolm's horrors had zapped fear into Saffi's heart. But when she saw where the trail had taken them, her heart skipped as if it had been jolted with electricity.

"Oh, honey!" Delilah put an arm around her shoulders. "Is that… is that where it happened?"

Saffi wanted to turn back into the forest where the fake demons dwelled, but her friend's sturdy hug held her in place.

"Just look at that!" Malcolm rounded the building with Bob in tow. The bejeweled tail of the actor's Goblin King robe flared out behind him as he shook his fist. At first, Saffi thought the fist was aimed at her, but he put his hands on his hips and faced the shed instead. "Do you see?"

Saffi squinted. Damage to the shed seemed minimal. Blackened boards showed where the flames had shot up one side, not surrounding the whole building as she'd imagined while trapped within. Beyond that, Saffi had no clue what Malcolm wanted Bob to see.

After failing to elicit a response, the actor lifted his arms skyward, either showing off his robe's long flared sleeves or directing Bob's gaze—and theirs—toward the shed's metal roof.

"Bird poop! All along the ridge. It's acidic." Malcolm dropped his dramatic pose, turned to Bob, and started issuing orders. "The ladder's in the shed. You need to clean that off before it burns through the metal."

Bob folded his arms and shook his head. "I'm a park manager, not a groundskeeper."

"Bob." The actor folded his hands as if pleading. "Be reasonable. The Spooktacular is *tomorrow*. You need to pitch in and do whatever it takes to make it happen."

"Hold on a minute, pardner!" Glenn stepped forward, thumbs tucked into his thick black belt, looking more like Sheriff Raymond than a shorter, far more stylish man should ever be able to do. "You all can't be having some fancy-pants Spooktacular here. I shut this place down, remember?"

"Pish tosh." Malcolm swept his right arm sideways, nearly

taking out Bob's eye with the pointed tip of his flared sleeve. "The Spooktacular will go on!"

Glenn looked perplexed. "How?"

"Lawyers, my love." Malcolm tweaked his friend's youthful cheeks. "Lots and lots of high-priced lawyers."

Half of Saffi's brain paid attention to their banter; the other half was stuck on the words "acidic" and "poop." She touched her cheek. *Remember*, Raven had whispered. The nightmare of something falling on her cheek and burning through to bone came back in full force. So did her memory of what happened as the shed started to burn. The cormorants had arrived, croaking a warning she'd been too slow to heed. *What next?* A deep breath helped Saffi remember. It also brought back yesterday's hacking cough. Delilah gave her a helpful slap on the back.

The cormorants had landed on the roof before the shed door slammed shut. Once the fire was set and smoke began to rise, the birds had shrieked, lifted off, and flown into the distance. All of that had happened *before* help arrived.

The dream burn was cormorant poop. *Gross*, but helpful, since only one person was outside the shed when the birds took flight: the person who set the fire. Traces of bird poop on clothing couldn't simply be washed away. The acidic drops would discolor the cloth. The sea ravens had gifted her a clue to the arsonist's identity. She could wait around for a suspect to show up wearing a telltale garment. Or she could con her way into the closet of the one person who could have unlocked the shed but didn't: Bev.

Yesterday had taught her a lesson she would not soon forget. Before going after her prey, she told Delilah and Glenn exactly where she was going and why.

"If you're not back in two shakes of a turkey's tailfeathers, we're coming in after you." Delilah gave her the squint eye.

Since the day Saffi arrived at the Haunted Wood, she'd had C.J.'s badge behind her. If she'd lost his confidence and support for good, there was no one she'd rather have at her back than Delilah Dunsmore.

. . .

"Just a minute!" Bev's voice sounded welcoming. But when she opened the door of her Jayco, her pale blue eyes iced faster than a windshield in a bomb cyclone.

"I was wondering if we could—" Smoke inhalation had left Saffi's voice raspy. She hacked into her hand to clear it. "Talk," she finished. "About what happened yesterday."

Bev stepped down from the trailer, forcing Saffi to back away from the door. So much for conning her way into closets.

"I know what you're thinking," Bev said. "I could have let you out of that shed, and I didn't. But you're wrong. After you called Malcolm, he dragged me out of the office without telling me what was happening. If I'd known, I would have brought the keys with me."

Saffi narrowed her eyes. "Would you? If it meant Malcolm would know you had access to the museum? To his loft?"

Bev stepped toward Saffi, fists clenched. She'd gotten used to how tall the park manager was, but, this close, her height felt far more intimidating.

"What do you think he'd say if I told him *you* had those keys. Used them to poke around in his stuff when he was away." She poked Saffi's chest to emphasize her point.

Some people thought tai chi forms like the ones Saffi practiced were simply for relaxation. Saffi knew otherwise. One waving-cloud hand later, Bev knew it too.

"Malcolm knows more than you think." Saffi released the hand she'd trapped against Bev's side. "And so do I."

Since Bev wasn't in the mood to cough up a confession, and C.J. wasn't likely to run those prints, Saffi made a quick call. Then she tracked down Delilah. She found her outside her trailer, sticking on a set of Halloween-themed press-on nails.

"Let me see!"

Delilah wiggled her fingertips beneath Saffi's nose. Each nail featured a mummy's wide eyes peeking out of its face wraps. Some mummies looked one way, some another. The effect was far more comical than creepy. "Looks like you're ready for the Spooktacular."

"Are you kidding? These are my everyday spooky nails. I'm saving the spectacular bling for tomorrow night."

Saffi chuckled, which made her cough for long enough to bring a furrow to Delilah's forehead. "Sorry. Smoke." She coughed once more, then sucked in a breath. "How would you like to explore offgrounds a bit?" she asked. "There's a place a few miles from here you shouldn't miss."

Delilah snorted, then pressed her right pointer finger to the center of her forehead. "The all-seeing eye tells me that the questioner wishes to follow a clue beyond these grounds. Hmmm..." Her lips vibrated so hard Saffi laughed. "But the questioner cannot do that unless a glamorous, though unsuspecting, redhead agrees to drive her."

"OK. You got me. But the place I need to go is genuinely gorgeous. Where's Glenn? He shouldn't miss this either."

"Oh, Honey. Glenn is a man on a mission."

"A mission?" Saffi made gimme motions with her hands.

Delilah obliged. "He was spiraling over whether the costume he brought with him was too Last Chance Cove for the Spooktacular. The last time I saw him he was sizing up costumes in the museum."

Saffi covered her mouth with one hand. "We'll never get him out of there."

Delilah pressed the "all-seeing eye" against her forehead. "It is decidedly so."

A few minutes later, Delilah's small red car bumped along the gravel road that lead into and out of the Haunted Wood. They passed one Malcolm-faced balloon after another, sagging toward the ground as the helium leaked out.

"Are those super creepy, or is it just me?" Delilah ducked her head to peer through the windshield.

"Definitely not just you."

When they reached the end of the drive, Delilah stopped talking to gauge the approaching traffic, then turned right onto Highway 101.

"It's not far." Saffi warned her. "The first left past the wetlands."

Seconds later, Delilah flipped up the turn signal and made a left onto Three Rocks Road. They took a right at the Sitka sign and wound up the narrow lane through the trees. As the car's red nose came out of the shadows, sunlight danced across the hood and up the windshield, dazzling their eyes. When her pupils adjusted, Saffi spotted one of the things she'd hoped to show Delilah. Elk dotted the hillside, their velvety noses to the ground as they munched their way through the grass.

"Turn here." Saffi pointed to the Sitka driveway.

"I don't know what kind of clue would lead you here, but... wowzers!"

Delilah braked the car so fast Saffi's seat belt stiffened. The barista grabbed her cell and jumped out to take pictures. She got back in, turned into the driveway, drove about twenty feet, then hopped out again. She repeated the routine every twenty feet as they crept up the hill. Saffi folded her hands, unfolded them, tapped her boots against the floorboard, and prayed for the patience that so often alluded her. She had called ahead to make sure Mere would be here, but, at this rate, they'd'reach the office after the sun went down. On the other hand, she'd conned Delilah into driving her with a promise of gorgeous views. So gorgeous views she would have.

Mere wasn't in the office when they arrived. Instead, a beefy thirty-something man with dark shoulder-length hair and a broad smile welcomed them inside.

"I'm here to see Mere." Saffi glanced around the warm, wood-paneled office as if expecting C.J.'s daughter to materialize.

"She's in the ceramics studio." The man stood as if ready to lead the way.

"I know where it is, but my friend hasn't visited. I don't suppose you could—"

"Show her around?" The man moved around the desk. "I can't think of anything better to do with my morning."

Saffi left a smiling Delilah and her eager escort outside the office door and headed up the stairs to the studio. She found Mere inside, carefully loading a massive kiln with pieces ready to fire.

"Hang on a sec." Mere bit her lower lip as she positioned a serene-faced mask on a shelf inside the kiln. As she backed away, her shoulders relaxed, and she wiped chalky hands on her canvas apron. When she turned toward Saffi, her moss-green eyes shone the way her father's did when he was trying to puzzle her out. "I reserved a block of time to fire these, so I have to finish loading while we talk, is that OK?"

Saffi hesitated. If one of her questions caused Mere to drop one of her amazing pieces, she would never forgive herself.

Mere chuckled. "Something tells me I'd better stop for a few."

Was reading minds in the Horseman DNA?

Mere pulled two wooden bar stools from beneath a roughhewn counter, their metal furniture-glides scraping the concrete floor. The counters, Saffi noticed, were lined with white clay masks and birds and whimsical conveyances awaiting their turn in the kiln.

"I'll be quick. I promise."

And she was, within the space of a few minutes she had described the photo Bev had taken and learned that Mere had, indeed, waved a paddle as she passed the dock on her way home from work one evening. Her full lips curved into a smile. "Bev loves taking silos. Says the mystery of not knowing who is in the photo allows every viewer to create a different story around the subject."

Bev wasn't wrong about that. Saffi had created two stories about the twilight kayaker as she tried to unravel the mystery of Lennie's murder. One cast Mere as the villain. The other revealed her to be a witness. Was either story true? Saffi had no idea.

"How well do you know Bev?" Saffi couldn't help remembering what Bev had told her when she asked if the paddler was a friend. *Not really.*

Mere drummed her fingers on the wooden counter, then picked up a wad of white clay and started kneading it between her palms. Saffi recognized impatience when she saw it, but Mere wasn't impatient; she was kinesthetic. Touch, movement, the feel of cold clay on her palms, seemed to help her remember.

"Truthfully...?" Mere rounded the clay into a ball. "I'm artsy. She's artsy. We talked a time or two. Then she banned me from the park." The artist grinned. "I suppose my sign-waving felt like an attack against her livelihood." Mere blew her strawberry-blond bangs off her forehead. "I don't hold it against her or anything. But, that day, I wasn't waving to Bev. I didn't see her. I saw Bob. He was wrestling that Black Lagoon creature of Malcolm's into the water."

The knowledge jolted Saffi. She'd seen that creature on the forest trail a few hours ago. Could Mere have mistaken what she'd seen for a prop? Something like, a body? Her brows creased. "You're sure it was the creature?"

"Sure as I need to be." Her mouth set in a line, and her green eyes flashed. "I told Bob to get that thing out of there before I reported him to Fish and Game. You can't just dump movie props into the river. Can you believe it? He said Malcolm *told* him to put that thing in there. Someone needs to teach that man a thing or two about protecting the environment."

Someone, being you? Saffi tried to school the judgment from her face.

"How long ago did this happen?"

Mere molded and pinched and smoothed the clay until her clever fingers shaped it into an exact replica of the lagoon creature's spiny fish head. The artist picked up a rag and wiped white clay from her hands, then shrugged. "A few days. Maybe a week? I'm not sure. I tend to lose track of days when I'm sculpting."

A chill ran along Saffi's spine. If Mere's creature sighting happened *before* Lennie's body was found, instead of after, Saffi's suspicions might have landed on the wrong end of the paddle.

THIRTY-ONE

The visit to Mere left Saffi more certain than ever that C.J.'s daughter had nothing to do with Lennie's murder. She wanted to strike the artist off her suspect list once and for all, but unless C.J. ran those prints and cleared her, she couldn't. Mere was an environmental activist. She had protested against the park and been banned by Bev. When sign-waving didn't work, she could have resorted to postcard threats to scare the actor into changing his plans. The next time Saffi saw C.J., she would insist that he have the cards checked. Unless, of course, he'd already burned the evidence.

If she could eliminate Mere from her list of suspects, Cecily Raymond would move to the top. The real estate developer had the strongest motive for scaring the actor into closing down the park. *Loot, loot, and more loot.* Bev, on the other hand, looked less and less like a suspect. If she had banned Mere to protect her job, she had no motive for sending the postcards.

Bob? Could he be the postcard perp? Almost every time she ran into him, Bob railed against Malcolm's "unreasonable expectations." But the most egregious demands had happened *after* Lennie's death. Like his wife, Bob needed the Haunted Wood to remain open, so much so that she could believe his story about planting the creature in the river. And if he hated the grunt work he was doing now, why would he kill the groundskeeper?

Motives, Saffi. Concentrate on motives. When she did, her thoughts popped right back to Cecily.

As Delilah turned from Three Rocks Road onto Highway 101, Saffi's head came up. "Is that honking?" She squinted into the distance, trying to figure out what was causing the sudden hullabaloo. Tiny car horns with reedy voices. Massive semi-trucks with booming basses. Blasts and burps and everything in between transformed the tranquil stretch of road into a cacophony of sound.

"Lord help my soul and body." Delilah clutched the steering wheel. "What is going on?"

It soon became evident: a line of RVs coming from the south had shut down the highway in both directions as drivers tried to maneuver their rigs into the narrow entrance to the Haunted Wood.

Saffi scooted forward in her seat. "How will we ever get back in there?"

A few minutes later, they heard the frenetic *whoop-whoop-whoop* of sirens.

"Uh-oh. The po-po is coming." Delilah took her hands off the steering wheel and let the Jetta's engine idle. "You didn't bring snacks, did you?"

Three police cars and the sheriff's SUV whooped along the wrong side of the highway and parked crosswise, blocking the southbound lane. Saffi hadn't seen so many flashing reds and blues since she'd driven through LA on her way north from Temecula last spring.

"We're definitely going to need snacks." Delilah opened the glove box and lifted the car registration. "See anything?"

Saffi couldn't see much, but the smell that wafted out was whiffy. "Beach agates. Shells. Sand. Is that a crab leg? Ooh." Saffi pressed her hand over her nose and her back into the seat.

"Oops. I wrestled that thing away from Archie the other day.

Forgot I'd tossed it in there." Saffi held her breath until Delilah gave up the hunt and slammed the glove box shut.

As her attention returned to the road, Saffi spotted a yellow-and-white camper van on the opposite side. "There's C.J.!" She opened the door. Had he cooled down since last night? Or would he tell her to stuff it if she asked for help? There was only one way to find out.

"Saffi Graywood!" Delilah tried to reach across her to grab the door handle. "If you abandon me in this mess I will—"

"I would never! I have a plan." Before Delilah could stop her, Saffi jumped out. She leaned into the Jetta before she slammed the door shut. "I'll get us in there. I promise."

Without gridlock damming the flow of traffic, Saffi would never have dared to dart across the 101. On straightaways like this, semis regularly flattened animals into unidentifiable grease spots. Right now, the only vehicles moving were the RVs Sheriff Raymond directed into the Haunted Wood. Those who couldn't manage the turn got an arm whirl, a pointed finger, and a scowl that said "move on or face the consequences." Saffi had no idea where he expected them to go, but she imagined at least some of them would end up waiting out the traffic jam in the lot beside the burned-out Otis Café.

When C.J. was a single vehicle away from the entrance, Saffi scooted across the road and jogged up to his driver's side door. He refused to roll down the window, so she begged him to help through the glass.

"Just distract Sheriff Raymond for a minute or two, OK?"

C.J. scowled as if she'd drained his reserves of good will, but his innate chivalry seemed to kick in. He motioned her away, got out of the van, and stomped over to the sheriff.

"Hey, Ray! I've seen monkeys direct traffic better. Want me to lend a hand?"

"Back off, Charley Horse!" the sheriff bellowed and charged toward C.J. like one of the bull elks she'd seen on her first evening at the Haunted Wood. C.J. immediately raised his hands in surrender.

"Chill out, Ray. Just trying to help."

The hubbub distracted the sheriff as Saffi had hoped, but it was not as easy-peasy, lemon-squeezy as she'd pictured when she came up with the idea. Before it was all over, both Delilah and C.J. ended up with citations. She was sure Sheriff Raymond would have written her up as well if he hadn't been called away to break up a brawl between an RV driver and a long-haul trucker.

Despite the fine Delilah now owed, she was impressed that they'd made it into the park ahead of the rest of the traffic jam. When she pulled the Jetta nose to nose with her Terry trailer, she lifted her hand for a high five, then offered to buy lunch.

"No way. Lunch is on Malcolm," Saffi countered. "And if I have anything to do with it, he'll be paying that fine as well."

Delilah grinned. "You go girl!"

Once they got out of the car, a whine from inside the trailer diverted Delilah's attention. "Archie's been cooped up long enough. I'd better take him for a walk before we eat."

Saffi nodded. "There's something I need to do first anyway." When it came to the postcards, Bev and Bob might be in the clear, but she couldn't shake what she'd overhead Bob tell Bev during the fire. He'd said that the hose was in the shed. The claim had been followed by a few telltale sneezes. He'd lied. The hose was not in the shed. Saffi had scanned the shed for it before Malcolm led her away. She needed to get into their trailer. Search the closets. If she found outerwear scarred by cormorant poop, she'd have evidence to put Bob at the scene of the fire at the exact moment it had been set.

Before heading to the Jayco, she did a quick circuit of the park buildings. She spotted Bob scouring the roof of the shed and waved. He did not return the wave and the reason was clear: he clung to the roof with one hand and the scrub brush with the other. The look on his face was a mix of terror, disgust, and rage. She didn't think Bob was behind the postcard threats. But if he was?

Malcolm Morton was pushing his luck. She circled back to the office and spied Bev through the window, checking in campers as rigs streamed into the park.

Saffi had just the opening she needed, and C.J.'s van was parked in its spot again. Would he help? Maybe. If a search of the Joneses' trailer provided a "get out of jail free" card for his daughter.

It had been refreshing to have a lawman supporting her sleuthing ability, but she'd lost C.J.'s trust. If she didn't regain it now, she probably never would. The knowledge started her feet marching toward his site and her mouth moving before he could storm away.

"I know you're mad. I get it. But I've been working all morning to cross Mere off my list."

C.J. clenched his jaw. "You can do that right now because she doesn't have a criminal bone in her body."

Saffi folded her arms across her chest. "She does, however, have a stash of protest signs and a walloping big motive."

He mirrored her closed posture. "That's quite a leap. From waving a sign to sending threats through the mail. Do you have a single piece of evidence to connect my daughter to those postcards?"

"I don't know." She skewered him with her eyes. "Do I?"

He knew exactly what she was talking about. "I sent the cards, OK? All of them, because, unlike *you*, I know my little girl's prints aren't going to show up on that postcard."

Clearly, he was still livid, but he'd done what she'd asked. Relief washed over Saffi.

"Saffi," he leaned forward until his weathered face was inches from hers, "this isn't a TV show where results come back between commercial breaks."

She knew that. She also knew some businesses could do finger-print checks in 24 to 48 hours. Surely the postal inspector's office could beat Whataburger's turnaround time.

"Fine. While we wait, I have some fresh information that

implicates Bob. I need to search his trailer for corroborating evidence."

"Do you even know what that is?"

Saffi put her hands on her hips. "Of course I do. It means something to back up information I've gathered." She told him about the missing hose that Bob had claimed was inside the shed.

C.J. stiffened. "Are you sure?"

"I'm sure. That, combined with Bev snatching the keys away from me the minute I mentioned exploring the shed, tells me the Joneses are up to something." She debated sharing her biggest reason for wanting to get into that Jayco: Raven's warning. Anything that smacked of "women's intuition" put a lot of men off. Detective Richards had understood about Raven, but he was Tolowa Dee-ni'.

C.J.'s tapping foot told her he was waiting for a more compelling excuse for invading Bev and Bob's space. Saffi threw caution to the wind and shared. Raven. The cormorants. The fact that he'd called them "sea ravens" which made her pay attention. The birds calling out before the shed door locked. Landing on the roof. The dream. The burn. The acidic poop. His brow furrowed. He crossed his arms. He shook his head. He rubbed a hand across his mouth, then he nodded.

"This might surprise you, but law enforcement relies on more than science and technology. The best officers share one quality."

"What's that?"

"Gut instinct. Everyone has it, but too many officers ignore it. You were suspicious of me from the get-go, and rightly so." His mouth quirked in a grin.

When he offered his lock-picking skills to get her into the Jayco, Saffi knew the lawman was back on her side.

"Five minutes," he cautioned, and she knew he was right. The longer she stayed inside the trailer, the bigger the chance Bev or Bob would notice C.J. prowling around and become suspicious. "I'll knock when it's time."

Once inside, Saffi headed straight for the master bedroom. She tore through the closet searching for an outer garment with the tell-tale evidence of bird poop. When she didn't find anything, she raced to the bathroom. She dug through the laundry basket, grimacing when all she found were socks, undies, sweatshirts, and Henleys. Not a single garment had bird poop on it.

Frustrated, she scanned the room for clues. The Joneses were up to something. What? The bathroom's cloying fake-flower scent brought on the hacking cough she'd suffered sporadically since the fire. She traced the smell to a basket packed like a packrat's nest with fancy soaps and bath bombs. She picked up a black bomb shaped like a rose and sniffed.

"Rose petals and lemongrass," Saffi whispered. What had Jyoti said about items going missing? Mugs. Fancy soaps. Books. Her grandfather's knife.

She stuffed the bath bomb into a pocket of her hoodie and hurried back to the bedroom. After pulling out a few drawers, she found one stuffed with gaudy souvenirs from parks across the country. Among the miniature spoons, keychains, and fridge magnets, she found a silver and mother-of-pearl penknife from a place called "Surfer's Paradise." Saffi stuffed it into her pocket as well. Maybe Sunny could identify the knife.

Rising indignation drove her through the rest of the trailer. Above the kitchen counter, she found a cabinet bursting with coffee mugs. She spotted a "Georgia on My Mind" mug beside a "California Dreamin'" cup. Plenty of RVers collected souvenir mugs from every area they visited, but RV cabinet space was too limited to allocate an entire cabinet to them. Especially when many of the mugs had other people's names. She found "Tina & Randy 4ever" on a wedding-themed mug and "Patricia's Brew" on the front of a cauldron-shaped mug. She also found a mug that read, *Oh. Em. Ghee.*

"Jyoti," Saffi whispered, remembering the favorite mug the young woman had told her was missing.

Behind the mug that clearly belonged to Jyoti, she found a cup that made her heart clench: the raven mug made by her artist friend back in Last Chance Cove. Saffi set the mugs side by side on the counter. None of the evidence she'd found proved that Bob had started the fire or dumped Lennie's body into the river. It proved something completely different: one of the Joneses was a complete klepto.

When C.J. knocked on the door to warn her that time was up, she took the two mugs she'd left on the counter: hers and Jyoti's. If Bev and Bob noticed, she hoped they'd get the message: *I know your secret.*

THIRTY-TWO

C.J. took one look at the fire in Saffi's eyes and knew she'd found something that had truly ticked her off. He took the mugs from her hands with a question in his eyes, but before she could explain, Delilah strolled up and tapped him on the shoulder. When he turned her way, she lifted her cell and snapped a picture. She held up her phone to show a pair of panicked sleuths. One with two mugs in his hands, one with frazzled hair and frantic eyes.

"Joining us for lunch?" Delilah tucked her phone in the back pocket of her jeans as if she hadn't just done something seriously stalkery.

"Uhm...? Sure. I just need to—" C.J. held up the mugs and glanced toward his van. The mugs would be as safe there as in her own rig, so Saffi nodded her OK. "See you in a few."

Once C.J. left, Saffi nudged her friend with her shoulder. "What's up with the pic?"

Delilah bared her teeth like an angry Archie. "Troy needs to see what he's up against. Swanning off to Texas like that. *Hmphf.*"

Saffi crinkled her brow in a frown. "Troy who?"

The shocked look on Delilah's face made Saffi burst out laughing. The pair lapsed into giggle fits as Saffi tried to wrestle Delilah's phone out of her back pocket, and her friend turned in circles trying to stop her.

"Truce!" Delilah stopped spinning and held up a hand as she tried to regain her balance.

"Troy hasn't messaged me a single time since he left for Texas." Saffi shrugged, then linked arms so the two of them could stagger to the tea house without falling on their faces. "And C.J. is all business."

Delilah snorted. "All business? And you call yourself a sleuth. *Mmm-mmm.*"

Well, maybe not all business, given how close they'd come to kissing once or twice. But if she shared that tidbit with Delilah, she would definitely message the photo to Troy. That, Saffi did not want. As they approached the Little Tea Shop of Horrors, Saffi was surprised to find a line outside. When the group of newbies in front of them started taking turns sticking their heads inside the Venus flytrap's mouth for snapshots, Saffi spotted Jyoti and waved. Jyoti returned the wave with a "come here" gesture.

"Let's go!" Saffi took Delilah's hand to hurry her along.

"Ooh! Friends with benefits," Delilah gushed.

When Jyoti blushed, Saffi rolled her eyes. "Don't worry. She means connections."

The swamped server ushered them to the table by the front window, slapped menus in front of them, then tapped a pen on her order pad as she waited. They chose a CharBOOterie Board for sharing and a Blobster Roll each after Jyoti swore they were made with lobster, not blobfish. Saffi had written about the jelly-bodied deep sea fish for her fifth *Bedside Reader.* "Blobby" had been voted World's Ugliest Animal in an online poll.

"Before you go, does this look familiar?" Saffi pulled the penknife out of her pocket and Joyti almost dropped her pad.

"Where did you find that?" she demanded.

"Not here," Saffi whispered. "Is it Sunny's?"

When the server reached for the penknife, Saffi shook her head. "Sorry. It's evidence. I'll explain later."

Jyoti stalked away with even more spice in her step than usual. Saffi could almost hear the wheels turning in her head as she tried to figure out who might have stolen her grandfather's penknife. *Welcome to my world, kiddo!*

"What was that all about?" Delilah asked. "And why do you smell like rose petals?"

Saffi took the black bath bomb out of her hoodie pocket and set it on the table between them. Delilah pinched her nostrils. "Strong, much?"

Saffi leaned forward and whispered, "It's Malcolm's."

Delilah spluttered. "No wonder he's such a sweetie."

Saffi tucked the bomb back into her pocket. The small café already felt close, stuffy, and warmer than usual, thanks to the new arrivals huddled around every table. She didn't want the soapy scent to overwhelm the tea shop's cardamon and cinnamon spices. The room reverberated with noise: voices bantered, chairs scraped, pots clanged. After scanning the space for familiar faces, Saffi spotted a few who could have been the stars Malcolm had promised would show up, aged past their prime, just like their host.

She turned away from the room to check the line outside the front window for—she had to admit—a certain helpful lawman. She watched, fascinated, as C.J. weaved his way from back to front using nothing but green-eyed surfer dude charm. Charisma got him through the door where a beefy arm blocked his way. Saffi raised a hand, and he pointed toward their table. "I'm with them." After a few begrudging seconds, the arm dropped.

Since Jyoti had sat them at a table for two, C.J. dragged an empty chair away from a nearby table and sat down facing the window. One knee pressed against Saffi's thigh. The other must have pressed against Delilah's because, pretty soon, her smile widened like those benefits she'd mentioned were within reach.

When the CharBOOterie Board they'd ordered arrived, the matte black tray held a truly *bootiful* variety of nibbles: cheese straws with almond fingernails—"witch's fingers," according to Jyoti—jalapeño popper mummies, and mozzarella eyeballs with olive pupils. C.J. tucked into the treats like he hadn't eaten in days. Saffi and Delilah exchanged flabbergasted glances as he reduced the board to little more than crumbs and rosemary sprig garnishes.

"These are great!" He swept cheese straw crumbs from his sweater as he reached for the last witch's finger.

Enough was enough: Saffi snatched it before he could munch it down. When their Blobster Rolls arrived, her rumbling belly was relieved that Jyoti had brought an extra sandwich for C.J., who rubbed his hands together with glee.

"Did I ever tell you you're the best server in the tea shop!" He tilted his head toward her.

Jyoti snorted. "I'm the only server, and you know it."

Delilah stiffened. "Are you kidding me? You're managing this crowd alone?" She narrowed her eyes. "Just let me get my hands on that Malcolm Morton." She lifted her pointer finger to Jyoti as if to say a "give me a sec," then picked up her lobster sandwich and took a bite that should have been bigger than her mouth. Several bites later, she made a scooching motion at C.J. He moved his chair back from the table to let her pass. Within minutes, a second server strode out of the kitchen wearing a Venus flytrap apron and carrying a pad and pen.

"Isn't she the best?" Saffi watched her friend wade into the fray.

With Delilah bustling around the tea shop taking orders, C.J. returned the chair he'd stolen and slid into the one across from Saffi. After scanning the room to make sure Malcolm hadn't made an appearance, she leaned close enough to whisper. "Have you verified Malcolm's story about buying the Smithsonian shipment?"

He reached across the table and snagged the last bite of her lobster sandwich. "You're too inquisitive for your own good, you know that, don't you?" If she hadn't wanted him to answer her question so badly, she'd have smacked his hand. How could he possibly fit more food into that taut belly? "How about you share first? Why did you steal those mugs from the Joneses' trailer?"

"I did not *steal* those mugs," Saffi hissed. "Bev... or maybe Bob did." She leaned closer, explaining what she'd found while searching the Jayco. The soaps, the souvenirs, the mugs—including her very own raven mug and the mug she was sure belonged to Jyoti. "I think they stole the Maltese Falcon."

C.J. glanced out the window, his gaze losing focus as if he were looking for holes in her theory. "The falcon theft doesn't fit the pattern."

"What pattern?"

"Kleptomaniacs don't steal for gain. It's a compulsion."

The truth of his words twisted in her gut. She'd written about celebrities with a compulsion to steal for her twelfth *Bedside Reader*. None of them needed the things they'd taken. Makeup. Cheap jewelry. Deodorant. Scarves. Trinkets, really. For a kleptomaniac, once the urge hit, the only way to feel relief was to steal.

Instead of conceding C.J.'s point, Saffi dug herself deeper into the same hole. "They didn't try to sell the falcon. They hid it. Probably after one or the other of them used it to kill Lennie."

C.J.'s brows shot up. "Bev or Bob? What makes you think that?"

"Something Mere told me."

"You talked to my daughter?" His eyes narrowed.

"Of course. How else could I strike her off my suspect list?"

"And have you?"

Instead of answering the question, Saffi shared what Mere had told her. "Right around the time Lennie went missing, Mere saw Bob dumping what she thought was a movie prop into the river. Gave him heck for it."

"Movie prop?"

"The Creature from the Black Lagoon." Saffi laced her fingers together and cocked a brow. When C.J. gave her a blank stare, she went on. "The creature that's on Malcolm's terror trail?" Saffi watched C.J.'s eyes go from skeptical to concerned to flummoxed.

"You think Mere mistook a dead body for a *movie* prop?"

Saffi considered the careful attention to detail Mere needed to create her exquisite sculptures. The timing and location of what the young artist saw made Saffi suspicious, but Mere had been sure of what she'd seen. If not for a *Bedside Reader* article Saffi had written a few months back, her suspicions might have been allayed. But she couldn't ignore the recent neuroscientific conclusions she'd uncovered: the human brain is predictive. What we "see" isn't solely based on what is actually out there. What we *think* we see is a bit like virtual reality. Based on its stored information, the brain completes the picture with what is most *probably* out there.

"We see what we expect to see." Saffi summarized her thoughts out loud. "When it comes to Malcolm and his minions, Mere expects environmental degradation. Not body counts."

"OK." C.J. linked his fingers. "Either way, Mere needs to tell the sheriff what she saw. I'll give her a call." As he started to stand, Saffi reached out to stop him.

"Hang on! You promised to tell me about the lead Malcolm gave you." She tapped the table. "Sit. Please."

C.J. hesitated, glanced around the room as if looking for an escape route, then sat. "I guess I owe you. Those items you spotted in Malcolm's closet helped break the Smithsonian case. While you were sleeping off the effects of smoke inhalation, I confronted Malcolm with what you had uncovered and persuaded him to give up the online identity of the seller."

C.J. took out a pen and wrote something on a paper napkin, then turned it toward her: chief_weasel_returns.

Saffi clutched the napkin in her lap. *The weasel!* The creature Malcolm needed to keep at bay was the Smithsonian thief. Was the weasel also behind the postcard threats? If so, Malcolm must have suspected his involvement all along. She'd put her life on pause, her edits on hold, not just to assuage her guilt over ruining Glenn's love life. She'd done it because she understood the fear she thought the actor had been facing. Fear of someone out there, watching, waiting, following, tormenting. Stalking. Dread washed over her every time she glimpsed a silver-and-black Mini-Winnie. She didn't know what she would do if her stalker pulled into the Haunted Wood. Run? Hide? Confront him?

C.J. broke into her fear loop to continue filling her in. "We're trying to connect the user name with someone we've had on our radar for years. He has a string of arrests for high-value thefts—even a few convictions."

"And?"

"Why do I feel compelled to tell you things?" The look C.J. gave Saffi was not businesslike... not at all. If Delilah had been at the table, she would have posted the photo she'd taken straight to Troy.

C.J. shook himself, as if casting off a spell. His eyes cleared, and he went back to business. "Our suspect's name is Kenneth Grahame."

The clatter of tableware and current of friendly conversation faded into the background as if a cone of silence had dropped over the table. Saffi could hear her own heartbeat, feel the pulse of blood in her veins. Her ears rang. Though she'd never have expected it, a wave of sorrow rose into her chest. Malcolm Morton, one of horror's most enduring icons, wasn't just a collector. He was a *criminal?*

No. It couldn't be. Not because he didn't have it in him, he probably did, but because she *liked* him. She liked his style, his flamboyance, his movie-screen-sized personality, his unexpected generosity. Sure, he could be an arrogant arse, but still... she liked him.

Without a word of explanation, Saffi pushed back her chair, stood up, and marched toward the kitchen.

"Saffi!" C.J. slid out of his chair. "Where are you going?"

"To see a man about a weasel."

THIRTY-THREE

It didn't take much to get the information she needed out of Sunny. He was, as his granddaughter claimed, as soft as fresh-baked naan and far more honest than his dear friend Malcolm might have hoped. When she left the kitchen, she knew the identity of the chief weasel. She took the back door out of the tea shop to keep C.J. off her trail. This was a conversation she wanted—no, needed —to have on her own. Even though she'd been bamboozled by the best, Saffi did not take kindly to bamboozlement. She found the actor on the grounds, micromanaging Bob as he strung twinkle lights across the park.

"Do you have a minute?" Saffi clasped her hands behind her back like a patient schoolgirl so she wouldn't wring the actor's neck in front of a witness.

"Can it wait, dear? The clock is ticking and, well, all these details! Who knew throwing a costume party could be so much work?"

Bob sneezed which, in this case, probably meant he knew exactly who was doing all the work, and it wasn't Malcolm Morton.

"I don't think it can. It's about the postcard perp."

Malcolm's triangular eyebrows rose in surprise. "You've found him? Or-or her?"

"I may be close." *Very close.* Saffi pressed her lips together.

"Fine! Keep at it, Bob, my boy. You'll have this place garishly grand in no time."

Malcolm tucked his arm through Saffi's and led her toward the barn. "Something else I had no idea about."

Saffi waited, certain that he'd fill her in. He did.

"Half the work of an RV park owner is managing the managers."

He stopped expectantly just inside the barn, but Saffi motioned toward the loft. "You might want a bit of privacy for this."

When they reached his living room theater, he sat on the sectional and pulled Tomago into his lap. "How's my sweet sweet kitten?" he purred.

She eyed the cat extending across his lap and onto the sectional with fear and suspicion. Tomago eyed her right back.

Noticing her look, Malcolm did his best to reassure her. "This cuddly mass of fluffy wonderfulness would not hurt a fly." He scratched behind the Maine Coon's ears, and the queen of cats purred her acceptance of his obeisance.

Saffi touched the spot where her scalp was still healing.

The actor raised his signature triangular eyebrows. "Unless she thinks she's protecting me."

Saffi took a seat on the opposite end of the sectional, as far away from what passed for a kitten in the Haunted Wood as she could get.

"So. Tell me." Malcolm stroked the Maine Coon as he waited.

"So much in this case relates to *The Wind in the Willows.* Willow Wood, the park you loved as a child. The postcards themselves, of course. And then, there's the chief weasel." Malcolm tensed, and Tomago flexed her claws, but Saffi kept going. "He was so easy to despise, wasn't he? When he and his weaselly band squatted in Toad Hall. I think the scene where Toad and his friends drove the weasels from the Hall was my favorite.

"I wonder how much of Kenneth Grahame was in the chief weasel. Or should I say, 'chief' underscore 'weasel'?"

Malcolm seemed to collapse in on himself, then forced his back to straighten. "Saffi, darling, I have no idea what you're talking about."

She was so very tired of the lies. So tired, she held nothing back. "The only reason you're not under arrest right now is that Sunny spilled your deep dark secret when I grilled him about the weasel the two of you were discussing the day of the vandalism. He swears that, while you can accurately be described as a weasel, you are not the chief weasel. In fact, you've spent half your adult life trying to keep the chief weasel at bay.

"I just have one question: did the weasel send those postcards? Because, if he did, I'm going to have a chat with Mr. Horseman about the fact that you've already violated the terms of your agreement with him. By, you know, not telling him that you know *exactly* who the chief weasel is, and you've known from the beginning because he is your *father*."

If Tomago hadn't been so heavy, Malcolm might have leapt to his feet. Since she was, the actor slid out from under her, nearly falling off the couch in the process. When he finally rose to his full height, he looked Saffi in the eye. "If I'd thought he'd sent those cards, I would never have invited you here. It would have been stupid—and I assure you, my dear, I am not stupid. I am just... trapped." Shadows chased across his black eyes like childhood memories gone to rot.

Once Malcolm started talking, he went into full-on performance mode, pacing the room, circling the couch, gesturing toward his audience of one to make points or beg understanding.

Malcolm's childhood wasn't as idyllic as the vacations to Willow Wood had made it seem. They were brief respites from the fear and drama of living with a pathological liar and a professional thief: Kenneth Grahame, Sr. The chief weasel, Malcolm disclosed, was the nickname he and his mom called his father after she divorced him during one of his prison stints.

"But the Smithsonian theft? How can your father be behind that? He must be, at least—"

"Eighty-seven." Malcolm stopped in front of Saffi, folded his hands, and looked down. "Living in a retirement home in Inglewood."

"Conveniently close to LAX." Saffi put her hands on her knees. "Malcolm, you're... you're a movie star. Your fans adore you. Why would you risk your reputation, your *freedom*, to possess a few more movie props? You have a whole museum of the things." She waved a hand toward the opening to the staircase.

"In a word," he collapsed onto the sectional, sending Tomago scrambling to the top, "blackmail."

Just as Malcolm said the word, C.J. emerged from the staircase, holding a cardboard carrier filled with coffees. "Sorry I'm late." He gave Saffi a look that said, "Giving a federal agent the slip isn't as easy as you thought, is it?"

She took the coffee drink he handed her with a look of chagrin. "Thanks." Her first sip told her two things: he knew her preference for spicy mochas, and, since her coffee had begun to cool, he'd been listening on the staircase for quite a while.

After handing Malcolm a coffee, C.J. pulled an asymmetrical art deco chair away from the wall and set it in front of the sectional almost knee to knee with the actor. "If you don't mind, I'd like to get this on record." He reached into one of the front pockets of the canvas field coat he now wore, took out a small recording device, and balanced it on his knee.

"Be my guest." Malcolm's hand shook as he raised the to-go cup to his lips. Then he heaved a great sigh and relaxed into the leather cushion behind him to share the rest of his sordid tale.

His mother—who had sole custody after his parent's divorce—had succumbed to breast cancer not long after he left his home in Portland to pursue an acting career. "I was going to make fistfuls of money. Bring her to LA. Buy a mansion with an ocean view. Give her the life she *deserved*." He pressed his lips together so hard the curled tips of his mustache trembled.

"She hid it from me, the cancer. If I'd known, I would never have left. She knew that. So..." Tears sparkled in the aging actor's eyes, his love and longing for his mother unfaded though her death had been decades in the past.

Saffi scooted close enough to put a hand on the actor's shoulder. "I'm so, so sorry, Malcolm."

"Yes, well... on to dear old dad."

At the first breath of his son's success, the elder Kenneth Grahame had weaseled his way back into Malcolm's life. Grahame Sr. had seemed thrilled. Supportive. Humble even, when he talked about his past. He had many regrets, he claimed. Three years behind bars had given him plenty of time to examine the life choices that had put him there, and he was ready to go straight.

"He'd just gotten out of prison and he *begged* me to help him. He was my father! How could I refuse?" Malcolm sniffed back what might have been real tears... or fake. He'd snowed Saffi one time too many for her to be sucked into what might be false emotions.

Malcolm had hired his father as his driver, giving him an apartment over the garage to live in and a generous salary. But, all too soon, valuable objects began to go missing from the actor's house. A painting. A vase. A vintage cigarette case that had once belonged to Marilyn.

Saffi and C.J. exchanged glances. "Monroe?" she squeaked.

Malcolm put the back of his free hand to his forehead in an exaggerated expression of angst.

"I sent the chief weasel packing, thinking I was well shot of the thieving old fart."

He wasn't. Kenneth Grahame, Sr. pulled his son back in with one more con. He was broke, he said. Living on the street. He'd been dumpster-diving on Sunset Boulevard and found something he thought might be valuable. With his record, he was afraid to approach a pawn shop to find out. Could Malcolm take a look?

Malcolm had lived in Hollywood for long enough to know that people with too much money tossed away valuables all the time.

He took a look. His father had found a gorgeous crystal cognac bottle, empty, and dusty enough that some overambitious cleaner might have tossed it into the trash without knowing its value.

After writing "Treasure or Trash" for *Bedside Reader*, #9, Saffi knew that bottles like the one Malcolm described had been sold for tens of thousands of dollars.

"Oh, no. You didn't."

"I did." Malcolm closed his eyes. "Gave him two grand for the thing. Enough, he said, to get him into an apartment and keep him off the street. My gut told me he hadn't found something so valuable in the trash, but... the dust." Malcolm lifted his hand off his forehead. "I convinced myself his story could be true."

It could have been, but it wasn't. Once he'd tricked Malcolm into buying the stolen bottle, he had him. Either his son helped him out from time to time, or he would tell the world he was a crook, just like dear old dad. From that time on, the chief weasel had maintained his lifestyle by selling stolen goods to his son in return for his silence.

"He was my first, and probably best, acting teacher." Malcolm took a sip from his coffee, heaved himself off the cushiony sectional, and carried the cup across the room to a faux-Grecian urn apparently doing double duty as a trash can. Then he turned to C.J. "Do we still have a deal?"

C.J. rubbed a hand across his mouth and chin. "I got the OK based on a single charge of receiving stolen goods. What you've just confessed goes way beyond that. My advice? Give that fancy lawyer of yours a call while you still can."

THIRTY-FOUR

C.J. took his leave, heading off to report what Saffi had just dug out of Malcolm. Before she followed, she took time to wheedle enough information from her down-for-the-count host to put her a few steps closer to catching at least one more crook—an arsonist. She poked and prodded until he remembered a few telling details about the fire. After she'd phoned Malcolm, he'd called 9-1-1 and rushed to the office to find out where his office managers kept the key to the shed.

"They'd left the office unattended." He shook his head. "Not the first time that's happened, mind you."

Bev, how could you? She'd told Saffi that Malcolm had dragged her out of the office so fast she hadn't had time to grab the keys. But she hadn't been in the office! So much for the park manager being Kenneth Grahame's helpful Ratty. She was an altogether different species of rat: *rattus perfidus*. The traitor.

Malcolm had found Bob at the shed running back and forth like a school kid at his first fire drill. Jyoti and Sunny had been there as well. They'd smelled smoke, heard screaming. Bev showed up a few minutes later, red-faced and apologetic.

"Oh!" Malcolm snapped his fingers. "That Cecily woman was

there, too. I suppose she'd been in the tea shop and noticed the commotion."

"What?" Saffi startled.

"The sheriff's wife. The one who wants the park to fail so she can scoop up my land for that ridiculous Riverside Ranch extension of hers."

Cecily Raymond? What possible motive could the real estate developer have for harming Saffi or C.J.? Unless... Saffi's suspicious nature cranked up a notch. The fire had given Cecily's husband that "one more terrible thing" she'd said he needed to close the park. Without Malcolm's lawyers stepping in, the Haunted Wood would already be shut down.

As Saffi considered the sheriff's wife's potential for murderous impulses, she caught sight of Tomago slinking along the top of the sectional. The colossal cat paused with her head so close to Saffi's face she felt the tickle of Tomago's whiskers. She held her breath and braced for another slashing attack. Instead, the queen of cats slid down the back of the sectional like whipped cream oozing over the side of a cup and landed as light as a feather in her lap. After a moment's hesitation, Saffi reached out to stroke Tomago. It was like petting the silky fur of an Angora rabbit.

The cat's purr was low and rumbly, its vibration eased the tension from her thighs and hips, its nearness provided comfort. Just like that, an enemy became a friend. How quickly things could change. Fast enough to stop any more madness from happening? Saffi could only hope.

She caught up with C.J. seated at his campsite with an ear pressed to a cellphone. He waved her to a second camp chair on the other side of the fire ring and motioned for her to sit while he wrapped up the call. "Mere," he explained. "She promised to talk to Ray tomorrow."

Saffi didn't have a lot of confidence in Sheriff Raymond. If he'd done his job—stepped up to find the killer—Saffi might be on her way home to Last Chance Cove by now. *Home.* She smiled. None of the places she'd landed in her three years of RV roaming had felt as much like home as Last Chance Cove. If Delilah and Glenn hadn't shown up at the Haunted Wood, she'd have been pining for the cove by now. Home wasn't just a place: it was the people who lived there.

The people here—Jyoti, Sunny, and Mere in particular—had charmed her. And C.J.? She glanced up from the fire and saw him returning her gaze. She was definitely not immune to the depths in those moss-green eyes, to his teasing, his ability to predict what she would say, his keen intelligence. The connection was real, but tenuous, as was her connection to the Haunted Wood.

Then there was Malcolm... what could she say about Malcolm Morton? She'd been captured in his orbit like a satellite. Since the moment she arrived, she'd spent her days spinning around him.

"What will happen to him—Malcolm?" she asked. "And to that despicable dad of his."

C.J. rested his elbows on his knees and stared into the fire he'd lit before she joined him. "Malcolm? I wish I knew." He shook his head and shrugged. "As for his dad, he's eighty-seven and living in a glorified nursing home. My guess is he'll lose his computer and Internet privileges and be forced to spend his final days reading books."

"Hey!" Saffi pursed her lips. "Reading is a privilege, not a punishment."

"Yes, it is. Especially your books. I'll make sure his *Bedside Reader* privileges are revoked."

C.J.'s praise warmed her from the inside out. A man who appreciated books. Her books. When she returned the favor by congratulating him on finding his man and recovering the missing items from the Smithsonian shipment, he scoffed.

"I had the entire postal investigation apparatus at my disposal but without those super-snooper skills of yours, I'd be living in that camper van for another six months at least."

"The skills that almost got you asphyxiated?"

C.J. stretched his arms above his head. "While simultaneously uncovering a missing falcon worth millions. So, now that my case is solved, how can I help?"

Saffi sighed. Tomorrow was Halloween. The postcard perp's deadline was almost upon them. Was there anything C.J. could do that she couldn't? Follow the forensic evidence, perhaps. Even if Lennie's murder wasn't connected to the postcards—and she still had no idea whether it was or wasn't—his death mattered. "Find out if the blood on the falcon matches Lennie's?"

C.J. hunched forward. "Much as I hate to do it, I might have to turn the falcon over to Ray. The murder case is his to solve, not mine... and not yours." The concern in his eyes made Saffi start doing that leaning toward his irresistible magnetism thing again. She stopped herself. *Concentrate, Saffi.*

"I get it. But... I'm not sure you should. After you left, Malcolm told me that Cecily was on the grounds when the fire started."

"Ray's wife?" C.J. picked up a slender log and added it to the fire. "Why would she be here?"

That was the million-dollar question. "I don't know. But if you turn that falcon over to the sheriff, and his wife is involved in this whole thing, we could lose our only piece of concrete evidence."

C.J. shook his head. "Not our only lead. We also have the postcard."

"Oh, so now you *like* my postcard fingerprint plan?" She batted her lashes, which could have been teasing or even provocative if she'd had sense enough to stroke on a bit of mascara. Since she hadn't, C.J. seemed to think ash from the fire had blown into her eyes.

"Sorry," he said. "I shouldn't have put another log on with the smoke blowing your way."

Smoke from campfires always seemed to blow her way. Moving made no difference. It would follow. This evening, her singed lungs fought back with a cough. Once it started, she couldn't seem to stop. "I'd better—" She held up a hand while a hacking fit racked her chest. "Go."

C.J. stood as if to walk her to her door but she shook her head.

"I'm fine. Really."

She dragged herself away from C.J. and unlocked her RV. Once inside, she gulped down a glass of water. A glance in the mirror above the kitchen sink showed a pink-cheeked woman with wild hair and determined eyes. Determination was enough to get her locked in a shed inhaling smoke, but was it enough to solve multiple crimes before it was too late? The last postcard had made the perp's intention clear: he or she would show up at the Spook-tacular. If Saffi didn't pin the perp before tomorrow night, she would have failed Malcolm. Failed Glenn. And—since her only excuse for abandoning her revisions was to find out who sent the postcards—she would have failed herself as well.

Saffi ran her tongue over her teeth. The coughing fit had eased, but her mouth tasted of ash. She left the kitchen sink for the one in the bathroom, brushed with peppermint-flavored toothpaste, and scoured her tongue with a scraper. She succeeded in banishing the acrid taste of smoke, but her eyes held the haunted look of someone who had come way too close to death. Her postcard fingerprint plan *had* been a good one, but she didn't have time to wait for results. She needed a new plan.

When an article left her brain spinning, she knew exactly what to do: go for a walk. As she left the trailer, she clicked the lock. Half the park could probably get inside, with or without a key, but she'd be darned if she'd make it easy. She set a brisk pace past the office and onto the forested river trail she'd walked with C.J. on the night of her arrival. It was exactly what she needed: the smell of tree resin, the chorus of birdsong, and the rustle of small animals in the underbrush, the air cool and clean enough to clear away the choking smoke she'd inhaled at C.J.'s campfire.

By the time she reached the dock, the robin's-egg-blue after-noon sky had deepened. Clouds that had settled along the coast-line were edged with gold, backlit as the sun began to sink toward the horizon. Her clenched shoulders relaxed. Her breathing slowed, her heartbeat settled, and her mind started to clear. The river barely rippled as it flowed toward the sea, just enough to keep a trio of harlequin ducks paddling their webbed feet to stay put. Saffi had to smile. The ducks' slate-blue feathers were sectioned off by black-and-white stripes. White dots and burnt-orange accents made them look as if they'd arrived a day early for Malcolm's party. The party that could either save the Haunted Wood, or destroy it.

The chill that rose through the cracks between the dock's weathered boards once again made Saffi acutely aware that Lennie's body had been found in the water flowing beneath her boots. Death felt close. Too close. The wetlands smell that usually reminded her of the richness of life now smelled of decay. The mysteries she'd tried and failed to solve—the postcards, the arson, and... most horrifying of all... the murder—coalesced into a sense of dread that seeped into her spirit as well as her body. That dread led her to a conclusion: she could not wait for C.J. and Sheriff Raymond to collect clues, examine evidence, compare notes, and—someday in the distant future—catch a culprit. She had to take the bull elk by the antlers and wrestle the truth out of her short list of suspects *before* the Spooktacular when the perp had promised to make good on his threats.

The clues she'd been collecting since she arrived at the Haunted Wood pointed to multiple suspects, but only one of them had a strong motive for shutting down the park. If she concentrated her energies on nabbing that person, she would have done what Malcolm brought her here to do. She could return to Last Chance Cove with a clear conscience and get back to those revisions she'd been avoiding.

By the time Saffi returned from her walk, late afternoon had darkened toward dusk, and with dusk came more campfires. She passed a group of horror film nerds gathered around a teepee of smoking logs, chugging beers. Their voices rose in pitch as they argued about which movie stars they'd spotted on the grounds. Saffi swiveled her head right and left, wondering if any of the people cutting across her path were actors whose flannel shirts and Patagonia jackets hid them in plain sight.

Over by the hollowed-out log office, a twenty-something held up a cellphone. The young woman centered herself beneath the light over the door as if it was a spotlight, pressed record, and started gushing about the Spooktacular taking place on Halloween.

"This is MoiraLessMagic, the podcast about all things mystical, magical, terrifying, and tragical, coming to you pre-dead at Malcolm Morton's Haunted Wood. We've been counting down the days to the biggest Halloween bash this Oregon backwater has ever witnessed. By this time tomorrow, we'll be at numbero uno!" She held one finger next to a face that would have been pert and pretty if not whited-out and lipsticked up like Elvira, Mistress of the Dark.

Between "tragical," "pre-dead," and "numbero," Saffi had heard enough. She followed a gaggle of guests toward the Little Tea Shop of Horrors. Half of them went inside. The other half split off toward Malcolm's trail of terrors, shining flashlights to illuminate the path. A few seconds later, shrill screams and manic laughter told her they'd found the chewed Bigfoot remains Archie had left in his wake.

It took longer than she'd hoped to wiggle her way inside the tea shop. When Jyoti caught sight of her hesitating at the doorway, she rushed forward. The young server's sleek black hair stood out around her head as if she'd put her hand on a plasma ball.

"I don't need a table," Saffi reached out a reassuring hand. "I was just wondering if you'd seen my friends, Glenn and Delilah."

"Yes! This way." Jyoti started walking toward the kitchen, but glanced back to see if Saffi had followed.

Saffi almost tripped over her own feet trying to keep up with the young server. "Delilah's still here?"

"Oh, my gosh." Jyoti glanced back at Saffi as she brushed stray hairs off her cheeks. "She saved my life. Literally. I'd be dead now if she hadn't stepped in. Do you know what she did?"

Saffi raised her brows and waited.

"Look!" Jyoti swept an arm toward two long tables set up just outside the kitchen. "The woman is brilliant. She convinced my grandfather to set up a buffet. All we have to do is keep the trays filled." She leaned toward Saffi and whispered. "She has my grandfather wrapped around her finger."

"The one with the all-seeing eye?"

Jyoti giggled. "The very one."

"I heard that!" Delilah's deep laugh added to the song of steam coming from the kitchen. A few minutes later, the barista strode past Saffi and Jyoti to set what smelled like a chai latte on a table in front of a customer. She wiped a smidge of foam from her hand onto the Venus flytrap apron she wore.

"Yikes! That thing is grungy enough to feature in one of Malcolm's movies!" Saffi pointed at the remains of Delilah's day. "Is Glenn here, too?" Saffi glanced around the teeming café expecting to spot her friend, but Delilah quickly enlightened her.

"He was in here earlier, trying to convince Malcolm to give him access to his wardrobe."

Saffi's eyes widened. "Maybe we should go over there."

Delilah glanced at Jyoti. The girl's eyes went frantic, but she regained her equilibrium quickly. "Go ahead. I've got this."

A few minutes later, they made their way up the winding staircase at the back of the museum. At the top, Saffi paused. No way was she poking her head above the floor without knowing if Tomago was lurking nearby. "Hang on." She held out a hand to stop Delilah, then yelled, "Malcolm! You up here?"

A muffled but frantic voice came from beyond the door that led into the actor's bathroom. Was the actor in danger? Saffi hurried up the final stairs, forgetting all about Tomago's claws. She heard shoes thump across tiles, and, seconds later, Malcolm burst into the living room, glancing back over his shoulder as if a demon might be on his heels. "Saffi! Thank the goddess."

The actor had exchanged the Goblin King robe he'd worn earlier for an oversized school-bus-yellow turtleneck, distressed jeans, and black-and-white checked sneakers. The minute he caught sight of Saffi, he pressed his hands on either side of his cheeks in an imitation of the face he'd made famous in "Last Scream in Paris," a low-budget film made on the downslope of his rise to fame.

When he reached the two friends, he lowered his hands. "I've spent my life playing monsters, but I've never seen anything like what Glenn turned into when he walked into my closet."

They literally had to drag Glenn out of Malcolm's wardrobe. "I haven't finished!" he yelped. "The shoes? Did you see the shoes?"

"I saw the shoes." Saffi patted him on the shoulder. "And I'm sure they'll still be here in the morning." She was almost as certain that Malcolm would bar her cookie-baking friend from his closet for life.

THIRTY-FIVE

Halloween morning arrived with blue skies, the oaky smell of early-morning campfires, and the excited chatter of many voices. A miscellany of music—from the coffee-shop comfort of smooth jazz to the jarring ground gravel of Tom Waits' "Whistlin' Past the Graveyard"—competed for attention from portable Bluetooth speakers. As Saffi stepped out of her RV, zipping her cozy caramel-brown cardigan to her neck, the background noise was drowned out by the not-so-pleasant rumble of trucks bearing tables and chairs, the makings of a very large tent, and a soldierly row of blue porta-potties.

Threatening postcards, a murder, a string of thefts, arson... nothing, apparently, could stop Malcolm Morton's Haunted Wood from opening with the panache she'd come to know and, grudgingly, love about the actor. Malcolm stood center stage, of course, orchestrating the arrival from the steps of the Little Tea Shop of Horror. The Venus flytrap peering over his shoulder looked ready to bite his head off, as did Jyoti who was trying to squeeze hungry guests past him.

"Saffi!" a familiar voice shouted. She turned to see Glenn strolling toward her, dressed like he'd walked off the set of *A Grave Mistake,* Saffi's favorite Malcolm Morton movie. She'd seen the purple velvet smoking jacket Glenn wore in Malcolm's closet while snooping. He'd paired the jacket with gray wide-wale corduroys that must have come straight out of his own Davy Jones collection.

"I thought we were saving the elegance for tonight?" Saffi gestured from his gray satin collar and matching cuffs to the tips of his ankle-high black leather boots.

"This old thing." Glenn smoothed his lapels, trying for an air of cool nonchalance, but his full-toothed grin and dancing brown eyes said he was floating higher than one of Malcolm's helium balloons.

Saffi hip-checked Malcolm to get his attention as they passed him on the tea shop steps, and he gave her a wink and a nod. She'd shared her plan for nabbing her number one postcard suspect with him, and he was all in. As she stepped inside, Sunny stuck his head out of the kitchen and nodded toward the table closest to the kitchen door. Delilah placed brunch menus on the table and took their coffee orders. Glenn's nervous energy manifested in an info-dump about the clothes in Malcolm's closet, but when the suspect currently at the top of her list walked in, Saffi flicked her eyes toward the door to stop him.

The suspect Saffi had personally invited to the tea shop's Halloween Brunch sashayed across the dining room in a ginger-brown suit and beige pumps to join them. Saffi made introductions, then slid a brunch menu across the table to Cecily Raymond.

"I'm so glad you called. I brought all the information you'll need." Cecily reached into her designer tote and pulled out a Riverside Ranch folder thick with colorful brochures, maps, and floorplans.

"Thank you." Saffi set the folder on the table and folded her hands on top of it. "I've been very curious about your expansion plans."

"Ask me anything!" Cecily placed her manicured hands on the table and leaned toward her. "Once today's hoopla passes and all these"—she glanced around her at the jean-and-hoodie-clad diners filling the tea shop and sniffed—"horror fans crawl back under their rocks, I'm sure Mr. Morton will reconsider my offer."

Cecily was no better at recognizing Hollywood's horror stars than Saffi had been. If she'd known she'd just dissed tables filled with potential clients for her exclusive development, she'd have crawled into her tote and snapped it closed over her champagne-blond bun.

As Saffi gathered her thoughts, she glanced inside the folder Cecily had given her. The developer had thoughtfully included brochures on other properties her LLC had built along the coast. Saffi's brain ticked off towns during a quick flip-through, noting Gold Beach, Bandon, and Coos Bay among them. Each of those towns had been marked with a red X on Saffi's map to indicate that a postcard had been mailed from there. Cecily might as well have written her own indictment.

"Actually," Saffi smiled her most wickedly sweet smile, "I invited you here with a different kind of offer."

Cecily's micro-bladed brows rose. She moved her hands into her lap and posed expectantly.

"And what might that be?"

Saffi nodded toward the table by the front window where C.J. cut into a stack of chocolate pancakes piled high with strawberries and whipped cream. He waved a forkful bigger than his mouth at her, then somehow managed to stuff it all inside without losing a single dollop of creamy goodness.

"You're going to love it!" Glenn gushed loud enough to be heard in the kitchen.

As planned, Delilah delivered two Mad Scientist Mochas to Saffi and Glenn and set a plate piled with postcards in front of Cecily. The real estate developer pushed back her chair so fast it fell over. It was exactly the reaction Saffi had hoped for. Only someone who knew exactly what those cards were would have freaked out the way Cecily did.

"Scary, aren't they?"

"What?" Cecily put her hands up. "I don't know what these are or what you think you're doing." She reached for her tote and pulled out her cellphone. "I'm calling my husband."

Glenn's dark eyes danced behind his silky brown bangs as he rose to right Cecily's chair. "I do love a good arrest with my brunch."

Cecily shot a lethal glare his way as she tapped her phone with a manicured nail. She didn't bother asking who he thought might be arrested, a sign of guilt Saffi didn't miss.

As the phone started to ring, Saffi nodded toward C.J. again. "That man over there... he's a postal inspector. Before Glenn persuaded me to find the person who sent those"—she nodded toward the plate of postcards—"I'd never heard of such a thing. Have you?"

Cecily held the phone to her ear, tapping the toe of her stylish pumps as she waited for her husband to pick up. "What does a postman have to do with anything?"

The ringing stopped, and the sheriff's deep voice answered. "Cecily, I'm in the middle of something here. Can this wait?"

Cecily's face hardened. "No, it—"

"*Not* a postman," Saffi broke in loudly enough to force Cecily to listen. "A federal agent."

"Hang on." She switched the cellphone to her other ear to muffle the sound of the sheriff berating her for calling him at work and expecting him to hold the line.

Saffi held Cecily's eyes to keep her attention. "Badge. Gun. The whole ball of wax. And if I hold up my right hand, he'll come over here and explain what happens to someone who sends threats through the mail."

"Cece!" Sheriff Raymond's voice got louder, as if his wife might have lost her hearing.

She punched the red circle to end the call and dropped into her chair like a puppet whose strings had been snipped.

Saffi had the dumbfounded developer right where she wanted her. She went on to point out that, thanks to Oregon's requirement to do background checks and fingerprint candidates for real estate licenses, Cecily's prints were on file. She'd handed over the business card Cecily had given her at the Historical Museum to the postal inspector. All of that was true. What wasn't true, and what Saffi hoped the real estate developer couldn't read in her face, was that C.J. was still waiting for the fingerprint checks to come back. Until they did, the only way to "prove" that Cecily was the postcard perp was to spook her enough to incriminate herself.

Saffi played her final card. "Fortunately, you didn't follow through on the threats. Unless..." Saffi furrowed her brow. "You didn't happen to lock me in a shed and set a fire, did you?"

The last bit of color drained from Cecily's face, and she clutched the table like it was the last life preserver on a yacht being attacked by a killer whale. "That is utter nonsense," she hissed. "You could hardly buy a property from me if you were *dead*."

True enough. Saffi sat back and scanned the room as she considered what to say next. She had come to love this ridiculous tea shop with its mismatched tables, mad menu, and carnivorous centerpieces. It felt cozy, even on the chilliest October day. The Indian spices that always lingered in the air warmed the space, and Jyoti's bright smile and bouncy black hair always made her feel welcome. Something tugged at Saffi's heart—nostalgia, she realized, for a place she'd not yet left, couldn't leave until every thread had been spun, every culprit captured. It was time to tempt Cecily deeper into the web.

"Good point. And, despite the fact that you're a manipulative money-grubber whose actions will probably make me miss my manuscript deadline, if you're willing to do one little thing to help smoke out a killer, that handsome postal inspector over there will make you a deal."

"What kind of deal?" Cecily demanded.

"The kind that keeps you out of jail, sweetie." Glenn beamed.

Cecily chewed her lipsticked lips, coating her front teeth in more than enough red gore for Halloween. Saffi could see the wheels spinning behind Cecily's blue eyes. *Could they really charge her with a felony? If they did, she'd never be convicted. She was a big-deal developer and the sheriff's wife.* Saffi had thought the scenario through earlier, so it was easy to imagine the thoughts ricocheting in Cecily's mind.

"Well?"

Cecily glanced at the cellphone lying on the table beside the plate of postcards. Her eyes had the considering look of a cornered fox.

Saffi started to raise her right hand to give C.J. a wave, but Cecily grabbed her wrist.

"Wait!"

Saffi wrenched her arm out of the woman's grasp. Cecily Raymond played the long game, and she played it dirty. Saffi was done waiting. The real estate developer had all but admitted that she'd sent the cards. Let her pay the full price. She pushed back her chair and stood.

"I'll do it!" Cecily yelped, and every head in the tea shop turned their way.

"In that case," Sunny and Jyoti approached the table with plates piled high with goodies, "breakfast is on the house."

THIRTY-SIX

Sunny's scrumptious brunch and Delilah's delicious spicy mocha left Saffi's belly just short of uncomfortably full. By the time they finished, Malcolm had left the tea shop steps and taken up a post in front of the red barn where a team of burly workers pounded stakes and placed poles around a massive outdoor canopy they'd already spread on the ground. Malcolm stood on tiptoe using his hands as a megaphone as he shouted directions.

"A little to the left. No! No! Your other left!"

The workers gave him the occasional wave and smile, more to entertain themselves than to acknowledge Malcolm, Saffi decided. These were locals, men and women whose muscles and sure movements proved they'd been doing this kind of work so long they'd learned to ignore the guy who paid the bills and do the job right.

Good, Saffi thought. With Malcolm in charge, the tent would probably collapse in the middle of the Spooktacular and flatten them all.

"See you tonight!" Saffi waved as Glenn headed into the campground to meet and greet Malcolm's rabid fans and famous friends. Saffi made her way to the actor, both to keep him from driving the workers bonkers and to remind him of his part in her plan.

"Yes, yes, darling." He patted her shoulder. "I know my role.

Spread the word that the Maltese Falcon will be on display in the museum tonight. I leaked the news to friends who joined me for breakfast. Notorious Hollywood gossips, one and all. I told them 'mum' was the word until I'd made the announcement." He winked. "Half the park knows by now." He leaned closer to whisper in her ear. "I've been drawing in audiences since before you were born, my lovely."

Saffi did the math in her head. Not likely, but if he wanted to believe that, who was she to stop him?

Pulling Malcolm into her plan had been easy. Convincing law enforcement to use the Maltese Falcon to trap the killer? Not so much.

C.J. had insisted that Mere tell Sheriff Raymond what she'd seen at the river. Afterward, he'd told the sheriff about the Maltese Falcon and its possible connection to Lennie's murder. The sheriff went ballistic and told C.J. if he didn't turn it over, he'd bring him up on obstruction charges. C.J. offered to do the same unless the sheriff agreed to Saffi's scheme.

In the end, Sheriff Raymond couldn't fault her logic, so he agreed, with the caveat that he'd have C.J.'s badge if such critical evidence went missing. If the statuette really was the murder weapon—which they couldn't know for sure until a medical examiner had done a blood match—Saffi's gut told her that the person who had wielded it would not pass up the chance to retrieve it.

"You'll be right there, standing guard," Saffi had assured C.J. "One pretend bathroom break and, if I'm right, our fly will swoop in and, *whap!*" She'd smacked her hands together. "You'll slap on the cuffs!"

But what if she was wrong, and the fly was a certain local real estate developer? If Cecily had done any of the most dastardly deeds—killing Lennic, cutting the brake lines on Malcolm's roadster, setting the shed fire—she would avoid the trap they were setting. That was a risk Saffi was willing to take. She'd come here to solve the postcard mystery, and Cecily's guilty reaction seemed to indicate that she'd done that. The postcard perp now knew that both professional and amateur sleuths would be watching out for Malcolm during the Spooktacular. Hopefully, that would stop her from following through on the final postcard threat. And if Cecily had not bludgeoned her former groundskeeper? The least she could do was help catch the person who did.

Saffi skirted the workers raising the tent and found a spot where she could watch the office without being seen. She'd made a point of avoiding Bev and Bob since she'd rumbled their trailer. If they had noticed the missing mugs, they would know someone was onto their sticky-fingered ways. Saffi would be at the top of their list, just as they were at the top of hers. Moments later, Cecily stomped past as if trying to crush gravel—or Saffi—beneath the heels of her pumps.

"Calm down before you twist an ankle," Saffi mumbled as she passed.

Cecily kept stomping. Seconds later, Saffi heard a gasp, and Cecily's stomp developed a slight limp. *Don't say I didn't warn you.*

It took all of Saffi's willpower to keep her eyes on the workers erecting the tent, but she had to. Bev was smart. If she saw Saffi watching, she would be suspicious, even if the person who opened the office door and stopped just inside when her cellphone rang was Cecily Raymond.

Saffi heard the ringtone, and Cecily's high-pitched, "What?"

To Saffi, Cecily's voice sounded too shrill. She could only hope the office managers didn't notice.

"A falcon? I don't understand. Someone murdered that caretaker with... a bird?" Cecily's shriek stilled for a moment, as if she listened for an explanation. Of course, the person on the other end of the call wasn't the sheriff. It was C.J., coaching her on what to say.

Don't look. Don't look! Saffi kept her eyes on the tent construction, not daring to glance Cecily's way. The workers stood, one on each corner and two in the middle, coordinating each move as they threaded pole tips through large metal grommets in the canopy.

Pole by pole the heavy canopy rose. In less time than it took Cecily to complete her call, the tent had been erected and stood, pegs staked deep in the ground and ties ratcheted tight enough to hold the party tent against the most spirited of gales... or galas.

"Well of course." Cecily's long pause ended. "If traces of blood were found on it..." Her voice lowered to an indecipherable mumble, but Saffi didn't care. She'd delivered the pertinent information in a voice anyone in the office could have heard. The post-card perp had done her job. With suspects—current and former—helping her spin a web, and C.J. ready to step in, Saffi was sure she could trap a big fat felonious fly.

Once all of the elements of her plan had been put in place, Saffi headed back to her RV for a quick nap. She needed fresh energy to deal with whatever happened at tonight's Spooktacular.

What she didn't need was to spot a man leaning against a black-and-silver Mini-Winnie two rows away, watching her every move from behind a pair of geek-chic black glasses, the kind made cool by Buddy Holly. Thin. Medium height. A pompadour of hair so black it had to have been dyed. Pale skin. Cheeks that looked rouged even from a distance. Saffi's brain catalogued his details as if for a wanted poster like the ones she'd seen in the Gold Beach post office. Was this her stalker? Or was he a film fan preparing to party hearty on a Halloween night?

A stare-off wasn't going to answer any questions. With so much at stake, she couldn't run. She couldn't even hide. She could, however, lock herself into her RV until Spooktacular time and worry herself to sleep.

By the time Saffi woke up, afternoon had barreled into evening. One look out her bedroom window revealed elaborately costumed guests emerging into the evening's chill. Saffi grabbed her cellphone.

"Have you looked outside?" she yelped when Delilah answered.

Glenn must have been close by because he squealed. "Isn't it *fabulous*?"

"No. It's not fabulous. I came here to sleuth, not attend an actual costume party with actual actors! These people are literally dressed to kill."

"We'll be right there."

A few minutes later, Delilah and Glenn burst into her RV and rushed up the stairwell. Delilah waved a business card in her face. "This was taped to your door." Saffi glanced at the card. It was one of Mere's. The artist had scribbled, *Dock. 8 p.m. Important!* on the back. As if tonight wasn't complicated enough.

Her friends pushed past on the way to her tiny closet. She clutched her elbows and paced the living room. Could she make it to the dock by eight without jeopardizing her plan? Worse still, could her friends find a gala-worthy costume lurking in the shallow depths of her wardrobe? *No, and no.* What was she going to do?

When Delilah handed her thick black leggings and a matching tunic, Saffi balked. "Half of Hollywood is out there and you're dressing me as a middle-aged ninja? What kind of friends *are* you?"

Glenn looked at Delilah. "She's right. We need Malcolm and we need him now."

Malcolm Morton wasn't the only one who could make magic. After raiding the museum, Delilah and Glenn returned bearing a treasure Saffi was afraid to touch, much less wear: the gown worn by the dragon queen in *Blood and Beauty*. If Saffi remembered correctly, Malcolm had played a knight tasked with ridding the country of a bloodthirsty queen who kept her youth by bathing in the blood of virgins. The queen, Saffi knew from her "Horrific History" article in *Bedside Reader*, #12, was based on a seventeenth-century Hungarian countess rumored to have done the same. *Ick.* But the dress was beyond gorgeous.

Glenn held the gown in front of himself and smoothed it against his body. The entire V-shaped bodice had been sewn with iridescent blue and green dragon scales, the skirt with matching feathers that shimmered in the light. "If you don't wear it, I will."

"Don't be ridiculous," Delilah said. "You're way too bony to fill this thing out."

"You're right." Saffi reached for the dress. "Soaking in all that blood plumped her out to exactly my size. Come along, serving girl." She bared her teeth at Delilah. "The queen needs assistance."

The dress had been designed to be easy to step into, for which Saffi was grateful, but Delilah lost more than one fake nail trying to zip, hook, and snap it closed.

"Stop breathing!" Delilah hissed as she tried and failed to hook the final closure. Their eyes met in the closet mirror, Delilah's pleading, Saffi's panicking.

"If this thing gets any tighter, I will! For good!"

A brisk knock on the bathroom door disrupted their standoff. "Tick-tock, ladies!" Glenn called. "We don't want the revels to start without us!"

Saffi sucked in her breath. A few seconds later, Delilah slid open the bathroom door, stepped into the kitchen, and curtsied. "Behold! The dragon queen. God help her if she needs to pee during this shindig."

Saffi groaned. "Can I go back to the black tights and tunic?"

Delilah held up her hands so Saffi could see her mangled nails. "Try and I'll pluck you like a chicken."

Saffi did her best to glide forward the way the actor who'd played the movie role had done. Scales tinkled. Feathers rustled. Her foot caught the gown's edge, and she stumbled into Glenn, nearly knocking him off his feet.

"You can barely walk in this thing. Can you sit?" He rested his chin on the knuckles of his right hand.

Saffi scrunched up her face. "No, I can't sit. Or eat or drink or chase bad guys."

Glenn's eyes widened. "Oh my goddess! Eating is out of the question." He had seen the devastation left behind when Saffi consumed one of his powdered-sugar wedding cookies.

"Can you kneel?" Delilah asked before Glenn could yank the dress over her head and run with it.

"I don't know. Why?"

"Because there's no way you're going to the gala with this hair!" She fluffed out Saffi's tempestuous curls.

Delilah plucked the raven pillow off the couch. Saffi lifted her feathered skirt and knelt while her friend teased, swooped, wound, and sprayed her hair into an elegant black-and-silver updo adorned with dragon scales and feathers. Glenn sat on the couch chewing his nails until she'd finished, then added a few swoops of green glitter eyeshadow and enough mascara to make her lashes droop. Saffi widened her eyes to keep them from sticking together while the goop dried.

Delilah stepped back to see the full effect, then deemed her, "Beautiful enough to charm the britches off every virgin at the party."

Saffi grimaced. "I prefer vintage over virginity, thank you very much." Although, a tub full of youth-giving blood would have been helpful at the moment. Her knees ached, her thighs burned, and her feet had gone numb. It took both her friends to tug her upright. She walked back and forth across the carpet, skirt lifted above her ankles, teeth gritted against the pain as her blood started circulating again.

"One more thing!" Glenn held up a finger. He dug into a tote he'd left in the stairwell and unfolded what turned out to be diaphanous black dragon wings. The bony spines protruding at the joints looked dangerous enough to poke an eye out if Saffi wasn't careful.

"Guys. This is too much. I have a murderer to catch, remember?"

"Saffi." Glenn slid the shoulder harness up one arm and then the other. "You're about to attend a Malcolm Morton extravaca-denza." He slid black loops hidden inside the wings a few inches above their bony tips onto her middle fingers. "There can never be too much."

The wings were surprisingly light. She thought back to the many times her tai chi teacher had shouted, "Open your wings,

Saffi" to correct her posture during a form. When she lifted her arms, air whooshed upward, and Glenn jumped back.

"Claws in, gorgeous!"

A chastised Saffi tucked her arms to her sides. For a moment, she'd felt as if she could truly lift off, but at the very least, she should let her friends flee before she tested her wings again. With the dragon queen's permission, Delilah and Glenn scurried off like a pair of Cinderellas, determined to outshine each other at the ball.

THIRTY-SEVEN

Saffi stood at the top of the RV's narrow stairwell and bit her lip. How was she supposed to squeeze herself, her scaled and feathered gown, *and* her wings down those stairs? She pressed her arms against her sides, holding her feathers down, but when she took her first downward step, one of the clawed joints grabbed a potholder off the wall. Glancing toward her shoulder, she saw it hanging there, stained with last summer's barbecue sauce, a testament to her decided lack of queenly qualities. She reached up and across with her left hand, wrestled the potholder loose, and tossed it backward. She could only hope it landed somewhere she could find it.

She faced the stairs again. *You can do it, Saffi. You have to.* The only way down, she realized, was sideways, so she turned. Arms pressed against the dress, ballet slipper tapping for the next stair, she started down, one step at a time. She made it to the bottom step without adding any more unwanted adornments—the umbrella had been a distinct possibility—let go of her skirt, and pushed the door open with her right hand, then stepped down and down again. A breeze swirled beneath her skirt, and she gave thanks to Delilah Dunsmore: guardian of friends without enough sense to put their cozy leggings on *before* struggling into their gowns. Only her best friend would have had the nerve to yank them up her legs and over her hips after the fact. Without Delilah's sacrifice, the evening's chill would have frozen Saffi's butt off.

As she fumbled her way out of the RV, Saffi's eyes had been on her feet. When she looked up from her ballet flats, she gasped. Night had fallen. Orange and purple twinkle lights had transformed the park into a place so macabre even her leggings couldn't keep her from shivering. Horrors unlike any she'd ever seen except on a movie screen roamed the park. She sidestepped a glimmering ice goblin rolling a giant golden globe beneath its feet and ended up in the path of a stilt-walking Frankenstein.

"All men hate the wretched!" he howled as he reached down to snatch a feather from her hair. She ducked just in time, and he clattered on, grabbing a jester's jingles and a voodoo priest's feathered top hat. His deep laugh echoed across the park as he juggled the hats above their frustrated owners' reach.

As Saffi made her way toward the tent, a killer clown with familiar bright-pink cheeks offered her a black rose. As she reared back, he squeezed a hidden bulb, spraying something as sickly sweet as chloroform. Though only a small amount reached her, Saffi's smoke-irritated lungs reacted immediately, and she coughed in his face. He double-stepped backward, putting himself into the path of the rolling gold ball.

"Look out!" Saffi yelped.

Her warning came in time for the ice goblin to hop off the ball but not for the clown to keep his feet. Had her stalker just tried to knock her out? A slight wave of dizziness hit but passed quickly. She hurried from the scene with a new appreciation of John Lennon's "Instant Karma." In the case of the killer clown, he'd been instantly knocked off his feet.

She hummed along with the song in her head as she wove her way toward the tent. It swarmed with costumed partygoers mixing, mingling, and—as the mummy limping past her had just done—moaning. Saffi had no idea how she would tell friends from foes with everyone in disguise. She crossed her arms over her chest. The last thing she wanted to do was claw someone's eyes out—unless she spotted that killer clown again. Twinkle lights strung along the tent's ceiling spines and edges cast a ghoulish glow. Speakers in each corner pumped Bach's haunting toccata and fugue from *Phantom of the Opera.* The familiar organ intro instantly wiped the "Instant Karma" earworm from her brain.

Dry-ice fog—tinted purple and orange by the twinkle lights—turned partygoers into phantoms, seen then not seen as they wandered the crowded space. Most seemed to be doing nothing more suspicious than over-filling plastic plates from the tiered trays placed on tables along the tent's edge. Sunny and Jyoti had outdone themselves. The seafood tower featured sushi, crab puffs, and prawns. The dessert tower held dark-chocolate strawberries, mini-tarts, and petit fours. The CharBOOterie Boards on either side of the towers reminded Saffi of the way C.J. had scarfed down the cheesy witches' fingers at lunch.

Thinking of Glenn's warning about spilling, Saffi avoided the food and inched her way toward the champagne fountain. She regretted the urge the minute she tried to snag a plastic goblet and her bony wingtips collapsed the carefully constructed stack.

"Let me." A reveler in a flying monkey mask tipped a battered green top hat. Her helper held a goblet beneath a champagne fountain then held it out to her. Saffi reached for the champagne without thinking, and her wingtip caught in the weave of a worn black broadcloth jacket.

"Oh, no!" Saffi looked directly into the person's eyes and met a familiar ice-blue glare. As she stepped back reflexively, the costumed reveler whirled away, and her wingtip tore through the priceless fabric of the missing Oz jacket. "Stop!" she yelled, as if the word held actual power.

The Wizard did not stop. As Saffi rushed through the dry-ice fog, trying to keep sight of the retreating figure, a short round reveler in a spotted-owl costume blundered into her path. The owl's feathers caught in her dragon scales, and it took so long to disentangle herself she lost sight of the Wizard in the green top hat. She thought she spotted the hat bouncing through the crowd inside the museum, but when she caught up with the hat it sat atop the head of a Mad Hatter character who had stopped at the popcorn popper to accept a bag from Jyoti.

"Everything OK?" Jyoti scratched beneath the stiff red collar of her Golden Age movie usher uniform.

Saffi caught her breath. "Have you seen anyone else wearing a hat like that?" Saffi pointed toward the Mad Hatter's retreating back.

Jyoti's brow furrowed. "No." She lifted the red and gold pill-box-style hat off her head and shook out her hair. "But I've been stuck here since the party started. Why did you put me on popcorn duty? This thing is hot as Hades."

Saffi reached a comforting hand toward the young woman, then jerked it back. The last thing she wanted to do was slash friends as well as enemies. "I'm sorry. But I need someone I can trust to watch the falcon when it's time for C.J. to take his 'break.'" She made air quotes with the bony tips of her wings.

Jyoti grinned. "Those things are wicked."

"In more ways than one." Saffi sighed. "No food. No champagne. No quick trips to the porta potty. No wonder the dragon queen always looked so cross."

She waved a wing at Jyoti and wandered toward the largest gathering in the museum: the one where C.J. stood guard, hands locked behind his back like a soldier at parade rest. Revelers flowed around him as they marveled at the Maltese Falcon. Locked inside a metal cage on the plinth that had been its perch inside the actor's loft, the black statuette brooded. It looked for all the world as if it knew it was bait for a killer, and it was pissed.

C.J.'s hooded green eyes constantly scanned the room and flashed past Saffi as if he didn't have a clue who she was. He was giving off his most serious federal agent vibes, and those, Saffi decided, were even sexier than the surfer dude allure he'd had when they first met. She wandered around the edges of the crowd until she was behind him.

"Hey, good look—" Before she could get the word out, he'd

whirled around, captured her left wrist and shoved it behind her back. Pain shot through Saffi's elbow but all she could think about was the priceless costume she wore. "The wings!" she yelped. "Don't break the wings!"

C.J. let go and walked around to get a better look at her. Confusion shifted to certainty, and his eyes went wide. A whistle escaped his lips before he could stop it. He ran his fingers through his stubby blond hair then leaned toward her to whisper, "Aren't you supposed to be in the tent?"

"Yes," she whispered back. "But I spotted Bev. She's dressed as the Wizard of Oz, and, get this, she's wearing Malcolm's missing jacket."

Before he could respond, feedback shrieked from the speakers in the tent. Malcolm was about to welcome his guests. He'd tried to talk them into fireworks, but C.J. had put his foot down. "If we were on the beach, sure. But no one shoots sparks into these woods on my watch."

Saffi was in complete agreement. Since she'd moved to the West Coast, she'd seen more than enough forests decimated by wildfire. Until the winter rains arrived in December, even coastal forests were vulnerable. A contrite Malcolm had settled for scaring his guests to attention with recorded screams and screeches.

"Better go. That is, if you're not going to arrest me." She blinked her over-mascaraed eyes at C.J. and watched his neck turn bright red.

The plan would never work with her lurking near the falcon. She had to be in the tent listening to Malcolm when C.J. stepped away from the statuette. She brushed past him like a dragon queen with ruffled feathers and swept out of the museum. She positioned herself near the champagne fountain just in time for the first recorded scream, the distraction Malcolm had scheduled for 7:30 to draw everyone back to the tent with a single exception: the killer. They were counting on the culprit to see Malcolm's welcome as a golden opportunity to retrieve the falcon.

As Saffi ducked inside the tent, a gorgeous couple dressed as

Jay Gatsby and Daisy Buchanan vamped toward her. Gatsby wore a dapper black tux with a pleated white shirt. Daisy, a silver spangled dress with matching T-strap heels. Gatsby's hair was slicked to his head. Daisy's lustrous brown bob was held in place by a gorgeous beaded headband. She held out a white-gloved hand and whispered, in a voice far too low, "Aunt Saffi. As I live and breathe."

Just as she realized that the Roaring Twenties beauty clutching her hand was Glenn, an ear-splitting scream rent the air. For the first time tonight, Saffi was glad she wasn't holding a goblet filled with liquid. Even though she knew it was coming, she couldn't stop her body from reacting. Her arms flew wide, and her wings nearly took off the tip of Glenn's nose. He lurched backward, saved from falling off his heels by Gatsby who caught him against her "manly" chest.

"Delilah?" Saffi peered at her friend.

"Lord have mercy, Saffi. Reel those things in before you gut somebody."

Malcolm gave a dark chuckle, pausing as if to appreciate the moment, then took the stage like the master he was. "Welcome, my lads and lovelies, to Malcolm Morton's Haunted Wood. Eat, drink, and shriek your hearts out."

The audience cackled, brayed, howled, moaned, and yelped. The Spooktacular had officially begun. Delilah and Glenn moved away from Saffi, partly to help scan the tent for unsavory characters but mostly to keep from losing an ear to her bone-tipped wings. For the next twenty minutes, Malcolm mesmerized his audience with stories of his rise to stardom, the movies he'd made—the blockbusters and the flops—the leading ladies he'd loved and lost, and the fans who'd stalked him.

"Several of whom"—he pointed to a werewolf biting into a chocolate strawberry and a voodoo priestess stuffing prawns into her mouth—"are in the audience."

The werewolf's mouth fell open, and the strawberry rolled off his tongue. The priestess tried to hide behind the voodoo priest with the feathered hat Saffi had seen earlier. But when Malcolm—always the showman—extended his arms toward them and clapped, the rest of the audience whistled, whooped, and clapped along. Before the night was over, Saffi suspected, the two stalkers would be signing autographs.

As a woman, she did not have the luxury of being blasé about being stalked. After everything that had happened, she could hardly believe Malcolm could joke about it. She'd heard enough. The moment to slip away to the dock had come.

THIRTY-EIGHT

The moon rose above Cascade Head, casting an eerie glow over the Salmon River. Halloween could not have fallen on a more perfect night. Clear. Quiet. Bone-chilling. The yellow kayak glided around the curve in the black river without a sound. Then its two-bladed paddle broke the silence with a soft swish.

As the kayak glided closer, Saffi crossed her arms over her chest. She hadn't expected Mere to be dressed for the Spooktacular, especially not as Charon, the boatman who ferried souls across the River Styx to reach the underworld. It was, she had to admit, a chilling touch.

"You're creeping me out with that skull mask." Saffi stepped forward with a wave.

Almost as if it had been lifted from the Halloween postcard sent to Malcolm, an owl swooped across the kayak's prow, then landed in a nearby tree and hooted. Was it the second owl hoot she'd heard in the park? Two hoots—a nothing burger. Three hoots, a warning that death was nearby. Saffi gave a nervous laugh. Skull face. Hooded black cloak. If the scribbled note to meet hadn't been on the back of Mere's business card, she'd have thought she'd made a massive mistake coming out here.

The kayaker used the paddle to drive the boat's nose up onto the sloping river bank then stepped out to drag it a few feet further.

"I need to get back to the party, so, what's up?"

Death didn't speak, just inclined its hooded skull face her way and motioned for her to follow. Saffi tried to cast off the chill, to attribute it to the cold air rising off the river. She couldn't. If art ever failed her, Mere could follow Malcolm's footsteps into a career in horror movies.

As they walked beneath the tree where the owl had perched, it issued a hoot so forlorn Saffi froze. *Three hoots.* She looked up into the tree. Bright reflections of the full moon lit the owl's coal-black eyes. It tucked its head into its chest like an old man waiting for her to understand the depths of his wisdom. Saffi's sudden silence must have alerted her companion. The costumed figure turned to face her, and the moon illuminated the figure's eyes.

Saffi stumbled backward. She'd seen those distinctive eyes before. They weren't the moss-green of C.J.'s daughter's. They were a ghoulish gray. As if realizing that its guise had been penetrated, Death's hands tightened their grip on the paddle. In one swift move, the figure whipped the paddle toward Saffi's head. Pain exploded behind her eyes, and then... everything went dark.

Saffi woke up with blurred vision and a foggy memory. She'd fallen on her back, crushing her wings beneath her. She lay there for several minutes, trying to ignore the dragon scales and broken feathers pricking her skin, the cold seeping into her bones, blinking until the two full moons she saw above her joined into one. When her vision cleared, she wondered why she was still alive. The answer reverberated along with the throbbing pain in her head. The killer's target had always been the same person: Malcolm Morton. The postcards had made that clear. If he didn't close the park before the opening—which, Saffi now realized, could guarantee the park's success—the postcard perp would come for him. To do that, the perp needed Saffi out of the way.

She sat up so fast her head spun. After it settled, she shifted to one hip, then onto her knee. Frigid water surged out of the mud, through the fragile feathers, soaking through her once-cozy leggings. She struggled to get a foot beneath her. As she pushed herself to a half-crouch, her stomach heaved. She thanked the dragon god she hadn't been able to eat or drink during the party. Bile burned her throat as she rose... slowly, arms extended as if her broken wings might still have the ability to lift her. Vertigo nearly washed her off her feet, and she swayed, broken-winged, a bird fallen from its nest. Tai chi had taught her to breathe—in and out, in and out, deep slow breaths. She closed her eyes and sent shoots down, through the cold damp mud, deep into the earth. Bit by bit, the spinning stilled and when she opened her eyes, for the first time in a long time, she could see clearly.

It took longer than it should have to stumble her way along the trail. By the time she reached the museum, the falcon was missing. She pushed past guys and ghouls queued up for bags of popcorn.

"Jyoti! Where is C.J.?" She locked her hands together to keep from swaying.

Jyoti ignored her question, instead gawking at Saffi's ruined gown with a look of horror. "Malcolm is going to freak."

Saffi imagined he would, considering the way he'd lit into Jyoti that first night when he'd flung out his arm and sent buttery orange gajar ka halwa sliding down the gorgeous silk sari she'd been wearing. He'd blamed Jyoti, though it wasn't her fault, and he would probably blame Saffi as well. So be it. There were more important things than Malcolm's costumes... his life for one.

Saffi glanced around the room, blinking as the crowd seemed to pulse around her. "C.J.?" she asked again.

Jyoti shrugged. "I haven't seen him since the falcon disappeared."

"Disappeared? What do you mean?"

Jyoti shrugged. "I swear I was watching, but that dude in the puffy owl costume got a bag of popcorn and stood right there stuffing it into his beak for like, ten minutes." She pointed to a spot right in the line of vision she needed to watch the falcon in its cage. "By the time he moved, it was gone."

"Did C.J. go after the thief?"

Standing so close to the popcorn popper, Saffi could feel waves of heat coming off the warming light. Sweat ran down Jyoti's forehead, and she wiped it away with the back of her arm.

"I'm sorry, Saffi. It happened during his fake bathroom break. He's been prowling the grounds ever since."

Saffi stepped away from the nauseating heat. "Why don't you call it a night? Malcolm's minions can do without popcorn for the rest of the evening."

The grin that spread across Jyoti's face almost made Saffi forget the mess she'd made of the evening. Death had whapped her in the head. The falcon was missing, and C.J. was nowhere to be found. Saffi desperately scanned the room, but it wouldn't stand still long enough for her to focus. She pressed a hand to her belly, trying to hold in the queasiness. "Have you seen Malcolm?"

Jyoti raised her eyebrows and looked toward the ceiling as if trying to remember. "The last time I saw him, he was sharing a glass of champagne with Death."

Someone turned up the sound system, blasting Bernard Hermann's "Prelude and Rooftop" from Hitchcock's *Vertigo* into the museum. Saffi's head throbbed with each chord. Costumed horrors surged around her, and she swayed.

"Death?"

"They went upstairs." Jyoti waved toward the spiral staircase that led to Malcolm's loft.

Vertigo. The spiral staircase. Death leading the star to his doom. Could this be any more like a horror movie?

"Jyoti, you have to find C.J.! Tell him to meet me upstairs."

She navigated the first spiral with one hand on the metal rail. The second spiral required both hands, one to stabilize her, the other to pull her up, step by step. She staggered around the final spiral, pain hammering her skull, flashes blurring her eyesight. By the time she realized she'd be useless to Malcolm in this state she'd reached the top, and it was too late. Death grabbed one broken wing and dragged her up the last step and into the living room.

The room whirled around her, but, somehow, she kept her feet. Her heart pounded. Her head throbbed. And when she caught sight of the actor lying on the sectional, his body still as death, she stopped breathing.

"Look at you. Hot on the trail of the person who whacked you on the head. I did that to keep you alive, Miz Grayfeather." Death chuckled. "As my wife likes to say, 'You can't sell real estate to dead people.' If you were as smart as you think, you'd have stayed down."

"What have you done to Malcolm?" Saffi demanded. She tried to ignore the way her words echoed in her throbbing head.

"Just a tiny little pinch of hemlock in his bubbly. Not enough to kill him. Just convince him to go back to LA where he belongs."

"So your wife can buy up his land?"

"She's driven, my Cece. Convinced a lot of folks to invest their life savings in the Riverside Ranch extension. If it doesn't happen, we're both ruined."

"So, the two of you are in this together."

"Cecily?" Gray eyes rolled behind the skull mask. "Cecily doesn't get grime beneath her nails. But what Cece wants, Cece gets."

"Did she know? About the postcard threats?"

Death shrugged. "Not until you served up that plate of postcards. She was staffing the museum gift shop when I bought them."

Saffi winced. She'd pinpointed the wrong perp after all. Much as she wanted to use the old "keep the villain talking until help arrives" method of defeating Death, if Malcolm had ingested hemlock, the actor didn't have that kind of time. And neither did she, now that she'd blundered into a crime scene. She scanned the room for a weapon, swallowing down the nausea she felt every time she turned her head. Why was the actor's decor so minimalist? There wasn't a single vase she could grab or framed photo she could frisbee across the room to slice across Death's smirking face.

Think, Saffi, think! There had to be something in this room she could use. *Anything!*

At last, she spotted what she needed.

"I need to sit." She wobbled toward the sectional without giving the despicable Sheriff Raymond time to stop her.

"Why not?"

She eased herself onto the leather cushion with her legs close enough to Malcolm's feet to feel blood pulsing through them. His pulse seemed slow, but, at least so far, he was alive. The relief that washed through her did little to ease her tension. The more time passed, the more likely the Spooktacular would be Malcolm Morton's swan song, and hers as well. She lifted his feet and eased them onto her lap.

"How sweet." Death walked close enough to tower over the two of them, arms crossed. "I believe this is the part where you ask a lot of questions designed to find out exactly what I did and how I covered my tracks."

Wouldn't you just love that? The amateur sleuth, desperate to understand the killer, allows him to soliloquize for an hour. Meanwhile, the victim's breathing slows, his muscles freeze up, his heart stops.

"No need. That blow on the head you gave me answered all but one."

"And what is that?"

Saffi quirked her finger, and the sheriff—being as full of himself as only Death and arrogant lawmen could be—obliged, leaning closer.

"How good are you in a cat fight?"

THIRTY-NINE

Here's the thing: cats are the ultimate stealth weapons. They can lay there, still as animal skins, biding their time until prey gets close enough and then... they not only pounce, they go straight for the throat.

When she'd spotted the Maine Coon on the back of the sectional, Saffi had remembered Malcolm's words: "Tomago wouldn't hurt a fly, unless she thinks she's protecting me." Saffi knew she'd found the perfect weapon. Having been on the receiving end of Tomago's claws, she almost felt sorry for Sheriff Raymond. *Almost.*

In the aftermath of the cat fight—which the sheriff definitely lost—footsteps rang on metal, coming from two directions: the spiral staircase and the fire escape. Delilah, Glenn, and Jyoti rushed into the room from the staircase. C.J. burst in from the fire escape, gun first, and before Saffi could say "He's the killer!" he had Death in handcuffs.

Glenn's flapper dress shimmied as he hurried to the sectional and knelt far more daintily than Saffi ever could have at Malcolm's side. "Tell me he's not dead." The kohl around his eyes had already started to run. Delilah put one hand on his shoulder and stuffed her other hand into the pocket of her Gatsby tux jacket, debonair, even in the face of death.

"He's alive," Saffi said. "But he's been poisoned. Hemlock."

Glenn gasped. "You wrote about poisons in last year's *Bedside Reader*! Please, please tell me you know what to do."

The weight of her inadequacy settled over Saffi's shoulders. Glenn had trusted her to find the postcard perp and protect his friend. She had missed so many clues. The dead otter on Malcolm's doorstep. The high school kid who took potshots at wildlife. C.J.'s antipathy toward the small-town sheriff who'd been named most likely to end up in jail by his classmates. The fact that Sheriff Raymond had been trying to shut down the park instead of investigating Lennie's murder.

Driven by desperation, she had relied on a feline to stop a felon. Tomago had defeated Death in the form of Sheriff Raymond, but defeating death itself? Could she count on her limited knowledge to save Malcolm? Or would she make things worse? The consequences of playing amateur paramedic could turn her slapdash sleuthing into a genuine tragedy. But with hemlock, every second counted. The paramedics would not be here in time.

"Saffi! Please!" Glenn begged.

She had never been able to resist those caring brown eyes with their fringe of black lashes. Saffi laced her fingers together and said a silent prayer. "I'll do my best."

She sent Jyoti to the popcorn stand for a container of salt while she fetched a glass of warm water from the bathroom. When the young woman returned, Saffi mixed the salt into the water while C.J. wrestled Malcolm into a half-seated position in the crook of the sectional. She dribbled the liquid down the actor's throat until he started to heave. She tried not to mind that he threw up all over what was left of the dragon queen's gown, but the smell... that she might hold against him.

After the actor finished heaving, they laid him back down on the couch under a duvet Jyoti found in his bedroom and tried to keep him quiet until help arrived. Delilah pulled Saffi into Malcolm's closet to release her from the tattered, vomit-spattered remains of her dragon queen costume. The loft was sorely missing in basic necessities, such as plastic garbage bags, so Delilah dumped the ruined finery into the vintage tub while Saffi raided Malcolm's closet. She ended up with an oversized black sweater that turned her into the middle-aged ninja she'd avoided earlier.

Fifteen minutes later, the same rescue team that had treated Saffi and C.J. for smoke inhalation rushed up the fire escape. Saffi explained what had happened, described what she'd done, and left them to their work. Glenn, on the other hand, could not be pulled away from Malcolm's side, not even when the rescue team loaded the actor into the ambulance. He climbed inside, tugging his flapper skirt over his bottom.

"How do you not freeze your balls off?" He glared at Saffi and Delilah as if the chill going up his spangled dress was their fault.

"Pants!" Delilah waved. "I'll bring you some. In the meantime, cross your legs and sit like a lady."

Saffi walked Delilah to her trailer, so stunned by all that had happened she couldn't say a word. How had her plan gone so wrong? The Maltese Falcon had been stolen... again. Malcolm had been poisoned. Sheriff Raymond had been arrested, but his wife was as innocent as someone with that much avarice could be.

As Saffi watched the ambulance pull away, she felt just as unsettled as she had before the Spooktacular. Something was off. Sheriff Raymond was guilty of following through on threat after threat, but he hadn't killed Saffi. He'd knocked her out. He wanted her alive to buy a pricey new home in Riverside Ranch. Unless the sheriff had lied, he hadn't tried to kill Malcolm either. He had dosed him with just enough hemlock to persuade him to return to LA. But Lennie *had* been killed, and the bloodied Maltese Falcon *had* been stolen.

Death had not been clutching the falcon when he offered Malcolm that glass of champagne. He hadn't carried it up the stairs to Malcolm's loft. In fact, when the statue was stolen, Death had been attacking Saffi down by the riverside. Where was the Maltese Falcon, and who could have taken it?

Something Jyoti said earlier niggled at the back of her mind. The puffy owl had blocked her view of the caged bird as he gobbled down a bag of popcorn. Could it have been the same owl that had blundered into her path when she tried to stop Bev in the tent?

"You coming to the hospital?" Delilah nudged her out of her reverie.

Saffi shook her head. "Something's not quite—"

"Saffi!" Delilah whirled toward her friend. "You caught the killer red-handed. The bee buzzing around that bonnet of yours? It's not a clue. It's a concussion."

Saffi lifted a hand to the sore spot on her head. "You're probably right. Maybe I should go lie down."

"Good idea. I'll leave Archie with you to make sure you do."

Saffi dragged herself into her RV and flopped down on the couch. She felt like she'd been put through an antique wringer washing machine and draped over a metal tub to dry, but her brain kept buzzing. By the time Delilah delivered Archie to her door, she had a plan in place. The second the tail lights on Delilah's Jetta disappeared behind the trees, she patted the terrier's dense white curls.

"Come on, buddy. Let's see if we can spot ourselves an owl."

They wove through a park transformed by tragedy. Beneath the eerie orange and purple glow of twinkle lights, costumed characters gathered in small groups around campfires, voices subdued. Malcolm's stalkers—the werewolf and the voodoo priestess—sat side by side, heads drooping toward their laps outside the zeppelin-shaped trailer. The ice goblin's golden globe had rolled to a stop against the tiny Casita in the next site. He tended a roaring fire and clinked beers with the jester who had lost his jingle hat early in the evening. Frankenstein had removed his stilts and leaned them against the killer clown's rig—the Mini-Winnie. Had there been actual chloroform in that sickly sweet spray she'd coughed back into the clown's face? She clutched Archie's leash with a shaking hand and forced herself to walk close enough to read—and memorize—the Winnebago's license plate. The clown tracked her progress, wide red lips stuck in a perpetual grin, flames flickering in his eyes.

Karma's coming, buddy. Just not tonight.

Two figures were noticeably, but not unexpectedly, absent from the firesides: Bev—in her Wizard costume—and Bob, who was exactly the right shape and size to wear that owl suit. Saffi urged Archie toward the Jayco. As they got closer, raised voices inside the Joneses' trailer made the terrier's hackles rise. He strained against his red leash, triangular ears flattened against his head. Before she could stop him, he added his sharp bark to the argument. As if someone had flipped a switch, the voices went instantly quiet. A curtain twitched enough for someone to peer out but not be seen.

Saffi raised a hand. "You can talk to me, or you can talk to the feds."

The curtain closed, and a few footsteps later, the door cracked open. "Isn't C.J. busy booking that murderous sheriff?" Bev asked.

"I certainly hope so," Saffi admitted. "Can we come in?" She nodded toward her canine companion.

Bev stepped back, and the door opened wider. "I can't say I'm happy to see you, but I figured you'd show up sooner or later."

The first two things Saffi noticed when she followed Archie inside were sitting on the kitchen island: an owl's head and a top hat. The third was Bob, hunched in one of the matching recliners with the Maltese Falcon clenched between his thighs. For some reason, the white tights he'd worn to complete his spotted-owl costume made him look even more childlike than usual.

Bob's whiskery mustache quivered, and his button-brown eyes blinked back tears. "Things started falling apart..."

"... the minute we pulled into this park," Bev finished.

"I was just trying..." He clutched the falcon's bony black head.

"... to protect me." Bev's voice trembled, and the ice in her blue eyes started to melt.

Archie's little head bobbed back and forth between the two as they finished each other's sentences. His tongue lolled, and Saffi couldn't tell if the little terrier found them immensely entertaining or seriously disturbing.

"Sit." Bev motioned Saffi toward the other recliner. She took the seat but kept Archie at her heel, hoping his natural protective instincts would kick in if Bob decided to throw the falcon statuette at her head.

"None of this is Bev's fault," Bob said. "She has a-a d-diagnosed disorder. It started after..." He glanced at his wife as if for permission. Bev backed against the kitchen island, arms folded across her chest, face frozen in agony.

The pressure that had been building in Saffi's head since Sheriff Raymond had clobbered her with a paddle increased enough to make her rub her temples. Bob wasn't the kleptomaniac. The thieving tendencies of the packrat belonged to Bev, Ratty. She should have known.

Bob took off his wire-rimmed glasses and blotted tears against his wrist leaving a tiny feather stuck to his cheek.

"After we lost Mouse," Bev finished his sentence while he tried to collect himself.

Saffi sat forward, stroking Archie's fur and hoping her movements would put the Joneses at ease. "Mouse?"

"Our baby girl," Bob whispered. "She was the dearest little thing you ever saw but... she came too soon." He reached for a box of tissue on the side table and vigorously blew his nose.

Bev couldn't seem to figure out what to do with her hands, so she stuffed them into her jacket pockets. "She didn't make it."

Tears burned Saffi's eyes, and, this time, they weren't for herself. Losing a child. Such a random, unfair loss. She knew Bev's pain all too well.

"I couldn't save Mouse," Bob said. "But I can save Bev from this-this thing that has her in its grip." He glared at Saffi and edged forward far enough to evoke a warning growl from Archie. Saffi rubbed his head to calm him, but she was ready to loosen her grip on the leash if Bob moved a tailfeather off that chair. "She never took anything valuable. Souvenirs. Mugs. Small appliances. Things nobody would even miss."

Saffi begged to differ. The raven mug Bev stole from her RV had been a crafted by her artist friend, Mellie. It meant something to her. She kept that information to herself and sat motionless, listening, hoping Bob would talk long enough to reveal whether or not protecting his wife had led to murder.

"When Malcolm slunk off to the city leaving us stuck here doing prep for his stupid party, Bev got the urge. Lennie had opened up the museum to deep clean the floor. She was sure she could get in and out of the loft without him noticing a thing, but when I heard that machine shut down, I knew I had to do something."

Something, according to Bob, was to sneak up the curving staircase, creep up behind Lennie, and knock the groundskeeper out with the item closest to hand: the Maltese Falcon.

"I didn't even hit him that hard." Bob's pointed nose sank toward his feathered chest.

"Man's head was thin as an eggshell," Bev lamented.

Everything that happened afterward had been part of the pitiful but perilous pair's efforts to cover up what Bob had done. Bev kept watch while Bob dumped Lennie's body in the river. Later, they'd hidden the falcon in the shed, locked Saffi and C.J. inside with the incriminating evidence, set the blaze. During the Spooktacular, Bob blocked Jyoti's view while Bev snatched the falcon from the plinth.

"I'm so very sorry." The owl blinked.

For the first time, Bev didn't seem to know what to say. Tears ran down her cheeks. She pulled the hand Saffi had accidentally scratched earlier out of her pocket and gave the tears an irritated swipe. Finally, she took a deep breath and straightened, then slipped the Oz coat off her shoulders and handed it to Saffi. "Give the woman the bird, Bob."

Bob's eyes narrowed behind his round glasses. "It's not too late, sweetheart. We can hook up the trailer and go. Sell this thing." He tapped a knuckle on the falcon's head. "Disappear. She might have figured out what happened, but she can't stop us."

Saffi tensed. Her grip on Archie's leash tightened so much an uneasy whine rose from his throat.

"Maybe not." C.J.'s deep voice from the Jayco's stairwell worked better than a fistful of ibuprofen to relieve Saffi's tension. "But I can."

FORTY

Between C.J.'s arrival and the Joneses' arrest, it was past midnight before Saffi crawled into bed. Since she hadn't set an alarm, she expected to sleep till noon. Delilah had other plans.

"Rise and shine, honeybuns!" She rapped on Saffi's bedroom window, bullied her out of bed, into the tea shop, and onto the bumpy gravel road before she'd fully opened her eyes. Ten minutes later, they pulled into the hospital parking lot, and Saffi stumbled out of the car. Having called ahead to learn Malcolm's room number, Delilah blasted past admissions and onto the elevator before anyone could inform them that they'd arrived before visitors' hours. They found the room on the third floor, three doors down. Imagining walking in on Malcolm mid-exam or sponge bath, Saffi sucked in her breath and squeezed her eyes into slits she could peer through without seeing more than she wanted to.

"Saffi Graywood, my hero!" As if on cue, the morning clouds parted, and the sun beamed a spotlight on the actor propped upright in a hospital bed. He folded the newspaper he'd been reading, pressed his hands together in prayer position, and bent his head. "How can I ever repay you?"

Saffi let out the breath she'd been holding. She had a few ideas, starting with not making her pay for the dragon queen dress she'd managed to destroy during the disastrous Spooktacular. Before she could answer, the shimmery snoring bundle in the recliner on the other side of the bed shifted and stretched out legs clad in pink sweatpants.

"Glenn?"

"Daisy Buchanan" rubbed a hand over his whiskery morning shadow and answered in a gruff voice. "Unless you brought coffee, go away."

"Oh, we brought coffee." Delilah rounded the bed and waved a tray filled with four to-go cups in front of Glenn's face. His eyes popped open as if she'd held a cotton ball soaked in isopropyl alcohol beneath his nose. "Forget Aunt Saffi, *you're* my hero." He reached for the closest cup and wriggled it free of the tray.

Once they all had a coffee in hand, Saffi raised hers in a toast. "To Malcolm Morton and his Haunted Wood."

"To Malcolm! Whoot!"

Glenn did an upper-body flapper shimmy in his seat, and Delilah fluttered ghoul-green glitter nails at the actor.

For the first time since she'd met him, Malcolm did not take a bow. Instead, he unfolded the newspaper and held it so they could read the headline.

"Haunted Catastrophe to Close," Saffi read aloud. She glanced at Malcolm, whose famous eyebrows and mustache drooped as he shut his eyes.

"My park has been deemed an ill-conceived piece of puffery by a horror has-been," Malcolm whispered, then coughed into his hand to clear what sounded like phlegm from his throat.

"Brian Bennion?"

Malcolm blew a soft raspberry but kept his eyes closed. "Showed up at first light and weaseled his way into my room."

Saffi took the paper from Malcolm's limp hands and read what Brian had written. Malcolm, it seemed, had told him exactly what he needed to make the front page: the threatening postcards, the murder, the poisoning, and... Saffi glanced up with surprise... the fact that his lawyer had already drawn up the paperwork for a land conservation easement. Local artist Mere Horseman would head up the board of trustees.

"This is... amazing, Malcolm, but... what about the RV park?"

When Malcolm opened his eyes, they weren't filled with despair, they sparkled. "I'll fill it with vintage trailers just like my mom had. Visitors will come from all over the state—the country, perhaps—to study and restore the wetlands and to conserve the remaining forest. Ecologists, foresters, wildlife experts, marine biologists like Mere's Poppa Horse. The museum will make an excellent nature center, don't you think? Hands-on exhibits. Classes."

Saffi folded the paper and smacked Malcolm lightly on the shoulder. "You had this in mind all along, didn't you?"

Malcolm's smile lifted the curls of his mustache toward his eyes. "Did you really think the great Malcolm Morton would retire to the woods in the middle of nowhere? *Moi?* Spend retirement surrounded by sycophants, tending my museum, and growing fat on Sunny's cooking?"

Saffi narrowed her eyes. "Uhm. Yes?"

Malcolm chuckled. "Me, too. Then Mere Horseman showed up with her protest signs and a vision for the future of this place I found irresistible. The Malcolm Morton Center for Ecology. Has a nice ring, doesn't it?"

Saffi had to admit, it did. It was the kind of legacy that would live long after the glitz and glamour of the actor's Hollywood years faded from memory.

"I'll retain ownership of the land," Malcolm went on, "and the loft will remain my home away from home, but the restrictions put in place by the terms of the conservancy will remain... well, forever!" Malcolm spread his arms wide then folded them across his chest and beamed brighter than the sunlight.

"Mere didn't say a word. She hated what you were doing so much, I thought *she* might be the postcard perp."

"Yes, well, I wondered about that myself." Malcolm chuckled. "I didn't sign a thing until you pinned the guilt on Cecily."

"Erroneously, as it turned out." Saffi sighed.

"You got the rotten scoundrel in the end, darling, and saved my life to boot. Not to mention discovering who killed poor Lennie, one of the only true innocents in this entire debacle."

He was right about that. Most of Saffi's suspects had been guilty of something, including Malcolm himself.

"Now, please, darlings. Shoo!" Malcolm flapped his hands toward them. "My doctor tells me I need plenty of rest for my body to heal. This time, I intend to listen."

When he closed his eyes, his face lost all animation, and, for the first time since she'd met him, Malcolm looked truly old. Saffi clenched her hands and clamped her teeth together. She hoped Sheriff Raymond's time behind bars drained as much life from him as his wife's greed and his own treachery had drained from Malcolm.

The three friends piled into Delilah's red Jetta. Saffi in the passenger seat and "Daisy" sprawled across the back, refusing to put on a seat belt because it might destroy the bangles on his flapper dress. By the time they made it back to the park, the RV exodus had already begun. Delilah squeezed the Jetta to the right as rig after rig plowed past on the left.

Saffi had been prepared to confront the clown she believed to be her stalker, but the silver-and-black Winnebago had disappeared while they were away. *Good riddance!*

She thought about emailing the Mini-Winnie's license plate to Detective Richards, but until the clown committed a crime in the real world, what could he do? Instead, she centered her laptop on her tiny dining table and opened her blog to craft a new post. This one would do two things: describe the creepiest Halloween bash she'd ever attended and salt in enough fake clues about her next destination to send her stalker far, far away from where she actually intended to be.

By lunchtime, the park was down to its original number of inhabitants, switching out Bev and Bob for Delilah and Glenn. Sunny set up the tea shop's small dining area with an Indian food buffet to rival anything LA had to offer. Somehow, they squeezed in enough chairs to add C.J. and Mere, who had kayaked over to join the crew, to the circle around the big table. Jyoti and Sunny served masala chai and pulled over two chairs to congratulate Mere and thank her for opening the way for their return to LA. Then everyone peppered the artist with questions about how she'd talked Malcolm into exchanging his dream for hers. Half an hour later, Mere drained the last of her chai and wiggled her strawberry-blond brows at Saffi.

"So?" Mere grinned "Who's ready for a hike?"

Saffi almost choked on the sip of chai she'd just taken. "Now?" Right now, all she wanted to do was crawl into her bed and nap away the coma from the carbs she'd just consumed.

C.J. clapped and then rubbed his hands together. "A hike is exactly what I need. We can take my van," he offered.

Saffi imagined herself climbing halfway to Cascade Head and running out of steam. She was about to say no when C.J. took her hands and gave them a gentle squeeze. "I guarantee you, the view is to die for."

After thanking Mere for the invitation, Jyoti and Sunny pushed their chairs back. "We are done being involved with all things that are to die for. Thank you very much," Sunny said. He and his granddaughter offered the table a namaste then fled to the kitchen.

Glenn and Delilah decided to stay behind at the Haunted Wood. They wanted to walk Archie and rest up for the return drive they'd be making come morning.

Saffi, on the other hand, squared her shoulders. "A view to die for? When you put it like that, how can I resist?"

As C.J.'s van turned onto Three Rocks Road, Saffi's phone dinged. She read the sender's name and the short but sweet note, then powered down her phone. C.J. parked the camper van in a dirt turnout near a trailhead just beyond Sitka. The trail began at a crooked set of plank-faced steps carved into a hillside above the road. Past the steep stairs, the path wound gently upward through temperate rain forest shadowed by moss-covered hemlock—a grim reminder of Sheriff Raymond's treachery—and aromatic spruce. Moss and mushrooms sprouted from downed trees, and ferns swayed in the ocean-fed breeze.

Mere led the way. They stepped over knobby tree roots, balanced on a log bridge to cross a burbling stream, and took turns spotting wildlife: petite red squirrels, shy deer, a giant speckled salamander glistening in the shallows below the bridge. As they came out of the forest onto a hillside of waving rye grass, Cascade Head rose above them. A peregrine falcon swooped over their heads, its cry both welcome and warning.

Saffi paused to shade her eyes and catch her breath, grateful to spot a series of switchbacks crisscrossing the headland. They wouldn't just make the climb easier. For a woman who spent enough time at a keyboard to put the occasional hitch in her giddyap, the zigzags would make reaching the summit possible.

Mere stopped halfway up the hill to turn Saffi toward the estuary. Her breath caught in her throat, not because her lungs were struggling for air—even though they were—but because the view was... to die for!

"Wow!" she breathed.

Where the Salmon River surged into the sea, a wide comma-shaped beach curved toward the estuary. Just beyond the sandy expanse a dense dark-green forest dipped its toes into the tide. Off to her right, waves swirled around the three rocky outcroppings for which the road had been named. Beyond that, for as far as her aging eyes could see, the Pacific, bluer than she had ever seen it, spread to the horizon.

A few switchbacks later, the three hikers settled onto a grassy knoll at the summit, silent in the face of splendor. The afternoon sun cast a golden glow across the hillside as a sea breeze ran its salty fingers through her hair. Both spent and invigorated, Saffi savored the moment, soaking warmth from the sky.

Hundreds of feet below where Saffi rested, knees pulled tight to her chest, waves crashed against the rocky headland. The sound reverberated upward then faded outward. She plucked a clover, counted its petals—three, not the luckier number four—and held it to her nose to inhale its sweetness. C.J. was right. The climb was more than worth it, and, for a few golden moments, murder was the last thing on her mind.

The rhythmic movement of legs, feet, hips, arms, and shoulders that had brought her to the top of this hill seemed to have purged her body of the specter of the Haunted Wood. She felt relaxed, at one with the verdant headland, the rippling sea, the father and daughter seated on either side of her, their faces turned skyward to soak up sunshine. A part of her longed to stay here, to witness the transformation of the Haunted Wood into a center for ecology and spend more time getting to know Mere and, most of all, C.J.

Saffi had been traveling long enough to understand the lure of alternate routes. That sideroad through the forest might lead to something incredibly exciting. It could also get you lost in the wilderness, mired in the muck, or stuck under a bridge without enough clearance for your rig. C.J. was a road she'd love to explore, but two things meant he would remain a road not taken. The first was his law enforcement career in LA. The City of Angels was about as far from Saffi's idea of heaven as a place could be, and she was pretty sure her writerly life on the road would hold little appeal for a big-city postal inspector.

The second thing that put C.J. in her rearview mirror was the ping she'd heard as they turned into Three Rocks Road. It was a message from Troy: *Texas couldn't hold me, but I know someone who can.*

Troy's words warmed her heart, but could she hold him? Could he hold her? Saffi wasn't sure. Her traitorous body kept leaning toward C.J., even as she fought to stop it. Maybe Troy's distance during this case, both physical and emotional, had created an opening for C.J. to step into. Maybe the way C.J. respected her sleuthing skills meant more to her than she wanted to admit.

Saffi did not know if returning to the cove, to Troy, would close the door to anyone else. But tomorrow, or the day after, she would ready her RV to travel. She would leave the Haunted Wood and the friends she had made here behind. Would she close the book forever? As she stared across the endless Pacific, tears blurred the sparkles on the brilliant blue ocean. Like Kenneth Grahame's classic *Wind in the Willows*, some books had to be read again and again to discover all of their wonder. Some people did, too.

C.J. turned toward her as if reading her mind and mood once again. "What next?"

Despite the invitation in his moss-green eyes, the warmth of his muscular hand reaching for hers, the knowing smile on his daughter's face, to Saffi, what came next—in this moment—was clear.

"Last Chance Cove is calling, and I must go home."

A LETTER FROM THE AUTHOR

Boo-coup thanks for reading *Death in the Haunted Wood,* the second book in my Pacific Northwest Cozy Mystery series. I hope you had a Spooktacular time! Like Saffi, when fog rolls in off the ocean my favorite thing to do is cozy up with a good mystery. If you're ready to buckle in for more mayhem along the "drop-dead" gorgeous Pacific Northwest coast, join other readers in hearing all about my new releases and bonus content by signing up for my newsletter!

www.stormpublishing.co/kim-griswell

I don't know about you, but I've discovered SO MANY good books by reading reviews. If you've fallen for the cove, the coast, and the characters, I hope you'll introduce other readers to Saffi and friends. Even a short review can make all the difference in encouraging a reader to discover my book. Thank you so much!

Like Saffi Graywood, I'm a rambling RV writer. I've explored the endless twists and curves of the Pacific Northwest's highways and byways in a 35-foot RV, on the back of a motorcycle, and in the tiny green Fiat convertible that inspired Jyoti's "Ladybug." Putting the top down for any amount of time requires multiple layers and a willingness to say, "OK. That's enough." Preferably before your nose or toes freeze off.

I modeled the settings for Saffi's chilling adventure at the Haunted Wood on real places that are a part of my story, as well as Saffi's. The Sitka Center for Art and Ecology is real, as is the Cascade Ranch development (though Cecily Raymond's Riverside

Ranch is a figment of my overactive imagination). The Salmon River flows into the sea in the shadow of Cascade Head. I traversed the trail Saffi hikes with C.J. and Mere many times during a two-month writing residency at Sitka. If you drive along Highway 101 just north of Lincoln City, Oregon, look closely. You might spot the remains of a defunct theme park moldering beneath the vines and bracken. (Then again, you might swerve into a ditch, so... keep your eyes on the road!)

I raise my Mexi-mocha mug to the baristas of the world and to you, the amazing readers who support my writing, coffee, and wandering RV habits. Thank you for being part of this amazing journey. I hope you'll stay in touch—I have so many more stories and ideas to entertain you with!

Kim

 instagram.com/griswellkim

 facebook.com/kimgriswellmysteries

 x.com/kimgriswell

ACKNOWLEDGMENTS

This book and the Pacific Northwest Cozy Mystery series that began with *Murder in Last Chance Cove* would never have happened without the aiding and abetting of so many people in my writing life. Some have been with me on this journey for decades, especially my long-term critique group, the amazing children's book writers Barbara Kerley, Mary Nethery, and Natasha Wing. When I said "It's time for a change" and genre-shifted from children's to cozy mysteries, they supported me every step of the way. I can never thank them enough for always being there for me and my writing.

Eternal gratitude to my husband, Rob, who keeps our RV running, supplies me with matcha lattes whenever I ask, and actually appreciates the fact that a wife who sits in front of a keyboard tapping away all day is working and cannot be expected to cook. Everything Saffi knows about driving, servicing, or parking an RV is because of Rob's expertise. Your love fuels every page.

Special thanks to the Ashland Mystery Festival in Ashland, Oregon, for bringing stellar mystery writers to town when I was thigh-deep in investigating how to craft a cozy. Abundant thanks to the Sitka Center for Art and Ecology in Otis, Oregon, for granting me a transformative two-month-long writing residency. Sitka immersed me in the environment Saffi explores in this book and connected me to nature in ways I had never connected before.

Though I've worked in publishing for my entire career, I have never encountered a more talented, energizing, forward-thinking, and collaborative crew than the people at Storm Publishing. I don't know how I got lucky enough to catch the eye of my incredible editor, Kate Smith. I do know that her enthusiasm is a breath of fresh air, and her expertise made this book much better than it would have been without her. I look forward to continuing our work together. Thanks also to Editorial Operations Director Alexandra Begley for keeping the wheels turning smoothly, to Anne O'Brien for such careful copy edits, and to everyone at Storm for being such an extraordinary publishing team. To Oliver Rhodes for conjuring the Storm, creating such a remarkable team, and being a publisher who actually connects with his writers—thank you!

I can't leave without a shout out to the fabulous baristas who fuel my writing, most especially those at Rogue Roasting Company in Ashland, Oregon. ROCO, you rock!

Last but never least, to every lover of cozy mysteries who picked up this book and rambled along with Saffi—sharing my stories with you is the number one reason I write. (That and it gives me the excuse to spend endless hours in coffee shops!) Thank you, with every beat of my over-caffeinated heart.